I0707578

REDEMPTION

T. Milton Mayer

Text Copyright ©2023 T. Milton Mayer
All rights reserved.
No part of this book may be reproduced, or stored in a retrieval system or transmaitted in any form or by any means, electronic, mechanical, photocopying, recording, or otherwise without written permission of the author or publisher.
Published by Simon Publishing LLC ®
Simon Publishing LLC is a registered trademark.
    https://www.simonpublishingllc.com/

ISBN: 979-8-988 2937-0-5 paperback
ISBN: 979-8-988 2937-2-9 hardcover
ISBN: 979-8-988 2937-1-2 eBook

Library of Congress Control Number: 2023919250

Cover Design by Robin Johnson, Florida Girl Designs
    https://www.gobookcoverdesign.com/

Printed by Ingram Spark and KDP Amazon

First Edition

5 8 6 1 4 7 5 9 3 5 7 4

REDEMPTION

a novel
T. Milton Mayer

Simon Publishing LLC

DEDICATION

To the Comboni Sisters and all missionaries
who dedicate their lives to bring a glimmer
of light to the darkest corners of the world.

EPIGRAPH

"The sound of the Gion Shoja temple bells echoes
the impermanence of all things;the color of the sala
flowers reveals the truth that to flourish is to fall.

The proud do not endure, like a passing dream
on a night in spring; the mighty fall at last, to
be no more than dust before the wind."

The Tales of the Heike
Translated by Helen Craig McCullough

ACKNOWLEDGEMENTS

This story was inspired by the missionary efforts of two individuals: Sister Mary Bernadette, a Comboni Missionary who spent decades teaching children in Kenya, and Mr. Jim Corbett, a lay missionary who dedicated years of his life to helping Nigerian orphans. Their stories provided essential background information for Redemption.

I would be remiss if I failed to express my profound gratitude to the staff of Simon Publishing LLC. Their professional expertise and heroic efforts made this book possible. Specifically, the input from editors Joanne Tailele and Jill Yris were invaluable in making this project a success. Also, special thanks to Robin Johnson at Florida Girl Designs for her talented work as cover designer.

Thanks to my many early reviewers who have offered their insightful suggestions and thank you to all my readers who have emailed me saying how much they enjoy my books. It's what keeps me writing.

Finally, I must thank my lovely wife, Lisa who encouraged me when I needed it most.

ONE

Opening Day
Great American Ball Park
Cincinnati, Ohio

Brett Buchanan

My agent had scheduled me for an appearance with Jimmy Fallon on The Tonight Show in a few days. I didn't like the idea of rehashing the sordid details of my past in front of a national audience, but the agent insisted the exposure would provide a much-needed boost to my public image. It had plummeted since the afternoon that forever changed my life. Memories of the day continued to echo in my mind. "Incident," they called it in the press. An absurdity. Only eight letters and three syllables arranged together to form a powerful, but misleading expression. A well-known actor beat his wife so severely, she was hospitalized. An incident. A drunk politician drove his car off a bridge into a canal, leaving his girlfriend behind to drown. An incident. Stables of high-priced lawyers and public relations experts were summoned into action. Their solution? Terms like criminal assault or negligent homicide were to be avoided. They're too harsh and much too inappropriate for the famous and powerful elite of the world. The word "incident" however, was vague and non-accusatory. When combined with the modifier, "unfortunate," a sense of inadvertent unavoidability was conveyed, something more likely to be forgiven by the public. The obfuscation of reality distorted the perception of fault. Money exchanged hands. Souls were bought and sold. Life moved on. After an apology, the actor blamed the unfortunate incident on his addiction to prescription painkillers. He completed a four-week stint in a rehab program and returned to television. Publicly contrite and only slightly tainted, the politician resumed his successful career. Likewise, a tarnished professional baseball pitcher was allowed to return to the game. After all, it was only an unfortunate incident. Humanity and accountability were sacrificed on an altar of privileged expediency, leaving disaster behind in their wake.

Already nervous, I pushed the negative thoughts aside. They were about to announce my name and I needed to remain focused. I hadn't pitched in over sixteen months. I rotated my left arm to be sure it was ready. After fighting my way through three operations and a year of physical therapy, it felt strong.

Opening Day was the equivalent of a national holiday in Cincinnati. Cloudless blue skies created the perfect setting for my homecoming. A photographer from Sports Illustrated stood in the dugout, taking pictures of me for this month's cover. The smells of popcorn, hot dogs, and beer wafted through the stadium. Ribbons of red, white, and blue bunting lined the railings along the front row seats as the center field flags fluttered gently in the mild breeze. The ballpark teemed with energetic anticipation of the beginning of a new season, one that might bring a return to the glory days of The Big Red Machine: the days of Pete Rose, Johnny Bench, and Joe Morgan: the days of World Series pennants. I looked forward to basking in the adulation of my fans again.

The familiar voice, deep and gravely, percolated up from the dark recesses of my mind. **"Your fans? Face it, Brett. How long would they stand behind you if they knew? There is only one way."**

The voice had become more frequent as this day approached. Pushing the thoughts aside was becoming increasingly difficult, the words tormenting, demanding to be acknowledged.

I forced myself to focus on the game as I took the mound. If I was going to be on Fallon's show, it was essential that I win.

I finished my warm-up pitches. Adrenalin pumped through my veins. The first batter for the Mets was a young rookie I'd never faced before. He approached the plate with a confident swagger. I read his eyes the same way I read those of every hitter I faced—the same way I used to read my father's eyes, looking for anger, searching for the signs that he was about to lash out. The rookie showed no indication of fear as he crowded the plate, trying to intimidate. *Cocky little bastard.* That might have worked for him in the minors, but he was in the big show now. The outside of the plate belonged to me. I threw a high inside fastball in front of the guy's chin. He jumped back and landed in the dirt. Message sent and received. When he stood, the arrogant look in his eyes was replaced by fear. *Good.* My catcher called for a slider. I ran my fingers across the seams until I found the spot. Wasn't sure if my elbow could handle the stress. It did and I struck the guy out three pitches later. It felt great to be back.

"You're not back, Brett," rumbled the voice. **"You never will be. The damage is beyond repair."**

Images of the incident flashed across my mind. I buried them and retired the next two batters. After that, every inning was the same. Three men up to the plate and three men down. Electricity filled the stadium. I was in a groove and cruising to a no-hitter. I had trained hard for this, was prepared for it—but I wasn't ready for the little kid. I'd been so immersed in the game, I hadn't noticed the boy until I returned to the mound in the top of the sixth inning.

He looks the same age as Jonathan.

I forced the thoughts of guilt aside and struck out the first two batters of the inning. The capacity crowd stood and cheered. I stole a glance at the boy, sitting in the first row, next to the Reds' dugout. I could almost feel his presence, his eyes fixated on the mound, studying my every move.

My heart raced. Painful memories from two years ago pressed down on me. I struggled to catch my breath and tried to concentrate on the next batter. My catcher called for a fast-ball, which I shook off. Did the same for the slider and the off-speed pitch. Everything was a blur. I blinked and squinted, but it didn't help. I couldn't see the signs anymore—only that little boy, standing a hundred feet away.

My catcher, Gunner, turned to the home plate umpire. "Time." He pulled off his mask and jogged to the mound, chewing a mouthful of gum. "What's up, Brett? Arm bothering you?"

The boy's eyes bore into mine. I looked away. "Arm's fine."

"It's been over a year since you last pitched. Nobody ever thought you'd pick up a baseball again after the accident. I'd understand if—"

"I said, the arm's fine."

Gunner spit onto the ground and looked up at the score-board. "Okay, okay, Brett. The arm's fine. I get it. Just focus on getting this guy out. I know these hitters better'n you. I'll call the pitches and you throw 'em where I tell you." He tossed the ball back to me.

"Sure, you call 'em."

Before Gunner returned to the plate, I asked, "What's with all the military uniforms in the crowd?"

Gunner glanced up at the stands. "Disabled vets. The front office gave 'em all complimentary opening-day tickets. Great visual for national TV. Guess the execs figured they could use some good PR after last season." He stared into my eyes. "Forget about them, buddy. We only have a one-run lead and this next guy can tie it up with a single swing of the bat. Your job is to get the son-of-a-bitch out. Now let's play catch."

Disabled veterans? Those were the guys who deserved recognition. They sacrificed themselves for a country too preoccupied with politics, sports, and the personal lives of Hollywood celebrities to care about what the vets did. All they got in return were a few lousy tickets while the players on the field, guys like me, made millions. It wasn't right. I picked up the rosin bag, threw it down hard in a small cloud of dust, and faced the next batter. The guy missed two fast balls out of the strike zone. The crowd went berserk, chanting, "Big Brett, Big Brett, Big Brett…" Normally, I'd feed on their energy, but not today. I again glanced over at the young boy, a man in uniform standing at his side. *Must be his father.* They were cheering along with the rest of the fans, but I heard none of them. It was as though I were the main character in my own farcical silent movie. I took off my cap, wiped my brow, and faced the center field Jumbotron scoreboard. The huge screen flashed, "Big Brett Buchanan, Cincinnati's Comeback Hero!"

The voice again rumbled up from the darkness of my soul. **"Hero? Are you shitting me? You're no fucking hero, Brett. You know what you must do."**

I couldn't ignore it any longer. The voice was right. A hero is one who risks all for a noble cause, one from which he receives no personal benefit, people like those war veterans in the stands. What have I sacrificed? Nothing. I shook my head, trying to clear my mind. Needed to refocus on the game, but it no longer worked. The reality of my "incident" crashed down upon me, sucking the air out of my lungs. The weight of those reckless decisions could no longer be denied. The boy and his father forced me to face it for the first time in my career, bringing everything into a painful perspective. Hero? The hypocrisy was suffocating. The game was only a distraction, a meaningless spectacle, a money-making charade. And the fans? They only considered me a hero when I struck out batters. If I started losing games, they'd turn on me faster than my ex-wife in divorce court. The multi-million-dollar contract extension no longer seemed important. In the overall scheme of things, what good was it? How big a home and how many cars did I need? Did money and fame bring happiness? No. Did the game help my family? It tore us apart.

"Time out," I said and walked across the first base line toward the kid and his father. Like many children attending the game, the boy wore a Reds cap, and had a baseball glove on his right hand in hopes of catching a souvenir foul ball. The initials

"C J" were printed along the strap. He looked up at me with the awestruck innocence of youth. I envied him.

"Is that your name, son? C J?"

"Yes sir. It's short for Christopher James."

"So, you're a southpaw?" I asked.

"Just like you, Mr. Buchanan." A wide grin lit up the boy's face. "I've been studying how you throw the ball. Someday I'm going to pitch for the Reds too."

"Are you any good?"

The boy gazed up at his father with a look of admiration and love in his eyes. It was the same way I used to look at my dad—before he went crazy.

"My dad says I am, so I guess so." C J beamed up at his father.

Great kid, like Jonathan. I patted him on the shoulder and turned my attention to the father, a man in his early thirties, dressed in Army fatigues. "What's your name, soldier?"

"Flannery, sir. Sergeant Gary Flannery." He shook my hand.

I nodded to the prosthesis that was now his left arm. "What happened?"

"Roadside IED in Syria, sir. It destroyed our Humvee. I tried to fight the attackers off, but they killed everyone except me. I'm lucky to be alive. Not sure why God spared me."

I never could figure out why God allowed half the shit in the world to happen. Disease? Wars? Death of innocents? Made no sense. I gave up on His so-called grand plan years ago. I looked down at the man's son, searching for an answer to the father's question. The muscles in my throat tightened. I could barely get the words out. "It's because—it's because He wanted you to come back to take care of your little boy here." Tears threatened, but I blinked them away. "Thank you for your sacrifice, sergeant." The man put his arm around his son and pulled him close.

Memories of better times—before Dad started drinking.

The fans stomped their feet. They were getting restless.

The umpire walked over. "Time to get back to the game, Buchanan."

"Just give me a minute!" I called into the dugout. "Anyone have a pen? I need a pen." The batboy handed me one. I removed my glove and wrote on the heel. "For C J, a future Hall of Famer." I signed my name and handed the glove to the boy. "It's a little big for you now, but you'll grow into it soon enough."

His eyes grew as wide as home plate. "Your glove? Wow, Mr. Buchanan. Thanks." The boy raised it up for the fans to see. The crowd erupted. The Jumbotron again flashed "Hometown Hero." C J looked at me. "But won't you be needing it?"

"Not anymore." I held the game ball and rolled it over in my hand until I found the right spot. I scribbled a note and gave the ball to the boy's father. "Sergeant Flannery, a True American Hero. Thank you." I signed it BB.

I walked into the clubhouse, never to return to a baseball diamond again. The manager ran behind me, right on my heels, huffing and puffing. "What the hell're you doing Brett? You don't just leave a game without talking to me first." He jerked his hat off his head. "No one walks away from a fucking perfect game."

I threw my hat into my locker. "I'm done."

The manager's mouth hung open. "Done? You mean your arm's shot?"

"Arm's fine."

The manager smacked his cap against his hip. "Goddammit, Brett. Then, what the fuck's wrong?"

I removed my shirt and tossed it over a chair. "Don't care anymore. I'm gone."

"Gone?" The manager looked around the empty room. "Gone where?"

The guy had always been fair to me, even during my worst times. I couldn't look him in the eye. "I used to have everything but never took the time to realize it. Now, I have nothing."

"Nothing? That's a load of horse shit, and you know it, Brett. You have a three-hundred-million-dollar contract, and twice that amount in endorsements. I don't call that nothing. You can't walk away from that."

"I already have more money than I can spend in ten life-times. It's not about the money."

The manager threw his cap against the wall. "Well, what the hell's it about then?"

My eyes fixated on one of the locker room benches. The top was marred by a large black smear left behind from a pine-tar rag. It had been there for as long as I could remember. The club had tried to paint over it several times, but the stain kept leaching through. I shook my head and looked up. "It's about life. I've been trying to cover up too many stains with too many coats of paint."

"Stains? What the hell're you talking about?" The veins in his forehead looked like they might explode any minute. He kicked over a stand of bats. They scattered across the clubhouse, slamming into the walls. Last time he was that pissed was when the Dodgers swept us in a four-game series at home. Cost us a post-season playoff berth. "You're not making any goddamn sense, Buchanan."

I pointed to the bench. "Stains. If you don't fix the source of the stain, it'll just keep bleeding back to the surface." End of conversation.

The manager shook his head, turned, and unleashed a string of profanities as he walked away. I stepped into the shower and allowed the hot water to wash the stain of baseball off my body. The stain on my soul was another matter. Once dressed, I called my agent.

His first words were, "What the hell is going on, Brett? You left during a perfect game. Is it your arm?"

"Not now," I said.

"Okay." My agent paused. "At least you had that brilliant photo op with the little kid and his disabled father. Fans loved it. Your endorsement value's going to double."

"Not interested," I said. "I'm finished with baseball."

"What? You can't be finished, Brett. You're under con-tract."

I refused to argue the point. "Find a Sergeant Gary Flannery. He was the one you saw on TV. If the family has a home, I want you to pay off the balance of their mortgage. If they don't own a home, buy them a new one."

The agent screamed so loud, I had to hold the phone away from my head. "What? Are you nuts?"

"Just make it happen. Make sure it's a big house in a nice neighborhood with good schools. And, I want you to set up a college fund for all his children. While you're at it, set one up for all the kids of wounded veterans in Cincinnati."

"That's going to cost a bundle, Brett. You don't have enough liquid assets to cover everything."

"Then raise the cash. Sell my ranch in Jackson Hole. It should go for thirty million at least. The home in Indian Hill appraises for over fifteen million. Put it on the market. Auction off my cars and memorabilia. They'll bring in another ten million. Put it all in a wounded veteran's trust and make it happen by the end of the month. If you can't do it, I'll find someone who can." I hung up before he could say another word.

I sat down and felt a little better, but not much. It was too easy. *Paint over a stain.* I had more money than I'd ever need, and the gift to the sergeant's family was only a small fraction of my net worth. Atonement wouldn't come by simply writing a few checks. It was going to take much more—probably more than was humanly possible.

The dark voice inside returned. **"Too many damn stains, Brett. There is only one way."**

When I left the stadium, I battled my way through a gauntlet of reporters, all peppering me with questions for which I had no answers. I always assumed that in one way or another, baseball would remain a part of my life. I was wrong. It was over. Like my mother once said after a beating, "Don't worry, Brett. Nothing lasts forever. The bad always comes to an end."

"Like Dad?"

"Like Dad," she said.

"What about the good?"

"Even that ends someday." She hugged me tight, her face bruised and swollen. "But never my love for you, Brett. That will never end."

The official story from the team's front office was that Brett Buchanan had aggravated his arm injury. It was a lie, one of many that had already been told. I drove straight home and climbed into a bottle of Jack Daniels for the first time in over a year.

TWO

Philadelphia, Pennsylvania
One year later

It was two in the morning when Officer Patrick McKeown and his rookie partner, Mike Rennie walked their usual night beat along East Tusculum in Kensington. "Don't know why we have to walk when we could be riding in a patrol car," said the rookie. "We'd cover a hell of a lot more territory."

McKeown removed his cap and ran a hand over his balding head before replacing the hat. "Sure seems like a waste of manpower, but the mayor wanted an increased visual presence in the district because of the uptick in drug-related crimes. Whatever the mayor wants, the mayor gets, even after the son-of-a-bitch tried to defund the department."

Mike shook his head. "It's all a bunch of political B. S." They walked on for a bit before the rookie turned to his partner. "You do anything today, Pat?"

"Nah. Too hot for me. Stayed inside and watched the Phillies game on TV. They're looking pretty good this year. Could go all the way." He kept his eyes on his surroundings, looking for anything awry. "How about you?"

"Took the wife and kids to the pool," said Mike "It's not my thing, but they like it."

"Good day for swimming. It was a real scorcher," said Patrick.

"Said on the news it was the hottest day in Philly in over

twenty years. You think there's anything to that climate change stuff they talk about?"

"Not sure what to believe," said Patrick. "I've heard pretty good arguments on both sides. I'm sure it's a long-term problem, but mostly, I think it's a political football. Both parties keep kicking it back and forth, trying to score points with the voters." He checked the alley across the street, looking for anything suspicious. "There's one thing I do know for sure. When it gets this hot, people get mean."

"Boy, you got that right," said Mike. "At least it rained before our shift started. Cooled things down a little."

"And kept the crazies off the streets. We've been pretty lucky so far tonight, but don't let your guard down. Shitstorms pop up when you least expect 'em."

"That's a big 10-4."

An hour passed and still, nothing had happened. "Think it'd be okay for us to take a break?" asked the rookie. "Maybe get a fresh coffee at Schmidty's?"

Patrick laughed. "I could use that. This night's been so boring it's hard to stay alert." He looked over his shoulder. "But like I said earlier, you still gotta keep your eyes open for trouble."

They were only a hundred feet from Schmidty's Tavern when they stopped at the sound of groaning. Someone was hurt. A crash echoed from the darkness of a small alley on the left.

"Shit, there goes our break." Patrick unholstered his Glock. "Just when I thought we were going to have an easy night." Mike did the same. They turned on their duty lights and entered the alley, keeping a space of ten feet between them. The stench of urine and wet garbage filled the air.

"Stay close to the wall so you make a smaller target," Patrick whispered. More moaning. Patrick scanned through the darkness and saw a body in the wash of his flashlight. A man lay face-up on the ground, his clothes torn and covered in a combination of vomit and blood.

"Holy fuck, this guy got the living shit knocked out of him," said the younger cop. "His face looks like hamburger."

Footsteps raced further down the alley. The rookie took off in pursuit, but Patrick called him off. "Waste of time. They have too much of a head start and they know this neighborhood much better'n we do. Probably ducked into and out of a half-dozen doors by now." He flipped on his shoulder radio and tilted it toward his mouth. "This is Officer McKeown. We have an injured Caucasian male in an alley just south of Schmidty's Tavern on East Tusculum. The guy's in pretty bad shape. We need an ambulance."

Patrick put on a pair of crime-scene gloves and bent over to study the victim. He checked for a pulse. "He's still alive, but barely." He again called into his radio. "Tell that ambulance to hurry!"

"He's lucky we were nearby and heard him. Otherwise, he'd be dead," said Mike.

"Look at his eyes," said Patrick. "Yellow as a duckling's ass. He's an alky. Probably been drinking at Schmidty's and got mugged after he stepped outside."

"Why roll a drunken bum? Doesn't look like he has a pot to piss in."

Patrick squinted his eyes. "Don't think he's a bum. Look at his clothes. They're torn, but they're pretty damn nice. I'm no expert on shoes but I'd bet anything he didn't get those at Walmart. I think this guy is well off and was probably flashing around too much cash in the bar. Maybe buying drinks for the house."

Mike looked up and down the alley. "I can't believe this idiot was too drunk to realize what could happen to him in a neighborhood like this."

Patrick spoke almost to himself. "Or maybe he wasn't that drunk after all. Maybe this is exactly what he wanted."

"What's that?"

"Nothing." Patrick checked the victim's pockets. "Let's

see if he has any ID." He pulled back, "Shit, he just pissed him-self."

Mike laughed and holstered his gun. "Muggers probably already took his wallet anyway."

Patrick handed him a pair of gloves. "Put these on and check down the alley. Usually, they pull out the cash and credit cards and pitch the wallet. See if you can find it. Maybe he has a driver's license. I'll stay with the vic until the ambulance arrives. Watch your step. Junkies like to shoot up in these alleys. There's probably needles lying around everywhere."

Mike turned on his light and disappeared into the dark-ness. After a minute he returned. "Found a few things." He held a brick and a wallet.

Patrick grabbed the brick and examined it. "Looks like blood. Got a few hairs stuck to it too." He looked down at the vic. "Our guy's pretty big. Maybe put up a good fight. The perps got into more than they bargained for, so they hit him in the head. Once he was down, the party began. Beat him to a pulp. Better bag the brick for the lab. Might be able to lift some prints from it." He checked the alley opening. "What the hell's taking that damn ambulance so long?"

Patrick checked the wallet. "A Gucci? Definitely not a bum." He opened it. "Here's a photograph. Looks like a wife and a little boy. Good looking family." He searched the wallet's com-partments. No money or credit cards. "Here we go. A driver's license." He pulled it out, checked it closely with his flashlight, and again studied the victim's face. "Holy Jesus, Mary, and Jo-seph. Know who this guy is?"

Mike glanced down at the victim and shrugged. "No idea. Should I?"

"That's Brett Buchanan."

The rookie stepped closer for a better look. "Big Brett Buchanan? The pitcher for the Reds? No fucking way. What the hell's he doing in this shithole neighborhood?"

"Who knows," said Patrick. "Last I heard of him, he walked away from an opening-day no-hitter last year. Just disappeared and has been off the radar ever since. Now he's lying in an alley in one of the worst neighborhoods in Philly." Patrick put the license in his pocket. "Did you read about what he did for the wounded veterans in Cincinnati?"

"Yeah. Something about a scholarship."

"More than that. He guaranteed a college education for the children of every wounded veteran in the city. That took a shitload of money. Not sure what happened here, but this guy doesn't deserve to be remembered like this. He's one of the good guys." Patrick looked to his partner. "Keep his identity under your hat. No need to publicize this mess. Tell the EMTs he's a John Doe."

The unconscious Buchanan twitched violently. "Shit, he's having a seizure." Patrick placed the empty wallet between Brett's teeth to keep him from biting his tongue. He again spoke into his radio. "Where's my fucking ambulance? If it doesn't get here soon, it'll be a trip to the goddamn morgue instead of the emergency room." Patrick pulled out his cell phone and made a private call to the precinct captain.

"Sir, we have a situation here."

THREE

Namguru Village
Nigeria, Africa

Debare

Six thousand miles away, in the eastern jungles of Nigeria, a boy watched in terror as fire erupted all around him, consuming everything in its path, the flames casting eerie reflections across rivers of blood. There was no escape. Out of the inferno emerged a monster, impossibly huge with burning red embers for eyes. He laughed, a maniacal sound, more like a screech. The boy tried to scream for help, but the words smothered in his throat. He tried to run, but the monster kept pulling him back. "This is where you belong, boy. This is where you will always belong, right next to the bones of your daddy and granddaddy. Here is where you will die."

The boy awoke in a panic. He cried out, frightened and trembling.

"Are you having another nightmare, Debare?" whispered his mother, gently shaking him awake, trying to not arouse her other children. "I told your father he shouldn't allow you to listen to those village elders, cackling with all their stories. They spend too much time drinking ogogoro and gossiping about the rumors of what happened to the north. It's old-men talk. Now, they've done frightened all you children to death." She kissed her son on the head. "Don't you worry, Debare. They're just stories. Such things could never happen in our small village. We have nothing anyone would want. Go back to sleep now."

A dream? But it seemed so real. Grandpa used to say dreams were windows into the future. Debare prayed they weren't. He would ask Reverend Tsumambu. He knew about such things. In fact, he knew everything about everything.

There would be no return to sleep. Afraid the dream might recur, Debare got out of the same bed he shared with his baby brother and older sister. They were still asleep. Apparently, their dreams were much nicer than his. He dressed in a faded blue t-shirt and old khaki shorts, the same ones he wore almost every day of the week. Pulling aside the curtain that served as the front door to their circular hut, he walked outside into the early November dawn. Peaceful mornings were his favorite part of the day, that moment when there seemed to be no time. Everything was quiet, the villagers still inside their homes enjoying an extra hour of sleep. Cattle and goats paced in their pens, awaiting the herdsmen to lead them out to graze. "It's Sunday," said Debare, while patting a small gray goat on the head. "You'll have to wait until after the church service."

The sun was just beginning to crest over the horizon, casting a blood-red glow through the hazy fog that still hovered over the low-lying areas. Beyond the tree-lined perimeter at the edge of the village was jungle, miles and miles of impenetrable jungle. At the limits of his visibility, a small herd of antelope grazed, glancing over their shoulders, searching for predators. The early calls of hornbills, fire-finches, and African Greys filled the air, welcoming the new day. To the east, the mountainous peaks of Gashaka-Gumti loomed over the horizon, marking the border with Cameroon. The sight was expansive in its magnitude, but also constricting in its reality. Just as with his grandfather and his grandfather's father before him, this space would comprise the entirety of Debare's universe. "Here is where you will die," the monster from his dream said.

Was it true? What would life be like somewhere else? Maybe one full of adventure in a far-away land where evil mon-

sters didn't burn down villages. On several occasions, he had heard Reverend Tsumambu talk about a place called America. There were no monsters there. Debare was sure of it. The Reverend said everyone in America was happy and rich. Food was available everywhere and they ate as much as they wanted, so much they all got fat, like the reverend. The Americans lived in big houses, so large each one had its own water well inside. He very much wanted to go to America someday.

That was someday, but today he would spend with his family, celebrating his seventh birthday. At least he thought it was his birthday. In truth, he didn't know his age or the exact date of his birth, and neither did his parents. His baby brother and his older sister had no specific date for their birthdays either. His parents arbitrarily selected birthdates and they decided that today the family would celebrate Debare's. The boy wasn't even certain what today's date was. Their village was too far removed from civilization for it to make much of a difference. Most days were the same, except that half were during the rainy season and the other half in the dry season.

He knew it was Sunday because Reverend Tsumambu had arrived in the village yesterday for a meeting with the village elders and to deliver his monthly Sunday sermon. Knowing he'd have to come in soon to get dressed, Debare took several final minutes to enjoy the moment. He took in a deep breath, the air cool and sweet. In the distance, a rumbling rolled across the sky. The birds stopped singing and most of the village dogs started barking. The animals in the pen stomped, appearing agitated. *Thunder? Can't be.* The rainy season was still months away. There were no clouds.

"Why?" he said to the otherwise quiet morning. "Why the thunder?"

His thoughts were disrupted by his mother. "Time for breakfast, Debare. You need to get dressed for church soon. Reverend Tsumambu brought a shipment of clothing from America. Yours are folded at the bottom of the bed. Make sure you wear them and be sure you put on the shoes."

The boy went inside and found his father, smiling and holding something covered in brown paper and tied with a piece of string. "What's that?" Debare asked.

"It's a birthday gift," said his father.

"Birthday gift?"

His father held out the small package. "It's from the Reverend. In America, children get surprise gifts on their birthdays and he thought you should have one. He handed it to me last night when he dropped off your new clothes."

Debare tore away at the brown paper wrapping. Inside was a white ball with red stitching on the sides. Scuffed and a little yellow from age, it seemed mysterious.

"They call it a baseball," said his father. "American boys play with them all the time. You've been asking so many questions about America, Reverend Tsumambu thought you might enjoy it. He told me that he'd like to take you with him when he goes there for a visit next year."

Debare's eyes widened. "America?"

His father winked toward Debare's mother. "He said if you can throw this ball well, they might even let you stay there."

Debare studied the ball closely and ran his fingers along the stitching. Surely it must have some magical powers if it could transport him to America. *I must discuss this further with Reverend Tsumambu.* He tossed the ball up in the air and caught it. Pleased with himself, he repeated the maneuver several times until his mother reminded him that it was time to get dressed for church. He carefully set his new gift on the bed. Once he put on his new Sunday clothes, Debare placed the ball in his pants pocket, not wanting to risk the possibility of losing a thing of such mystical powers.

After a Sunday breakfast of fried onions and eggs, the family walked the short distance to their church, a small open sided building with a thatched roof. A humble wooden cross was affixed to the top, leaning slightly toward the Gashaka-Gumti mountains in the East.

The family took their usual seats on one of the dozen parallel wooden benches near the back. Everyone stood as the village elders led them in an introductory song. Debare couldn't concentrate. He kept thinking about the powerful gift that would transport him to America. He reached into his pocket to be sure it was still there. He felt the ball's reassuring smooth surface and the ribbed stitching.

Just as the Reverend was about to begin his sermon, the same thunder from earlier in the morning rumbled through the village. There were still no clouds in sight. With each second, the noise grew louder.

Evil exploded out of the jungle from all directions like some ferocious monster breathing fire and destruction on everything in its path. A half-dozen trucks barreled straight out of the trees toward the church. The sound of gunfire was deafening. *What's happening?* Debare's heart pounded wildly in his chest. People screamed and stampeded in all directions, knocking each other over. Shaking uncontrollably, Debare crouched down behind the bench next to his family. Most of the attacking men jumped from their trucks and shot anyone who tried to run. Reverend Tsumambu raised his hands in the air and stepped forward. "Please, don't shoot. This is the house of God and we are peaceful people. We don't have much, but please take whatever you need and leave our people alone. We—"

He never finished his sentence. A devil with a black beret leveled his rifle and fired a half-dozen shots into the Reverend's chest. Then he fired at Debare's father when he tried to help. More shots and more deaths until blood covered the ground creating rivulets of red. A soldier grabbed a girl by the hair and pulled her from the arms of her mother. He looped a rope around the girl's neck and dragged her away, crying, and kicking her legs. She was tied to other girls who had been treated the same way. Her mother punched at the soldiers and yelled, "No…no… please no…" until she was shot.

"What about the babies?" asked one of the attacking men.

"We have no use for 'em," replied a soldier with large burn scars on his face. He turned his attention toward Debare's mother. She caressed her son's cheek. "Goodbye, Debare. Always remember, I love you." She ran, clutching Debare's baby brother in her arms. His mother enjoyed only a few seconds of freedom before the bullets pierced her chest. She and her baby fell to the ground, next to Debare's father.

The invaders herded the rest of the congregation together in a tight group. The villagers hugged each other, praying for mercy. There would be no protection offered by God this morning. Adults and the youngest children were slaughtered without hesitation. The older boys and girls, including Debare's sister, were bound with rope and forced onto the trucks. All but Debare.

This is where you belong, boy. Here is where you will die.

Within minutes, fire and death had consumed the entire village. Debare crawled out from his hiding place and sat on the ground next to the bodies of his parents. Screams of the dying and the smell of incinerating flesh burned into his senses, his young mind unable to comprehend the savagery of the massacre. Out of the flames arose a devil wearing a black beret and carrying a blood-stained machete, his face splotched with droplets of blood. He grinned, exposing a large gold fang.

Debare cried out, "The devil's coming to get me. Please help me, God. Why don't you do something?"

The demon with the gold tooth raised his machete and spoke. "This land is no place for Christians. You tell 'em, boy. You tell them what Shakar does to Christians in Nigeria." Just before Debare blacked out from the pain, he reached into his pocket to retrieve his magic ball, praying it would make the evil go away.

FOUR

Comboni Orphanage
Taraba Valley, Nigeria

Sister Annie

Sister Annie had just finished giving the last of the DTaP and MMR shots for the day. She placed a smiley-face Band-Aid over a little girl's injection site and sent her back to class. Sister Mary Margaret's voice exploded from outside. "We have another one." She rushed into the tiny clinic, carrying an unconscious young boy in her arms. His right arm had been partially amputated.

"Name?" Annie asked as she placed the child on the examining table.

"Don't have one. Don't even have a village. One of our delivery drivers found him in a ditch along the side of the road."

The boy's stump was caked with blood and debris. It was badly infected. Anne held his left wrist. "Pulse is rapid and weak." She checked the boy's pupils. "He's in septic shock and we're low on meds. Look inside the delivery truck for any IV supplies or antibiotics. Hurry."

Using forceps, Annie began removing insects and dirt from the wound. She rinsed it with a sterile solution and applied gauze dressings soaked in disinfectant.

Sister Mary Margaret returned with a large cardboard box. "This is all I could find."

Annie rummaged through the box until she found what she needed. "Great." She withdrew an IV kit and a bag of Ringer's lactate solution but struggled to find a vein. "Vessels collapsed. He's lost so much blood, he's volume depleted." After several failed attempts, she said, "We're losing him. Quick. Get a surgical pack."

Sister Mary Margaret found one and opened it. Annie pulled out a scalpel and poured alcohol over the boy's left ankle. "Need to do a cutdown to expose a vein." A minute later she had established an intravenous line and ran several hundred ccs of the Ringer's solution. She rechecked the boy's pulse. "Better, but not great." She ran another bolus of the fluid. Rooting through the supply box, Annie found a vial of intravenous antibiotics and added it to the IV solution.

After several minutes, Sister Mary Margaret said, "He seems better."

"He's stable at least, but he needs blood. Ideally, I'd transfer him to a hospital, but the nearest facility is over a hundred miles away, across rough terrain. He'd never survive the trip. I'll have to do the best I can with what I have here." She removed the gauze dressing, pulling away necrotic, infected tissue with it. "We need to change this every two hours."

"They smell like bleach," said Sister Mary Margaret.

"It is bleach, but that's the only disinfectant we have." Annie sat in a wooden chair next to the stretcher, her fingers on the boy's wrist, monitoring his pulse. She stared at the hut's gray, cinder-block walls, her eyes focusing on nothing in particular. When she began her surgical residency, she never expected to find herself like this, in the remote jungles of Nigeria. With her father and three brothers working in Minnesota as successful surgeons, she always assumed she'd follow in their footsteps. She'd graduated from medical school at the top of her class, wide-eyed and naïve, a new doctor ready to embark on her life's mission of relieving the suffering of others. She was accepted into a premier surgical residency program to study under some of the world's most accomplished surgeons, but the program didn't prepare her for the dark side that had infected far too many corners of medicine.

After her first year of training, Anne's life turned sideways. One of the surgeons on the staff was a younger man: charming, intelligent, and handsome. He was already recognized as a leading expert on the treatment of pancreatic cancer. Rumors were that he was on the short list to be the new Chief of Surgery at a prominent Boston hospital. Annie gradually found herself drawn to him. They went out on a date and he was a perfect gentleman–until he wasn't.

Her official complaints to the Chief of Surgery and the human resources department were dismissed as being unsubstantiated. The surgeon was never disciplined. The administrator wanted to avoid anything that might cast a shadow on the residency program or the hospital's image. The entire incident was swept under the rug and Annie was encouraged to resign. Other women eventually came forward to substantiate her claims, but for Annie, it was too late. Her father secured a residency position for her in another city, but she had seen enough of organized medicine.

Five years later, she was a member of the Comboni Missionaries, living in an orphanage in the middle of the mountain jungles of Nigeria. The clinic was pitifully small with a ramshackle tin roof, outdated equipment, and inadequate supplies, but it was here that she had found the greatest happiness and sense of fulfillment.

FIVE

Charles de Gaulle International Airport
Paris, France

Brett

It had been over a year since the attack in Philadelphia. During that time, I spent another cycle in rehab, and that's what led to this trip. I rubbed the scar over my left brow. The physical wounds had healed but the headaches persisted, like the worst hangover in my life. That was saying a lot, coming from an alcoholic. "Post-concussion syndrome," the doctors called it. "Should clear in another few months." Didn't make any difference what anyone called them, they still felt like a jackhammer inside my skull. I didn't even remember what happened that night, only that I was badly beaten and woke up in the hospital three weeks later, minus several million neurons. Figured maybe it was worth it if the attack knocked some sense into me.

My flight to Charles de Gaulle International Airport landed an hour behind schedule and I rushed to disembark the plane, the pain in my head pounding harder with each step. I popped a couple of Aleve tablets. In a way the pain was a blessing, a small distraction from the deeper ache inside my soul. There were no pills for that. A fellow passenger on the flight from Cincinnati tried to keep up with me as I walked, but he struggled. Even though I was thirty pounds heavier than my playing weight, the guy couldn't match my long stride.

"I enjoyed traveling with you Big Brett," said the man in a loud voice when he realized he'd never be able to keep up. "Thanks for the autograph. My son's going to love it," he almost yelled as I pulled farther ahead.

"My pleasure," I said over my shoulder and at the last minute turned right. I hoped to avoid any further conversation regarding baseball. The Charles de Gaulle International Airport was a huge maze of wide halls and misdirection. My inability to understand French made finding the next gate all the more difficult. I was way behind schedule and had to run to get to my connecting flight in time.

Must hurry. It was as I increased my pace that the memory hit, so hard it almost stopped me in my tracks, ripping through my heart, shredding my insides. It always happened this way. I never knew when it would call out, but when it did, it did so with a vengeance. The day could be rolling along smoothly and then, out of nowhere, something would trigger it. *Faster.*

I passed a food court, a series of specialty stores, and duty-free shops until I found the Air France gate for my flight to Nigeria. I ran down the jetway.

"That was close. We were just about to close the door," said a lovely raven-haired flight attendant. She was dressed in a blue pencil skirt, and a matching blazer over a white blouse. Her name tag read, "Aryianna." She smiled as she escorted me through the first-class cabin.

I fastened my seatbelt and settled in for the ten-hour flight to Nigeria. Why was I traveling all the way to Africa? Unlike the typical tourist, it wasn't the adventure I was seeking, but rather a sense of purpose in what had been a wasted life, one scarred by a loss of vision as to what was important. I had always been a goal-oriented person. Initially, that meant becoming a great major-league pitcher. The resulting fame and wealth led to my own destruction. I needed a new goal. Without one, I would wander through life aimlessly, a return to alcohol an inevitability. This trip was to provide an opportunity to recapture what were the remaining fragments of my life, to make some level of atonement, and to purge the guilt-driven emptiness that had penetrated deep into the essence of my being. The idea started with a talk and slideshow given by a nun. Sister Mary Margaret, she called herself, one of the most compelling speakers I'd ever heard. By the time she finished her presentation, I had donated five-hundred-thousand dollars to her African ministry. However, just like the money I gave to Sergeant Flannery, the disabled veteran, it wasn't enough. It couldn't help to calm the darkness plaguing my soul.

Paint over a stain.

An older woman took the window seat next to me. Conservatively dressed in a long linen skirt and a light-blue blouse, her only accessories were a simple pearl necklace, a Tag Heuer watch on her left wrist, and a beaded cross-body purse. "Good morning." she said with an aristocratic British accent.

"Good morning, ma'am," I said.

That was the extent of our conversation. There was no look of recognition in her eyes. *Good.* I had been hoping for comfortable anonymity once I left the U.S. She reached into her purse and withdrew a book on the life of Dian Fossey, the primatologist. Probably headed to Uganda to see the mountain gorillas. Definitely, not an American sports fan. Not going to have to endure another long baseball discussion.

My sense of relief soon faded. A large, rotund man lumbered past, checking the overhead seat numbers, reading each one out loud as he went. His excessive weight was overshadowed only by his blaring voice. The quintessential ugly American. The man stopped to study the sign just opposite me, checked his boarding pass, hiked up his pants, and plopped down into his seat with a grunt, his bloated face covered with sweat. A wave of stale cigar smoke and too much cheap cologne followed him.

Shit. At least he's not right next to me.

The heavy man stared. I buried my face in a magazine, trying to ignore him, hoping he wouldn't recognize me.

The pilot announced that our flight was third in line and would be taking off in a few minutes. The flight attendant named

Aryianna stopped and flashed a flirtatious smile. "Would you care for something to drink, Mr. Buchanan?" She was tan, with seductive dark eyes. Stunning.

"A glass of tomato juice would be fine." I returned my attention to the magazine.

She dropped the smile and turned to the fat man across the aisle. "Would you care for something to drink?"

"Sure would, doll. Whatever you're selling, I'm buying— definitely buying," he said, loud enough to be heard throughout the cabin. "How about a Maker's Mark on the rocks."

After she left, the man leaned across the aisle toward me. "Did I hear her call you Buchanan? I thought I recognized you. Aren't you The Brett Buchanan?"

I cringed. My headache worsened. "I guess that depends on who 'The Brett Buchanan' is?"

The man laughed—too loud. "Big Brett Buchanan. You know, the left-handed one who used to pitch for the Reds. Two perfect games, three-time Cy Young Award winner and an MVP award to boot. Probably would've won a couple more if you'd kept playing. No doubt about that. A guaranteed Hall of Famer the sports announcers used to say."

"I guess that's me." I sank lower in my seat and tried to focus on the magazine. This was going to be a long flight.

"I can't wait to tell my friends who's sitting next to me." He leaned closer and asked, "Do you mind?" Without waiting for a response, the guy tried to take a selfie of the two of us. I pulled back.

The beautiful flight attendant rescued me. "We're ap- proaching the runway and the pilot's ready to take off. You'll have to turn off your cell phone and put it away now, sir." In addition to being beautiful, she was also clever.

"Just a second, babe. I want to take a pic first."

"I'm afraid I must insist."

"Bitch," the man said under his breath, but loud enough for the flight attendant and me to hear. He turned off his phone and returned it to his pocket. I figured I had been saved and mouthed a "Thank you," to her. She smiled in return. It was a brief reprieve. As soon as the plane reached its cruising altitude, the guy again pulled out his phone and snapped the selfie.

Terrific. Soon it would be on Facebook and all over the internet. Brett Buchanan, the drunk, was headed to Africa.

"Had to do that, Brett. May I call you Brett? My buddies would never believe me if I didn't send them a pic. I'm actually sitting next to Mr. Perfect."

Another cringe at the nickname. *Mr. Perfect? You wouldn't say that if you knew the truth.*

"I saw you pitch that perfect game against the Dodgers a few years back. Now that was a real work of art. One to zip. Had to be one of the best games ever."

"I had a good defensive team playing behind me that day," I said with my standard reply.

"Good defense? I don't think so. It was your ninety-eight mile an hour fastball and a slider even God couldn't hit. As I recall, you struck out nineteen batters that afternoon. You don't need a good defense if the other team can't even put the ball in play. Let me buy you a drink."

"Thanks for the offer, but it's a bit early in the flight for me. Think I'll stick with my tomato juice."

"Suit yourself."

The flight attendant returned and again offered me a smile. The scent of her perfume washed over me. When she bent over to serve my drink, the top two buttons of her blouse had come undone, exposing the edge of a lace bralette underneath. There was a time when I would have jumped all over such a suggestive offer, but not today. That part of me died after the incident. I had no room in my heart for an intimate encounter, not even a one-night stand.

A large, blue diamond pendant hung from her neck, resting just above her cleavage. Distracting. It was almost identical to one I had purchased for my wife on the occasion of our fifth wedding anniversary. Had to cost at least a hundred grand. *On a flight attendant's salary? Unlikely. Another job, maybe? Must be good at whatever she does.*

The fat man across the aisle leered at her. "Now that's a beautiful piece of jewelry you have there, honey. Aaannnd it's sitting in such a deliciously sweet place. I envy that pendant. I'd pay anything to change places with it." He winked at her. "And I mean anything."

Aryianna ignored the comment as she unceremoniously set his bottle of Maker's Mark and a glass of ice before him.

"Thank you, doll. In my business, I fly a great deal. In fact, I've been all around the world, and I don't think I've ever seen a gal as beautiful as you serving drinks. Whatever you're selling, I'm interested." He winked again.

As he poured the drink, the aroma of the bourbon played with my senses. I yearned for the alcohol's numbing effect, the dissipation of the pain lingering deep within me. My mind took a drink, relishing the taste and the pleasure of the burning in my throat, promising relief. The familiar voice of addiction wormed its way through my mind, as the seductive sounds of the amber liquid splashed over the cubes of ice.

Come on, Brett. You've got this thing under control now. You've had a tough couple of years. If anyone deserves a drink, you do, certainly more so than that obnoxious fat ass across the aisle. It's not like you're going to go out on a bender. How much trouble can you get into at forty-three thousand feet in the air?

"Plenty," I said.

"I'm sorry," said the British woman next to me. "Did you say something?"

"Uh, nothing. I was just thinking out loud about the cost of this trip."

She chuckled. "I understand completely, but there's something about Africa that seems to make it worthwhile."

The fat man took a mouthful of his drink, swallowing hard, gulping it down. I yearned for the taste, just one sip, but knew it would never end with only one. Within the next few days, I'd find myself passed out and beaten in an alley somewhere, my watch and money stolen, just like in Philadelphia.

"Isn't that what you needed, Brett?" the dark voice echoed in my ear. **"To be punished? Isn't that the cost of atonement? You know what must be done."**

I ignored it. I'd been sober for thirteen months, one week, and five days, but I was nowhere near being out of the woods. I never would be. You never control the alcohol; it controls you. Alcohol had become my mistress, a best friend to whom I could confess all my woes, but it was far from being a friend. It was a demon that destroyed my family and almost killed me. I wasn't about to let that happen again.

I reached under my shirt and found it, my one-year sobriety medallion. Earning it was one of the most difficult things I had ever done, certainly much more so than pitching the perfect game against the Dodgers. I held it tightly in my hand, quietly saying the Serenity Prayer, the same one I recited every morning, "God grant me the serenity to accept the things—"

My thoughts were abruptly interrupted by the fat drinker. "How's your arm, Brett?"

I had been asked the same question thousands of times over the past several years and hoped I'd never have to answer it again. An unrealistic expectation. "Better," I replied without elaborating.

"Think you'll ever pitch again?" the man asked.

I wanted to yell, "Never," but responded with my standard rehearsed reply. "God willing." I needed to deflect the conversation away from myself. I had seen his type many times before and knew what to do next. The result was as expected. Pompous asses like him loved to brag about themselves. I asked, "What is it that you do?" The result was a vocal avalanche, almost sucking the air out of the plane. Once started, there was no stopping it.

"Funny you should ask. I'm actually in the import lumber business. Been very successful at it, in fact. Ship wood from all over the world to the US to sell to hardwood floor companies. That's why I'm flying to Africa. About to negotiate a blockbuster deal with some Arabs. Going to expand my business by over two hundred percent. It'll make me the third largest importer of hardwood in America." The man looked at me, as if inviting a response. When none came, he pressed on. "Started my own company seventeen years ago with only a hundred dollars in my pocket and—"

Blah, blah, blah.

I reclined my seat back as far as it would go but wasn't so naïve as to think I would actually be able to nap. Sleep was a friend who had deserted me ever since the incident. When the lights were out, I was left alone in the dark with nothing but the frightening prospect of having to face my own past.

Perhaps the insomnia was part of my punishment. Sleep was a luxury I didn't deserve. One must earn the privilege of enjoying the peaceful sleep of the innocent. Maybe after this trip?

I didn't know why, but somehow my instincts were telling me that in Africa I would finally find a way to quiet the turmoil inside. An inexorable force in the form of Sister Mary Margaret was pulling me there. So here I was, flying off to a remote dark corner of the world, trying to discover some tangible meaning to my life, something not provided by wealth or the ability to throw a baseball.

I was born with a gift. Yes, I had worked hard to perfect it, but the ability to throw a ninety-eight mile an hour fastball was simply given to me. That gift destroyed my life. Dedication to the game had become a displacement of purpose. I had elevated it, the money, and the associated adulation of the fans ahead of my own family. The price was steep and was paid by those who loved me most.

Like I had done countless times before, I relived the events leading up to the incident. Forcing myself through the painful process was part of my recovery, a form of spiritual self-flagellation. During my six-month stint in an Atlanta rehab center, I had been taught to reflect back upon my life, looking for changes or different decisions that might have prevented my fall into alcoholism. One could never know what might have happened on the paths not chosen. The key was to understand why the paths selected were bad. I had put myself through the same painful exercise many times before, but it was a long flight and I decided to begin the process again, anything if it would help grant me the inner peace I so desperately needed. I closed my eyes and allowed my mind to remember.

Mom was the cornerstone of my childhood, the one who held my hand when I was sick, and the one who comforted me in times of sorrow. She was my anchor of stability in times of trouble, which were many. My father was a violent drunk. It's not an excuse for what I became. It was simply a fact. Dad would knock Mom and me around on a regular basis. I blamed myself for not protecting her.

"You've never been good at protecting the ones who loved you, have you, Brett? You should have done more."

The words ricocheted through my mind, like an endless loop, each inflicting a deeper level of anguish. I clenched my fingers around the armrest, trying to choke the voice out of my head. I didn't protect Mom, and Dad beat her to death. I didn't protect my family and lost them. I was alone and had no idea of what might lay ahead.

36

SIX

Abuja, Nigeria

Brett

Weeks without sleep and the long flight must have caught up with me. I dozed off and was awakened by an increasing pressure in my ears. We were changing altitude. A gentle tap on the shoulder. "We'll be landing in about an hour, Mr. Buchanan. Would you like something for breakfast?" It was the sultry voice of Aryianna. The top buttons of her blouse were again fastened, but her cleavage remained clearly visible. I ordered orange juice, coffee, and eggs. The fat lumber importer across the aisle was still talking, this time to an unfortunate elderly man sitting next to him. "I hope they repaired those giant potholes in the runway. I read where some of the major airlines are refusing to land here until things are fixed. Rumor has it that the damage was caused by terrorist revolutionaries!"

Revolutionaries? Terrific. What was I getting myself into?

Thirty minutes later, the pilot's voice came over the loud-speaker. "We are beginning our initial descent into the Nnamdi Azikiwe International Airport in Abuja. Please return your seats and tray tables to their upright position. Turn off all electronic devices. We'll be arriving at our gate twenty minutes early. The skies are clear with light winds from the west. The temperature in Abuja is 33 degrees Celsius. That's 92 degrees Fahrenheit for our American passengers. Local time is 1:45 p.m. I hope you enjoyed your flight and thank you for flying Air France."

Upon disembarking the plane, I found the beautiful flight attendant waiting at the door. "I enjoyed meeting you, Mister Baseball Star." She emphasized the last three words, drawing them out, almost singing each syllable. She shook my hand, squeezing it slightly. When I withdrew it, I found she had handed me a napkin with the Air France logo on the top. Turning it over, I found a hand-written message. "I'm staying at the Abuja Hilton for a few days. Drinks and dinner later? Call me…Aryianna."

The same hotel where I was booked for the next several nights. I put the note in my jacket.

<hr>

I'm not sure what I expected when I left the plane, maybe a third-world airport housed in a small, cinder-block terminal with a corrugated tin roof, where a few attendants rolled steps up to the side of the plane. I was surprised to disembark through a sky bridge. The Abuja International Airport was a modern facility with thousands of travelers hustling about much like in any major airport in the United States.

A tidal wave of other passengers swarmed around me as we merged with an even larger herd of bleary-eyed travelers, frantically rushing about, trying to make connections to other cities and countries throughout Africa. Every few hundred feet, pairs of military guards wearing black uniforms and carrying automatic rifles conspicuously patrolled the halls. They were there to make a point. No disorderly or threatening activities would be tolerated, something to be expected considering the rumors of recent terror attacks on the runway.

Fortunately, the airport terminal signs were written in English, so I had no difficulty negotiating my way to customs and immigration. Voices of a dozen different languages filled the air. Two of the lines were labeled "Non-Residents," and that's where I headed. They were long, but the immigration staff handled the crowd with admirable efficiency, something else unexpected in a third-world country. Not that timeliness was essential. This was to be an experience in which my life was to slow down, to allow me the chance to reassess my very existence.

Within fifteen minutes, a voice from behind one of the glass cubicles said, "Next." I stepped forward and pulled a passport holder from my jacket pocket, a gift my ex had given to me for our first wedding anniversary. It was a leather-bound Louis Vuitton, embossed with my initials, BB on the front, and a Cincinnati Reds logo on the back. I covered the logo with my fingers and made a mental note to throw the thing away. I withdrew the passport and handed it to the man, but not before he saw the Louis Vuitton markings. I smiled. He frowned. Bad sign. "Welcome to Nigeria, Mr. Buchanan. The reason for your visit?"

"Pleasure. I'm on vacation and plan to do some sightseeing."

The agent unfolded my visa, looked up, and narrowed his eyes. A look of distrust. "Not many Americans come here for ninety days just to sightsee." Some people, including this guy, hated Americans, especially ones sporting a customized, thousand-dollar passport holder. He examined the papers for several uncomfortable seconds. His jaw muscles twitched. "Just a minute please."

"Is there something wrong?" I widened my smile, trying to look as friendly as I could.

"One moment." The agent picked up a phone and had a long conversation with what was probably a supervisor. "Yes, sir," said the agent into the phone. "I understand completely, sir." He concluded the conversation and stamped my passport—too hard. Without so much as another look, he turned to the line and said, "Next!"

What was that all about?

I continued down a short hall toward baggage claim where I retrieved my duffel bag and a small pull-behind suitcase. I had nothing to declare at the customs counter and was waved through toward the exit. Outside, a wall of oppressive heat and humidity smacked me in the face. Within minutes, my shirt was soaked with sweat. The suffocating smell of exhaust fumes crawled up my nose, threatening to remain there. Cabs lined up three deep, jostling for position to pick up fares, the drivers honking their horns incessantly and yelling at each other, as though it would actually help their situation. Unlike inside the terminal, any sense of order had been abandoned. I had hoped for a more laid-back country where I could reflect on the mistakes of my life and find a new direction. This was as bad as any large metropolitan area in the U.S.

Clouds of gray dust rolled past, stinging my eyes. Squinting, I scanned the cars looking for the Hilton Hotel courtesy shuttle. It wasn't there. A large black Lincoln limousine pulled to the curb directly in front of me. A chauffeur got out and held up a white sign that read, "Buchanan" in large black letters. He was a bull of a man, stocky, well-groomed, and wearing a funeral-black suit and tie over a crisp white shirt, precisely tailored to fit neatly over his tight muscular chest. The shirt stood in stark contrast to his shining, ebony skin. Chiseled facial features and a muscular body said he might be a former athlete or maybe military. A bulge under the left side of his suit coat suggested he was armed. *Why?* His dark brown eyes remained in perpetual motion, darting in all directions, probing everyone around him with fiery determination and a promise of retaliation if any threat was suspected. Those nearby gave him a wide berth. Some people naturally had that don't-fuck-with-me appearance and the guy standing in front of me definitely had that look. The driver approached. "Mr. Buchanan," he said with a British accent. Something else unexpected. It was more a statement of fact than a question. I didn't know how, but the man obviously knew it was me, but I had made no arrangements for a limousine service.

"Yes, I'm Brett Buchanan. How did you know?"

"Easy guess, sir. You're by far the tallest white man in the airport." The chauffeur held out his right hand and introduced himself. "Desmond Pierce, sir. Mr. Cabot from the U.S. Embassy instructed me to pick you up and take you to him." His eyes continued to survey his surroundings as he spoke.

Cabot? From the embassy? An uneasiness hovered over

me. "I was scheduled to be picked up by the Hilton Shuttle. I don't even know you, Mr. Pierce, and I don't know anything about a Mr. Cabot. The only people who are supposed to be aware of my visit here are the nuns at the Comboni Missionary."

"Of course, Mr. Buchanan. Mr. Cabot is aware of these things, sir. He helped to expedite your situation with the immigration agent."

Situation with the immigration agent?

I'd been warned about the possibility of kidnapping for ransom in Nigeria, but that wasn't supposed to be a concern in large metropolitan areas like Abuja. "I need to see some identification."

The man withdrew his wallet and showed his card, confirming him as a member of the U.S. Embassy staff. British accent? Didn't make sense. I hesitated, still a bit uncertain. The hotel shuttle was nowhere to be seen, but jumping into a random vehicle didn't feel like a great idea. Desmond had already loaded my things into the trunk of the Town Car. When he opened the rear door, it didn't appear to be an offer to enter the limo. It was a command. Hesitantly, I took a seat, and as soon as the door closed, an automatic lock engaged. I checked the handle. It didn't move. My back muscles tightened and my pulse quickened. I was trapped inside with an armed man who I didn't know, and I had no means of escape. I immediately regretted my decision to get into the car. I fumbled in my pocket for my cell phone. Did they have a 911 number in Nigeria?

The limo pulled away, headed for downtown Abuja. Desmond repeatedly checked the car's rearview mirror as he drove. *Is he checking on me? Maybe, sizing me up? For what? Was his ID fake? Did he plan to rob me? Kidnap me?* In this foreign country, I couldn't be sure.

Despite my concerns, nothing suspicious happened. I relaxed a little and gazed out the passenger window at the country that would be my home for the next several months. Abuja could be any large city in the West: tall skyscrapers interspersed with parks and a multitude of other green spaces. Ornate fountains and lush gardens dotted the landscape. Streets were lined with western clothing stores, art galleries, Apple and Microsoft outlets, jewelry stores, electronics businesses, and restaurants. The city was vibrant and teeming with prosperity. Rivers of energetic pedestrians crowded the sidewalks, a magnificent potpourri of contrasting colors and cultures. The majority were Africans but there was an eclectic mixture of Europeans, Asians, and representatives from the Middle East. Most of the native Nigerians dressed in the traditional African attire of flowing boubou robes, Kufi caps, and brightly colored Ankara fabric dresses. Others appeared to be caught up in a struggle to live in imitation of western cultures, wearing suits, dresses, t-shirts and jeans, seemingly casting aside generations of local cultural tradition. All rushed about with a sense of urgent purpose. As they walked, some carried on animated conversations via cell phone earbuds. Others stopped momentarily to study iPad screens. I had a hard time reconciling what I was seeing around me with the dismal pictures of famine and poverty presented by Sister Mary Margaret of the Comboni Mission six months ago.

The driver spoke over his shoulder. "You look surprised, Mr. Buchanan."

"I am. I didn't realize Nigeria was so modern—and affluent."

"Some of it is. The city of Abuja was created out of almost nothing forty years ago. It was well-planned from its inception and was designed to be the crown jewel of the Nigerian government, a modern replacement for the old capitol in Lagos. Now it's one of the most rapidly growing cities in the world, which is both good and bad. The increase in population has not been associated with a proportional increase in jobs so there are large pockets of poverty and social unrest. You haven't been exposed to those yet."

"Yet?" I received no response.

Desmond remained busy, checking the rearview mirror. I initially thought he was looking at me. Apparently not. He made a hard turn to the right across several lanes of traffic. Horns blared. I almost rolled sideways in my seat. "What's going on?"

"We're being followed. Been on us since the airport."

"Following us?" My pulse raced. I turned my head and looked out the rear window. "Nobody's even supposed to know I'm here."

Desmond checked the mirror again. "Apparently someone does." He made another hard turn, this time to the left, down a narrow street. "It's a gray Mercedes sedan. Still there. Two cars back."

"Who are they?"

He accelerated down the narrow street. "Hard to say, but they're definitely interested in you. Could be kidnappers, but they seldom strike in the large cities. Too risky."

"Seldom?"

"Insurgent sympathizers might consider the risk worthwhile, especially a large group like Boko Haram."

"The ones in the news?"

"Yes." Another turn and I fell against the door. "Could be the Ministry of Intelligence. They're like a combination of the FBI and CIA."

"That's good, right?" Something told me I should be worried. I feared that maybe the car was actually trying to save me from being kidnapped by this Desmond fellow.

"Could be good or bad," Desmond replied. "It's a matter of perspective. Here in Nigeria, it's impossible to know who to trust."

I thought of the delay at the immigration counter. I was definitely worried. "I don't know how that's possible. I've only made contact with Sister Mary Margaret. She made all the hotel and travel arrangements in her name."

"There are no real secrets here in Nigeria, Mr. Buchanan. Someone is very much aware of your presence. Don't worry. I'll lose them before we reach the embassy."

He swerved around a delivery truck and drove directly into approaching traffic, dodging cars coming at us head on. Horns blared. I was convinced we were going to die.

I didn't know who to trust. Was Desmond my savior or my kidnapper? Was the car following us the good guys or the bad ones? I had no way of knowing.

SEVEN

American Embassy
Abuja, Nigeria

Brett

Despite Desmond's driving, we didn't die. He maneuvered down several side streets to be sure he lost our pursuers. Twenty minutes later, he turned the car onto Diplomatic Drive and drove along a ten-foot-high, cinder-block wall crowned by festooned coils of razor wire. We approached a set of heavy wrought-iron gates, adorned by a United States Embassy plaque, and guarded by a pair of armed marines. Looked like they meant business. They waved our limousine into the embassy compound where Desmond parked in front of a three-story building, stark in color, boxy in design, and lacking any sense of architectural nuance. It looked more like a fortress than an embassy. Regularly spaced, vertical black slashes served as windows, their patterns giving the appearance of a recent attack by some enormous clawed beast. Hoped it wasn't an omen.

Desmond opened the passenger door. "I'll wait for you here, Mr. Buchanan."

I left most of my luggage in the trunk but retrieved my pull-behind carry-on bag. A receptionist met me as soon as I entered the lobby and escorted me up a flight of stairs to a second-floor office. The sign next to the door read, "Ambassador Sebastian E. Cabot." Sounded stuffy. With a name like that, I fully expected to see a spacious room with Ivy-league college diplomas hanging on the walls and an aristocratic old man sitting behind a desk, wearing an expensive three-piece suit and a Harvard University tie. Instead, the room was comfortable, but functional, with minimal accessories, just a single photograph of President Richard Wagner hanging on one wall and the official seal of the United States Department of State displayed next to it. A large map of Nigeria occupied almost the entire wall opposite.

An athletic looking man with a square jaw and military haircut sat behind an unimposing desk, holding a phone tightly against his ear. His short-sleeved white shirt exposed muscular forearms. Clouds of gray ran through his temples. He looked more like a rugby coach than a U.S. ambassador.

A United States flag stood prominently next to his desk. An ashtray, overflowing with a dozen half-smoked cigarette butts, sat in front of him. A fresh one had been recently lit. A canvas package about the size of a large briefcase lay on the right side of the desk. A yellow sticky note on the top had my name written on it.

The ambassador was involved in a heated phone conversation with someone, and that person appeared to be on the receiving end of a verbal smack-down. He looked up and saw me at the door, held up a finger, forced a smile, and mouthed, "One minute." He returned to his conversation, his face bright red and the veins on his forehead bulging. "I don't care if he is the goddamn Minister of Natural Resources, and I don't care how fucking powerful he is! Do what you have to do. If you're not up to it, I'll find someone who is." The man scowled and the color of his face deepened to a violaceous purple while the person on the other end spoke. "Okay, use the damn woman, but I don't trust people who play both sides of the fence. Keep close tabs on her, and you tell her twenty thousand is all I'm paying. Not a penny more. With what we have on her, she should be doing it for free. You'd better not fuck this up or your next assignment's going to be in Afghanistan!"

He slammed the phone down and crushed out his cigarette. The guy was not a political animal who spent his evenings attending endless state functions. He was an arm twister, here to make things happen. CIA? After a few seconds and a deep breath, the redness in his face disappeared. He stood and walked around his desk. His scowl transformed into the wide smile of a classic diplomat. "It's a pleasure to meet you, Mr. Buchanan. We don't get many celebrities here in Nigeria. I'm Sebastian Cabot."

I shook his hand. "Call me Brett."

"Okay, and you can call me Cabot." The Ambassador looked at the phone. "Sorry about the language. This job can be exasperating, and I'm forced to wear many hats. Diplomat one second, and a tough boss the next."

I liked the guy. "No apology necessary. It pales next to what I was used to hearing in the clubhouse at the ballpark. Reminds me of my manager trying to deal with a bunch of overpaid, prima donna baseball players."

Cabot returned to his desk and lit up a new cigarette. He inhaled deeply and blew the smoke up to the ceiling. "It's frustrating here. We give over a billion dollars in aid to this country every year and we've been getting little in return on our investment. Like in many third world countries, corruption is endemic in Nigeria. It's woven into the very fabric of the country's economy. Graft is so pervasive that our attempts at assistance seldom have an impact on the average citizen. Cash and goods simply make their way into the pockets of public officials, and too often, terrorists. It's crazy. We give money to people who help fund terrorists who in turn attack us."

The veins in his forehead again bulged. He was venting. "It's been going on for a long time, but our new President is demanding more accountability. My job is to turn things around and tighten the screws on some people."

Cabot regained his composure and changed the line of conversation. Back to being a diplomat. "Would you care for something to drink?" He offered a bottle of Dasani water. "It's very hot this time of year and it's easy to become dehydrated." I accepted. After I took a drink, Cabot added, "I can get you something stronger if you like."

"No, thank you. Water'll be fine." I could see it in his eyes, like reading those of a batter. It was the answer Cabot was hoping to hear. Looked like the ambassador had done his homework on me and was aware of my history. Guess he wasn't keen on the idea of a drunk American celebrity stumbling around Nigeria, getting himself into trouble.

"How was your flight?"

"Uneventful until I heard about the terrorist bombings of the airport's runway."

Cabot grimaced. "I'm afraid the revolutionaries get blamed for almost everything that goes wrong in Nigeria. Not that they don't deserve it, but they didn't bomb the runway. In fact, the potholes are the result of shoddy construction when the runways were extended years ago to accommodate the larger jets. It seems the contract for the job was awarded to a builder who just happened to be the former President's brother-in-law. They both made millions on the deal. It's a prime example of the corruption that infects the Nigerian government. Unfortunately, it's not a rare occurrence in this country. To make matters worse, the U.S. footed a majority of the bill."

I leaned forward in my chair. "I'm sure you didn't bring me here to discuss the politics of the country. Why'd you have me picked up at the airport?" I still wasn't so sure about the chauffeur. "Is there a problem?"

Cabot's eyes twinkled at my apprehension. "You were in good hands with Desmond." He nodded toward the case on his desk. "I needed to give you this package, but first, I want to discuss some basics with you."

Basics? I didn't know there were some basics. "Like?"

"Nigeria can be a dangerous place for those who are unprepared. One of my jobs is to make sure American citizens are ready for what they encounter here, especially celebrities like you. Nigeria is one of the world's largest exporters of petroleum and rare earth minerals. Blue-diamond fields have recently been discovered in the state of Taraba. You might think that this would make the citizens wealthy, but most of them aren't. Well over half of Nigeria's two hundred million people live in abject poverty, struggling to survive on less than a dollar a week. Widespread poverty has led to unrest, and that has led to the emergence of political uprisings and crime. That can pose a danger for tourists like you. Once you travel out into the bush, you'll realize what we're up against.

"Like the terrorists?"

He nodded. "That and much more. The most militant group around here is called Boko Haram. They control wide sections of the country outside the metropolitan areas."

"I'm aware of them. Don't they have ties to al-Qaeda?"

"Yes, but mostly they're little more than gangs of thugs who cloak themselves in their religion under the guise of fighting oppression. Their real purpose is to accumulate power through intimidation. They rape, pillage, and murder innocents whenever and wherever they have the opportunity."

"Why doesn't the government just flush them out? Nigeria has a military and that would seem to be a simple solution."

"One might think so, but the problem is that Nigeria is predominantly a Muslim country. Radical groups like Boko Haram have sympathizers and spies everywhere, even in the highest levels of government. Bottom line is you can trust no one here unless you've paid for them yourself. There are a half-dozen Nigerian Army generals and colonels on my payroll. I compensate them very well, but I still don't trust even them."

Cabot stood and walked over to the large map of Nigeria hanging on the side wall of the office. "I want to show you something, Mr. Buchanan." The ambassador placed a white pin over Abuja. "This is us." He inserted a red pin in the middle of an area to the east, a place devoid of any roads, towns, or villages. "This is Taraba Valley, the place where you are headed. Just to let you know what you're up against, the Comboni Orphanage is over three hundred miles away, in the middle of nowhere. The land between here and there is uncivilized territory that is often under the control of armed terrorists. The nearest active village to the orphanage is over fifty miles away. Most other towns in the vicinity have been abandoned."

I studied the map. "Abandoned? Why?"

"Usually Boko Haram. Sometimes the army. The locals are afraid of both. I want to caution you to always be aware of your surroundings. It's a different world out there, one with its own culture and set of rules. Anytime someone donates a half-million dollars to a mission in remote Nigeria, it's going to raise a few eyebrows, especially in our own State Department. It also draws the attention of many jackals who'd like to get their hands on some of that cash. Believe me, they know who you are."

I thought about the car that tailed us from the airport.

"That's the problem when you try to give a substantial amount of money to charities in third world countries. Government officials take much of what's donated for themselves." Cabot looked at the package sitting atop his desk. "I assume that's the reason you had this sent to the Embassy."

He handed me the package. Two hundred thousand dollars was heavier than I expected. I placed the canvas bag in my pull-behind.

"You must have a lot of clout to have it shipped directly to my office by special courier. Good idea, though. Sending it as a diplomatic pouch allowed you to bypass the greedy fingers of customs officials."

I shrugged. "What can I say? The Assistant Secretary of State is a baseball fan."

Cabot continued, "I think I know what's in this bag, and again I want you to be very careful. In Nigeria, just a thousand dollars is an unimaginable amount of money, ten times more than most people in this country can earn in a year. Some would kill for much less."

Including Desmond? Can I trust him? I zipped my pull-behind closed and got up to leave.

"There's just one more thing before you begin your journey. Once we're finished, Desmond will take you to the Hilton."

"How'd you know where I'm staying tonight? I don't remember telling you."

Cabot almost smiled. "It's my job to know what U. S. citizens are up to in this country, just like it's my job to know about that pretty flight attendant you met on the plane. Be careful with her, Brett. She's not who you think she is."

The blue diamond pendant.

"Like I said, trust no one. Everybody here has a price, no exceptions. You may be a sports hero back home, but to groups like Boko Haram, you're just another piece of kidnapping bait who's probably carrying a great deal of cash. That kind of situation can be problematic for the State Department."

"I'll try to stay out of trouble." Problem was, trouble had a way of finding me.

"Just stay alert. You're going to be in the deep jungle, about as far from civilization as one can get. There are still areas out there with tribes that have had almost no contact with the outside world. That makes them exceedingly dangerous. I'm not sure why you feel a need to visit that orphanage and I'm not going to waste my time trying to talk you out of it. It's a no-man's land where there are no laws. If you get yourself into trouble, I won't be able to send in the cavalry. My primary responsibility is to the United States government, but I can offer you something." He handed me a business card that read, "Major Desmond Pierce" and included several contact numbers.

"If you find yourself in a serious jam, see if you can get to a radio. He might be able to help you out."

I studied the card. "Major? Desmond's military?"

"Former military." Cabot offered no further elaboration as to what Desmond's job was. He certainly wasn't just a chauffeur. I turned the card over and saw the name "Doctor Livingstone" hand-printed on the back.

"Who's this?"

"Your name if you ever have to make the call. We don't want eavesdroppers hearing that the famous Brett Buchanan is in trouble."

Cloak and dagger stuff. The guy definitely must have been CIA in a former life. I played along. "The proverbial Mr. Livingstone?"

Cabot smiled. "Seems appropriate for someone headed out into the darkest reaches of the jungle." He paused for a second before continuing. "One other thing before you leave."

"Yes?" There always seemed to be one more thing.

"Better take that watch off your wrist and hide it. Nothing says I'm a rich American wanting to be robbed more than a guy wearing a fifty-thousand-dollar Patek Philippe."

I looked at my watch. *Shit!* I hadn't even thought about that. I just put it on automatically every morning. It was a gift from my wife on the occasion of my thirtieth birthday. I've worn it every day since. I slipped it off and put it in my pocket.

"You're not going to need a watch where you're headed anyway. Time becomes irrelevant when you're out in the jungle. You'll be too busy trying to stay alive."

EIGHT

Hilton Hotel
Abuja, Nigeria

Brett

As Desmond drove me to the Hilton Hotel, I reflected on my conversation with the ambassador. Maybe I made a mistake in coming here. I knew it was a third world country but never realized how dangerous it could be. People get killed here. I gazed at the late-day crowds on the sidewalk and wondered what awaited me outside the city.

Like the embassy, the hotel was protected by a ten-foot security wall creating the impression of a fortress. Desmond drove the limousine through a guarded security gate and around a huge fountain until he stopped under the portico. When he helped the bellman load my luggage onto a cart, his suit coat pulled aside, exposing a shoulder holster containing a pistol.

Images of the car pursuing us ran through my mind in rapid succession.

Desmond turned to me. "Try to stay up as long as you can tonight. It'll help you get acclimated to the time difference."

Staying up wouldn't be a concern. Sleeping had always been my problem.

"I'll pick you up at nine tomorrow morning. Mr. Cabot arranged for me to give you a tour of Abuja. Can I get you anything before I leave?"

"No, I'll be fine. See you tomorrow."

"As you wish sir."

Before turning to enter the hotel, I asked Desmond. "Did you grow up here? Your English is perfect."

"Nigeria was a British Colony until the 1960s, so English is our official language. It's spoken almost everywhere, but there are over fifty local languages and dialects mixed in. In the jungles to the east, there are a few tribes like the Zambuti that have their own culture and speak a language only a few people understand."

"Mr. Cabot mentioned the remote tribes."

"If you are unfortunate enough to run into them, you could be in trouble."

"Trouble? How would I know?"

"Can't miss them. They're pygmies, red pygmies. They suffered centuries of attacks from white men and other tribes. The Zambuti survived only by retreating into the mountain jungles of Gashaka and Cameroon. They're isolated and paranoid. That makes them extremely dangerous. You must be careful around the orphanage if they're wandering about. Many believe them to be cannibals."

"Cannibals? Terrific. Any other good advice for me?"

"About a hundred different things, from diseases, poisonous snakes, and even more venomous humans, but it's impossible to cover everything. You're going to have to learn as you go. My best advice is to trust no one, and always be aware of your surroundings. Surviving the jungle will be your biggest challenge."

Exact same advice as from Cabot. *Terrific.*

Desmond placed the last of my bags on the bellman's cart. "Will there be anything else, Mr. Buchanan?"

I had a half-dozen more questions about Desmond and his association with Ambassador Sebastian Cabot but was too tired to pursue the matter further.

I took control of my pull-behind, turned and walked into the impressive lobby. It was a contemporary hotel, eight stories tall and contained all the amenities you could ask for in any major American city. Banks of glass-enclosed elevators were arranged against the far wall. Next to them was the entrance to the hotel's restaurant and a large bar where too many individuals appeared to be drinking their dinner. I approached the registration desk where a sophisticated young woman checked me in. "Do you need anything else, Mr. Buchanan?"

"No, thank you. I'm fine for now."

"I'll have the bellman take your bags to your room." The man offered to take my pull-behind. I gripped the handle tighter. "I'll take this one myself. It has my important business papers."

On the way to my room, I stopped at the hotel's small gift shop and bought a bottle of Aleve and a bottle of Evian. My headache still pounded inside my skull and Desmond's chaotic, demolition derby race to the embassy didn't help. I opened the Aleve and took two pills with a mouthful of water.

The room wasn't quite what I had expected from a Hilton. The nauseating scent of too much cheap air freshener failed to hide the underlying smell of mold and stale tobacco smoke. The ceiling was marred with several blistered water stains, probably from a leaking pipe. It looked like the hotel management had tried to paint over them, but the stains still leached through. *Paint over stains.* They can't be covered up. You need to cut them out and fix the source.

I sat on the edge of the bed and looked around the room. Had Mr. Cabot bugged it? Probably just being paranoid but it wouldn't surprise me. There was something mysterious about the man and he wasn't telling me everything he knew. He had his own agenda, but I had no idea what it could be. Certainly, I wasn't at the top of his list of concerns, and the presence of Desmond didn't make any sense. I reminded myself of what Cabot had said. "Trust no one."

I unzipped the canvas diplomatic pouch Cabot had given me and emptied the contents onto the bed, two hundred thousand dollars in fifty-dollar bills. I stared at the pile of money. What the hell was I going to do with it? The room had a lock but that wasn't very reassuring. Cabot said people in this country would kill for almost nothing. I stuffed most of the cash into the room's safe. What didn't fit, I hid under the mattress. Clever. Ha. No one would think to look there. I checked the door lock to be sure it was engaged. Then, I wedged a chair under the door handle, something I learned once from a James Bond movie.

The pills started to work their magic and the head pain abated. I returned to the edge of the bed. Surprisingly comfortable. Now what? The room was quiet—too quiet. The walls reeked of solitude. This was when things were most difficult for me, alone with nothing else but the ravaging thoughts of my past, relentless strobe lights of pain that never allowed me peace. I should've done more. Should have done more to protect my mom from Dad. Should've done more to protect my family. The memories ricocheted through my mind, unearthing events I didn't want to relive, the only solution in the past being the Jack Daniels or to put a gun in my mouth. The bitter taste of the cold metal between my lips cured me of that idea. I tried to bury the thoughts as deeply as possible, but one memory I could never erase was the last call from my ex-wife. It was several months after she had married an insurance salesman from Toledo.

"Hello, Brett," she'd said.

"Hi, Rachael. It's great to hear from you." My heart fluttered, excited at the possibility she might be calling to say her recent marriage had been a mistake. Maybe she wanted to get back together.

"How are you doing?" she asked, her voice distant and aloof. Her tone told me this was not going to be a friendly chat. She always had the artful ability to cut me to the bone and make it sound pleasant. The unspoken translation of her words was, "Are you still drinking?" It destroyed my mood of optimism.

"I'm fine," I replied, forcing my voice to be just as cool as hers. "What's up?"

"I wanted to let you know first-hand, before you heard it

from one of our friends. My husband and I are expecting our first child."

First child? Her words plunged into my heart like a hot knife. "Yeah? Well, thanks for the heads-up." I wanted to yell into the phone, "You self-centered, heartless bitch. How could you do that to me? First child? What about Jonathan?" I said nothing. She had already disconnected the call anyway. Not so much as a goodbye. Sadness pressed down, suffocating away whatever small hopes I might've had for reconciliation.

That was six months ago. The conversation seared an irrevocable scar on my heart.

I searched the room for something, anything to distract me and fill the emptiness. On a table sat the ever-present Gideon Bible. I flipped through the pages and tossed it back down. God never did anything for me.

I yearned for someone to talk to and searched my jacket pocket where I found the napkin Aryianna handed me as I left the plane. The lingering scent of her perfume drifted over me. The message on the back read, "Drinks and dinner?" The unwritten implication was obvious. After considering the possibilities for a minute, I crumpled up the note and threw it in the wastebasket. I repeated Cabot's words aloud. "Trust no one."

I pulled out my wallet and removed a few photographs. Why they were still there, I couldn't explain. They were but shimmering echoes of a once-beautiful life. Wonderful memories. The problem with memories was that too many were filtered through a lens of what we wanted to remember. The bad ones were conveniently erased and stored deep in our subconscious until they clawed their way to the surface. *Unfortunate incidents.*

The first photograph was of my son, Jonathan. I held it closely, tears threatening my eyes, a few escaping down my cheeks. I wiped them away with the back of my hand. "Sorry I'm not with you little guy. Maybe soon." I gently laid it down on the night table. The next photograph was one of my wife and me taken during our honeymoon in Maui. I didn't need a picture to remind me of how she looked. I could draw every beautiful feature of her from memory: the sparkle in her blue eyes, her slight overbite, the mole under her right breast, the wrinkle in her nose when she smiled, and her deliciously soft curves. I knew every one of her dreams, her fears, even her most private secrets, and she knew mine—until I started drinking.

By the time I stopped, it was too little too late. Everything was gone. There was no forgiveness from her, only a tolerance of my presence. We always believed that the strength of our love would be too strong to erode. We prayed that, with time for healing, there would be enough to pull us back together. However, erode it did, slowly, relentlessly, until nothing remained but an abyss from which there was no escape. What I had done had extracted a heavy toll. Mistakes, especially ones as monumental as mine, always come back to gnaw away at the essence of your soul, sucking the lifeblood out of everyone around you, draining them dry until nothing is left.

Our marriage had been poisoned and there was no antidote. We married because the thought of not spending the rest of our lives together was incomprehensible. After the incident, the pain of staying together was far greater than the pain of separation. The divorce was an inevitability. Nothing left but these old photographs.

I missed her still, so much so that the mere thought of her left me breathless. I gazed straight ahead, remembering the times when life held so much promise. The minibar came into focus, only five feet away, staring back at me, calling my name. All I had to do was simply lean forward and pull open the door. Easy-peasy. The solution to my anguish. I longed for a drink, just a little something to soften the ache in my heart. I wrapped my fingers around the handle but jerked my hand back. "No," I said to myself, refusing to become my father.

The raspy voice whispered in my ear, ***"It's too late, Brett. You've already become your father. You destroyed everything, just as he did."***

"No, it's not," I screamed at the empty room. I had excised the malignancy of alcohol from my life, and I intended to keep it that way. Mistakes could never be reconciled in a bottle of whiskey. Atonement would be impossible without sobriety. I simply had to make it through this day—then one more—then one more.

Perhaps it was time to set all those memories aside, both the good and the bad. I wished I'd been a better husband, a better father, a better person, but I hadn't been. I'd spent enough time over the previous several years punishing myself for the past. What was it my AA sponsor had told me? "Don't waste your time looking back, Brett. The past isn't where you're headed." I studied the picture of my wife one last time, caressing her image with my finger. Then, I tore the photograph into small irreparable pieces and flushed them down the toilet. Took off my wedding ring and tossed it into the trash can. Long overdue. Like my mother once told me, all things come to an end, both the good and the bad.

"It's time," I said to the empty room, "time to cut out the stains."

NINE

Apartment of
Miniser Uguhru Muhammadi
Abuja, Nigeria

Aryianna

He didn't call. Aryianna figured the American must be too tired from jet lag to meet up with her. *Pity, he's rich and alone. There is that wedding ring he's wearing, but that's seldom a problem. Married men make the easiest marks.* The offer was still out there. Maybe tomorrow. She would change her plans if he called. She checked the seams on her nylons to be sure they were straight before putting on her black dress and stilettos. After a subtle spray of Chanel® N°5, she was ready.

The limousine arrived at the Hilton at eight o'clock. It took her to what the Minister liked to call their "Love Nest." She hated the name and detested the man. He was a pig, but she had slept with worse fat, ugly men over the years. Uguhru certainly wouldn't be the last. It was part of the business. Aryianna tolerated them as long as they provided her with the comforts and luxury she demanded.

When she entered the apartment, Uguhru greeted her with a glass of champagne and kissed her on the cheek. His large lips quivered when he spoke and his horizontal, wide mouth reminded her of a toad she had once seen in a television cartoon. *Toad*

Hall, it was called.

"I was afraid you wouldn't be able to make it, my dear," he said.

She forced a smile. "You know I wouldn't miss our weekly meetings for anything, Daddy." She almost choked on the word, but that's what he liked to be called. Freud could have written books evaluating that little quirk. "You're the only reason I continue on the Paris to Abuja rotation. It gives us more opportunities to be together."

He stroked her hair. "How do you like your new condominium on the Champs Elysée?"

"It's wonderful, Uguhru. Thank you so much."

"A woman as beautiful as you deserves the best." He caressed her cheek for several seconds, turned, and retrieved a small box from the hall table. It was gift-wrapped in silver paper and a matching bow. "Speaking of which, here's a little something I bought for you."

Her mouth widened. "I wasn't expecting this." She was. Gifts were part of the deal. "You shouldn't have." She opened the present and found a rectangular velvet box containing a necklace with a large central diamond pendant hanging from the center. *Must be at least a ten-carat stone, twice the size of the last one he gave me.*

Uguhru fastened the necklace around her thin neck and kissed her on the shoulder. "It contains rare blue diamonds mined here in Nigeria, eighteen carats in all." He turned her around to face him. "Now let me look at you." She twirled around. He devoured every inch of her with his eyes. "You look exquisite, my dear. The necklace is stunning on you, but I find all that clothing to be a bit distracting. We should christen your newest piece of jewelry. What do you think?"

Aryianna forced a smile, stepped back, unzipped her dress, and let it fall to the floor. Her body glowed in the room's soft light. Uguhru took her hand and led her to the bedroom where the satin sheets were already turned down and waiting. He turned to her, removed her bra, and began caressing her breasts while creating a trail of kisses along her belly. Kneeling before her, his lips focused on a spot between her legs, slowly coaxing her panties to the floor with his fat fingers.

Clumsy oaf.

"Is this what you like?" he asked.

"Oh, yes," she lied. She was afraid she might vomit in her mouth, but this was the price she had to pay.

"Say it. I want to hear you say it."

"This is what I like, Daddy. Please don't stop."

Aryianna looked up at the ceiling and thought she might scream at any second, not out of pleasure but from disgust. *Just get on with it, toad.* She forced a moan and tightened her muscles, faking an orgasm, hoping things might end sooner. Thoroughly satisfied with his performance, Uguhru pushed her down onto the bed and laid next to her. She touched him, hoping her hand would be enough, but it wasn't. It never was. He could never perform without the help of her mouth. The mere thought of him caused her to gag, but she fought it back. Too much was at stake, the money, her lifestyle—and Shakar.

After he finished, he got up and walked to the kitchen, a repulsive sight, ripples of fat hanging over his sides. His naked body waddled across the floor like something bred between a hippo and a bowl of Jell-O. Clutching the new diamond necklace helped to erase the image.

As soon as she was sure he was out of the room, she reached over to the nightstand to grab her clutch. There wasn't much time. She retrieved the tiny device and scanned the room for a hiding place. She heard him in the kitchen, opening the wine cabinet, meaning she had less than a minute before he returned. She found the perfect spot, behind one of his nude wall paintings. It was a dangerous proposition to plant an eavesdropping device here, but she was caught in a dilemma with no good options. If Uguhru discovered it, she wouldn't leave the condo alive. If she didn't plant it, the American ambassador would expose her, and she'd spend the rest of her life in a Nigerian prison, a fate worse than death. At least the Americans were paying twenty thousand dollars for the risk. *Cheap bastards should be paying fifty.*

By the time he re-entered the bedroom, she was already back under the sheets. He carried two crystal glasses and a bottle of Château Lafite Rothschild. She sat up and took a sip. At least the toad had good taste in wine.

Uguhru sat on the bed next to her. "So, how are things with our friend?"

She paused and held her breath, hoping he wouldn't mention Shakar's name. The Americans were probably already listening. "We maintain contact."

"Has he received this month's cash transfer?"

"I believe so. If he hadn't, he would have definitely asked me about it." Uguhru was wandering into dangerous territory. Any indication of a relationship with the leader of Boko Haram could potentially lead to a death sentence.

Uguhru frowned, "His progress has slowed over the past several months and my associates are growing impatient. He must expedite this situation. I don't care what it takes."

"I'll let him know of your displeasure," she said, forcing herself not to look in the direction of the hidden device. She had to be careful to manipulate the conversation in the direction she wanted. Too much information could hang her. Too little might anger the Americans. She finished her wine, put on a robe, and checked her phone to see if Mr. Buchanan had tried to call. Unlike Uguhru, that would be a job she'd enjoy. Perhaps a tryst with him could wash away thoughts of her evening with the toad. She was disappointed to see that the man wasn't interested. She would try again before she contacted Shakar.

"Do you have to be somewhere, my dear?"

She closed her phone. "No, I'm just a little tired tonight. The wine and time change have gotten to me."

"I should probably head home anyway. Must get back to the wife and family. Same time next week?"

"Of course, Daddy." Aryianna got dressed while Uguhru called for a government limousine to take her back to the Hilton.

She gave him the obligatory kiss on the cheek and left. During the ride back to the hotel she pulled the necklace out of her purse and inspected it closely. They were all grade-A blue diamonds, rare, and very expensive. She had done well. Despite her repulsion, this had been a very profitable evening: three-hundred-thousand dollars' worth of jewelry from the toad and twenty thousand from the Americans. *Better yet, there's still Mr. Baseball Star. I'm not finished with him yet.*

TEN

Hilton Hotel
Abuja, Nigeria

Brett

The wake-up call came at exactly six-thirty. It wasn't needed. As usual, I hadn't slept. After dressing in khaki pants, a white, short-sleeve linen shirt, and comfortable shoes, I retrieved my cash from the safe and the mattress. I placed the money in my pull-behind and headed down to the restaurant.

A breakfast of eggs and some type of mysterious sausage was surprisingly good. *Maybe wildebeest?* The waitress poured a second cup of coffee, black and strong, just how I liked it. I took a sip and heard the seductive sounds of expensive high heels clicking along the restaurant's marble floor. Aryianna looked radiant in a light floral dress and strappy white heels. The receptionist escorted her to a spot several tables to my left. She took her seat and crossed her legs the way some women do, showing just enough bronzed thigh to garner attention and titillate. She didn't need to. Every pair of eyes in the room were already fixated on her, the men staring lasciviously, the women with contempt in their eyes. When she saw me looking in her direction, she smiled and cast her feminine charms in my direction. I checked my watch. Running late. Tempting, but I had no time for this. As I got up to leave, I stopped at her table. "Hello again, Aryianna." I switched the pull-behind handle to my left hand and extended my right.

"Hello to you, Mr. Buchanan," she said, taking my hand, her skin soft and inviting. The scent of her perfume wafted over me. She looked even more gorgeous this morning than yesterday. The most primitive parts of my brain triggered a release of testosterone. Gazing up at me, she pouted slightly. "I was a little disappointed when you didn't call last night." The words purred in her mouth. "Would you care to join me for breakfast?"

"Thank you, but I just finished and I'm late for an appointment this morning."

She continued to hold my hand. I didn't pull away. "What're your plans for later today, after your meeting? Something fun, I hope. Abuja can be an exciting city if you're with the right person who knows where to look."

"I'm actually going on a tour, but I'm not so sure how exciting it's going to be."

"I hope it's not one of those frightfully crowded bus tours. They can be so unpleasant, all those sweaty people jammed together. Perhaps you should cancel your plans and allow me to show you around. I'm very familiar with Abuja." She squeezed my hand. Another jolt of testosterone, more localized this time.

"Thank you for the generous offer, but this is a private tour that was scheduled months ago." It was a lie. I didn't know about Desmond's plans until yesterday, but avoiding the truth seemed like a good idea when dealing with Aryianna. *Trust no one.*

Her provocative lips turned down at the sides. Erotic. "Too bad. I think we'd have a wonderful day together. Maybe we could meet for drinks later tonight? It would be fun to get together."

"Maybe. I'll let you know." I released her hand. "Must go. I have a car waiting to pick me up." At the door, I looked back. She stared at me with intensity in her eyes. For a second, it reminded me of the hypnotizing look of a snake just before it strikes. She flashed another smile which I returned.

Desmond was already waiting, holding open the passenger door of the same Town Car he drove yesterday.

"Good morning, Mr. Buchanan."

"Good morning, Desmond."

"How did you sleep, sir?"

"Fine," I lied. "What do you have planned for us today?"

"First of all, sir, do you have any Nigerian currency?"

"No, I haven't made any exchanges yet. Should I?"

"There's a major shortage of U.S. dollars in Nigeria. They're in big demand and they're valuable. Converting dollars into Nigerian naira is easy and can be done at any time. The other way around is almost impossible so I'd keep most of the money in U.S. currency. You will need some spending cash, however. I would suggest converting about ten thousand into naira. We'll start out the day at the Citibank."

Desmond pulled out of the hotel, took a left, and soon encountered heavy traffic, horns blowing and drivers weaving their way around slower cars. The sounds and smells were reminiscent of New York City during a typical business week. I checked in all directions. No one appeared to be following us, but large numbers of small television cameras covered the roads and sidewalks. "What's with all the cameras?"

"They're part of Abuja's CCTV system."

"Closed circuit TV like they use in London?"

"The same kind but not quite as extensive. With the rapid increase in population, there's been a proportionate increase in crime. The camera systems were intended to be a deterrent, but they've become a double-edged sword. The cameras can be of great assistance in tracking down perpetrators of a crime. However, they can also be a liability for any innocent person who would prefer to maintain a low profile while in this country."

"Like me?"

"Precisely. The cameras can give the wrong individuals

information regarding your whereabouts, so from now on we should try to avoid them as much as possible."

How were we supposed to do that? The cameras were everywhere. As we drove, we passed dozens of banks. "I think Abuja has more banks than Manhattan," I said.

Desmond nodded. "We have more than our share, Mr. Buchanan. Nigeria is one of the major money laundering countries in the world. It's the level of corruption here that makes the conversion of illegal money to legitimate currency so easy. Illicit cash from all over the Middle East and South America flows through here. Farmers do grow some cannabis in Nigeria, and the country has many drug dealers, but most of the drug business comes in the form of illegal currency. Mr. Cabot has been working hard behind the scenes to eliminate it, but he's been facing an uphill battle."

"Why's he concerned about money laundering in Nigeria? Isn't that their problem?"

"From America's standpoint the problem is that once the money is washed, much of it is distributed through dozens of shell corporations and ultimately funneled to fake charitable organizations in the Middle East. They're ostensibly established to provide humanitarian aid to refugees, but they do very little to help the displaced and impoverished. In actuality, most of that money makes its way back to fund terror organizations in the West."

Desmond slowed the car. "Ah, here we are." He pulled into a parking lot surrounded by a complex of ten-story, glass buildings. I opened the car door. "You should wait here, sir," said Desmond. "It would be best if I handled the conversion as a member of the U.S. Embassy. We frequently complete these types of currency exchanges, and I have contacts who know how to remain discreet in such matters. If you do it, I'm afraid the transaction will raise some eyebrows. Questions will be asked by certain individuals, people who we don't want to be aware of your presence here. Nigerian revolutionaries like Boko Haram have eyes everywhere. We certainly don't want them to know that Mr. Brett Buchanan is walking around the country with ten-thousand dollars' worth of naira in his pocket—and more in his suitcase."

I handed him the ten-thousand dollars, locked the car door, and watched him disappear into the building.

When he returned to the limo, Desmond handed me the envelope of naira currency. "Hide as much as you can in your shoes just in case your pockets are picked."

I removed my shoes and hid the money in the bottoms. They were now too small and uncomfortable.

"Now, we need to deal with the contents of that package you received by diplomatic courier. Carrying that amount of money around in the backcountry in your travel case might look strange and draw suspicion. I think our next destination should be the Jabi Lake Mall so we can purchase a backpack for you."

"And maybe some hiking boots?"

"Certainly, sir."

The mall was almost the equivalent of Michigan Avenue in Chicago. Every name brand company was represented there: Tiffany's, Nike, Louis Vuitton, a complex of 3-D cinemas, and more. The stream of upscale western stores seemed endless. We tried three different sporting goods store locations before I found one selling size fifteen hiking boots. Desmond led me to an outfitter where I purchased a black nylon backpack that wouldn't draw any unwanted attention. At the car, I transferred the dollars from my pull-behind into the backpack, and put on my new boots. Much more comfortable. We returned to the mall for lunch.

"I'm surprised by the level of affluence in Nigeria. It's not what I expected."

"It's the result of an influx of oil, rare mineral mining, and precious stone money," said Desmond. "It's created an entire community of billionaires and made multimillionaires of many government officials. They own fleets of private jets, luxury cars and live in huge mansions. After lunch, we'll see the Nigerian capitol building. Then it's off to the largest Muslim Mosque and the largest Christian Church in Abuja. Finally, I'll drive you through a few of the more opulent gated communities in the city."

***

When finished seeing the sights, Desmond said, "Now I'm going to take you to an area that the Bureau of Tourism and the Chamber of Commerce don't want you to see. It's dangerous and how most of Nigeria lives."

We headed down the highway, past a multitude of new car dealerships: Lexus, Porsche, and Mercedes. A red Ferrari blew past us. *Faster!* Another punch in my gut. The four-lane highway narrowed to a single-lane road as it passed through a middle-class neighborhood that slowly transformed to simple concrete block homes. A short distance to the east, the paved surfaces of the city gave way to gravel roads pocked with potholes. The once smooth drive became something akin to a rough amusement park ride. After several minutes, Desmond brought the limousine to a stop at the top of a small overpass. He parked the car and we got out. I was immediately hit with a wall of fetid stench, so strong it made me nauseated. The acrid air burned my eyes.

Desmond stood next to me and gazed down. "The city of Abuja is merely a sideshow, a beautiful painting covering the real-life picture of the slums." He extended his arms wide. "I present to you, Nigeria."

Below us on both sides of the small overpass, spreading out almost to the horizon, was a sea of squalor. Piles of burning garbage smoldered everywhere. Young orphans, clad only in rags, scoured through them in a desperate search for food. Shacks assembled from scraps of old wood and cardboard, were packed so tightly together, there was barely enough room to breathe. Some had tin roofs, but most relied on patchwork layers of muddy tarps and plastic garbage bags to protect them. The material flapped in the breeze like a thousand flags waving in surrender against the relentless assault of hopelessness. Narrow roads of mud cut through the neighborhoods, creating small streams of raw sewage along the sides. Individuals walked about aimlessly with no apparent purpose. In this cesspool lived hundreds of thousands of destitute families simply trying to survive another day.

"Depressing, isn't it?" said Desmond. "This is probably what you expected in Nigeria."

"It's worse," I said.

"This is only one of dozens of such slums scattered about the nation's metropolitan areas. Over half the country lives in abject poverty like this."

"It's so shocking to see this much despair in such close proximity to the affluence you showed me only several miles away."

"Yes, the striking contrast is something that's difficult for visitors to comprehend, but the opulence provided by the flow of oil and gemstone mining never reaches these people. Their numbers grow daily. Those from outlying areas migrate to the cities with hopes for a better life for themselves and their families. It's a promise that seldom materializes. The government only remembers them during political campaigns when they make promises they never intend to keep. It's all a ploy to win votes. Once the election is over, the poor are again abandoned until the next election cycle."

"So, on and on it goes without resolution, campaign promises made and soon forgotten. Sounds like politicians in the United States," I said.

"That's correct. The slums are a problem no one in the cities wants to see. Except for a few brave souls, most of the news media avoid reporting on the issue for fear of governmental reprisals."

I shook my head, the reality of the situation settling deep in my gut like a rock. "Out of sight, out of mind."

"The overriding problem is that the government has been trying to fight the Boko Haram insurgency out in the remote villages, but ironically, they have allowed this breeding ground for revolution to grow here, right in their own backyard. The major metropolitan areas are encircled, almost under siege. If nothing is done, the slums will enlarge, eventually consuming the cities. As the number of disenfranchised exceed the privileged, the present systems will all come crashing down."

A commotion erupted below the overpass, to our right. A screaming crowd led a young woman to a shallow pit in the ground where they forced her to kneel. She sobbed and extended her arms as if pleading for mercy. The first stone hit her in the left cheek. A barrage of rocks followed, relentless punishment raining down upon her. Her bloodied body bobbed away with each strike until she resisted no more. She fell onto her side and curled into a fetal position, bleeding profusely. It reminded me of the night my father murdered Mom, her face bloodied beyond recognition. I did nothing to help her.

I paced back and forth in front of Desmond, frantically waving my hands. "They're killing the woman. We must do something."

"Nothing we can do," said Desmond, a hopeless look in his eyes.

"Don't you have a gun? Maybe fire a few shots?"

"Too late," he said. "It's a local custom. The woman was probably caught being unfaithful—or perhaps she was merely the victim of a rape."

"Rape? The victim gets stoned?"

"The community usually assumes the woman did something to provoke the attack. Either way, according to Sharia law, the punishment is stoning to death."

A man, maybe the leader, walked out of the crowd, carrying a heavy brick. He ended the woman's misery with a final blow to her head."

"Probably her father. Honor killing, they call it."

"Father?" A coil of rage filled my stomach. "Bastards," I screamed at the insane brutality of it. Too loud. The crowd turned to face us and a group of young men pointed in our direction.

"They don't like outsiders interfering, especially westerners," said Desmond. "We should leave."

"There they are," a voice shouted from the end of the

overpass. A stone hit the trunk of the Town Car, followed by another hitting the roof. A group of young men rushed toward us.

"Get them!" one said.

The attackers were still a hundred feet away, but they were closing fast. Desmond pulled his Glock from his shoulder holster and fired a few shots into the air to slow them down.

"Quick, get into the car."

I hesitated.

Another shot. "Now!" he said.

Within seconds, the group had us surrounded, pounding on the hood with their fists and spitting on the windows.

I leaned back and wiped sweat from my brow. "They came out of nowhere."

"That's the way things happen here, Mr. Buchanan. One minute, everything appears to be under control, and then, in the blink of an eye, disaster. It happens when you least expect it so you must always be alert, especially out in the backcountry."

"Is that why you brought me here, to see this?"

"One reason, yes, but I want to reassure you that you're safe with me. Our car is an armored vehicle, and the windows contain bullet-proof glass. Short of a direct RPG attack, we're perfectly secure. I'd never bring you here in any other type of vehicle. However, when you leave the city, things will be different. I won't be able to protect you out there."

The crowd grew more violent and started rocking the car, trying in vain to turn it on its side. Their faces were just inches away, separated from me by only the plate of window glass. A maniacal hatred burned in their eyes. It was almost like being surrounded by a pack of wild animals. I was convinced that if they could get inside the car, they would likely rip Desmond and me apart with their bare hands.

"This is where the seeds of Boko Haram and revolution are sown," said Desmond. "This is where they germinate and flourish. In many ways, Boko Haram is the bastard son created out of the arrogance and corruption of the government elite. Mr. Cabot wanted you to see this. We couldn't tell you about it. Our words would have had no meaning. You had to personally witness the mindset you might be facing if you proceed with the rest of your trip. It's worse out in the backcountry. We both want you to think long and hard about traveling out to the orphanage. It sits in a world that, until now, you've never imagined. Mr. Cabot recommends that you head back to the U.S. and let Nigeria handle its own problems."

Desmond inched the Town Car forward until we were clear of the mob. Then, he accelerated. A half-hour later, we passed through the wall that surrounded the hotel, the need for such extensive security measures now obvious.

Desmond exited the car and opened the passenger door. "If you still want to proceed with your plans, what time would you like me to pick you up in the morning, sir?"

"Seven. If I have a change of mind, I'll let you know."

"And Mr. Buchanan?"

"Yes?"

"Tomorrow, I'll pick you up at the side door." Without looking up, Desmond glanced through the corner of his eyes toward the cameras mounted in the ceiling of the porte-cochere. "The CCTV. You wanted to keep a low profile."

I understood. When I got to my room, I locked the door. The events of the day had taken their toll. My headache returned with a vengeance, and I took three more Aleve. I desperately needed a drink, but I clutched my sobriety medal until the urge passed. A light on the phone blinked, indicating I had a message. Aryianna? I pushed the button and listened to her sultry voice.

"It was nice to see you at breakfast this morning, Mr. Buchanan. I'm scheduled to fly out tomorrow, but maybe we have time to get together for dinner tonight and perhaps a nightcap in my room. I'd enjoy it—and I think you would also."

She left her room number for me to call. I sat on the bed and considered her offer. I needed something to clear away my thoughts of the brutal killing I had witnessed, anything to remind me I was still a human being. Aryianna was a beautiful, sensual woman, but after what I had seen today, I found the thought of an intimate evening to be repugnant. I deleted the message and took a hot shower. Afterward, I scanned the room service menu, but wasn't hungry. I tossed it aside and sat in a chair. Mr. Cabot was right. This could be a dangerous mission and there was a definite possibility that I could die here. But what difference would it make? Death might be a welcomed escape from the misery and alcoholic life that had consumed me. I needed something in my life and firmly believed that somehow, Africa was the place where I might be able to find it. If I fled back to the U.S. now, a return to my old friend Jack Daniels would be an inevitability. Like recovery from alcoholism, self-discovery wasn't the result of a sudden epiphany, but rather part of a long journey, one fraught with pain and uncertainty. Absolution had to come at a price. "Hell, you are dying anyway, Brett," I said to the empty hotel room. "Better to die, trying to do something good."

I contacted the front desk for a wakeup call in the morning, knowing it was unnecessary.

ELEVEN

Okamu Airport
Abuja, Nigeria

Brett

I dressed in khaki cargo pants and an army-green t-shirt. Seemed like an appropriate color for the jungle. I hid the Nigerian money in my socks, laced up my hiking boots, and threw the new backpack of cash over my shoulder. Desmond arrived at the side door of the hotel promptly at 7:00 a.m. He said nothing about the conversation from the previous day. My decision had been made.

Desmond was now dressed in more casual attire of jeans and a black t-shirt pulled tightly over an impossibly wide chest. He loaded my luggage into the Town Car and made no attempt to conceal the belt holster on his right side. Once the car headed out, I asked, "I'm not sure I understand your official position, Desmond. If you're a citizen of Nigeria, how'd you wind up working for Sebastian Cabot and the United States government?"

"Suffice it to say that I owe Mr. Cabot a great deal." That was it. He offered no further elaboration on the subject. Desmond continued to look straight ahead. "By the way, Mr. Cabot said it was good you didn't have drinks with that pretty flight attendant last night. She isn't exactly what she appears to be."

"How'd you find out about her?" My question was rhetorical. Just as I suspected, Cabot must have bugged my hotel room.

Trust no one.

Desmond looked at me in the rearview mirror and smiled. "Her full name is Aryianna Rhamani, an Iranian national living in Paris. She's a dangerous woman who's suspected of maintaining contact with several Nigerian insurgent groups, including Boko Haram and their leader, Shakar Bhutah."

"Are they romantically involved?"

"We don't believe so. She doesn't appear to be interested in any underlying political agenda and she has no strong personal ideological beliefs. She's strictly motivated by what's best for her from a financial standpoint. She's up to something bad, but we don't know exactly what it is. The Nigerian Ministry of Intelligence has had her under surveillance for some time now. The problem is that she's a paramour of Uguhru Muhammadi, the Minister of Natural Resources, so she's been untouchable. He has protected her and in return, she grants him special favors."

"A prostitute?"

"It depends upon what you call a prostitute, but basically yes, she's a highly paid and very connected call girl who's slept with over half the most influential leaders in Nigeria. In exchange for sexual favors, she receives protection, expensive gifts, and promises of a luxurious lifestyle. She's for sale to anyone willing to pay the price. That begs the question of why she's shown such interest in establishing a relationship with you, Mr. Buchanan."

"Maybe it's my charming personality." I laughed. Desmond didn't. "I don't know. We only met by chance on my flight from Paris. It's not like our crossing paths was arranged."

"Maybe it was by chance, maybe not," said Desmond. "She can be a dangerous woman and she's been implicated in several suspicious deaths in Abuja, but Minister Uguhru's friends in the government shut down every investigation of her before they got started. No one's been able to tie her to anything substantial thus far. She's smart and elusive, but Mr. Cabot has made some serious progress. He's able to do things others can't."

"Things?" I asked.

"Suffice it to say you don't want the Nigerian government believing that you have a relationship with her. They're already nervous enough with Boko Haram out there." The Town Car took a left and began heading east through an industrial area.

"You already know where I'm headed? I haven't given you directions yet."

"Certainly, sir, the Okamu Airport."

"But how did you know?"

"Mr. Cabot told me where to take you. As I said before, he makes it his business to know these things. In all honesty, it wasn't hard to figure out, given the fact that you're headed out to Taraba Valley. There's only one pilot in Abuja who'd be crazy enough to accept a charter flight that far out into the wild country."

Crazy enough? I didn't ask him to explain. Sometimes it was best not to know.

The Town Car made a right turn and headed down a long gravel road. At the end stood a cluster of rusted metal buildings, a gas pump, and a half-dozen small planes that looked like they hadn't been in the air since World War II.

Desmond brought the car to a stop. "Here we are."

"This is it?"

"Yes sir, the Okamu Airport."

An older man crouched over the engine cowl of a small single-engine plane, a cigarette hanging from the corner of his mouth. It bobbed up and down as he cursed wildly, banging on the motor housing with a wrench. "Come on, you stupid son of a bitch!" When he saw Desmond exit the car, he stood straight and smiled, exposing interrupted rows of nicotine-stained teeth. An impossibly long ash dangled precariously from the end of his cigarette, threatening to drop into the plane's engine at any moment. He wiped his brow with an oil rag, replaced it in his back pocket, and spit out the cigarette. After crushing it under his boot, he walked over to our car. He lit a new cigarette and tossed the match to the side, ignoring the dozens of barrels of aviation fuel nearby. He took a long drag and inhaled the fresh smoke deep into his lungs. "Mr. Buchanan, I'm Nigel, your pilot today." The man smelled of a mixture of engine oil, body odor, and stale cigarette smoke. His face was partially concealed by a three-day growth of beard. On his head, a tangled rat's nest of hair looked like it hadn't been combed since before his last shave. At least there was no trace of alcohol on his breath, just the unmistakable odor of dental disease that had been ignored for too long. He and Desmond shared a few words and it appeared as though Nigel was trying to tell a joke. Desmond didn't laugh. I doubted that Desmond had ever laughed in his life. He unloaded my bags onto the ground and drove away without a word.

The Town Car disappeared down the gravel road, kicking up a large plume of dust along the way, leaving me alone with the pilot. I studied the man, then the plane, and then back to the pilot. I couldn't decide which one looked more battered. "Will this thing fly?"

"Of course, she will," said Nigel with a cockney accent. "The old girl hasn't crashed yet. Still has a lot of good hours on 'er." He patted the side of his plane like one would a pet dog. "Hop in."

I climbed into the passenger side. After Nigel loaded my bags into the rear, he struggled into the pilot's seat and turned the ignition key. A groaning protest rumbled from the plane's engine. "Come on, baby." Just as it seemed the battery would die, it turned over with a belch of black smoke spewing from the exhaust pipes, casting a thin cloud of oil over the windshield. A bad omen. Nigel revved it up and when the rpms were right, he released the brake. The plane lumbered forward, slowly picking up speed until it became airborne with less than ten feet of runway left. Tree branches scraped the bottom of the fuselage, but Nigel seemed to pay no mind. It appeared to be business as usual.

We headed east, toward the morning sun. The metropolis of Abuja slowly yielded to the cardboard jungle of shacks from the same slum Desmond had shown me the day before. From this altitude, the individual poor souls looked tiny and insignificant, but the slum appeared as large as an ocean. The squalor extended out to the horizon as far as the eye could see. Cabot was right. Businessmen and tourists only saw what the government wanted them to see. Despite the glitz of the city proper, this was a land unimaginable by western standards, a place modern civilization had forgotten. In time the densely compacted shacks began to separate. They slowly grew farther apart until there were only miles of dry flat grasslands dotted with occasional small villages and farms. Linear cuts of dark green crossed the barren land where it was traversed by the few small streams that hadn't yet dried up. Before us a savannah sat high on a plateau, and beyond that, mountains in the far distance. As the elevation changed, the parched earth gradually transformed into a lush jungle.

"We're about thirty miles out," said Nigel. They were the first words he had spoken since taking off over two hours ago. "I assume you've arranged for transportation when we land. It'll be another hundred miles to your destination."

"The Comboni Mission made the arrangements," I said.

"I hope so, for your sake." Nigel flicked at the gauges on his instrument panel with his fingers. A laughable maneuver. None of them appeared to work anyway. He pointed straight ahead. "There it is."

"There what is?"

"Your destination."

"I don't see an airport anywhere around here."

"See that small white building at two o'clock?"

I leaned forward and strained to see the structure. "That's an airport?"

"Yes, at least it used to be. The government abandoned it about ten years ago. Eastern Nigeria's been pretty much wiped out by decades of war and disease. Most survivors have migrated to the big cities."

"But there's no runway!"

"Of course, there's a runway. You think I'd land this baby without a runway? Look beyond the building and to the right.

You see a pile of boulders?"

I searched the ground for a few seconds. "Yes, just above the grass. Looks to be a couple feet tall."

"Continue to look east and you'll find more rocks. Beyond those are more piles in a straight line."

"I see them."

"Now if you look fifty feet to the north, you'll see another line of boulders. Between the two lines is the landing strip."

"That's the runway? You're kidding. There must be a couple hundred animals down there."

"Yep, wildebeest mostly. They help to keep the runway grass from getting too high. It's a little too crowded right now. Need to clear things out a bit."

"Are those zebras?"

"A few. Usually, they're only found in the national parks, but every once in a while, a small herd'll wander over here. They generally don't last long. The villagers tend to hunt 'em down. Poaching's against the law and the locals could go to jail, but they take the risk if they have a family to feed. Actually, what I'm about to do is also illegal but it's the only landing area for a hundred miles." He flicked his finger at another gauge. "You might want to fasten your seatbelt."

I searched. "There is no seatbelt."

"Of course, there is. Not allowed to fly without one. It's on either side of your seat."

I reached over and found the frayed ends of two nylon straps. "This is my seat belt? Where's the buckle?"

"Gone. You have to tie it. Double knot. Make sure it's tight." He handed me a small towel. "Put this between the straps and your stomach for padding."

"Padding?"

"In case we go down. Don't want to rupture your gut if we crash."

Sweat trickled down my face. "Crash? I thought you said this plane's never failed you."

"Only twice."

Twice? We're fucked.

"Here we go." With that, Nigel pushed the stick forward and the plane made an abrupt nosedive. My stomach jumped up into my chest, threatening to heave any second. The plane suddenly leveled off only twenty feet above the ground and accelerated. My insides somersaulted. Animals scattered in all directions.

"Trees ahead!" I said and braced myself against the back of my seat.

"Yep." Nigel pulled back on the stick, bringing the plane's nose upward. The branches were so close I could see the veining in the leaves. I folded over and prepared myself for the crash. Nigel pushed the stick to the side and the plane banked hard to the left as he pulled around to make his approach. He landed before the animals had a chance to return.

Three rough bounces later, Nigel taxied to the far end of the strip, turned one hundred eighty degrees, and pulled next to the small concrete block building. Its walls were pockmarked with dozens of bullet holes. Bad sign. The plane shuddered to a stop, the engine threatening to die at any second. Nigel turned the nose to face back down the runway and kept revving the engine to keep it running.

I let out a deep breath. Didn't believe in a God but I thanked Him anyway when I stepped off the plane. I slung the backpack of cash over my shoulder while Nigel quickly tossed my duffel bags to the ground. He disappeared inside the plane and returned with a white Styrofoam cooler.

"What's that?" I asked.

"Don't know. I was told to give it to you to take to the orphanage. I'm not paid to know anything else." Nigel gazed in all directions. "One problem with all these wildebeest and zebras is that they tend to attract predators."

"Predators?" I looked around and saw nothing but high grass and trees. "You mean like lions?"

Nigel climbed back into his plane and lowered the window. "Yeah, maybe lions. They like to hide in the tall buffalo grass. Hard to see 'em. Sometimes other things hide there too. This isn't a good place to be hanging around for very long." He gazed out. "You said you got a ride? I don't see one anywhere."

"It was supposed to be waiting for me."

The pilot scanned the area. "Well, like I said, I don't see a car." He paused as if considering the options of leaving me alone or taking me back to civilization. "You got a gun?"

"No."

Nigel shook his head. "Who in the hell comes out here without a weapon? I saw a pack of hyenas near the end of the runway. Nasty creatures. Powerful jaws that can crush through bone like nothing. They surround their prey, always attacking from the rear and biting at the legs, trying to tear a tendon or muscle. Once they bring something down, they don't waste time killing it. They start eating while the poor animal's still alive."

"Eat them alive?"

"Yep. They gotta fill themselves up before something bigger and badder steals their kill. I suspect they were stalking that wildebeest herd looking for an old one to attack. They ran off when we landed, but they might be coming back. Since the wildebeest herd scattered, you're the easiest meal around." He disappeared into the back of the plane and when he returned, he sat behind the controls and tossed something out the window. It was a rusty revolver, probably older than the plane. "It's a forty-five. You know how to use one?"

"A little. Just point and shoot." I balanced the weight of the gun in my hand. I'd seen enough movies to know I should check to see if it was loaded. It was.

He yelled over the sounds of the engine. "If something gets too close for comfort, just pull the trigger. Even if you don't hit anything, the noise alone should scare 'em off. Save the last bullet for yourself."

"For me?"

"You don't want to find yourself on the menu while you're still breathing. Most times though, it's the two-legged type of animal you have to worry about."

"What if the sound doesn't scare them off?"

"Just pray your ride gets here soon. I need to take off before anyone decides to come by to check things out. They don't get planes around here very often and when they do, the bad guys tend to show up. Like I said, hope your ride gets here soon. Good luck!"

With that, Nigel revved up the plane's engine. It belched out more black exhaust, and lumbered down the runway until it was in the air. A cloud of red dust coated my tongue. I took a gulp of water from my canteen as the plane disappeared into the distant haze, leaving me alone in the middle of nowhere. Even at this early hour, the air was already heavy with humidity. There was no breeze, just the suffocating heat. I wiped my brow and did a three hundred sixty-degree assessment of my situation. In the distance, I heard the mooing of wildebeest while zebras brayed, a cross between the sound of a donkey and a dog. All around me, acres of high buffalo grass melted into the far horizon, perfect cover for anything that wanted to hide until the last minute. To the east, small foothills slowly rolled into tall dark green mountains. I was alone.

Terrific. Should have listened to Desmond. What the hell ever drew me to this god-forsaken place? The cries of wild animals pierced the morning. I didn't know much about the wildlife in Africa, but I'd seen enough programs on The Animal Planet to know, they weren't the cries of an animal in distress. They were the sounds of predators, hungry predators, and they weren't very far away. Maybe those hyenas.

Looking out across the savannah, I studied the landscape, searching for possible threats. I feared that if I blinked, I might miss something. *Is that grass shifting from side to side?* My heart raced, skipping beats. It was subtle, but there was definite movement, and it wasn't from the wind. There was no wind. Pulling back on the hammer of my gun, I aimed in the direction of the disturbance.

"Keep one bullet for yourself," the pilot had said. I squinted and studied the grass. "Where's my damn ride?" There, in the distance to my right, a Jeep kicked up a rooster tail of thick red dust behind it. "About time!" I said, just before everything went black.

TWELVE

Middle of Nowhere
East Nigeria

Brett

Through a veil of semi-consciousness, I pulled hard against something. My face was pushed against the dirt, filling my mouth with red clay. I tried to spit it out but had no saliva. My eyes burst open at the sound of gunfire. Something hit the ground hard next to me. It was a man and the back of his head was gone. At least I was still breathing. Couldn't say as much for the guy lying next to me. His bloody hands clenched around one of the straps of my backpack. I was still holding the other one.

"That was close, Boss," said a voice from someone standing over me. "You can get up now if you're able." I rolled over and the man extended a hand to help me to my feet.

"Muth fuf of muf," I managed to croak out.

"That's because that dead asshole lying next to you had his foot on the back of your head, pushing your face into the ground. He wanted your backpack and was trying to smother you to death to get it. Even though you were barely conscious, you wouldn't let him take it. Must be something important— valuable enough to die for."

The man sported a headful of dreadlocks making him look more Jamaican than African. He offered me a bottle of water to rinse the clay out of my mouth. I swished a mouthful and spit out the mud, then guzzled the rest.

"You must be Mr. Buchanan." He handed me another bottle of water. "I'm Vincent."

"Vincent—?"

"Just Vincent."

"You were supposed to be here an hour ago."

"Sorry for the delay, Boss, but I had a little trouble with my vehicle."

Vincent was slender and tall but still stood four inches shorter than me. In a holster hanging low on his right hip, he wore a six-gun. The grip was comfortably worn to the contours of his hand. Vincent looked like he just stepped off the set of one of those Clint Eastwood spaghetti westerns. I could even hear that same eerie music in the background. Probably from the concussion.

Vincent held an automatic rifle, pointed to the ground. He was dressed in faded blue-jeans, a Bob Marley t-shirt, and running shoes. The man's eyes were concealed by large, mirrored blue sunglasses that he made no attempt to remove when he introduced himself. I figured he must be hiding something. I didn't like it when I couldn't see another man's eyes. Couldn't read them and as a pitcher, I relied on my ability to read an opposing batter's eyes. It was an art I learned out of necessity when I was a boy. By reading my father's eyes, I could tell if the man was simply on a rant or was close to attacking. That was my clue to tell my mother to run.

Should've done more to protect her.

A large scar traversed the entire left side of Vincent's face, disappearing under the glasses. The guy looked like he'd lived a hard life and been in his share of battles. Maybe he was former military or maybe even a criminal. One thing was for certain, Vincent was no stranger to violence.

My head throbbed. I now had a new headache to join the one from Philadelphia. They were like two giant black holes on a collision course as they migrated toward one another across my skull, threatening to become the mother of all migraines. I felt along the back of my scalp and discovered a sticky lump. My hand was covered with blood. "What happened? Was I shot?"

"You were ambushed by a gang of thugs. One of 'em hit you in the head with the butt of his rifle. They must have seen the plane landing and figured you'd be easy pickins. You would've been if I hadn't gotten here when I did and shot their leader. The others ran off into the bush."

Shit. I'd been mugged again. If this kept up, my brain was going to look like a plate of scrambled eggs. I looked at Vincent. "You saved my life. I'd be dead if you hadn't stopped them. Thank you."

"All part of the job, Boss." Vincent surveyed the area, looking for the other men. "Hopefully, the hyenas'll get 'em." He returned his attention to me. "They sure were interested in your backpack. They didn't go for anything else, even that expensive watch of yours."

Damn. I'd still forgotten to get rid of the damn watch. I checked the backpack and was relieved to see the cash still there, but the robbers must have known what I was carrying. How was that possible? I recalled the ambassador's advice and looked at the dead man on the ground. *Trust no one.* Maybe the pilot tipped them off, but why would he give me a gun? Maybe this Vincent guy was in on it, but why would he save my life?

"That pilot had no business leaving you here alone until he was sure I'd already arrived. East Nigeria can be a dangerous place, especially for a white man on his own." He checked the horizon, "We should leave, Boss. Think you can travel?"

"Yeah, I'll be fine." I pulled out my bottle of Aleve. Empty. Shit. "You happen to have any aspirin or ibuprofen?" A class 5 hurricane was raging inside my head.

Vincent laughed. "There ain't no medicines around here for at least a hundred miles. I do have this though." Vincent set his rifle down on the back seat of the Jeep and pulled a small flask from his pocket. "This might help."

"What is it?"

"The locals call it Ogogoro."

It smelled like turpentine, probably the Nigerian equivalent of moonshine whiskey. I yearned for a drink, if for no other reason than to help quiet the jackhammer smashing at the back of my skull. I declined. Drinking alcohol in any form would be a slippery slope that could lead me nowhere but trouble.

Vincent loaded my luggage into the back of the Jeep. He found the unused revolver lying on the ground nearby. He picked it up and studied it for a second. "Good thing you didn't need this gun, Boss. You'd be dead by now. The damn firing pin's broken. Where'd you get this piece of shit?"

"The pilot gave it to me." *Trust no one.*

We both heard it, something behind us. We spun around in time to see two men charging out of the buffalo grass, each carrying a rifle and aiming in our direction. Several errant shots whizzed past my ears. In the blink of an eye, Vincent drew his six-shooter from its holster and dropped both men in their tracks. Two shots and two men dead, just fifty feet away.

"Who were those guys?" I asked.

"Not sure. Don't much care as long as they're dead. I suspect they were the buddies of the guy who had his foot on the back of your head a few minutes ago. Probably thought they could get the jump on us while we weren't paying attention. Amateurs. Maybe friends of the pilot who gave you a worthless gun and no way to protect yourself."

Vincent walked over and kicked the two bodies. One of them groaned and Vincent put a bullet in his head. He must have noticed the shocked look in my eyes. "Did him a favor, Boss. Put him out of his misery before some hungry pack of hyenas started feeding on him while he was still breathing." He gathered up the dead men's rifles and put them in his Jeep. "They must think you're carrying some real valuable shit. Maybe in that backpack of yours. One thing's for sure, they knew something."

That damn pilot.

"We should go, before someone else shows up," said Vincent.

I nodded to the dead bodies. "What about them?"

"What about 'em?"

"Shouldn't we at least bury them or something?"

"You got a shovel?" asked Vincent.

"No."

"Neither do I, so I guess we leave 'em right where they are. This land has a way of cleaning up after itself. By this time tomorrow, they'll be all gone."

We finished loading my bags and the Styrofoam cooler into the back seat. Before we took off, Vincent handed me a rag and a fresh bottle of water. "Better rinse that blood out of your hair and the dirt off your face. You look like you've been in a war zone, and I don't want to have to explain what happened."

"Explain to whom?"

"Anyone interested enough to ask."

THIRTEEN

East Nigeria

Brett

As the Jeep took off, I asked, "Did Mr. Cabot send you?"

"You mean Mr. Sebastian Cabot from Abuja? No, he didn't send me. I just got a message that someone needed to be picked up out here. At first, I thought it was a joke. Who'd ever want to fly all the way out into the middle of this hell-hole place, but I was guaranteed payment, half up front, so here we are."

The Jeep's canvas top had been torn away over the years and the seats were worn through to the padding. Vincent handed me a length of thick rope. "Here's your seat belt."

Seat belt? A rope? At least Nigel gave me a towel to cushion my gut. I started getting more and more worried about this trip.

"Fasten it to the seat and tie it around your waist. Secure it tightly. We're headed cross-country and you're in for a bumpy ride ahead."

"Bumpy?" Was he speaking metaphorically or literally?

"The rainy season leaves the roads with deep ruts and I don't want you bouncing out if we have to run for it."

"Run for it?"

"The locals call this region a death trap and not only because of the surface conditions." He stared straight ahead. "Once we get to a regular road it'll be a bit better, but not much." Vincent pushed on the accelerator and the Jeep lurched forward. The gears groaned like a coffee grinder. Any small remnants of a suspension system protested. Something loud snapped under the chassis.

"What was that?"

"Nothing important."

"Sounded pretty damn important to me."

He stared straight ahead. "Hang on. It's gonna get rough."

"It's already rough. Think I just lost one of my kidneys." The ride was spine jarring. My headaches now had headaches and were getting worse by the minute.

A mile later, Vincent pulled under the cover of a copse of trees. "We need to take care of a few matters before we go any farther. You're still wearing that expensive watch and I assume you're carrying a substantial amount of cash in that backpack of yours. That's what those men were after when they jumped you. Give them to me now."

Shit, I was getting mugged again. I looked around and we were isolated. Couldn't see anything that resembled a road. I could try escaping but I'd never make it in time. Vincent was too good a shot, and it's hard to outrun a bullet. This would be a great place to hide my body. Cabot had told me that just a hundred dollars was more than most Nigerians made in a year, and I was carrying a hell of a lot more than that. I untied my rope seatbelt, jumped out of the Jeep, and raised my fists. "What? You planning to rob me? Not again. Gun or no gun, I'm not going to let that happen."

Vincent bent over in a wild laugh. He raised his hands in surrender. "No Boss. I'm not going to rob you."

I lowered my fists.

"All you white people think we blacks wanna rob you. If I was going to do that, I'd have done it fifteen minutes ago by the landing strip and blamed it on the thugs who attacked you. Like I said before, your body would have been completely gone within a day. The hyenas woulda seen to that."

I stared at him, but couldn't see his eyes with those big

sunglasses. Maybe, he was only covering his ass and waiting for a better opportunity to shoot me. Someone probably knew he was picking me up and eventually, any investigative trail would lead to his door, if he even had one.

Vincent laughed some more. "What I want to do, Boss, is to keep other people from robbing you. You're not in the United States anymore and there are very few laws out here. The only one that counts is the law of survival and that means people take whatever they want, whenever they want, from whomever they want. That includes lives. We don't want others finding out how much money you're carrying. We also don't want them knowing that a famous American baseball hero is traveling through the backcountry of East Nigeria. You're an attractive target, Mr. Buchanan. You'd fetch a sizable ransom if you were kidnapped. That's why I need your wallet, passport and any other valuables you might be carrying."

I never told him I played baseball.

I turned over everything, including the backpack with the two-hundred-thousand dollars. Vincent didn't open it. He checked my wallet and removed any papers that could identify me as a U.S. citizen. He removed all but fifty-dollars-worth of Nigerian naira and told me to hide the rest. The cash joined the rest of the money I was already hiding in my socks.

When he saw my stash, Vincent again laughed. "Clever, Boss. Who'd ever think to look in someone's socks. Shit. Everybody hides their cash there, Boss." He took my Patek Philippe watch and gave me a Rolex to wear instead.

"A Rolex! This isn't much better than wearing my own!"

Vincent simply smiled in return. "Trust me."

I wasn't supposed to trust anyone.

Vincent lifted the Jeep's rear seat and pried open a long metal compartment hidden under the floorboard. He stowed all my valuables inside. Next to them sat a cache of grenades, automatic rifles, and ammunition inside an open nylon duffel bag.

"What's all that for? You planning on starting your own private war?"

"Can't be too careful, Boss," replied Vincent.

"Are you a smuggler? Do you run guns, maybe even to Boko Haram?"

A momentary glare flickered in Vincent's eyes before the look gave way to a forced smile. "A man must do what a man's gotta do to survive out here." Vincent removed the Styrofoam cooler from the rear seat. It was wrapped tightly with gray duct tape. "What's this?"

"Don't know. I hadn't ever seen it before this morning. The pilot told me to deliver it to the orphanage."

Vincent pulled a knife from his pocket, pushed a button on the side and a six-inch switchblade sprung out. He cut the tape from around the cooler and opened it. Medications. "I hope they didn't send any kind of drugs in this thing. If we get caught with narcotics, it'll be bad for us. You don't get a jury trial out here. Justice is quickly meted out with a bullet." He emptied the contents of the cooler onto the Jeep's seat. Wrapped in ice packs was a selection of different antibiotics. In addition, there were vials of immunization medications. Vincent checked inside the cooler for a false compartment. There was none. "At least they didn't use you as a mule to carry dope. It happens sometimes."

"The Comboni Sisters would never do that," I said.

"Probably not, but someone else along the supply chain could have, including that pilot who left you here to die. You never know." Vincent packed the medications back into the cooler and stopped for a minute.

"What?" I asked.

"I'm not sure how to handle this stuff. If I leave it sitting in the open, people might think it contains drugs. Out here, some'd kill you in an instant to get their hands on 'em. If I hide them under the seat and the army finds them, they'll shoot us for smuggling drugs. We're screwed either way." Eventually he decided to load the cooler into his hidden compartment. If the army found it, they'd shoot us anyway for smuggling the guns. Vincent got back behind the wheel and headed east until he found a road. Once there, he pushed on the accelerator.

Faster. Go faster. Another punch in the gut. I thought life would slow down here, but everywhere I went I always seemed to be in a hurry. In America, it was always for the sake of speed. In Nigeria, it appeared to be the need to escape danger—maybe even head toward it. I didn't know for sure which one I was doing.

FOURTEEN

First Checkpoint
East Nigeria

Brett

It only took an hour of traveling down the road before I under-stood the significance of Vincent's concern regarding the cash and cooler of medications. Our way was blocked by a line of cars stacked up behind an army truck painted in camouflage.

"It's our first checkpoint, Boss."

Two armed Nigerian soldiers stood in the middle of the road, pointing automatic rifles at the cars while a third one manned a large machine gun in the bed of the truck. Yelling erupted in front of us. The two soldiers pulled a man from his car and forced him to the ground, his fingers locked behind his head.

"What happened?" I asked.

"The guy made a mistake."

"What kind of mistake?"

"A bad one."

Bam. The loud shot startled me. If it hadn't been for my seatbelt, I'd have jumped out of the Jeep. One of the soldiers had shot the man in the back of his head, spraying blood across the grass in front of him. No one paid attention. Business as usual. The soldiers trained their weapons on us as Vincent came to a slow stop and waited for one of the military men to approach.

"Captain Azikiwe! He's the one wearing the beret. He'd

sell his own mother for a few dollars," Vincent whispered through clenched teeth. "Say nothing and do only what I tell you to do." He and the captain got into a heated discussion, yelling at each other in a language that seemed to be a combination of English and another one I didn't understand. Vincent waved his arms around wildly. The captain responded by raising his rifle and aiming. Vincent held his hands up in submission and acted irritated. He turned to me and winked. "He wants what's in your wallet. Calls it a travel tax. Give him the money. He also wants your watch. Try to look a little pissed off when you hand it to him."

I put on the act and removed the Rolex and all the cash from my wallet. I handed them to Vincent who turned them over to the captain. The man shook the watch and listened to it. Satisfied that it worked well, he told one of his men to back up their truck and let our Jeep pass.

A hundred yards down the road I asked, "What was that all about?"

"I've dealt with this captain before. It's how things are done in Nigeria. It's a way of life here, kinda like bartering. We get safe passage for another hour in exchange for your wallet-full of naira and the watch. No search of the Jeep, no questions asked, and no bullet in the head. All things considered, I'd call it a pretty good deal, but the captain didn't get what he thought." Vincent laughed. "The Rolex was fake. I have a dozen of 'em in that compartment next to the guns. As soon as I get a chance, we'll pull over and I'll get another one out for you to wear. You'll also need to pull another batch of naira from your sock and put it in your wallet. That won't be our last checkpoint."

"What if they had found the cooler or your guns?"

"We wouldn't be around to worry about it." Vincent pushed on the accelerator and the Jeep again lunged forward.

FIFTEEN

Kanguna, Nigeria

Brett

Thirty miles beyond the first checkpoint, we entered the outskirts of a small town. "Kanguna," Vincent called it. The road was flanked on both sides by small vegetable farms. Owners herded goats along dirt paths while women pushed wooden carts loaded with firewood. In the center of the town sat clusters of shops, housed in small cinder-block sheds that were at one time painted in bright hues of yellow, blue, and red. Like festering sores, those layers of color were peeling away, exposing the gray concrete underneath. The sides of the buildings were scarred with bullet holes and splattered with dark red splotches I could only assume were from dried blood. Battles had been waged here and by the looks of things, it wasn't that long ago.

The men wore loose pants held up with belts or lengths of twine while women wore faded wraparound dresses. T-shirts displayed symbols of western culture: NY Yankees, Jimi Hendrix, Snoop Dog. Some wore old Nikes while others walked around in tire sandals. Many remained barefoot. The front of each shop opened like a wooden garage door exposing the items for sale inside. Farmers displayed their crops of fresh fruits and vegetables, carefully arranged on makeshift tables. The food selection was limited, and the quality looked poor. The smell of smoke filled the air as men tended fires made in old oil drums. They grilled indiscernible creatures that had been impaled on stick skewers. After cooking, they were chopped into bite-sized pieces. I pointed to the charred critters. "What are they?"

"Don't know," replied Vincent. "Could be almost anything. Looks like when they were alive, they had fur and four legs." Slabs of some types of meat hung from tree limbs, unrefrigerated in the midday sun, blanketed by a variety of winged insects. A merchant carved off slices with a machete. Vincent said, "As disgusting as it looks, meat is a delicacy that many in the market can't afford."

It was no wonder disease was such a prevalent problem in the country. Few if any precautions were taken to protect the health of the community. As if in answer to the problem, we passed a section devoted to items of witchcraft and native cures for any and all ailments. Spread out on the ground were lemon-sized beetles, snake heads, pulverized horns, and dried parts of dead animals that defied description. A chorus of voices filled the air, people hawking their products and haggling over prices, desperately trying to entice a buyer.

"People come from remote farms and small villages to gather here every day, hoping to make enough money to feed their families. It's an ongoing struggle for them," said Vincent.

Several stalls contained piles of shirts and pants. "Where'd they get the clothing to sell? Most of it looks like it comes from the U.S."

"Most of it does, Boss. I think they call it Goodwill."

"But those items are donated. They're supposed to be free. Why do people have to pay for them?"

"Capitalism, Boss. Missionaries have been trying to teach the locals how to run a business in order to establish a local economy besides farming. This helps them understand the concept. The merchants buy the clothes for pennies and sell them for a few cents more. They don't make much profit but, it's a start."

"It looks like the locals are learning well."

"They're trying, but over the past several years this village, like many others in remote Nigeria, has been slowly dying. If you look closely, you'll see that most people aren't buying, just selling. It's a matter of numbers. This town has been bleeding inhabitants for years. Some have given up and moved to the larger cities in the hopes of finding a better life. Many have left to work in the newly discovered diamond fields farther to the east in the Mayo-Sina region. Several hundred thousand have flocked there with shovels or any other tools they can get their hands on, hoping to find a stone and get rich. It's usually a futile attempt, leading only to more poverty and death. The only ones who get rich are the mine owners. The local people continue to starve. Meanwhile, small towns like this one suffer a slow death."

"Maybe we should stop and buy a few things. Maybe help them a little."

"Real bad idea, Boss. Stopping anywhere is not an option. You're not going to make friends out of these people by throwing around a few hundred dollars. That's a lot of money, more than most of 'em will see in their lifetimes. As soon as they see a white man pull out his wallet, they'll swarm us, looking for more. It'll take no time at all before it turns into an angry mob."

We pressed on toward the far outskirts of the town. The area looked more depressed than what we'd just left. Almost all the cubicles and stalls sat empty. More bullet holes marred the sides of the buildings. Blood had been shed here. I yelled, "Stop!"

Vincent slammed on the brakes, bringing the Jeep to a screeching halt. My seatbelt rope dug into my gut. Vincent jerked his head from side to side. "What?"

"Back up."

"I told you, there's no stopping along here, Boss. Too dangerous."

"Back up, I said."

Vincent frowned and put the Jeep in reverse. Gears protested.

I looked down a narrow dirt street. "Over there." I pointed to our right, a spot a hundred feet away. "There's a mob back there and they're beating a young boy with clubs. They might kill him!"

"I suspect they will, Boss. Probably caught him stealing."

"But he's only a boy, thirteen at the most. We have to do something for him."

"In Nigeria, a teen is already considered to be a man and is held accountable for a man's actions. It's called jungle justice. There's nothing we can do."

"We have those rifles of yours. We can save him."

"Our guns aren't going to help us against a violent mob like that one. They have blood in their eyes. They're angry, and right now that boy is as good as dead. You might want to help but believe me, he's not some innocent kid. There are thousands of others just like him in Nigeria. They'd shoot both of us in a heartbeat if it meant something was in it for them."

A tire hung from around the boy's neck. "But why the car tire?"

"It's called necklacing, usually saved for cases of treason or murder. Maybe he killed someone while stealing. The tire's soaked in gasoline. Once they've finished with him, they'll light it. A lesson to others. Then everything'll be over."

"We can't let them do that, Vincent. I have money. I can repay what he stole!"

"For what? You think if you make reparations, they'll just let him go? No! Like I said, he's already as good as dead."

Some of the mob turned toward the Jeep and pointed in our direction. Even at this distance I saw hatred in their eyes, the hungry look of those who have nothing to lose. I saw that same look when Desmond and I were attacked near the Abuja slums, when the poor woman was being stoned to death. Several of the men headed toward our Jeep. Vincent stepped on the gas and the front tires lifted off the ground. I instinctively grabbed the dash as my head snapped back. Headache got worse.

"You mentioned the money, Boss. How much, exactly?" asked Vincent.

"Enough."

Vincent appeared to consider the situation for a few seconds. "Like I told you, there's nothing you can do for the kid. If you offer them your money, they'll take it and then still kill the boy. Probably us too. You won't be doing anybody any good if you're rotting in a ditch somewhere. In many areas of the world, death is a way of life. You'll see some things in my country that you might call an atrocity, but you must always keep in mind that you are a guest here. You're not in the United States anymore. We have different rules. There's no due process. The people here have their own ways of dealing with problems and what you just witnessed is only one of them. Don't try to interfere. You don't want to find yourself on the receiving end of their justice system. Their judgment is swift, ruthless, and not fair. Remember this, you have only one responsibility out here. That's to survive, not take care of every sorry soul you see."

When safely out of the village, Vincent slowed the Jeep. I craned my neck to look back in time to see a plume of black smoke rising from the village, the kind you see when rubber burns. The screams were mercifully brief. A sense of nausea welled up in my stomach. Should've tried to do something for the boy.

The gravelly voice hit me. **"What *you should've done was to protect your own family, Brett. You didn't. You were too preoccupied with you.*"**

So far, this country was not providing the chance for the atonement I needed. How in the hell did I get myself into this mess?

It was the nun.

SIXTEEN

East Nigeria

Brett

I met Sister Mary Margaret as part of my twelve-step program. After I was found passed out in an alley in Philadelphia, my agent arranged to have me placed in a new rehab program. This time, it wasn't another country club retreat like Monterey where they hide celebrities from the public so they can dry out in private. This one was the real deal, more like a boot camp. The program focused on addicts whose lives were already on the brink of destruction, a broad cross section of society including lawyers, corporate executives, blue collar workers, and the homeless. Many were forced into rehab by judges in lieu of jail time. No one in the center cared about previous lives or levels of influence. All were treated as equals. Every resident was required to live at the facility for at least six months. During that time, just one deviation from the rules resulted in dismissal from the program with no option to return. Any chance to regain a normal life was lost. Twice-a-day group discussions with counselors and other addicts were mandatory: every morning and evening. There were no considerations for the schedules of the rich and famous. We were all the same, substance abusers. No one received special treatment, not even baseball celebrities.

One of the requirements was that the residents attend some type of religious service at least once a week. For me that meant returning to my roots in the Catholic Church. The intent was "To improve our conscious contact with God, to pray for the knowledge of His will for us, and to foster the strength to carry that out." Much to the chagrin of the nuns at my orphanage, I never bought into the whole God thing. Mom was devoutly religious, and He never did anything for her. I spent most of the church time ignoring the message being delivered. I doubted that any God could help me. He certainly wasn't there during my childhood.

On one Sunday, our group attended a service at the Church of St. Paul the Apostle. It was a magnificent, old building with vaulted dark ceilings that forced you to look up toward heaven. Intricate stained-glass windows along the sides depicted various scenes from the Bible. The smell of incense filled the air.

After the priest completed the initial part of the mass, the congregation sat for his homily. Instead of delivering a sermon, he introduced a nun who had been invited to deliver a presentation. She stood behind a polished walnut pulpit, a resting lamb ornately carved in the front. She wore an old-fashioned, sky-blue habit with a large silver crucifix hanging around her neck. A fiery determination glowed in her eyes as they gazed at each and every member in the congregation. When she spoke, I had the feeling she was talking directly to me.

"I want to thank Father Miller and everyone here at Saint Paul's for allowing me to speak to you today. My name is Sister Mary Margaret and I'm a member of the Comboni Missionary Sisters. Usually, when an outsider speaks during the priest's sermon, it means that person is going to ask you to open your wallets and checkbooks for donations."

A wave of nervous chuckles rippled through the church.

"I'm afraid I'm no exception to that rule, but before you dismiss me as just another person begging for money, I'd like you to take just a few minutes to hear my story."

She poured a glass of ice water from a pitcher, her microphone picking up the sound of water splashing into the glass. She took a sip and set it in front of her on the lectern. "Such a simple thing to do, pour a glass of water," she said, her eyes seeming to lock onto mine. I wasn't sure if she knew who I was, but I felt a connection with her.

She continued. "God has blessed this country of ours, this United States of America, and we should be proud of what we have accomplished. The U.S. has become the most successful country in the history of civilization. We live in a democracy governed by laws that protect all. If we are hungry, we simply drive to the nearest grocery store or restaurant to buy whatever we want to satisfy that hunger. Our options are endless. If we feel uncomfortably hot or cold, we push a few buttons on a thermostat and are rewarded with a perfectly temperature-controlled environment. If we happen to become ill, we can see our doctor and he prescribes medicine to cure us."

She stared at the glass of water still sitting in front of her. Tears of condensation ran down the sides. "And if we become thirsty, we can turn on a faucet. Instantly we have a glass of clean, fresh water." She took another sip and set the glass back down. "In some areas of Africa, women must carry heavy jugs of water for miles, back and forth, twice a day, just for the privilege of enjoying a simple drink. Food is a scarce commodity. Thousands of hungry little orphans die of starvation every week. For them, each day is a life and death struggle to survive. When they are afraid or are hurt, they can't reach out for the comfort of a mother's arms. There is no father to protect them. They have no family to care for them. Parents die from famine, disease, or attacks by terrorists. I'd like to show you how the orphaned children look when they first arrive at our shelter. I must warn you that the photographs you are about to see are graphic and disturbing. What you must keep in mind is that for us in this country, these are merely pictures. For these children in Nigeria, it's their daily lives. First slide please."

She paused, allowing the parishioners to study the slide and digest the horror they were seeing. There were dozens of children, half-naked and covered in sores, their bellies distended from malnutrition. Many of them were Jonathan's age. Their blank stares bore into my soul. There was no childhood spark in those eyes, just an emptiness, devoid of any hope for the future. It was almost as though they had resigned themselves to the inevitability of their impending death.

Sister Mary Margaret continued. "This is how these same children look after only two months of proper food and medical care in our orphanage." I leaned forward in the pew and studied the pictures closely. Gone were the ravages of malnutrition. Their bright eyes were now full of hope. Despair was replaced by wide smiles. "We are able to accomplish these miraculous changes in each of these innocent children's lives for only a dollar a day. That's less than the cost of a cup of coffee."

She let her message sink in for a minute. "We at Comboni Sisters don't venture far beyond the reaches of civilization for the purpose of recruiting souls. We do it because it needs to be done. Our mission is to go into the impoverished, dark corners of the world to provide resources such as food, clean water, medicine, and schools. Our primary purpose is to eliminate their anguish. Once that is done, we preach the good news of creation for any who might be interested. Our reward is not in amassing converts. It's seeing the happy faces of these young children."

The good Sister turned to face the screen. "One of my favorite stories involves the time a young girl was brought to us just a few years after we started the orphanage. She was a member of the Zambuti, an isolated mountain tribe that had rarely been encountered by the outside world. There had been rumors of their existence, but until that day, I had never seen one. The people spoke a language that none of us had ever heard before, so regular communication was all but impossible. The tribe appeared at the edge of the jungle one morning. At first, I was terrified. They were pygmies, almost naked, covered from head to toe in ornate red tattoos. After a few tense minutes, a young woman stepped forward. She was carrying a little girl, listless and near death. The child couldn't have been older than three. She was gasping as though each breath would be her last. The mother handed the child to me and said the word, 'Maageek.'

"It took me a second to realize what the mother wanted. Her child was obviously sick, and she wanted me to heal her with magic. I carried the little girl to our makeshift clinic and had one of the other nuns examine her. The child had severe tonsillitis to the extent that she was septic. The problem was as simple as a bad case of strep throat. It took several days but we were able to cure her with several dollars-worth of penicillin, a treatment usually taken for granted in our country—but a life saver in Nigeria.

"Her parents and many members of her tribe remained at her side twenty-four hours a day until she was ready to leave. Our reward was that a few days after they disappeared back into the jungle, the girl and her parents returned. They had given the girl a small red tattoo on her right cheek, a crucifix just like the one I wear around my neck. It wasn't that they wanted to convert to Christianity. They had no idea what our religion was about, but they did want to show respect for our culture just as we had respected theirs. They were good people, so what could we convert them to? In their own way, they were following the same principles of Christianity as we do, perhaps more so. I only have a single photograph of her smiling face and those of her parents. They wouldn't allow any more to be taken because they believe pictures have the power to steal a person's soul."

I sensed that there was something else to the nun's story, but she was reluctant to share it. She was definitely holding something back, a fact that made her feel guilty. I could see it in her eyes, but what could it be? The woman was like a living saint. What could a nun from Africa possibly have to hide? Maybe it was because she was asking for money. It was almost as though revealing her secret would somehow jeopardize all that she had worked for.

Sister Mary Margaret continued for another twenty minutes, discussing the need for donations, but I was unable to pay attention. The pictures she had shown were gut-wrenching. It was a sobering display of how little those in other parts of the world had in contrast to life in America. Though my life as a child had been tragic, it paled in comparison to the lives these young children were forced to live. As an adult, I had allowed myself to be consumed by the self-centered pursuit of fame and hedonistic gratification, making my own life a travesty while too many in the world suffered. I made my decision. The following day, I called my agent and arranged for a half-million-dollar donation to the Comboni Missionary Sisters. The gift helped to ease the guilt about my personal sins, but I was still unable to get the plight of those young African children off my mind. Just as when I helped the amputee veteran at the ballpark, writing a check was too easy, especially for a man of my wealth. Just another coat of paint.

A month later I made the fateful decision to travel to Nigeria. I needed to witness first-hand what was going on there. Somehow, I believed that in Africa, I could find what I was looking for, a rebirth.

SEVENTEEN

East Nigeria

Brett

After exiting the town of Kanguna, we passed vehicles headed in the opposite direction. They spewed out thick clouds of black exhaust. "Shit cars," I used to call them when I was an arrogant teenager—before I became a self-absorbed adult. I remembered something I once read while in rehab, "The arrogance of success often digs its own grave." The irony was painful.

Vincent seemed to read my mind. "Everything is relative, Boss. They may look like clunkers to you, but out here, they're the equivalent of a Rolls Royce. Except for the military, you won't see many cars in East Nigeria. Too expensive."

The flow of cars slowed to a trickle, mostly replaced by carts pulled by men or women, hunched over, carrying loads of firewood or goods. Where they were headed, I couldn't tell, but they appeared determined to get there. Time crawled by. We continued driving together in silence for the next hour, the only sounds being the Jeep bumping across deep ruts, and the scraping complaints from the car's undercarriage. The pitch of the road steepened and the air grew cooler, a welcomed change from the oppressive heat of the lower altitudes. Dry grass gave way to heavy green brush and groves of small trees. We were climbing the plateau I had seen earlier from Nigel's plane. Along the way, we drove through several creeks, their drying beds a latticework of deep cracks.

"During the rainy season we wouldn't be able to forge through here," said Vincent. "Too deep. In another month it'll be bone dry."

Small groups of women collected whatever water they could find in isolated pools to take back to their homes. Like acrobats, they balanced the heavy jugs atop their heads, some with a baby hanging from a cloth pouch on their back. Little faces stared out toward emptiness without any spark of curiosity in their eyes. Clouds of black flies swarmed around their tiny heads, landing near their eyes or mouths, trying to steal a drink.

I thought about Sister Mary Margaret's words about how difficult it could be to get water in Africa. "How far do they have to carry those jugs?"

"There's a small village a couple miles down the road, so I guess that's where they'll be headed. Once the creeks dry up completely, they'll have to walk all the way to the Taraba River. That's over five miles, just one way and they must make the trek every day."

At the top of a hill, Vincent slowed the Jeep. "There's another checkpoint straight ahead. Remember, say nothing. Let me do all the talking."

Everything happened about the same as the last roadblock, except the soldiers seemed a little more nervous and animated. Unlike the disciplined soldiers at the first checkpoint, their uniforms were stained and frayed. Looked like these men were second stringers, relegated to this more distal assignment. No one appeared to be in charge, all yelling at the same time, shouting orders I couldn't understand. I stared straight ahead and said nothing, which seemed to irritate them more.

"Stay cool," said Vincent. "These guys aren't the army's brightest. It'll be over soon."

The soldiers searched my luggage and found nothing of value. They settled for my fifty dollars and my watch, another fake Rolex.

"They were agitated," I said as we pulled away.

"Boko Haram's been in the area."

"How could you be sure they weren't just going to shoot us?"

"I haven't dealt with these particular guys before, but I knew they wouldn't shoot. I have a good instinct for these things."

"But what if your instincts were wrong and they decided to thoroughly search the Jeep? They would've found your secret compartment."

"Then, we'd do what we must to survive. Run, if we can."

"And if we can't run?"

"Plan B."

"Plan B? What's plan B?"

Vincent didn't respond. He looked straight ahead. "There's the next town."

The few homes scattered on either side of the road appeared to have been abandoned. Pens that once held livestock, now sat empty. All that remained of market stalls were the skeletal remnants of their wooden frames. The smell of putrefaction permeated the air. A dog, so malnourished he looked closer to death than life, wandered about, patrolling the dusty ground, searching for scraps of food. Its fur was matted with blood and his right ear had been torn in two. He stopped and sniffed at the carcass of some small creature. It looked similar to what I had seen the men cooking earlier in the last town. This one had obviously been dead for some time. Excited by his good fortune, the dog grabbed the treasure in his mouth and quickly escaped into the bush.

"What happened here?" I asked Vincent.

"Boko Haram. Last month they strapped a young girl with explosives and forced her to walk into the market. Eleven villagers were killed. Female children were taken to be trafficked as sex slaves in the Middle East markets. Boys were conscripted into their army. Boko Haram has been systematically burning down Christian villages for years. Occasionally they'll even attack Muslim towns to recruit more members for their army.

Their stated goal is to destroy the present Nigerian government and replace it with an Islamic Caliphate. Mostly though, they're simply common thugs who use their organization as an excuse to pillage, rape, and murder. They conquered a large section of the country in the northeast, but the Nigerian army claims to have taken back much of that territory. I don't know if it's true, but the claims have pissed off the Boko Haram leaders. It's made them even more aggressive."

"Why hasn't the army tracked them all down and destroyed them?"

"They've tried, but in doing so, they've become just as ruthless and predatory as Boko Haram." Vincent rubbed the scar on the side of his face. "That's how I got this. Wrong place at the wrong time." He paused, maybe in a not-so-distant memory. "Anyway, the army's been unable to completely eradicate the insurgents because they're like ghosts. Some retreat into the jungles and the mountains near Cameroon where it's impossible to find them. Others hide their uniforms and dissolve into the remote villages for a while, only to return to the main camps when called upon. Locals are afraid to turn them in. There are worse punishments for betrayal than simple death."

"Like necklacing?"

Vincent nodded. "That and more. One of their leaders is a man by the name of Shakar Bhutah. Some say he's possessed by the devil himself. I saw him once when I was driving through a village in the northeast states. He's big, but not tall like you. He's big around. His gang was trying to recruit new members for his army and it wasn't voluntary. Those who didn't join were either beaten or shot. I got out of there fast. Shakar is insane—and smart."

"Dangerous combination."

"He's not someone you want to anger. While he's cutting your heart out, he grins, showing off his gold front tooth. Considers it a trophy. Got it from a government official he once clubbed to death."

"Stop the Jeep."

He ignored my request. "I told you before, it's not safe around here."

Several elderly women, wearing faded head wraps and tattered dresses, tended roadside stands where they were selling bottles of water, beans, peanuts, and firewood to buyers that didn't exist. The usual army of flies attacked them, but they seemed to be oblivious to the onslaught, their desperate eyes gazing out toward a future, which could only offer them despair. I couldn't take my eyes off one of the women. She stared at me, her eyes fixated on mine. She was the victim of the harsh jungle world, her dark skin leathered and worn like the dried-up creature the dog had found. We were from different cultures, from opposite sides of the world, but on some inexplicable level, I felt a connection with her, a commonality of the anguish in our souls. She was a victim of her environment, things beyond her control, but my anguish was self-inflicted by my own bad decisions. I had the opportunity to climb out of my despair. She couldn't. I had to do something for her.

"Just stop for a second," I said. "Pull up next to that old woman. Look at her. She's no threat." When the Jeep came to a halt, I got out to inspect the woman's goods. I wanted to help her in some way, prepared to hand over my entire backpack of money, but what could she do with so much cash? There was nothing to buy. She was too old to head toward a different life in the city. This was her home, the only life she knew.

"Don't buy the water, Boss," Vincent warned me from behind. "The old women scour the roadsides and pick up whatever plastic bottles they can find. They fill 'em with creek water. That stuff's about as clean as a toilet. Drink out of one of 'em and you're going to have the shits for a month. Same goes for the peanuts and beans. Probably all rotted."

Ignoring his advice, I dug into my socks for money and purchased the woman's entire inventory of eleven bottles of water and three sacks of peanuts. I gave her a fistful of money, probably hundreds of times the amount she was asking. I smiled and took her hand in mine, her skin rough, but soft at the same time.

"No tell," I said to her. She nodded, seeming to understand. I told her to hide the money, advice that wasn't necessary.

I got back into the Jeep and Vincent again floored it. The car sped off in a cloud of dust. I looked back as the old woman clenched her new-found wealth and smiled. She hid the money under her head wrap as she watched our car disappear into the distance. After we were out of sight, I tossed my recent purchases into the depths of the bush. The bottles would be available for recycling by others.

Vincent stared at me. "Why didn't you just give her the money, Boss?"

"I wanted to give her more than cash. I wanted to give her a sense of dignity. In some ways, that can be more important than the money."

EIGHTEEN

East Nigeria

Brett

Our Jeep strained toward higher elevations, struggling so much I thought we might have to get out and push. The road gradually deteriorated into a dirt path, partially overgrown with weeds and scrub brush. Trees reached across the path to join their counterparts on the other side, almost as though the jungle itself was trying to devour us, Jeep and all. The foliage grew thicker, creating a canopy that ultimately blocked out the sun. We pressed on, as if driving into the dark maw of a giant creature. Fear nibbled at the back of my brain. I felt like Wiley Coyote in one of those old Road Runner cartoons when he chased the bird into a dark tunnel, directly into an oncoming train. What was I heading toward?

It was unexpected. We drove around a sharp bend and saw what looked like another checkpoint in a small grassy clearing. *Why here?* This time the road was obstructed by a rusted, white Ford pickup truck that lacked any official military insignias. It had no machine gun mounted on the back.

Vincent slammed on the brakes and brought the Jeep to a sudden halt twenty feet away. The plume of dust that had been stalking us continued forward, engulfing us in a cloud of red. I coughed and by the time the air had cleared two soldiers approached, carrying automatic rifles.

"Shit," said Vincent.

"Another checkpoint?" I asked.

"I don't think so, Boss. They're not wearing uniforms and they don't look Nigerian. Probably mercenaries from another country. Our little watch trick isn't going to work this time."

"So, whatta we do?"

"No matter what you hear me say, keep your mouth shut. We might get lucky enough to survive this."

"Survive?"

"Trust me on this, Boss."

Are you kidding? I was told to trust no one.

The soldiers' eyes darted around in all directions as though in search of danger, but we were the only ones around, and we weren't holding weapons. Wide-eyed, the two men acted like cornered animals on the verge of shooting anything they might perceive as a threat, their rifles pointed directly at us. We were trapped with nowhere to run.

"I have this," whispered Vincent. "These guys don't look very bright, and that's a break for us." He smiled, but a momentary look of concern on his face betrayed his confidence. Keeping his eyes trained on the two men, he retrieved a handgun from under the seat and chambered a round. "Take this. If things go sideways, you don't have to do anything but point and shoot. Don't panic and only fire if you must. Just be careful you don't hit me."

As it turned out, the formula for success began the same way as at the prior roadblocks. People were essentially the same, whether in America or Africa, whether wealthy or poor, army or thugs. Ultimately, human greed provided the solution. I glanced at Vincent, past his grin, and into his determined eyes. In them, I now saw the look of a predator.

Vincent spoke first. He held his hands in the air as a sign of surrender. "I'm transporting this missionary to the Comboni Orphanage in the Taraba Valley. He's carrying a backpack full of money, a lot of money."

They lowered their weapons slightly, and one of them

took a step closer. "How much money?"

"More than you've ever seen before," said Vincent. "More than either of you can make in a lifetime as a soldier."

So much for trust. The son of a bitch just sold me out. I tightened my grip on the handgun and vowed to shoot Vincent first.

"Show me," the soldier demanded as he aimed his rifle directly toward the center of Vincent's chest.

Keeping his hands raised, Vincent cautiously exited the Jeep. With his left hand he lifted the rear seat compartment and removed my backpack. Placing it on the hood of our Jeep, he unzipped it and stepped back. "It's in here. Take a look."

One of the men picked up a stack of fifty-dollar bills and thumbed across them. His eyes widened. For the two men, it was more money than was even imaginable. Now it was theirs for the taking. They grinned in excitement until they froze at the unmistakable click of a weapon being cocked. It happened too fast to register in my mind. Vincent gave no warning. He didn't hesitate. He pulled his six-shooter from its holster and dropped both men in less than a second. By the time the last man fell, Vincent's gun was already back in its holster. Two shots fired, two dead men on the ground.

"What the fuck, Vincent," I screamed. "Why?"

"Because they were about to do the same to us."

"But you didn't give them a chance. You could've threatened 'em first, but you murdered them in cold blood!"

"I had to go to plan B or we were going to die. Remember what I told you about life in the jungle? The number one rule out here is survival, and we weren't going to survive another minute if I hadn't done what I did. Once they saw the money, we were as good as dead. No time for meaningless threats."

"But you don't know that for sure."

"Did you notice anything when they smiled?"

"No. I was too worried about getting shot," I said. "Smiled? What?"

Vincent walked over to the closest body. He pushed the

man's lips apart with the tip of his gun and apparently found what he was looking for. "Just as I thought. These men weren't regular soldiers. They're definitely not Nigerian. At best, they were mercenaries trained to join Boko Haram. Probably deserted and became pirates. I wanna show you something."

I climbed out of the Jeep and joined Vincent. He knelt next to the body, pushed the dead man's lips aside further, and looked up at me. "You see his teeth? They're stained green. That's the result of chewing khat."

"Khat?"

"It's a stimulant leaf that's chewed by Somali military to give them energy. It's the reason these guys were so agitated. They were stoned out of their minds and would've shot us no matter what happened. If we didn't give them the money, they'd shoot us. If we did, they'd kill us anyway. Out here in the jungle, there are no good guys and there are no bad guys. Just alive guys. I told you that if things went bad, we run, and if that doesn't work, then—"

"This is your plan B?"

Vincent stared at the bodies. "I know what I'm talking about, Boss. The thing I know best is how to survive. Last year my youngest brother was cut down the same way by guys like them." Vincent checked our surroundings. "We'd better clean this up and get out of here before someone decides to investigate the source of those gunshots."

We loaded the two bodies into the back of their rusted pickup truck and drove it as far as we could into the jungle. As we returned to our Jeep, Vincent said, "Don't worry. If they're found, the army'll blame it on Boko Haram. This is how they deal with deserters."

I wasn't worried about them being discovered. I was more concerned about how easy it was for Vincent to do what he did.

Two miles later, the head of another Somali mercenary stared down at us, its lips pulled back in a death grin, exposing green teeth. Covered with a swarm of flies, the head was impaled atop a wooden spike, the eyes and tongue cut out. I prayed it had been done after the man died, but suspected otherwise. A black flag hung from the pole just below the head.

"Boko Haram," said Vincent. "It's a message to anyone who would consider desertion."

My eyes fixated on the head. Couldn't turn away. It reminded me of *Lord of the Flies*, a book I once read in high school, the story of a group of children stranded on an island without adult supervision or laws. The result was homicidal anarchy. "This is Boko Haram territory?"

"Wherever they are at any given moment is their turf. Today, that means right here."

Vincent pressed on the accelerator, pushing the Jeep deeper into the darkness of the jungle. I couldn't say for sure which direction we were headed. All I knew was that the more distance we put between ourselves and the dead Somalis, the better. This land was supposed to provide me with an opportunity to rediscover my life, to provide peace and a sense of purpose. Thus far it had only been a place of bottomless despair and horror. We seemed to be heading further back in time to an era when there was no civilization—and even less humanity. *Lord of the Flies.*

NINETEEN

Cameroon Jungle

Shakar Bhutah

Spent and sweating, Shakar lifted himself off the girl. He enjoyed the young ones. What they lacked in experience, they made up for in endurance. Even better, they were malleable and could be trained. Fear was a great motivator.

"Leave," he said and rolled over onto his back. Staring at the ceiling of his tent, he grinned at the thought of it. He could smell the fear on others. He fed on it. Fear made his wives exceedingly anxious to please, but he was becoming bored with some of the older ones. They were starting to resist and make demands. Time to sell off a few of them while he could. Even at nineteen, they should still fetch a decent price.

The twelve-year-old girl exited the hut, still half naked and in tears. She belonged to Shakar as one of the wives the Colonel took after an orphanage raid a year earlier. He had kept the prettiest ones for himself. The others were given to his men or sold on the Middle East sex-slave markets. His thoughts were interrupted when Tariq Ziyad, one of his lieutenants, pushed the curtain aside and entered the tent. The lieutenant was ten years older than his leader and had been the veteran of several civil wars for which he was rewarded with extensive burn scars on his face.

"Sir," said Ziyad, as he saluted the Colonel.

Shakar turned to face him. "Allah came to me in a dream last night. He wants me to rid the world of all infidels. I am to start with Africa and then expand to Europe, Asia, and America. He promised to give me all I would need to accomplish my destiny. Once I have fulfilled his commands, he will install me as ruler over all lands."

"Praise Allah and his wisdom," said Ziyad. "He made an excellent choice in selecting you as the point of his spear." He paused for several seconds, allowing Shakar to bask in the glow of his words. He added, "I have some information, sir."

"What is it?"

"I'm afraid it's bad news, sir. We suffered another defeat in the north. It was an ambush, sir. Our men were badly outnumbered."

"What about the Somali mercenaries we trained?"

"They ran as soon as the fighting started."

"Worthless cowards. Should've never trusted them. Hunt 'em down and kill them all."

"Already dispatched a team to do it, sir."

"What of our own men?" asked Shakar.

"Only seven survived."

"That means seventy-eight are heroes with Allah in Paradise, but seven of them failed to fight to the death. Take them out and shoot them in front of the other men. Do it slowly. Start at their knees and work your way up. An example must be made of those who fail to fight for Allah and our cause."

"As you wish, Colonel. You are right. An example must be made. The Nigerian Army has already reclaimed much of the territory we took last year."

"That's because we've been recruiting cowards who are unwilling to fight." Shakar was a man seldom distracted by the nuisances of reality. The fact was his army consisted of too many untrained boys who were no match for the seasoned Nigerian forces. Ziyad dared not mention this.

"You are right, as always, sir. We need to do something. Some of our people are afraid that our cause is hopeless and they're leaving." The news was worse than he was reporting. Shakar's army was collapsing from desertions. The lieutenant had to walk a fine line lest he become the victim of the Colonel's snake-like temper. It was quick, unpredictable, and lethal. It forced Ziyad to avoid reporting the true seriousness of any situation. It could be perceived as a criticism of Shakar's leadership and result in a bullet to the back of the head, or worse.

Still naked, Shakar sat on the side of his cot and stroked his wiry beard as he considered the desertion problem. He jumped up, his fury growing. He paced the floor of his command tent, back and forth like a caged animal. Ziyad dared not take his eyes off the man for even a brief second. Failure to do so could be a fatal mistake. That was when most predators attacked, when you were most vulnerable. He prepared for a rapid retreat if Shakar lashed out in his direction. The Colonel seldom needed a reason to kill, he simply needed a convenient target to quiet his wrath. Ziyad didn't want to be that target.

Shakar pulled on a pair of camo pants and buttoned his shirt. "I have a better idea. Shooting's too good for those cowards." He walked over to pick up his club. A bad sign. The worse the Colonel's mood, the more likely he was to turn to the club and the more likely there would be brutal bloodshed. It looked like a giant femur bone with a large knob protruding at an angle from the top. It was stained red and matted with human hair. Shakar turned to Ziyad. "Round up all our men in the judgment area. Place the seven cowards in the middle and bind their hands behind their backs."

It took only fifteen minutes. When the seven arrived, Shakar forced them to kneel in the dirt, facing away from him and toward the rest of his men. "An army's purpose is to fight for a just cause and can anyone deny that ours is just?" There was no response from the several hundred men standing at attention before him. "We have been commissioned by Allah to carry out His holy jihad. In order to be an effective fighting force, soldiers must function as a unit, under the command of their leader. That unit becomes weakened if there is a lack of resolve on the part of any individual soldier. These men kneeling before you lacked that resolve and failed to support their unit. They ran, and in doing so defied the will of Allah. Those actions led to our defeat and the death of seventy-eight brave soldiers. You can't win a war by retreating. It must be won by fighting until you are no longer able to take a breath. Anything less than that is tantamount to treason and there is only one way to deal with traitors."

The Colonel walked up behind the first kneeling man on his left. He wound up and swung his heavy club, striking the man along the back of his skull, creating a sickening crunch as bits of red bone and gray tissue exploded out from the man's head. The six remaining kneelers sobbed.

Ziyad turned to Shakar. "Impressive display of authority, sir. You sent a forceful message to the rest of the men. Insubordination will not be tolerated. Look at them. I think they all pissed their pants."

Shakar grinned at the sight of the terror he caused, his gold tooth reflecting in the sunlight. "Nothing makes a leader more respected than when his men fear his presence."

"Absolutely, sir. It makes me wonder. Since these men are so frightened, maybe they've learned their lesson—something that I'm certain you've already considered yourself. Of course, you understand matters of command much better than I, but do you think these men should be allowed to live?" Ziyad cringed and glanced at the club, still dripping with blood. Shakar didn't raise it, a good sign. Ziyad pressed on. "Their stories of your power and resolve will be heard by all throughout the country. You will become a legend. It's unlikely that anyone else would ever disobey your orders in the future."

The rage in Shakar abated as he appeared to consider Ziyad's words. He said, "Lieutenant, I think the rest of the men got my message. Take the remaining six and flog them. Then, return them to their unit. We need as many soldiers as we can get."

Ziyad breathed a silent sigh of relief and did as ordered. When finished, he returned to the Colonel's tent to see if he would face any consequences for his suggestions. All was forgotten.

Shakar had moved on to other issues. More importantly, he had retired his club to the corner, but resumed his pacing. "I'm tired of losing ground, Lieutenant. I'm tired of running. I'm tired of hiding in these shithole jungles of Cameroon. And I'm tired of these damn desertions," Shakar screamed. "My sources of funding are in jeopardy. I need to make a statement to the Nigerian people and the government. I need to let them know that we are not going anywhere and that I intend to win this war. Soon, I will be ruler of the new Islamic State of Nigeria! It's Allah's will, and He will not be denied. But first, we need to teach the deserters a lesson. Track every one of them down. Go to their villages, pull them out of their huts, and shoot them."

"There must be hundreds of them, sir."

"Then your men better carry a lot of bullets."

"What about their families?"

Shakar stared at his club for several seconds. "Leave them alone for now, but make sure they and the rest of the villagers see what happens to all who desert. If that doesn't stop this, we'll begin to execute a family member and force the deserter to select which one dies." Shakar grinned, a look on the wrong side of sanity.

He dismissed his lieutenant, reached into his pocket, and retrieved the message from Aryianna. He read it for the third time. The first part was a warning from the Minister Uguhru and his partners. They were growing impatient over his lack of progress. The usual funds were deposited in his Iranian account, but they were threatening to withdraw future support if they didn't see more results. "That slimy fat jackal! Someday I'm going to get my hands on him and snap his neck in two!" For now, Shakar needed the man's money. He had to come up with a token plan that wouldn't be too dangerous. He couldn't afford to lose any more men.

The message appeared to be useless information. It read, "American celebrity arrived in Abuja. Might be worth pursuing. Not sure where he's headed. My usual finder's fee?" That was it. There was no further information about the man other than his name was Buchanan. Shakar couldn't recall any famous American leader by that name. "Probably one of those do-gooder actors from Hollywood," he said to himself. "They're always sticking their noses in Africa's business. Makes 'em feel less guilty about being so rich and famous. They can tell all their movie friends about how wonderfully generous they are." He was about to tear up the note and throw it away but he paused. *Maybe...*

He brought the note closer to his face and sniffed it. He hadn't seen her in over three years, but he remembered her scent and the softness of her skin. He was certain she was still as stunningly beautiful as ever and the thought of all the things he would like to do to her aroused him. He again brought the note to his nose and inhaled deeply. She was an incredible woman, as cunning as she was beautiful. "Once I am king, I will take her as my queen," he said to the empty tent. The mere thought of it excited him. Shakar made a mental note to arrange for the usual transfer of twenty-thousand dollars into the woman's Swiss Bank account. He called for his lieutenant. "Ziyad!"

"Sir?"

"I need some information on an American by the name of Buchanan. He should've arrived on the flight from Paris to Abuja a few days ago. Check with your contacts in the government. I want to find out who he is and why he's come to Nigeria."

"Yes, Colonel."

When the lieutenant turned to leave, Shakar added, "Send for one of my new wives."

TWENTY

Comboni Mission
Taraba Valley, Nigeria

Brett

Except for the occasional ray of light fighting its way through the triple canopy of trees, we hadn't seen the sun for several hours. The strong smell of dampness and rotting vegetation filled the air. Our Jeep struggled through a series of steep switchbacks until it sputtered to a stop in a clearing at the crest of a small mountain. A verdant valley stretched out below us, a sea of green extending to the north and south as far as I could see.

"Here we are, Boss." Vincent got out of the Jeep and extended his arms. "Taraba Valley."

I was speechless. I had traveled across many continents, but had never seen anything as spectacular as this valley. Had I been a poet, I might have been able to come up with the words that could do it justice. As it was, the best I could say was, "Magnificent."

"That it is, Boss. The word Taraba means 'Special Place.'"

I'd been searching for a special place, one that might give me a new life. I hoped the valley lived up to its name.

Vincent gazed at the panoramic sight spread out before him, seemingly mesmerized by the magnitude of the view. "Along the far side is the Taraba River. It slowly winds its way along the southern end of the valley."

Beyond that, a high mountain range silhouetted against the fading blue sky, a majestic backdrop for the valley below. Vincent pointed toward the mountains. "That's the Gashaka-Gumti National Park with more jungle for another fifty miles, all the way into Cameroon."

A cacophony of a thousand bird calls along with the growls of too many wild animals encircled us. The jungle pulsated with prehistoric mystery, a step back in time, like a scene from Jurassic Park. Overhead, a single large eagle cruised the skies in search of a late afternoon dinner. I raised my face and basked in the light of the sun. It was beginning its downward journey behind the distant mountains and was already casting a golden glow along the clouds. The valley was a spectacular sight, pure and untainted by civilization, as though it were a symbolic Garden of Eden, the kind of place where I could leave my old life behind.

Vincent pointed down into the valley. "There's the orphanage."

I searched. "I don't see anything but jungle."

"Look directly out at one o'clock, several miles north of the river," said Vincent.

There it was. A small tapestry of cultivated farm fields stood alone like an uncharted island in an endless expanse of dark green. A chorus of birds signaled their final serenade for the day.

"We'd better head down," said Vincent. "I don't have headlights on this Jeep, and we don't want to get stuck out here after dark. It's beautiful now, but dangerous when the light's gone."

The road slithered its way back and forth down the side of the mountain until it entered the valley floor. As the sun disappeared behind the mountains, streaks of lavender glowed along the undersurface of the clouds. Dusk threatened to bring with it the stirring of the creatures of the night. Vincent pushed the Jeep to its limits, racing through the dwindling light, so fast he almost missed the Comboni Orphanage sign. Faded and warped from the onslaught of decades of torrential rainy seasons, the sign remained standing in defiance of the forces of nature. He turned the wheel, carving a sharp left around the sign, missing the road and slicing through heavy foliage. The car ricocheted through the underbrush, giant leaves slapping me in the face, reawakening my headache, a volcano about to erupt inside my skull.

Vincent found a narrow gravel road, and after another mile, we arrived at a large open area where the trees and underbrush had been replaced by a lawn of manicured grass. The orphanage was a compound of a dozen huts and cinder-block buildings clustered around a central courtyard. As we pulled to a stop in front of the main building, a tall woman wearing the billowy blue habit of a Comboni nun approached. A large silver crucifix hung from her neck and she walked with a purposeful gait that said she was the one in charge.

"Mr. Buchanan."

"Sister Mary Margaret," I said.

She chuckled and walked over to the Jeep. "I'm only called that when I'm out fundraising. For the younger children in the orphanage, Sister Mary Margaret was too much of a mouthful. They couldn't pronounce it, so my name became Sister Maggie." She extended a hand, her grip firm and her skin calloused. "Welcome. We've been expecting you for hours. I was getting a little worried."

"We got hung up at a number of checkpoints along the way," I said.

"Yes, we've heard the army has stepped up their activities recently. Apparently, Boko Haram has been spotted in this part of Nigeria." She turned to Vincent. "And you are?"

"I'm Vincent."

"Vincent...?"

"Just Vincent, ma'am."

Staring at Vincent, I furrowed my brow. "Don't you already know him?"

"No, I can't recall that we've ever met," said the nun.

"But didn't you send him to pick me up at the airport?"

"No, we hired Patrice." She turned to Vincent. "What happened to Patrice?"

"Bad case of dysentery. He asked me to drive for him."

My pulse quickened, the words "trust no one" echoing in my mind.

"Funny, he's never mentioned a Vincent," Sister Maggie said. She stared at the holster hanging from Vincent's hip. "A gun, Mr. Vincent?"

"Yes ma'am. Needed it for protection while traveling through Boko Haram territory."

She scoffed. "Not around the children, Mr. Vincent. Most have already been traumatized by firearms."

"Yes ma'am."

"Well, in any case, it's getting late, and we only have a few minutes of daylight left. You two must be tired and hungry. I kept the generator running so the cook could make some warm sandwiches. After you eat, I'll show you to your quarters. Once you're in for the evening, I'll turn off the generator. Fuel's running low and we must conserve as much as we can." Before leading the way to the dining hut, she added, "Don't wander around outside in the dark. For the past few months, we've had a female leopard prowling through the camp at night. I think she's hunting to feed her cubs. You two are probably too big for her to tackle, but there's no sense in taking chances. After we turn the generator off, it's lights out and pretty much pitch-black outside."

Terrific! What do I do if I need to take a leak?

As if she were reading my thoughts, she said, "There's a flashlight on a table inside the hut. If you have to use the latrine, just flash the light several times and one of the guards will escort you."

I hope he has a gun.

"If you need water, the borehole is just fifty feet in front of your hut. Everyone's in charge of retrieving their own water, even the children."

"Borehole?"

"Yes, the well. You can get water there when you need it,

but wait until daylight."

Before she left, I asked, "Do you happen to have any aspirin or Aleve?"

"Why?" she asked. When I showed her my head, her eyes widened. "You've been bleeding Mr. Buchanan. What happened?"

Vincent stepped forward. "We hit a bump and he fell out of the Jeep."

I glared at him for a second. *Why lie?*

"You need more than aspirin. Let's head over to the clinic," said Sister Maggie. "You helped pay for it. You might as well get to use it."

Vincent patted his holster and whispered, "I'd better go with you in case that leopard's prowling about." He lifted the Styrofoam cooler of medications onto his shoulder. Once we entered the cinder-block clinic, he set the cooler on a stretcher.

"What's that?" asked Sister Maggie.

"Medical supplies for the orphanage," replied Vincent.

She smiled. Looked like she was warming up to Vincent despite his revolver. I hadn't decided what to think about him yet.

Sister Maggie turned to leave. "I'll send someone in to fix your wound. I'm afraid you're going to need some stitches."

After she left, I spun around to face Vincent. "You didn't tell me you weren't the regular driver. Exactly what happened to their normal driver, that Patrice fellow?"

"Like I said, bad case of dysentery. Happens all the time in Nigeria, Boss. It's the water."

"You shoulda told me."

"No purpose in it. We had no time to discuss things. If you recall, I had to get you outta there as quickly as I could. You were about to be murdered."

Another nun, one much younger than Sister Maggie, entered through the clinic's only door. She smiled and studied me with lovely, intelligent eyes.

I introduced myself. "I'm Brett Buchanan, Sister. And this is Vincent."

She smiled at him. "Vincent?"

"Just Vincent, ma'am."

Her smile faltered for a second. "I'm Sister Anne Marie. I understand you have a pretty nasty cut on your head, Mr. Buchanan." She had me lie down on a long, wooden table covered in a crisp white sheet. "Now let's see what we have here." She examined the wound. "This is fairly deep. How long ago did it happen?"

"About seven hours," replied Vincent.

"We should be okay then. If you'd taken much longer to get here, the wound would've been too contaminated to suture." She withdrew some instruments from a drawer. "I'm afraid we don't have any local anesthetics. We ran out last month, so this is going to hurt a little."

She was like no nun I'd ever known. The woman's fingers were delicate, her touch gentle and cool. As she went about the business of cleaning my wound, she spoke to me, her voice soft and soothing, almost mesmerizing like my mother's when she tried to console me after a beating.

I became lost in her words as my mind wandered, remembering the nights when Mom and I would sit on the roof outside my bedroom window, hiding from Dad whenever he went on one of his drunken rampages. She'd wrap her arm around me and point to the constellations in the night sky: Leo, Centaurus, Ursa Major. I'd always look first for the Big Dipper, which was the easiest to find. However, my favorite was Orion's Belt, a family of three stars clustered together in a line, like a child in the middle with a parent on either side to protect him. That was the way it was supposed to be, but not for me. All I had was Mom. I often wondered if a boy living on that star could be looking back at me. Maybe he would question if my world was a nice place to visit. I'd tell him to stay away. Earth was not a friendly place, especially with my crazy Dad around.

"All finished, Mr. Buchanan," Sister Anne Marie said about thirty minutes later.

"Already? I barely felt a thing. You're very good at this, Sister."

She chuckled. "I get a lot of practice with all the children. They always seem to be getting scrapes and cuts." She placed the finishing touches on the bandage. "I'm sure you suffered a concussion so it's important that you rest for twenty-four hours and keep the bandage clean. We'll remove the stitches in five or six days, depending upon how well it's healing." She gave me something to drink. "This should help with the head pain." It was a thick green liquid that tasted sweet and lacked any scent of alcohol. "Let me know if you're having any problems."

When she turned to leave, I said, "Thank you."

She smiled and disappeared through the door. I was surprised that I felt such little pain. I kept thinking of her gentle touch and soothing voice.

Sister Maggie had left sandwiches for us in our hut. When finished eating, I eased myself into a wooden chair in front. I didn't know if it was the concoction Sister Anne Marie had given me, but my headache was completely gone. Sister Maggie turned the generator off, extinguishing the lights. A wave of blackness flooded the valley, the night as dark as any I'd ever experienced. I gazed up at the moonless night sky through a break in the trees. Without the presence of harsh city lights, I saw millions of stars in an infinite expanse of the universe, a concept beyond human comprehension. Like Carl Sagan used to say, "Billions upon billions of them, more than all the grains of sand on all the beaches on earth." Much of what I was seeing was the way the stars looked in the past. It took that long for the images to reach us. If that boy in Orion's belt saw me, he'd be seeing things that happened centuries ago, long before Dad killed Mom. Did it mean that on some celestial plane, my mother still existed, a stream of cosmic images awaiting the inevitability of her own violent death? My head was swimming, probably from Sister Anne Marie's pain liquid.

"You'd better get inside, Boss. That leopard's liable to wander by soon."

Vincent hid his guns under his cot but took one out to keep at his side. When I looked at him, he said, "I always keep one with me, locked and loaded. You can never be too careful out here. It's a matter of survival."

Exhausted and probably a little stoned, I collapsed on my canvas bed and rested my head on a flat pillow. The cot smelled of mildew, and it was much too short for me, an inconvenience I would have to accept. After all, this was probably the best Sister Maggie's orphanage had to offer. I suspected it was their equivalent of a penthouse suite.

Despite everything I had seen that day, I rested well—that is until the animals of the night started scurrying about. I was glad I didn't have to get up to use the latrine. At one point the female leopard prowled outside, growling, and searching for a meal. The only thing keeping it out of our hut was a flimsy cloth curtain over the doorway. I wondered if she realized how easy it would be to get to us. I heard Vincent pull his rifle closer. After an hour of expecting the big cat to enter our hut, I fell back to sleep and dreamt of Jonathan.

TWENTY-ONE

Comboni Mission
Taraba Valley, Nigeria

Brett

A pre-dawn breeze rustled the trees outside my hut. For the first time since the "incident," I had slept most of the night. Whatever the nun had given me last evening worked. The pain in my head had completely dissipated. Looking over to my right, I noticed Vincent was gone. He'd taken the nylon bag containing the guns with him. In a panic, I immediately searched the cot for my backpack full of cash. It was still there. I opened it and checked to be sure. Nothing missing. Still, I decided I'd better keep a close eye on Vincent whoever he was. What was he up to so early in the morning?

Our hut was a round structure, made of bent saplings woven together and sealed with a mixture of straw and mud. The conical roof was capped by layers of dried buffalo grass tied together in bundles. Hand-hewed wooden planks provided the flooring, constructed so that it sat a foot above the ground, probably to keep slithering critters out. Woven palm mats covered the bare areas.

I sat on the side of my cot and checked inside my boots for snakes or whatever else might be crawling around in there. After slipping them on, I pushed aside the curtain door and stepped outside. The Jeep still sat where we had parked it last night, so at least Vincent hadn't run off. Didn't trust the guy. As soon as I could find a good place, I planned to hide my backpack with the two-hundred-thousand dollars.

There was a small porch area, also elevated and large enough for two, wooden ladder-back chairs that had been repaired more than once, but never painted. The seats were worn smooth over the years, but surprisingly comfortable, even for a man of my size. A small three-legged table sat between the chairs, a bowl of water and two towels on top.

Sitting in the same chair I had used last night, I spread my feet wide and feasted upon the beginnings of a new day. The sunrise cast a soft orange glow through the morning mist. The ethereal beauty surrounding me stood in defiance of the violent jungle sounds I'd heard during the night. The earthy smell of freshly turned soil filled the air, the scents of an innocent lifestyle, scents promising a chance for rebirth. Goats and chickens wandered about the grounds freely. Across what had to be a hundred acres of farmland, I made out the image of a small herd of Thompson gazelles peacefully grazing on grass, a split-rail fence keeping them from the crops. Birds tuned up for their morning symphony, ushering in the new day. Absent was the hustle and bustle cacophony of civilization: no cars, no televisions, and no radios. I inhaled the clean cool air deep into the bottoms of my lungs and drank in the solitude of the tranquil morning. It was pure and unspoiled, only the beauty of life everywhere. "Special place," Vincent called it. He was right.

The orphanage compound was substantially larger than it appeared last night. There were several concentric circles of buildings arranged so that the doorway of each faced the central courtyard. Some of the buildings were huts like my own, but many were made of a hodgepodge collection of cinder blocks of different fading colors, like they were waiting for a new coat of paint. Strategically placed openings were cut out of the walls as glassless windows for light and ventilation. The most prominent of the structures was an open-sided church, constructed of poles lashed together to support a thatched roof. It looked precariously unstable, like it wouldn't survive the slightest gust of wind. Still, here it sat where it had probably been for over several decades, bravely resisting the elements. A humble wooden cross adorned the top.

Like my own hut, the church sat on a wooden floor about a foot above the ground. Benches arranged in parallel rows served as pews while a small table draped with a yellow cloth appeared to be an altar. A mobile blackboard had been pushed against one side. The church apparently also functioned as a school for the children. One item seemed impossibly out of place. I never expected to see a piano this far from civilization. *How did Sister Maggie get an old upright all the way out here?* I chuckled. If anyone could pull it off, she could.

Further away, near the fields, sat several buildings that looked like they might be barns. Beyond those, extended acres of cleared farmland, ready for the next planting. The entire space of buildings comprised an area the size of a football field. A hundred feet around the perimeter, the well-manicured grounds gave way to a heavy wall of jungle, so dense I couldn't see more than a few feet into it.

If there was a heaven, this would be it. The place was mystical, promising a new chapter in my life. I bathed in the peaceful quiet until my memories destroyed the moment. Out of nowhere, the voice hit me like a runaway freight train, arising from the darkest recesses of my mind, deep, rumbling, and foreboding.

"You don't deserve this, Brett. Too many stains. You know what you must do."

I pushed the thoughts aside when two nuns walked across the courtyard toward what looked like the well. One of the nuns wore the same billowy light-blue Comboni habit as Sister Maggie, but the other wore an all-white veil that started just behind her hairline and draped down the small of her back. There was just a single stripe of blue binding along the hem. Each woman carried several large plastic jugs, which they immediately set about the task of filling with water. I recognized the younger of the two. She was the same one who had stitched up my head last night, Sister Anne Marie. Each of the nuns took turns with the hand pump.

I rushed over to them. "Can I help you with those? They look heavy."

Sister Anne Marie said, "You're supposed to be resting for a few days, Mr. Buchanan."

The older nun added, "Thank you, but we'll be fine. We do this four or five times every day, so we're used to the work." After they finished pumping the water, the two headed back toward an open mess hall built in a fashion similar to the church. At the last minute, Sister Anne Marie turned and smiled.

I gave a wave and returned to my hut, taking a seat on the small porch. The sun had to crested over the horizon and promised a beautiful day. A thin layer of mist continued to hover over the lower lying areas. I leaned back on the wooden chair and again allowed the untainted tranquility of the morning to wash over me as I enjoyed the sunrise. After several minutes, Sister Anne Marie returned to my hut carrying a pot and a plate of small cakes, her habit blowing gently in the breeze.

"We thought you might like some fresh coffee, Mr. Buchanan."

I hadn't really noticed the night before when she was suturing my scalp, but when I looked into her eyes, they were a brilliant blue, filled with an innocent tenderness. Her hair was mostly hidden by the veil, but chestnut-blond bangs peeked out. She wore no makeup, which was to be expected with a nun, but she was astonishingly beautiful just the same. There was a natural radiance in her that I rarely saw in other women. She set the coffee pot down on a small table and poured a cup. I took a sip. It was black and hot, just the way I liked it.

"Would you prefer some cream and sugar?" she asked. Her voice seemed to softly sing when she spoke.

"No, this is perfect. Thank you, Sister Anne Marie."

She laughed in a way that lifted my spirits. "The children here call me Sister Annie."

"Sister Annie it'll be then." I sipped my coffee. Not wanting her to leave yet, I asked, "How long have you been in Nigeria?"

"It's been a little over five years now."

I was about to ask more questions but was interrupted by a voice from across the courtyard. It was the older nun from the well this morning, "We need you back in the kitchen, Sister Annie."

"I'm afraid I must go," she said. After a few steps, she looked back. "Enjoy your morning, Mr. Buchanan."

"Brett. Please call me, Brett."

"Enjoy your morning, Brett." Her smile seemed to light up the darkest recesses of the surrounding jungle.

I sat back down on the chair and enjoyed the early sun as it continued its daily journey upward. I took a bite of one of the small cakes. It was delicious, a surprising treat. How could they possibly make something this good way out here in the middle of a jungle? I ate another. As the hours melted away, I allowed my mind to wander aimlessly, but kept drifting back to thoughts of Jonathan and how much he would enjoy this place.

Several groups of children and a few adults made their way toward the church. *Must be Sunday.* I'd lost all track of time.

The boys were dressed in black slacks and white button-down shirts, while the girls wore white dresses. All were grinning and happy. There were fifty or sixty of them, mostly children, but more adults than I would have expected at an orphanage. I wouldn't be joining them in church today, nor any other Sunday for that matter. Despite the rehab center's rule regarding weekly church attendance, God and I weren't on the best of terms—hadn't been for a long time. I blamed the so-called Creator for what had happened to my mother—and for the incident. As the open church service began, Sister Annie took a seat in front of the piano and played a hymn I didn't recognize. The pious voices of the children's choir filled the air. It was a haunting, chanting type of singing that wafted out of the church and through the trees. It was as close to a spiritual experience as I'd ever had in my life.

The moment was interrupted when Sister Maggie walked past my hut. In the morning light, I saw the deep furrows in her brow and the lines across her face. Life had been difficult, but a determined spirit burned brightly in her eyes. She was a woman used to winning her battles, no nonsense, and didn't suffer fools. "How did you sleep last night, Mr. Buchanan?"

"Very well, all things considered. I woke up to that leopard prowling through the compound."

Sister Maggie chuckled. "She's been doing that most every night. She has cubs to feed."

"So, you warned us, but it was still a little unnerving."

"I'm afraid she got one of our goats. We herd them up at sundown and lock them in the barn, but occasionally one of them strays off, a fatal mistake on their part. We can't afford to lose too many of them. They're our only source of milk for the children."

"Why don't you just shoot the leopard? That should take care of the problem and then you'll lose no more goats."

She shook her head.

"We could never do that, Mr. Buchanan. The jungle is her home. The animals have been here for millennia, and we're only guests. Besides, we don't allow any guns in the orphanage."

I stared across the compound. She had seen Vincent's revolver but didn't know about the automatic rifles Vincent kept at his bedside. A part of me was glad they were there. Yesterday's trip from Arusha confirmed that the jungle held the potential for unexpected violence.

"Will you be joining us in church this morning, Mr. Buchanan? It is Sunday after all."

"I think I'll pass this morning, Sister. I'm still getting settled in." I cringed inside at the lie as soon as the words came out of my mouth. It was a lame excuse and I could tell she saw right through it.

She stared into my eyes for several uncomfortable seconds. "Sunday worship isn't mandatory here. It's strictly voluntary, but most do attend."

Trying to change the subject, I said, "I see you have quite a few adults in attendance. I mean in addition to the half dozen nuns here."

She looked over at the church. "I guess we do. Most of them grew up here as orphans. They decided to remain after they became adults. A few married and are raising a second generation of families along the periphery of our farm. Others simply wander in and like what they see, so they also stay."

"It's a little like a small Israeli kibbutz."

She laughed heartily, which was surprising. In all my years of living in the orphanage, I'd never seen a nun laugh. She looked into my eyes, seeming to explore my mind. "I've been wondering about you, Mr. Buchanan. Why are you here, visiting our little kibbutz as you call it? Some people come to Africa for adventure, some because they are searching for a more noble purpose in their lives, and others come to leave old lives behind. Which group are you in?"

I laughed, too nervous. "I'll let you know as soon as I figure that one out."

Her eyes locked onto mine, seeming to probe the depths of my soul, searching for my secrets and perhaps the source of my pain. "You know, Mr. Buchanan, each of us experience events in our lives that change us forever. Sometimes we make unwise choices and follow the wrong paths. Mistakes, even seemingly unforgivable mistakes, plague us all, clinging to our conscience like a dark shadow. I've certainly made my share. It's how we respond to those tragedies that defines us for the rest of our lives. The author C. S. Lewis wrote, 'You can't go back in life and change the beginning, but you can start where you are and change the ending.' The first step in healing is allowing yourself forgiveness."

I shifted in my chair, uncomfortable with the conversation, and tried to change the subject again. "I have an unrelated question. Maybe you can explain."

Sister Maggie furrowed her brow. "Yes?"

"I've noticed that you and most of the nuns wear a gold band on your left ring finger."

She looked at her hand. "They're like wedding rings, a symbol of our devotion to Christ and the obedience of God's law."

From across the courtyard, the priest's voice bellowed out, "I will go unto the altar of God."

"Unto God, who giveth joy to my youth," the congregation responded in unison.

Sister Maggie looked over toward the church and said, "I'm afraid I must go, Mr. Buchanan. It's time for Mass." Her eyes again studied me. "I pray you find what you're looking for in Africa. Relax and allow this land to fill your heart. Remember, everything comes in its own time." As she walked toward the church, she made the Sign of the Cross. I was amazed at her uncanny ability to read me so well after knowing me for such a short time.

As soon as she left, Vincent returned, his hands covered with dirt.

"Where've you been all morning?"

"Had to find a good hiding place for my guns. I couldn't exactly have a bunch of orphans running around with loaded automatic rifles. I don't think the good Sister approves of 'em."

I needed to do the same with my backpack of cash, especially with Vincent prowling about. I didn't trust the guy and two hundred-thousand dollars could tempt anyone. Vincent was still holding one of his guns, partially hidden at his side. He noticed me eyeing it.

"I always keep one close by, just in case. It's best to have one and not need it rather than need one and not have it."

Those words would ring uncomfortably true over the coming months.

TWENTY-TWO

Comboni Mission
Taraba Valley, Nigeria

Brett

The following day, I again awoke just before dawn. The leopard had made her nightly visit, and this time it sounded as though she was just outside my hut. I laid awake for a while wondering if the thin walls of the hut could keep her out if she really wanted in. Certainly, the curtain covering the doorway wasn't much of a deterrent. I looked over to my right and was relieved to see Vincent in his cot and his rifle still at his side. He was wearing his blue sunglasses. What the hell was that about? Who sleeps with their glasses on? Didn't trust a guy who hides his eyes.

I walked out onto the small porch and took my seat in one of the old wooden chairs. Another bucolic morning. Just like yesterday, two nuns came out to the pump carrying several large jugs. I was disappointed to find that Sister Annie wasn't one of them. I enjoyed the coolness of the morning and soon coffee was brought to my tent, but again it wasn't Annie. "Annie?" What was I thinking? *It's not Annie you fool. She's almost a nun, for God's sake. It's Sister Annie.*

After pouring the coffee, the nun said, "As soon as the children finish eating, breakfast will be available." She looked over in the direction of the dining hut. "I'd say in about thirty minutes."

Once the children scattered off to their classroom, I joined Sister Maggie at a table and ate a breakfast of scrambled eggs, fried onions, and garri, a biscuit made from ground tubers.

"It's sweet," I said with a surprise.

"Honey, a rare treat," said Sister Maggie. "One of the men found a hive not far away. He harvests just a little each month so the bees don't relocate." She took a sip of coffee. "When you're finished, I'll give you the grand tour of our orphanage and show you what we've done with your generous donations."

Vincent had just taken a seat next to me. "Donations?" he asked.

"Yes, Mr. Buchanan was kind enough to gift us several hundred thousand dollars to improve the facilities here at the orphanage." As soon as the words came out of her mouth, she appeared to regret saying them, as though she had shared more information than she should have. She changed the subject, "Will you be returning home this morning Mr…?"

He seemed lost in thought before responding. "Vincent ma'am. Like I said last night, just Vincent. No, I won't be leaving today. If it's all the same to you, I'd like to stick around for a while, maybe check out the area."

Sister Maggie folded her napkin in a perfect square and centered it in the middle of her plate. "There's not much to see except the orphanage compound and the jungle, but suit yourself. We might ask you to help with a few things while you stay. Everyone here is expected to earn their keep." She looked outside. "That Jeep of yours looks old. You must have repaired it on several occasions. Do you know anything about truck motors?"

"Yes ma'am, a little. Why do you ask?"

"You'll see."

After a second cup of coffee, we stood and followed Sister Maggie across the courtyard toward a barn where we found an old flatbed truck. She rested her hand on the hood. "We've had this thing for over twenty years, and it's served us well. Then, it just up and died. This is why I asked if you knew anything about truck motors, Mr. Vincent. Would you take a look and see if you could get it running again? Without it, we've had no reliable transportation." She patted the truck's hood. "What do you think? Can you repair it?"

Vincent stared at me. I shrugged. "I'm afraid I'll be of no help on this one."

Vincent walked around the truck, kicked the tires, and lifted the hood. "I've never seen anything like this before. It's even older than my Jeep. When was this thing built?"

"I can't say for sure," replied the nun. "I purchased it secondhand a long time ago. Got it for a good price though. It even has a toolbox behind the driver's seat."

"He'll be happy to fix it for you, Sister. Won't you, Vincent."

"I guess," said Vincent as he removed his shirt. A latticework of scars spread across his back. I hadn't seen them before. Probably got them the same way he got the scar on his face. He had been in more than his share of battles. He leaned over the motor. "Jesus Christ. This goddamn thing's a dinosaur." He looked up. "Sorry Sister."

She laughed. "I've heard much worse over the years, Mr. Vincent. However, maybe you could eliminate your use of the Lord's name in vain." She and I left him to work on the truck while we continued with the tour. Once on the other side of the barn, a deep grunting sound startled me. "Holy shit." I jumped back and stumbled to the ground. Before me stood a colossal beast, as big as a pickup truck–and it had huge horns.

"I'm sorry, Mr. Buchanan," said Sister Maggie. "I should've warned you. This is Otis, our Cape buffalo." She patted the animal on the neck and scratched behind his ears. "Thanks to you, I was able to purchase him to help with the plowing. I'm seriously considering buying a second one. If we can clear another one hundred acres, we can be fully self-sufficient from a food standpoint."

The huge animal was tethered to a tree by a thin rope, so flimsy I was convinced he could snap it like a thread. Otis grunted and shook his head. I jumped up and stepped back, away from the animal.

"Watch out," said Sister Maggie just before I tripped over something.

I looked down to see what it was. PVC pipes? "What're these for?"

"They're a small part of our first set of purchases with your donation, Mr. Buchanan. I also ordered an electric motor. I planned to convert our bore hole over to an electric pump system so we wouldn't have to carry those heavy water jugs from the well every day. I was hoping to be able to run water directly into all the buildings."

"Why hasn't it been installed yet?" I asked. "You need more money?"

"Oh, no. Our pump was stolen during a supply truck hijacking. The driver was killed in the process. Over half of our scheduled deliveries never make it here."

"Boko Haram?"

"Either them or the military. One's as vicious as the other."

"What do you need to get this project done?" I asked.

"Mostly the pump, and manpower to dig the trenches and lay the pipe," she replied. "Twenty years ago, I would have done it myself, but I'm afraid I'm a little too old for that now. We also need to run electric from our generator to the pump. An electrician must do that, but handymen are afraid to come this far out to do the work. They all say it's too dangerous because of the terrorists."

We took a wide berth around Otis and continued with the tour as she showed me the boy's and the girl's dormitories. Half were constructed of mismatched concrete blocks and were marred by the same bullet hole patterns and scorch marks I had seen several days ago in the villages. Other dorms were made of flimsy woven sapling walls much like my own hut. "We're hoping to replace these with new buildings in the future, but we can't get the necessary supplies."

"The hijackings?" I asked.

"I'm afraid so."

A short, rotund man in a black cassock approached us with a worried look on his face. Around his neck hung a large crucifix, similar to Sister Maggie's. "I'm sorry to interrupt, Sister, but they need you in the communications hut right away. We've had another supply truck ambushed. Both drivers are dead."

She turned to me, her nostrils flaring and her eyes blazing with anger. "I'm afraid I must excuse myself, Mr. Buchanan. This problem demands my immediate attention. The good Father will have to take over from here."

TWENTY-THREE

Comboni Mission
Taraba Valley, Nigeria

Brett

The priest and I watched as she rushed away. "She was in such a hurry she didn't get a chance to introduce us. I'm Father Norbert, the orphanage priest."

He had one of those round faces that seemed to defy age, but streaks of gray in his hair suggested he was mid-forties. I shook his hand. "Brett Buchanan. I'm just a visitor." I paused for a second to watch Sister Maggie rush up a small hill. "You mentioned she was headed for the communications hut. You have access to telephones?"

He shook his head. "No, just a radio. It was installed six months ago thanks to a generous benefactor who I can only assume was you. If you look up the hill to the left of the rise, you can see the hut. Just behind it, there's a tall tree with the antenna fastened near the top."

I searched for a few seconds. "Got it, but even with the antenna, how can you make contact with the outside world from this far down in the valley? The nearest town must be well over fifty miles away, and it's on the other side of the mountains."

"We tie into the GPP network."

"GPP?"

"Gashaka Primate Project. It's an organization that has

been working to protect endangered gorillas and chimpanzees in the Gashaka-Gumti National Park. The rangers established a network of radio towers that covers over ten thousand square kilometers of the region. That way, they can communicate with each other and mobilize a rapid response team if poacher activity is spotted. The boundary of the park is only ten miles from here and the rangers have allowed Sister Maggie to tie into their system. We only have sufficient reception for several hours a day, so communication with the outside world is still limited."

Father Norbert checked on Sister Maggie's progress as she continued up the hill toward the radio hut. "She's gone," he said and turned to me. "You wouldn't happen to have any cigarettes on you, would you?"

"Sorry, I don't smoke."

"Pity, I thought all Americans did. I'm dying for a cigarette, but the good Sister doesn't allow them in the compound. Corrupts the children, she claims." He again looked in the direction of the communication hut. "I tried to sneak some of the tobacco the locals use, but that stuff can drive you crazy. I don't know what's in it, but when I smoked one, I hallucinated for half a day. Thought I was being chased by demons. Sister Maggie was so mad I was afraid she'd ship me back to Rome." He laughed hard. "It was probably God's way of telling me I shouldn't be smoking anyway. Still, I'd give almost anything for a real cigarette."

I chuckled. Priest or not, everyone was plagued by a vice or two. Father Norbert was a regular guy, the kind you could share a beer with, if I still drank. I immediately took a liking to him.

"You said you were a visitor. We don't get many casual visitors in the jungle, Mr. Buchanan."

"Call me Brett."

"Okay Brett, what brings you here?"

"Long story. It was mostly because of Sister Maggie. I met her when she gave a talk at a church back home in the U.S. She discussed the Comboni Sisters and specifically their work with orphans here in Nigeria. I was an orphan myself, so I found her story intriguing. She's a very compelling speaker. Before I knew it, I was writing out a check with a lot of zeros."

"Compelling speaker she is," said Father Norbert with a hearty laugh, so loud it almost shook the ground beneath us. "She possesses the perfect combination of saintly charm and dogged tenacity that makes for a very serious fundraiser."

I joined in the laughter. "On a more serious note, after my donation, I wanted to come to Nigeria in order to see in person what was being accomplished here. I must admit I'm impressed that an orphanage compound like this could be carved out of the jungle in the middle of nowhere."

"Sister Maggie is beyond a doubt, a remarkable woman." Admiration sparked in his eyes. "She could have requested a different location, one safer and more comfortable, but she insisted on going to the darkest corner of the world where the people had the greatest need. She and four other nuns traveled up the Taraba River just over thirty years ago. At the time, there was only a primitive, small village where ivory was being shipped by boat down river toward the ports in Lagos. Once the elephant population was decimated by poachers, the ivory trade disappeared, and the village suffered. Sister Maggie hired some of the locals to help clear the land and used the lumber to build their first school. It also served as their home and a church."

We stopped as a small troop of baboons lingered along the path fifty feet in front of us. "Are they dangerous?" I asked, wishing I had one of Vincent's guns.

"Usually not, but they are pests. Different troops wander through from time to time. They steal our fruits and vegetables." The priest raised his arms, ran, and shooed them away. The largest male turned to face him, growled, and bared his teeth, large menacing fangs. Having made his stand, he soon ran away to join the rest of his troop. Father Norbert continued with his tour. "For the first five years, it was a slow process for the nuns, and the obstacles were overwhelming. Within months, one of them died of malaria. Then there was trouble with the local tribe. They had their own religion, which was a mixture of idolatry and witchcraft, so trying to convert them to Christianity wasn't a realistic option. Many of the tribal elders believed the presence of the nuns had offended the tribe's own gods. It made for a strained relationship."

"Sister Maggie remained undaunted?"

"Always. She ultimately went to the Vatican and convinced them to assign her more nuns and money to continue their work. She's been actively recruiting donors ever since. We now house over sixty young children, a school, and a newly expanded health clinic."

"So, you were sent here to help Sister Maggie?"

"I think that was the original idea. One condition they placed on the money for the orphanage was that I accompany her back to Nigeria. I was only five years out of the seminary and ready to take on the world, convinced that I was going to have a major impact on the direction of the Catholic Church. I worked hard and was rewarded with a position at the Vatican. My ultimate goal was to negotiate my way up into the inner circle of papal advisors. The church was trying to increase minority representation from third-world countries so my chances for advancement were better than good, but everything backfired on me. When Sister Maggie came to the Vatican, one of the Cardinals decided that since I was Nigerian, it would be a good idea for me to accompany her back to the orphanage. That way, the church could keep an eye on what she was doing and how the Vatican's money was being spent. There was no way a young priest like me could say no to a Cardinal, so I packed my bags, intending to make my mark here and return to Rome to resume my career as soon as possible."

"But you never made it back."

The priest gazed up at the cloudless sky. "Never did and I don't regret it for a minute. You might not expect it, but the Vatican was a center of intense political ambition and competition. I fell victim to its seduction of power, but once I left, I realized the inherent corruption the pursuit of power brings, even in the church. It leads to a compromise of one's core values. I'm grateful to no longer be a part of it. Now, my time is devoted to ministering to the religious needs of the orphanage." He gazed around us. "There's a compelling force that draws you to the jungle. I think it's the peaceful simplicity that pulls you in. Life is distilled down to its basic elements without the distractions of modern civilization and its associated materialism." He chuckled and patted his belly. "It's a bit primitive but as you can readily see, I haven't suffered by being here."

The two of us walked together in silence, taking in the scenery and sounds of the jungle. Father Norbert appeared to be lost in thought.

"That was sixteen years ago, and I wouldn't have traded my time here for even the most prestigious appointment in the Vatican. I must admit, things were a little tumultuous at first. I'm afraid I was a little too full of myself and tried to impose my vast leadership and organizational skills on the orphanage."

"You tried to take over?"

"Yes. Bad idea on my part. It didn't take long for the good Sister to pull me aside one day and set things straight. She very respectfully informed me that she would agree to defer to me in most matters spiritual. However, she also let me know in no uncertain terms that this was her orphanage and she was going to manage it in any way she saw fit. She told me that if I wanted to run my own orphanage, I was welcome to wander out into the jungle and build one."

I tried to suppress a smile. "So, what'd you do?'

"Like I said, I was pretty full of myself. I puffed out my chest and went to the tool shed. I retrieved a machete and an ax and set out on my own. I was going to show her." He paused to study a small yellow and red bird that was feeding her hatchlings. "Got lost in less than an hour. The sun was hidden above the trees and I couldn't tell east from west. Started getting nervous when the light began to fade. Didn't want to be out there in the jungle at night. I swallowed my pride and started yelling for help. Thought I was going to die for sure. I might have, if the good Sister hadn't sent out a few of the adults to keep an eye on me while I wandered about. I was only a half mile away from the orphanage when they caught up to me. Must have been walking in circles for hours. By the time I got back my body was covered in scratches, rashes and dozens of bug bites."

He laughed and slapped me on the back. "Maggie never said a word. Didn't need to. Her point was made. All in all, it was a great experience. The jungle changed me somehow. It was almost as if it gave me a rebirth, a new perspective on life, and a new set of priorities. A career at the Vatican no longer seemed so important."

Rebirth. I found the concept of a new life reassuring.

An iridescent blue and yellow butterfly landed on his hand. He held it up in the air and it lingered there for several seconds before flying away. "I learned that despite its beauty, one must always respect the jungle. It can be violent and merciless. At the same time, you have to lose yourself in it to find out who you are and what's important in life. God was letting me know I wasn't as important as I thought I was."

"A divine smack-down," I said.

He slapped my shoulder. "That's right, a divine smack-down! That's a good one, Brett." Once again, he shook the valley with a hearty laugh. "I've never heard anyone put it that way before, but it pretty well sums things up. Sister and I still have our spats, but we've gotten along well ever since."

Almost like an old married couple. We continued to walk side-by-side in silence, the only sounds being twigs snapping under our feet and the chorus of birds singing in the trees. I gazed at the farmland in front of me and wondered whether the nun`s owned the land. I asked Father Norbert.

"I don't actually know for sure. They've been here so long, no one's ever questioned the ownership of the land. I'm sure it must belong to someone." He stooped to study a green chameleon perched on the branch of a bush. He coaxed it onto his forearm, its body swaying side to side while its eyes scanned independently in all directions. "This is Camille. She's been hanging around the orphanage for years, almost like a pet." After a minute, he returned the animal to its branch where Camille immediately snatched a bug with her long tongue. "I seriously doubt that anyone possesses an official deed for the land. Perhaps it's owned by the government. Maybe Nigeria has squatter laws here just like in America. All I know for sure is that if someone tried to take it from Sister Maggie, they'd have a major battle on their hands, one that they would probably lose." Laughter sparkled in his eyes.

The look dissolved as though an ominous dark cloud were blocking out the sun. I looked around, searching for the reason. "What is it?"

"I love this land, but it's a little sad. I'm afraid all of this will come to an end one day."

"Why?" I asked.

"There is an impermanence to all things, Brett. It's an ancient Buddhist teaching. Everything comes to an end, whether it be health, prosperity, relationships, or life." He spread his arms wide. "Even this valley is vulnerable. It could be due to divine intervention, the natural progression of things, or through the self-centered conceit of mankind in its pursuit of material wealth. I fear that civilization with its attendant greed and corruption will eventually creep into Taraba and ruin everything." A loud screech pierced the day. A large African eagle soared overhead, gliding across the clear blue skies. With his talons, he grabbed a smaller bird in midair. One life ended so another could survive. "As I said, all things come to an end."

He used the same words as my mother.

"That's why we must preserve and enjoy this world God has given us—before it slips through our grasp. I just pray it doesn't happen in my lifetime. In the meantime, we should feast on all that this land has to offer." The sparkle returned to his eyes and he patted his belly. "That's exactly what I plan to do."

"Maybe the jungle has its own form of civilization," I said. "One not based upon progress or industrialization, but one that has actually surpassed that of the modern world. Maybe that's the jungle's salvation. Maybe it will last forever."

"We can only pray, Mr. Buchanan, but I do worry about an evil infestation from the outside world."

TWENTY-FOUR

Comboni Mission
Taraba Valley, Nigeria

Brett

My walks with Father Norbert became part of my daily routine, one I looked forward to each day. He and I stood at a fence, watching some of the children playing soccer. "They look happy," I said.

"As happy as could be expected considering their parents and family were massacred by terrorists or died of disease."

I nodded toward the children. "There are a number of young boys here who are missing their right arms—too many to be just a coincidence. What happened to them?"

"Boko Haram. When they raid a village, they generally kill the adults. When they're finished, they round up the children. Girls of all ages are sold off in Middle East sex-slave markets. Trafficking in children has become a multibillion-dollar a year, global enterprise. The younger they are, the better the price they fetch. The boys are conscripted into Shakar's Boko Haram army. If they refuse to fight, they're shot. Those boys considered too young to fight have their right arm cut off as a warning to any who might question Shakar's authority. We haven't seen as many such victims recently. I believe Shakar has realized there's also a market for the very young boys amongst some circles of the Middle East wealthy."

I shook my head in disbelief. I thought I had a rough childhood. I experienced more than my share of cruelty in life but it was nothing compared to the level of merciless evil these poor kids have been subjected to.

"Come walk with me," said Father Norbert. "One of the locals came up with a pretty good tobacco substitute. I need a cigarette and I don't want Sister Maggie to see me."

"But she's working in the communications hut. I just saw her heading in that direction before coming over here."

"Makes no difference whether she's inside or not. The woman's uncanny. I'm convinced she can see through walls and around corners. Sometimes I think she might have been a witch in a previous life." The two of us laughed as we continued to joke about some of the nun's superpowers.

"I'm afraid it's an art shared by many women, especially wives and mothers," I said, before feeling the crushing failures of my past. The voice didn't speak. It didn't need to. The pain was already inflicted. I had failed to protect my family just as I had failed to protect my mother.

We walked side by side in silence. Once the priest thought it was safe, he lit up and inhaled. "Not bad." He exhaled and grinned. "I needed that. It's the small pleasures in life that make us truly happy." He took another puff from the cigarette and asked, "Tell me, Brett. Are you happy here?"

"Yes," I said, though I still hadn't been able to shake away the darkness of my past.

"I'm sure it's been a big adjustment for you, living out here, leaving behind the comforts of life in the U.S. In time, though, you will come to appreciate the magnificent complexity of God's creation. It's a moment when you become one with the jungle. There's often a temptation to wander into it, to explore the unknown around us, but I must caution you to stay close to the orphanage."

"Terrorists?"

"Partially, though we haven't seen that activity near us. It's more the jungle itself. You might see it as a beautiful collection of different trees and wildlife, but it's more than that. The jungle is alive, a magnificent, complex creature in its own right. It's a wonderful blessing but it can devour you if you fail to respect it."

"Like what happened to you?"

"Yes. I was lucky to survive."

"How do I do that, learn to respect the jungle?"

"It's something you'll eventually learn as you realize and accept your limitations." Father Norbert looked ahead. "Ah, now there's a face that can brighten even the darkest corners of the jungle!"

Across a wooden rail fence, in the middle of a small clearing, stood a slender woman, tall, with short chestnut-blond hair. Dressed in a t-shirt and khaki shorts, she was tossing a tattered old baseball back and forth with a young boy. She threw with the fluid grace of an athlete. Even from this distance, her wide smile and soft blue eyes were striking.

"Amazing isn't she," said the priest.

"She doesn't throw like most women."

"I've been told that she grew up with three older brothers. I imagine playing sports was a matter of self-preservation."

My eyes returned to the two tossing ball, and saw something I hadn't noticed at first. My attention was directed so much toward the attractive woman, I hadn't noticed the boy. Just like the other boys I had watched playing soccer, this one had only one arm. The child's right one had been severed mid forearm. Kicking a soccer ball with just one arm was one thing, but playing baseball was an entirely different matter. He caught the ball with a glove on his only hand, then tossed it into the air while tucking his glove under what remained of the right arm. Catching the ball with his bare left hand, he was ready to throw it back to the woman. He repeated the maneuver over and over in one seamless motion without any evidence of difficulty or extra effort. There was no outward indication that the boy was self-conscious about his limitation, just the obvious enjoyment of playing toss. It was perhaps baseball in its purest form, a game played just as it was meant to be, for fun. It reminded me of the times when Dad and I used to toss ball in the side yard. He always had a can of beer nearby. After he lost his job, the beer was replaced by a bottle of whiskey. That's when everything started to fall apart.

The boy told the woman, "I've been working on a curveball. Wanna see it?"

"Sure thing, Jenkins," she replied, dropping into a catcher's crouch position, and pounding her fist several times into her glove. "Let's see what you've got, hotshot."

I turned to Father Norbert. "Jenkins?"

"Jenkins," the priest replied with a wide grin on his face.

"Seems like a strange name for a boy in the middle of Africa."

Father Norbert gazed out toward the two still playing toss. The boy and woman hadn't yet realized we were watching. "When he was brought to us a year ago, the boy had no memory of his name or family. He was found, near death, along the side of a dirt road, half of his right arm gone and the stump badly infected. A few locals delivered him here and Sister Annie slowly nursed him back to health."

"Sister Annie. She's the one who stitched up my head."

Father Norbert nodded but said nothing for several seconds. He gestured toward Jenkins. "When he arrived, all the boy had with him was that tattered baseball. The cover was yellow from age and stained with blood, but he wouldn't part with it. He screamed when we tried to take it away. He said something about powerful magic. It's been a mystery."

"And the boy doesn't remember what happened?"

"No, but we believe his family and village were massacred by Boko Haram. He doesn't have any recollection of the events of that day." Father Norbert watched the boy for a few seconds, frowning. "I guess it's fortunate he doesn't remember."

"So that's how he lost his arm, just like the other boys?"

"Unfortunately. It's a tragedy for all of them, but Jenkins is special somehow. He's become an inspiration for the other boys. Most are bothered by their disability, but Jenkins almost embraces it as a challenge. He's always upbeat, always smiling."

"And the name?"

"As I said, he held that baseball close to him at all times. He had a fascination with America and believed that if he could learn to play the game well, the ball's magic would be his ticket to move there someday. No one's had the heart to tell him otherwise, so he continues to practice throwing whenever he gets the chance."

"Everyone needs a dream of a new, better life."

"Exactly," replied the priest. "Sometimes it's the only thing that keeps us going. Anyway, when we were finally able to separate the boy from the ball, we found that there was some writing on the side. It was signed with the name Jenkins."

"So that became the boy's new name," I said.

"Seemed appropriate. A couple months later, a driver of one of our delivery trucks brought an old sports magazine. He knew Jenkins loved baseball and thought he'd enjoy reading it. The magazine had to have been at least thirty years old. Half of the pages were yellow or torn, but the boy was thrilled, and paged through it almost every day. On the cover was the picture of an African-American player by the name of Ferguson Jenkins."

"His own name."

"Yes, and the headline said, 'Greatest Pitcher in America.' The boy ran to Sister Annie and said, 'He looks just like me. Someday I'll be the greatest pitcher in America too!'" Father Norbert paused for a few seconds to watch the game of toss. "Would you like to meet him?"

"I'd enjoy it. That boy has overcome more adversity than any child should be forced to endure, and did so with remarkable courage."

"Jenkins." Father Norbert waved the boy over.

"Brett, this is Jenkins, our star baseball player." The compliment elicited a wide grin of enthusiasm from the boy. His large inquisitive eyes looked like those of a child in a Margaret Keane painting. It was a look that generated an immediate liking for the little guy. There was an innocent excitement there that I hadn't seen in a long time. He reminded me of Jonathan. I looked at the boy's amputated arm and wondered. How could a supposedly all-merciful God inflict so much pain on someone so innocent? He abandoned this boy like He abandoned my family. Exactly the way He abandoned me.

"Jenkins, this is Mr. Buchanan."

With his only hand extended, he shook mine. "Nice to meet you Mr. Buchanan."

"The pleasure's all mine, Jenkins. I enjoyed watching you throw the ball."

"Thank you, sir. You're the famous American baseball player Sister Annie's been talking about?"

Sister Annie was talking about me?

"Did you ever play against Ferguson Jenkins?"

"He was a bit before my time, but I did have the opportunity to meet him on several occasions. He was a great pitcher for the Chicago Cubs. More importantly, he was a good man."

The boy responded with another wide grin. "Then that's what I'm going to do, pitch for the Chicago Cubs. Could you give me some help?"

"I'd be glad to, Jenkins."

"It sounds like I'm about to be replaced as pitching coach," said a soft voice from several feet away. I recognized the way she walked, graceful like a dancer, but athletic at the same time. She was pretty from a distance, but up close, she was stunning with glacial blue eyes that sparkled mischievously when she smiled. She seemed out of place here in the middle of the jungle. As she turned to face me, her chestnut hair blew gently in the breeze.

Father Norbert introduced her. "Brett, this is Sister Annie, our doctor."

She extended her hand. "Hello again, Mr. Buchanan."

I was so flustered I didn't shake her hand. "Annie? I mean Sister Annie? Why are you—?"

"Dressed like this?" She completed my question. "Rules

regarding our wardrobe have loosened over the years, especially out in the jungle where full habits tend to be impractical. Of course, some of the older nuns like Sister Maggie still prefer to wear the more traditional dress of Comboni nuns."

Father Norbert laughed. "You'd best not let her hear those words, 'older nuns.'" All four of us shared in the laughter.

Sister Annie seemed to glow when she did. "I still wear my habit when in church or even in the clinic, but most times I dress casually. Sister Maggie cuts me quite a bit of slack since I'm still a novitiate."

"Only nun to be a novitiate for over five years," muttered Father Norbert.

She ignored his comment and handed the ball back to Jenkins. "That was a great curve. Keep working on it. Why don't you have the good Father here help you?" She turned to me. "I guess you'd like to see some of what we did with your money. Come on, I'll give you a tour of the clinic. You didn't get to see much of it the night I fixed your scalp."

I touched the spot on my head. I'd forgotten all about the laceration and it was time to remove the stitches. I turned to Jenkins. "I'll be back later to give you some pointers."

TWENTY-FIVE

Boko Haram Camp
Cameroon Jungle

Shakar Bhutah

"**B**astard!" Shakar had already been in a bad mood because of the continued desertions, but now he was closer to the breaking point. He had just read the most recent note from Aryianna, crumpled up the paper and threw it in the corner. He paced the tent for a minute with his club in his right hand, swinging like a pendulum at his side. He wanted to smash something, anything. "That fat toad, Uguhru would be a good start."

Shakar retrieved the note and read it again. "A message from our mutual friend. He told me to let you know that he and his partners are tired of your indecisive inaction. (His words, not mine.) They want to see something happen soon or they plan to decrease financial support down to twenty thousand dollars a month."

There was no signature but Aryianna's scent on the paper was unmistakable. "That fat fuck threatens Shakar?" he screamed to the tent. "He doesn't know anything about leading an army. He's never fought a war. He's never even held a damn gun! I can't feed an army and replenish our weapons on just twenty thousand."

Shakar was tired of dealing with Uguhru. The Minister and his friends stood to make hundreds of millions while he and his army took all the risks, did all the work, and got crumbs in return. He needed to break free of Uguhru's financial thumb. "Once I have conquered Nigeria, I'm going to deal with that slimy toad. I'll crush him with one hand!"

"I have good news, sir."

Shakar looked up to see Lieutenant Ziyad standing at the opening of his command tent. Ziyad breathed a sigh of relief when Shakar set the club aside.

"What is it?"

"I was able to arrange for the sale of one of the wives you told me to unload."

"How much?"

"Five hundred dollars, sir."

"Five hundred dollars? That's nothing. She should have brought ten times that amount."

"She is over twenty, sir. There's not much of a market for the older ones," said Ziyad, keeping one eye on the club.

"What about the other one?"

"Kashandi? No interest sir. The buyers all said her face was too scarred and half her teeth were missing." He paused before adding, "That, and she has the child."

"It's her own fault. She had a big mouth and complained constantly. Now what am I going to do with her and the kid? I don't need a kid."

"Maybe hand her over to the men, sir. I'm sure they'd enjoy having another woman, even one like her."

"Maybe," said Shakar as he picked the club back up and paced around his tent. "I need something to appease our backers." He stopped and grinned, exposing his oversized gold tooth. He had an idea that would help solve his problem with the woman, and hopefully Uguhru. He described his plan in detail to Lieutenant Ziyad. "Make it happen as soon as possible," he said.

"As you wish, Colonel." The lieutenant remained in the tent.

"Is there something else?"

"Yes, sir. I have more information about the American

you told me to investigate."

Shakar had forgotten all about the celebrity from America. "And?"

"His name is Brett Buchanan, sir. They refer to him as Big Brett but he's not a movie star. He's a sports hero, one of the most popular celebrities in the United States. He plays baseball."

"Baseball? I don't know much about it except that it's a little like cricket. So, why's he here in Nigeria?"

"No one seems to know, sir. Our contacts were able to monitor his activities on the Abuja camera surveillance system. He stopped at the American Embassy and spoke to the ambassador for several hours but didn't meet with any of the Nigerian political leaders. He spent several days doing some sightseeing. An American Embassy limousine picked him up at the Hilton hotel and headed to the Citibank building."

"He needed Nigerian currency. Any idea how much he exchanged?"

"No, sir, and I haven't been able to find out."

"Bet it was a lot. What then?"

"His driver took him to the Jobi Lake Mall to do some shopping and have lunch. Picked up a backpack and boots. That was it."

"Backpack and boots? Is he planning on hiking the parks?"

"Can't tell, Colonel. After the mall, they headed east down the main highway. That's when we lost them. No camera surveillance that far out."

"Why would they head there? There's nothing but the slums where I grew up. Why would he want to visit the slums?"

"Like you said, Colonel. Maybe he's just another rich American looking to spread some cash around to make him feel good."

"Maybe." Shakar paced the tent, still swinging his club at his side, trying to formulate a plan to get some of the American's money. He had nothing.

Ziyad continued. "After several hours, Buchanan was returned to his hotel and has not been seen since."

"Somebody must know what he's up to. Keep checking with our contacts in Abuja. See if you can turn someone in the American embassy. I don't care what it costs."

As the Lieutenant saluted and turned to leave, Shakar added, "Good work, Ziyad. Take one of the new girls for yourself for a few days, but make sure it's not one of the virgins. I don't want to ruin their value. Once they're sullied, they're only worth half as much."

"Thank you, Colonel." His facial scars twisted his mouth into a sneer.

TWENTY-SIX

Comboni Mission
Taraba Valley, Nigeria

Brett

The clinic sat along the east side of the compound, just behind the first circle of dormitories. It was newly constructed with cinder block and freshly painted a tan color. It looked to be about a thousand square feet. The roof was strange, appearing as though it were covered in glass.

"It's part of Sister Maggie's plan," said Sister Annie. "Our generator is old and not always reliable, so she had the roof constructed out of solar shingles. They provide enough power to run the clinic twenty-four hours a day if we have to."

"What about at night?"

"We can thank you and the Tesla Corporation for the solution to that problem. Come inside and I'll show you." Mounted against a back wall, was a two and a half foot by four-foot gray box. "It's called a Tesla Powerwall and it enables us to store electric power in its battery packs. We can draw upon the stored electricity at night if we need it. We now have air conditioning for the sicker children and a refrigerator for our more temperature-sensitive medications. It's all thanks to you, Mr. Buchanan."

"Please, call me Brett."

"Sorry. I forgot. Brett it'll be." She chuckled. "And you can still call me Sister Annie. Now, let's take care of those sutures." After cleaning the wound with alcohol, she removed my stitches. There were only nine and it took less than a few minutes. I barely felt them. "Your gift was so generous that Sister Maggie planned to install solar panels in the dining hut and all the dormitories."

"But?"

"That's when our truck deliveries started being hijacked. We've lost almost everything she's ordered over the past four months."

"Boko Haram again?"

"Probably, but it could also be the Nigerian Army. There's a great deal of corruption in this country."

"So, I've heard."

Sister Annie took me outside and pointed to the large pile of PVC piping. "This was another part of Sister Maggie's plan. She wanted to attach an electric motor to our well and pipe fresh water throughout the orphanage."

"I tripped over them last week and knocked half the pipes over." I picked one up and studied it. "And the project couldn't be completed because of the hijacking problem?"

"That's it. I think we still need the motor and wire to run power from the generator to the pump. We also need an electrician to help hook everything up."

I considered the problem. "Maybe I can help with that. I'd like you and Sister Maggie to compile a list of everything you need for her projects. Include a new generator, concrete, cinder blocks, paint, extra solar panels, food, medical supplies, and anything else you might need. I have a little bit of clout with several influential people in Abuja and I might be able to solve your hijacking problem."

The next day, Sister Maggie accompanied me to the communications hut. Once connected to their intermediary system in the GPP, I spoke into the radio. "I need you to patch me through to Mr. Desmond Pierce at the American Embassy. Tell him Mr. Livingstone needs to speak to him."

TWENTY-SEVEN

Comboni Mission
Taraba Valley, Nigeria

Brett

I sat in my usual chair in front of the hut, enjoying my morning coffee and a stack of the small cakes when Sister Maggie approached. "I want to thank you for arranging for the delivery of our supplies, Mr. Buchanan."

"I was lucky enough to have a few contacts in the American Embassy in Abuja. Hopefully everything will arrive as ordered."

"The other Sisters and I will pray for it." She furrowed her brow and appeared to be in deep thought. She leaned over as if she wanted to whisper something to me in confidence, but changed her mind and leaned back. "I was talking to Jenkins the other day. He was quite taken with you. You've become his new hero."

Her eyes said that's not what she really wanted to discuss. She was holding back on something important, but I decided not to pursue it. "I don't think hero is the right word." I was no hero. "We do seem to share a bond though. Maybe it's because I too was an orphan." I watched Jenkins as he skipped across the courtyard, talking to some of the other children. They were laughing. "He is a special boy."

"Yes, he is, and one of our most promising students. He's

unusually intelligent and would be an excellent prospect for college in Abuja, but for now he has his heart set on pitching baseball in America. The Chicago Cubs, he said." She stared at me with a concerned look in her eyes. "Is that even possible, with his arm situation?"

"The odds of anyone playing professional baseball are slim. It's almost easier to get struck by lightning, but I've watched him throw. He's very good and can certainly play at some level. Will he be able to love what he does? Definitely."

"I just don't want him to become distracted by an impossible dream."

"Neither do I, but we should never discourage him. It's the innocence of youth that promises a future of endless possibilities. Everyone needs hopes and dreams. They're the things that make life worthwhile, even if they seem out of reach."

"I guess you're right." Sister Maggie gazed out over the land she had cleared. "This was all an impossible dream only three decades ago and now it's a successful orphanage, albeit with some serious financial problems." She appeared to be preoccupied by an unpleasant thought. "We must be careful with dreams. Sometimes the quest to attain them can contain the seeds of our own self-destruction, especially if we seek them at the expense of everything else."

Her words rang painfully true, forcing me to reflect on the same mistakes I had made. We remained quiet, digesting the trend in the conversation. Why did she raise the issue of self-destructive decisions? I couldn't help but feel there was some pressing issue on her mind, something she was reluctant to discuss. It was the same feeling I had when I first heard her speak at the church. What could be bothering her?

TWENTY-EIGHT

Comboni Mission
Taraba Valley, Nigeria

Brett

Days slid into nights, one leading to the next, each becoming another week, then a month. Every morning, I'd awaken before dawn after having listened to the leopard prowling about during the night. Coffee and a stack of small cakes would typically be delivered shortly after I sat on my chair. Initially there were three, but after several weeks I asked if it could be increased to five. More often than not, Sister Annie delivered them along with the pot of coffee. Each time she did, I'd ask her to join me. She'd politely decline, saying she had to return to the kitchen. To my delight, one particular morning she brought the coffee and poured two cups. Without comment, she sat down next to me as though we'd been doing it all along.

I took a bite from one of the cakes. They tasted like madeleines, only better. "These are delicious. What's in them anyway?"

"They're Sister Maggie's secret recipe. I think it might be the goat's milk and a few special ingredients. They can be addictive."

"Don't I know it." I leaned back and rubbed my belly. "Everything is delicious here, maybe too good. I'm sure I've put on at least fifteen pounds in the past month. That's on top of the thirty I gained after I stopped playing ball. Starting to look more and more like Father Norbert every day."

She chuckled. "You're a long way from that, but it can easily happen here. The nuns are excellent cooks."

"And, Sister Maggie has those secret ingredients."

I don't know what changed, but every day since that morning, Sister Annie joined me for coffee and cakes. We would chat about life and the orphanage. I cherished those moments, learning more about her history. I discovered she was from Minneapolis and her father was a surgeon.

"So how does a girl from Minnesota wind up in this dark corner of Africa?" I asked.

Her usual smile faded as she took a deep breath and set her cup on the table. The pensive look on her face said this was something she wasn't ready to discuss. I apologized for asking. "I'm sorry, it's actually none of my business why you're here."

"That's okay. The abbreviated version of the story is that I was looking for some sense of purpose in my life when I stumbled upon a lecture being delivered by Sister Maggie at my church. She was accomplishing some wonderful things in this part of the world and I wanted to be part of it. Within six months, I was living at a Comboni Sisters Convent preparing for a life as a nun. Five years later, here I am."

I laughed and she stared at me with a confused look in her blue eyes. "I had the same experience when I listened to her. That's how I wound up here!"

"She does have that effect on people. She's somehow able to draw you into her world." She turned toward the kitchen. "I've completely lost track of time. I'm needed to help with breakfast for the children. Then I'm scheduled to teach a class on health and nutrition." She picked up the cups and pot and headed across the courtyard. Halfway, she looked back and waved. I waved in return.

It had been a great morning. I leaned back in the chair and

patted my belly just like Father Norbert did. I'd become soft and doughy since leaving baseball, but it's worsened ever since I got here. My t-shirts were too tight and my pants hard to fasten. It was those damn cake things every morning and they were only pre-breakfast. I'd been eating four or five meals a day. "Got to stop," I said to the morning. It had been a long time since I'd been concerned about the way I looked. Needed to get back into shape and start doing something before my girth got too far out of hand. After finishing the last of the five cakes, I vowed to eat no more.

I jumped up, put on my boots, and ran the one-mile trek down the orphanage drive toward the main entrance road. Five years ago, I could have done it without breaking a sweat. The added weight, time, and alcohol had taken their toll. Halfway back, I doubled over with a stitch and could barely catch my breath. I slowed to a walk, but was forced to stop when a troop of baboons blocked the dirt road. Had to be a couple dozen of them. They looked different than the ones Father Norbert had chased away a month ago. These were larger and more muscular. "Usually not dangerous," Father Norbert had said, but usually wasn't the same as never. I took a deep breath, raised my arms over my head and shouted, just as Father Norbert had done. "Get outta here." It worked well for him, but apparently my size didn't impress this group. A huge alpha male turned to face me. Looked like he had been shooting up steroids. A vertical red stripe ran along the top of his nose and a thick mane circled his head and extended down his back. He roared like a lion and charged at me, exposing giant fangs, each as big as a butcher knife. He wasn't afraid of me, especially since he had so many buddies backing him up. "Respect the jungle," Father Norbert had told me. I lowered my eyes and slowly backed away. The baboon accepted my subjugation and led his troop on their journey. To where, I didn't know and didn't care, as long as it was in the opposite direction of where I was headed. Once I was sure they were gone, I ran and made it back to my hut in half the time it took to run out.

Twice-a-day jogging became part of my daily schedule. A few dozen push-ups and a hundred stomach crunches rounded out my routine for the next month.

It was time to start being productive, so I searched the barn until I found several shovels and a pickaxe. I headed up the hill behind the church to clear some land behind two large trees. The following day, I began the process of digging the trenches for the water pipes to the huts, several hundred yards of them, a foot deep. Removing large buried rocks and cutting through tree roots, added to my exercise program. The pounds melted away and I started to feel healthier, one with my surroundings. The intensity of the harsh voice arising from the dark corridors of my mind abated. I embraced the uncomplicated freedom of the wilderness and understood what Father Norbert had said about the jungle. "There's a compelling force that draws you in here. It's the simplicity of purpose."

Within a couple months, I saw the results of my workouts. My gut was gone. I hadn't cut my hair since I got here and it was almost down to my shoulders. "Damn, Brett. You've gone native. Fucking Tarzan of the jungle." I screamed out the Apeman's victory cry, "Ahheeahheeaheah." The nuns and students stared at me in shock. Sister Annie suppressed a giggle. She had three older brothers.

Sister Maggie smiled.

TWENTY-NINE

Mubi, Nigeria

Shakar's Wife

Kashandi walked through the edge of the village of Mubi, the place where she was born and raised—until she was kidnapped five years ago. She headed toward her family's home where she handed over her baby. Without explanation, she said. "I must go. There isn't much time." Her mother begged her to stay and tried to hug her. Kashandi pushed her away, tears in her eyes. "Please understand. I have no choice. I must leave." She looked to her father. "Do not follow me. Make sure everyone remains inside, no matter what you hear. Wait for a few minutes. Then, I need you to escape into the jungle and remain there until it's safe." Her family members looked confused and protested, but she stopped them. "I love you all. I'm sorry."

It had been almost five years and though she was only nineteen, she looked several decades older, her face scarred and her mouth mostly toothless. At first, the villagers didn't recognize her, but then, one of the older women finally exclaimed, "Kashandi? Is it you?" The woman rushed over to hug the girl. "Praise God. It is you." The woman turned to the crowd. "She has returned! It's a miracle. Kashandi has returned to us."

She brushed the elderly woman aside and struggled down the village's main road, limping toward the center of Mubi. It was the place where she had spent most of her childhood and the place from which she had been taken when Shakar and his men raided her village. Alone, Kashandi continued toward the central market area, the shrapnel vest pulling on her shoulders, the straps digging into her skin. She couldn't feel the pain. Her mind was too preoccupied by what she was about to do. She had been raised as a Christian and knew she would be in hell with Satan within the hour, but there was no other way. She couldn't allow her baby and family to be slaughtered by Shakar.

Tears streamed down her cheeks as she slowly approached the market. She forced away the impulse to scream out a warning. Shakar's men were watching. Before long, a crowd gathered around her, welcoming her back, hugging her, and wishing her well. There were cousins and friends she had known her entire life. There were families who had helped care for her when she was a young child. There were former classmates from school. They had no idea what was about to happen, how they were about to be betrayed. Overcome by guilt, Kashandi stared into their eyes and whispered, "Run." When the crowd continued to encircle her, she screamed at the top of her lungs, "Run! I have a bomb!"

It happened before any of them had a chance to react. Ziyad was standing under a copse of trees a hundred yards away. Seeing what she had done, he pushed the detonator button and rushed toward her family's home. There was a price to be paid for betraying Shakar.

Cabot

Several hundred miles away, Sebastion Cabot sat in his office when he received the call from Desmond. "It was in Mubi, sir. Sixty-seven confirmed dead," said Desmond. "Twice that many were injured."

After Desmond elaborated more details of the bombing, Cabot threw his ashtray across the room, smashing it against the huge map of Nigeria. All his efforts, working behind the scenes, trying to ensure stability and humanity in the region, were not working. He needed to turn up the heat. He said to Desmond, "It's time to play hardball. We're going to tighten the screws on that Iranian woman, our Miss Aryianna Rhamani. Shakar's head will roll for this!"

THIRTY

Home of Uguhru Muhammadi
Ministry of Interior
Arusha, Nigeria

Aryianna

After sex, Uguhru and Aryianna shared a bottle of Dom Perignon White Gold champagne. Aryianna held her glass pensively but didn't taste it. Uguhru stared down at her naked body on the sheets. "What's wrong with you tonight, my dear? You seem distant and preoccupied."

"I'm sorry, Daddy. Guess I'm just tired. I pulled an extra shift between Frankfurt and Paris, and then had to do a quick turnaround for the Abuja flight. I'm worn out." She knew Uguhru would check out her story. He was a stupid toad, but he wasn't a fool. If she were caught in a lie, he might execute her, but she had planned her cover story well. He would find everything to be as she claimed, but exhaustion wasn't the reason for her quiet mood tonight. She wanted to avoid any possibility of a conversation that might refer to Shakar. There was that bug she had been paid to plant several months ago and she was positive their conversations were being monitored. She cursed herself for agreeing to hide the device. It wasn't worth the twenty thousand the Americans paid her, but she'd had no choice. They were blackmailing her, and she faced a lifetime in a Nigerian prison if she failed to cooperate.

"Have you heard back from our friend?" he asked.

Damn! She had hoped this wouldn't pop up before she had a chance to leave. Uncharacteristic droplets of perspiration formed along her upper lip. She hid them with a sip of the champagne. Aryianna had to walk a fine line here. "Not recently." She hoped he wouldn't pursue the matter further. He did.

"His work in Mubi was impressive, but he accomplished nothing. Yes, he killed dozens of locals but that bombing did nothing for my business. You tell Shakar that my partners and I are fed up with his delays. We will not be placated by trivial suicide bombings. Unless we immediately see some tangible results, we'll be forced to eliminate all financial support." He handed her a piece of paper that contained a name. "Since he has been so ineffective, my partners and I have selected his next target. There will be no negotiating this matter. Tell Shakar that if he fails to carry out this attack, he's on his own. I will no longer provide him with protection or money."

There it was. She was tied to the attack in Mubi. Worse, a terrorist attack was being planned and she was complicit. Everything was caught on tape. She and Uguhru were discussing a treasonous association with Colonel Shakar Bhutah. She was trapped. By acknowledging a relationship with one of the leaders of Boko Haram, she would be arrested and tried for sedition. That was assuming she'd even get the chance to see the inside of a courtroom. More than likely, she'd suffer a horrible death in a remote interrogation facility. She couldn't be coy and try to act like she didn't know what he was talking about. Uguhru would see through her act and know something was wrong. She'd never make it out of his condo alive. She was stuck between two bad choices. Her only viable option was to go along right now and try to make a deal with the Americans later.

"Make sure you give this note to Shakar immediately," said Uguhru.

She looked at it and smiled. It gave her another option, one that just might save her skin.

THIRTY-ONE

Comboni Mission
Taraba Valley, Nigeria

Brett

"Great throw, Jenkins," I said. "Next time, try not to aim the ball so much. Just look at my mitt and fire away at it." Jenkins took his windup and threw his hardest fastball. It popped into my catcher's mitt directly in the center.

"Wow! Now that's what I call bringing the heat. Throw another one but this time, kick your right leg a little higher as you throw and push off with your left. The key to throwing hard isn't just the arm. It's the momentum of your whole body behind the pitch. That's what the great pitchers do. Let's try a few more of those and then, we'll work on your curveball."

After another half hour of practice, I stood straight and groaned. "Legs are getting stiff."

"It might be from all that digging you've been doing behind the church with Mr. Vincent."

I looked around. "Speaking of which, I'd better get back over there to help him. We're only half done and we need to finish with the pipes before they deliver the pump."

"What're you building?" asked Jenkins.

"When I spoke to one of the engineers in Abuja, they said we'd need a reservoir tank to provide steady water pressure. The pump alone can't do it, so we'll pump the water up the hill into a thousand-gallon tank. That way, gravity can provide water pressure even when we can't run the generator."

Jenkins nodded as though he understood, but his eyes were blank. He looked disappointed that I couldn't spend more time with him.

"While I'm working on the pipelines, I want you to paint a small X on the side of the barn, about the size of a dinner plate. Stand about sixty feet away and practice hitting it. Paint the X at a different height each day. Once you hit it consistently, try it with your eyes closed. Study the position of the X, see it in your mind, and throw. Never aim."

<hr>

Over the next two weeks, Vincent and I continued the process of working on the pipe trenches. I was surprised he stuck around, but he worked hard. We removed the larger boulders and tree roots with the help of Otis. When we were just about finished, I stopped and leaned on my shovel to rest. A rumbling roar arose from several miles away. It sounded like thunder, but the rainy season was still months away. Children rushed out of their classrooms and dormitories to see what was happening. Jenkin's eyes widened and he tugged at me. "Bad devils are coming. We need to run."

The ground shook like an earthquake. Jenkins pulled me behind one of the huts to hide. He trembled uncontrollably. Minutes later, a caravan of trucks drove down the entrance road, a large cloud of red dust following them. "It's alright, Jenkins. These men are friends of mine."

There were four fully-loaded flatbed trucks accompanied by three military escort vehicles, two in front and one protecting the rear. Sitting in the passenger seat of the first was Desmond, outfitted in military camos and sporting an automatic assault rifle over his shoulder. He was accompanied by a Nigerian general. *Must be one of the select military officers on Cabot's payroll.* It seemed incongruous that a man like Cabot would have to bribe a general to provide protection, but corruption was the way of the world in this country. I resented the fact that I'd been forced to participate in the system. It seemed hypocritical, tantamount to making a contract with the devil, and I prayed that there would be no repercussions for what I had arranged.

Desmond and the general walked up and shook my hand. "It's good to see you again, Mr. Buchanan. To tell you the truth I'm a bit surprised you're still alive."

"Still standing," I said.

"Still standing, indeed," said Desmond. "From the looks of things, you've done much more than survived. You've prospered here." He turned to the portly man next to him. "This is General Bhendari Jabba. He arranged for the military escort."

I shook the general's hand and looked over my shoulder to introduce Vincent. The bastard had disappeared.

The children and the nuns helped unload a three-month supply of beans, rice, potatoes, yams, and onions. They stored them in the barn where the critters of the night couldn't get to them. The soldiers helped stack cinder blocks, cement and solar panels near the children's huts and the church. It took eight men to unload the new generator and secure it behind the church. When the soldiers began to unpack the plastic water tank, I was confused. It was huge, four times larger than expected. I turned to Desmond. "What's this?"

He nodded. "It's a four-thousand-gallon tank. I spoke to one of the engineering consultants in Abuja. He said the system you requested was too small and wouldn't be sufficient for the orphanage's needs. You'd have to fill it too often and the generator wouldn't be able to keep up. With the larger tank, it can be filled once daily and the water needs of the entire compound can be delivered by gravity twenty-four hours a day."

I groaned. "We need to get that thing about a hundred feet up the hill behind the church to provide the necessary water pressure. Even when empty, it must weigh over five hundred pounds and the truck can't get it up there. I'm not sure we have the manpower to do it."

Sister Maggie joined the conversation. "That's no problem. Otis can handle twice that amount."

"Otis?" asked Desmond.

"You'll see," I said. "I've already cleared a space that should be large enough."

We spent the next two hours securing the tank to a harness and coaxing the huge buffalo to pull it up the side of the hill. Once there, we stabilized it behind two large trees. The last job was to unload the pump next to the burr hole and move twenty barrels of generator fuel behind the church building.

As the sun began to set, Sister Maggie turned to Desmond. "Will you and your men be staying with us for a while, Mr. Pierce?"

"I'm sorry Sister, but I must leave with most of the men tomorrow morning. Our electricians and a half dozen of the military will remain behind until all the heavy lifting, construction, and electric work have been completed."

He turned to me. "Could I have a minute of your time in private, Mr. Buchanan?" We walked over to my hut. "Not quite as lavish as the Hilton, but cozy," said Desmond.

"It's all I need in life right now. What'd you want to discuss?"

"As I told the good Sister, most of the soldiers and I will be leaving in the morning. The general would like to be paid before he departs."

"Of course. I almost forgot."

"As you requested, the cost of the supplies will be billed directly to your lawyer in the States, but the general's men will require cash."

"How much?"

"Thirty thousand."

"Thirty thousand? Dollars?"

"The cost of protection is high in Nigeria, especially this far out into the jungle. The trip is fraught with danger."

"Protection from Boko Haram or the army?"

"Both, I'm afraid."

The bribery payment left a bad taste in my mouth. I shook

my head in disgust at what I had to do. "Excuse me for a minute." I walked a hundred yards into the jungle to retrieve the cash from its hiding place. When I returned, I said, "Am I going to have to make arrangements for a more regular protection detail?"

"Probably, unless things change with Boko Haram. I can guarantee that there will be no more hijackings by the Nigerian Army. Mr. Cabot spoke to General Jabba personally and let him know that if the hijackings didn't stop, his lavish lifestyle was going to change for the worse."

I smiled. "I guess the entire corruption thing can be a double-edged sword."

"It does provide a great deal of leverage if you know how and when to use it. Mr. Cabot is an expert at such things." Before leaving to give the cash to the general, Desmond said, "Take care, Mr. Buchanan. We don't want to see anything happen to you."

I returned to the last truck to be unloaded. Included with the shipment were a dozen baseball mitts, bats and balls. Jenkins' eyes lit up when he saw them. It made the thirty thousand well worth the expense.

***

They were gone early the following morning, before I had a chance to say goodbye. Desmond was a mysterious man, but I liked him and learned to trust him implicitly. While waiting for my morning coffee, Vincent showed up.

"Where the hell have you been, Vincent? We needed your help unloading the trucks."

"I had urgent matters to attend to."

"All night? In the middle of the jungle?"

Vincent shrugged. "General Jabba and I have a history." He rubbed the scar along the side of his face. "Had to make myself scarce. It was best that he didn't see me here."

"History? What kind of history?" Vincent didn't answer. Though I trusted Desmond, Vincent was an entirely different matter.

A week later, everything was set except for the final electrical and plumbing hook-ups. I was attaching the new water lines to the interior faucets of the mess hall when Sister Maggie stopped to watch me for a few minutes. Finally, she said, "We can't thank you enough for all you've done, Mr. Buchanan. You've been a Godsend."

"I'm glad I could help. We still have some work to do but you should have water in every building within the week."

"I realize you have contacts in Abuja, but this military escort had to be expensive. I know all too well how things work in Nigeria."

"Money well spent, Sister."

She hesitated before saying, "If you need any help with the finances, please let me know." She stared at the ground and kicked at the dirt. She seemed embarrassed and walked away.

What was that about? Except for what I had given them, the orphanage seemed to run on a shoestring budget. How could she possibly help with finances? It was another Sister Mary Margaret mystery.

THIRTY-TWO

Small Village
Cameroon Jungle

Shakar Bhutah

Ziyad and Shakar checked their army. "How're we doing with recruiting?"

"We came across a couple dozen Zambuti."

"Zambuties? The pygmies?" Shakar laughed.

"They're fierce warriors who were prepared to battle to the death. They fought us well even though all they had were spears and arrows. They were no match for automatic weapons though. I hoped we could train them."

"Fight to the death? Sounds like the kind of men we need. So, where are they?"

"Had to shoot them, sir. They were like wild animals. Impossible to train."

"What the hell did you expect from cannibals? Next time, shoot them on sight and don't waste my time. I need real soldiers, ones who won't desert in the face of battle."

Shakar turned his attention back to the crowd of villagers. "Next deserter." He asked the soldier standing next to him, "How many are left?"

"Five, Colonel. You've already shot seven."

"Waste of good bullets." Shakar said, his club at his side. He adjusted his black beret and scanned the crowd of several hundred villagers standing before him. His men kept their rifles trained on the group in case any of them decided to run or protest. "They don't look frightened enough. We can't expect to stop this rash of desertions if the people don't fear and respect us. I need to send a stronger message." Shakar paused and commanded, "Bring out the final five for their trials. I'll do them all at the same time. Make sure you bring their families also. I want them to stand next to the accused."

After they were marched out into the open, Shakar selected one who had just pissed himself. His eyes were hollowed out and his skin hung on his skeletal frame like a rag. Despite the beatings he had already received, he fought against his restraints as he was dragged in front of Shakar and forced to kneel. The man looked in panic at the seven bloodied bodies already lying on the ground. His family and those of the other four sobbed uncontrollably.

"You have been charged with desertion." Before the man had a chance to reply, Shakar pronounced his judgment. "I find you guilty. The punishment for your treason is death." Shakar looked at the man and asked, "Do you have a son?" He didn't answer. Shakar looked to the crowd and shouted, "Does this man have a son?" There was no answer. A demonic grin consumed Shakar's face, a ray of sunlight reflecting off his notorious gold tooth. "If someone doesn't point out this man's son, I will start shooting you one by one until I get an answer."

The group of villagers pushed a young boy of about nine forward.

"That's more like it. All I ask for is a little cooperation and loyalty." Shakar withdrew his sidearm and ejected the clip. He removed all bullets except one, replaced the clip, and chambered the only round. He paused and motioned for the man's son to step forward. Shakar placed the gun in the boy's right hand and, holding his own hand firmly around the boy's, he pressed the barrel of the gun against his father's forehead.

"No—please no! Have mercy," cried the boy's mother.

"Shoot him!" commanded Shakar.

The boy sobbed and shook his head no.

"Are you disobeying a direct order from your commander, soldier? Are you disobeying the word of Allah? You're a traitor just like your cowardly father." Shakar immediately turned the weapon on the boy and fired a round into his head. His lifeless young body fell at the feet of his father. As the man sobbed, Shakar nearly decapitated him with the club. The crowd froze in fear.

"Next coward," said Shakar.

For the next man, the result was the same, a child being shot and the deserter being clubbed. For the three final executions, there were no more protestations from family members. Sons shot their fathers in the head within seconds of receiving the gun. The ground ran red with the blood of Shakar's victims.

When all was finished, Shakar looked at the crowd and proclaimed, "I am a merciful leader, am I not? I have given each of you the chance to save the lives of your family members, but how have you responded to my mercy? You betray and disrespect me. In doing so, you disrespect Allah. I will tolerate it no more. From now on, the punishment for desertion will be death for the deserter and all members of his family."

He put his hand on Ziyad's shoulder and pulled him close. "Take every man and boy who can carry a rifle." He looked up and pulled his sidearm as a vehicle sped into the village. It came to a sliding stop ten feet away, kicking up a storm of dust. The driver jumped out and spoke to Ziyad.

"What is it?" Shakar asked.

"Our contacts in the village of Katanga report that a convoy of delivery trucks passed through the town several days ago. They were headed northeast."

"Did our men intercept them?"

"They couldn't. The convoy was protected by the Nigerian Army. It looked almost like a military assault."

"I'm surprised those bastards didn't hijack the trucks themselves. That's what they usually do and then blame us. Where were they headed?"

"East, down the main road, but it's a hundred miles of empty jungle. There's nothing out there except for a small Christian orphanage and it's too tiny to be of any significance."

"And you say there were four trucks?"

"Yes, that's in addition to the three military escort vehicles."

"That's a lot of firepower to protect trucks delivering supplies to a small orphanage. There must be something else going on there. Not many people have enough influence to arrange for that kind of operation. It would take someone with a great deal of cash to bribe enough army officers for an escort of that size."

"That's what I thought, sir, so I did some more digging. Many of the military men said everything was arranged as humanitarian aid through the American Embassy. Not only that, the men were paid in American dollars."

"Americans? What could they be up to?" asked Shakar. He paced back and forth, holding his club and processing this new information. "I need to know what's going on around that so-called orphanage. The Americans might be funding the establishment of a peripheral military compound. I can't allow that to happen." He paused for a few seconds. "Select a few of your most reliable men and have them do some surveillance."

"Yes sir," replied Ziyad. "I'll send two of my cousins. They're excellent warriors and ready to support your cause with their lives."

THIRTY-THREE

Comboni Mission
Taraba Valley, Nigeria

Brett

I was still putting the final touches on the new water supply to the kitchen when Jenkins ran across the courtyard. "Mister Brett, come quickly!" The boy's eyes were wide with panic.

"What's the problem?"

"Strange red creatures just crawled out of the bush."

"Red creatures?"

"Yes. People. They look like little devils!"

"Little? How small?"

"Taller than me, but not much."

"Tell the other children to stay away from them." I rushed inside the kitchen where I found Sister Maggie helping the other nuns prepare lunch. "I need you to come with me. I think those pygmies of yours have returned."

"The Zambuti? It's been over fifteen years since I last saw them."

We walked together and saw them a couple hundred feet away, at the edge of the jungle. A wide smile spread across Sister Maggie's face. "Amazing people. They've remained hidden in the mountains between here and Cameroon for centuries. They're extremely shy and avoid almost all contact with the outside world. They distrust Christians because early missionaries destroyed images of their gods and tried to force Christianity upon them. Trying to erase the local culture of these third-world societies has been the undoing of the initial missionary movement. This is the same tribe I describe in my lectures back in the States."

"The little girl who almost died of strep throat?"

"We treated her with antibiotics for a week. After she recovered, they disappeared back into the jungle."

"Until now," I said.

"Until now," she replied.

As we drew closer, I identified a group of three short, muscular men whose bodies were covered in mosaics of red ochre tattoos. They were completely naked except for clusters of fresh leaves tied around their waists like small loincloths. One of the men stepped forward as we approached. He was almost half my size but stood proudly erect with an air of being the man in charge. He wore a headband of braided palm leaves and his hair was slicked back with red clay. In his right hand, he held an ornate spear with a blade at one end and a spike on the other. It looked lethal but it was more than a weapon. He carried it like a scepter. The shaft contained images, carved from ivory, and inlaid with multiple pieces of light blue glass. The spear appeared to be ancient, as though it had been handed down for centuries. The man who held it would be a leader, a chief, highly respected by his tribe. A knife with a matching handle was sheathed in animal-hide strapped to his waist. The other two men stood on either side of the chief, each holding a bow loaded with a red arrow. The scene looked like an old photograph from *National Geographic.* I studied the group for signs of aggression, but couldn't tell if they were friendly or meant harm.

"What's the deal with all the red tattoos?" I asked.

Sister Maggie studied the people. "From what I was able to ascertain the last time I saw them, the tattoos depict their family history and any heroic accomplishments."

"What do they want from us?"

"I suspect we're about to find out. Put on your friendliest

smile and follow me slowly. They have their own code of social interaction, so don't make any sudden gestures. If they see anything that could be perceived as a threat to the chief, we all could wind up dead."

I scanned the edge of the thick trees. "I don't see any weapons except a few arrows and that spear."

"They don't need guns. Too cumbersome and loud. Their strength comes from their cunning and speed."

"But they're so small. What can they do?"

"Don't make the mistake of underestimating them because of their size, Mr. Buchanan. The chief alone is more than capable of handling himself, even against a man twice his size and half his age. It's the reason he's chief. It's not an honor handed down as a birthright. It must be earned. He has demonstrated to the rest of his tribe that he's a ferocious warrior. He's revered by his tribe almost as much as they idolize their gods. His fellow tribesmen would consider it an honor to sacrifice their lives to protect him."

I again scanned the perimeter of the compound. "Tribesmen? But it looks like there's only these three guys."

"That's the point. You can't see them, but right now there are probably over two dozen arrows pulled and aimed directly at us. You don't see them or hear them unless they want you to. When you do, it's usually too late. The locals call them the 'Red Ghosts.' They're masters at being able to melt into the jungle. It's what makes them so dangerous."

"Terrific." I forced what I hoped was a friendly smile.

Father Norbert approached, followed by Vincent who was carrying one of his assault rifles. "Zambuti pygmies!" Vincent snarled. "Nasty creatures, barely human. I've heard they're cannibals." He raised his rifle and within a second, a red arrow sprung from somewhere in the brush and landed between his feet.

"No," said Father Norbert. He reached over and placed his hand over the barrel of Vincent's gun, carefully pushing it toward the ground. "If you try that again, the next arrow will be through your neck. Now drop the rifle before you get us all killed."

Vincent mumbled something about goddamn red devils, but did as he was told.

Sister Maggie took another step forward. "Let's see if we can find out what this is about. Mr. Buchanan, come with me. The rest of you, stay back. And for God's sake, Mr. Vincent. Don't shoot anyone."

The nun took several more cautious steps forward and began the process of trying to communicate with the chief using a combination of hand signals and a language the likes of which I had never heard. When the chief talked, his speech was punctuated with a series of clicking and grunting sounds much like the use of consonants in western languages. The chief said a word that sounded like "maageek," the last consonant being one of his clicking sounds.

Sister Maggie nodded her head, and repeated the word "maageek." She motioned for the chief to follow her. He didn't. Instead, he stepped aside, and a mostly nude woman emerged from the dense brush, carrying a listless child in her arms. She had stripes of decorative red clay braiding in her hair, and a tattoo of a red crucifix on her right cheek.

"The tattoo," I said. "She's the one with tonsillitis whose life you saved."

Sister Maggie nodded in agreement as she checked the woman's child. He was a boy of about five and had a deep gash running down the outside of his right leg from the knee to his ankle. The chief turned to Sister Maggie with a desperate look in his eyes. "Maageek?" he again asked.

"Magic," she replied with a gentle smile and led them to the medical hut.

<hr>

When we entered, Sister Annie was putting the finishing touches on a knee bandage for a whimpering little girl. "It's just a scrape and it should be fine," she reassured her. She smiled when I entered the room. The smile quickly faded when she saw the pigmy woman carrying the injured child. Her response was immediate, but controlled. She cleared the examining table and laid the child on his back. "Leg's badly infected," said Annie. "He's septic."

"Septic? Can you stitch it up?"

Annie examined the wound closely and shook her head. "Can't. This gash is at least two days old and it's grossly contaminated. God only knows what type of organisms are in there. See those red streaks running up the child's leg. It's cellulitis. If I suture this closed, the bacteria will become trapped and the leg will abscess. He could even get gangrene. We have to leave the wound open and let it heal from the inside out."

The mother looked at Annie and asked, "Maageek?"

"I will try," replied Annie with a less than convincing tone. She asked Sister Maggie to escort the few tribe members outside. The mother and chief refused to leave. Annie turned to me. "There's no time to transfer him to a hospital. It would take days and he'd never make it in time. We have to take care of this on our own." She began cleaning the wound with forceps. "I don't know what kind of germs are causing the infection, but it's probably a mixture. The good thing is that antibiotics have been used sparingly in this part of the world, so most bacteria haven't had the chance to develop wide-spread resistance. Hopefully, basic medications will be effective." She opened a cabinet and rummaged through it. "Damn. We're out of IV sets. I'll need to improvise."

"What can I do?"

"Look inside that cabinet on your left. On the second shelf, you'll find a large bottle of Cefuroxime. It's Ceftin."

After a minute of searching I said, "Got it."

"Take out two tablets and put them into that mortar you see on the countertop. Use the pestle to crush them into a fine powder."

While I worked on the antibiotics, Sister Annie rinsed the child's wound with warm water, washing away all dirt and debris.

"Ready," I said.

Sister Annie dissolved the powder in a small amount of water and spoon-fed it into the little boy's mouth. "We have to give him a dose every six hours at first. If we don't see improvement pretty soon, I'll have to try something else. Now, could you go to the kitchen and get me some bleach?"

"Bleach? As in Clorox?"

"Yes, better get two bottles."

Ten minutes later I returned with the bleach. "What's this for?"

"It's a trick my father showed me. Laundry bleach, like Clorox, is little more than sodium hypochlorite. It's an excellent bactericidal on wounds like this." She diluted it with water. "We'll soak dressing gauzes in it and pack them into the wound. When the dried gauze is removed, it'll pull away all badly infected and necrotic tissue with it." After dressing the wound, Annie gave the child sips of water. "There's nothing more for us to do now but force fluids, wait and pray."

"What if he doesn't make it?"

"I don't even want to think about that possibility. It could mean trouble for us and the entire orphanage."

"Then I guess we'd better make sure he lives."

For the next seventy-two hours, Sister Annie and I maintained a vigil at the child's side, forcing oral fluids, giving antibiotics, and changing the dressings. Throughout the entire time, the Zambuti mother never left her child. The chief, who I assumed was the child's father, stood guard at the door, chanting some type of prayer over and over. Other tribe members appeared, standing and praying outside the clinic.

The endless days and nights bled together until on the fourth morning, the child cried. Annie did also. Joy and satisfaction washed through me. Other than Jonathan's birth, it was a sensation stronger than anything I had felt before, something baseball had never given me. She hugged me and kissed me on the cheek. "He's not completely out of the woods yet, but he's going to make it."

I walked outside to stretch my legs. I searched for the tribesmen, but couldn't see any sign of them.

Sister Maggie joined me. "They're still out there, Mr. Buchanan, just out of sight in case they're needed."

I continued gazing into the underbrush. "Amazing people. Their unqualified devotion to the child is admirable."

"You're right. Though we might consider them to be primitive and uncivilized, we could learn a great deal from them," she said. "They have no outside distractions, no cell phones, no televisions, and no blind quest to accumulate material things, just love and selfless devotion to their family and tribe. They live in peace with all who don't try to enforce their own agenda on them."

After two more weeks of dressing changes, the wound had just about completely healed, and the boy was ready to be discharged from the clinic. By the following morning, the Zambuti had already disappeared. No notice was given and there were no goodbyes. They simply vanished into the jungle without any trace that they had ever been here.

Sister Annie walked into the treatment room, and when she returned, she held a small hand-carved ivory crucifix. It had a blue stone in the middle. "The Zambuti left this on the child's bed."

THIRTY-FOUR

Comboni Mission
Taraba Valley, Nigeria

Brett

It had been a week since the pygmies had disappeared and I was putting the finishing connections on the water line leading to one of the new children's dormitories. When Sister Maggie approached, I quickly pulled on my t-shirt. "Good afternoon, Sister. I'm afraid you caught me by surprise." I jammed my shovel into the ground and leaned on the handle.

"Good afternoon to you, Mr. Buchanan. It appears as though you're making good progress on the water system. It looks like everything is just about ready."

"I tested the pump and filled the storage tank. You should have all the water you need in about an hour as long as there aren't any leaks or last-minute glitches."

"I'll pray that there won't be, but life always seems to offer surprises." She furrowed her brow and looked around as though perplexed by a problem smoldering just below the surface. I had seen that look in her eyes several times before.

"Is there something I can help you with?"

"I've been watching you for the past several months, Mr. Buchanan. You're honest, stable and not prone to overreaction. I like the way you handled yourself with the Zambuti. I can tell, you're a reliable man who can be trusted with sensitive information."

Reliable? There are many who wouldn't agree with you, especially my ex. "Information? What kind of information, Sister?"

"I need to tell you something I've never shared with anyone before, not even Father Norbert." She lowered her voice to a whisper, her words slow and measured. "You must promise you'll never share the details of our conversation with anyone."

I couldn't imagine where this was going. "Of course."

Sister Maggie looked around as if to be sure no one was watching us. She reached into the pocket of her habit and withdrew something in her fist. When she opened her hand, I was shocked. She was holding a brilliant, polished stone about the size of a baseball. It had a faint blue color.

"It looks like a diamond, a huge diamond."

"Exactly."

"But how? Where did you get it?"

"You remember the young Zambuti girl I told you about during my talk in America?"

"Yes. The one with the tonsillitis, the mother who just brought her boy to see us. You said the tattoo on her cheek was drawn out of respect for you and your beliefs, a way of saying thank you for what you did."

"Yes, but what I haven't told anyone is that the tribe also left this precious stone behind as a gift."

This must have been the information she was withholding when I first heard her speak, but why? I took the gem from her hand and held it up to the sunlight to check it more closely. I had purchased my share of precious stones in the past and was familiar with their quality. I rotated it in my fingers and inspected it from all sides. "It's almost flawless. Must be worth a hundred million, at least! How did the Zambuti get their hands on a diamond, much less one so large? And polished?"

"Diamond fields have been discovered in Southeastern Nigeria, just fifty miles from here. I think the Zambuti must have uncovered a nearby pocket long ago."

"Don't they realize what this is worth?"

"Monetary value is not a concept they understand," said Sister Maggie. "The Zambuti consider the diamonds to be religious symbols. I think they left it behind for me as a religious exchange for the magic we provided. They see its power as a way to protect the orphanage from evil."

"You realize this stone alone could solve all of your financial problems forever? You could do whatever you wanted in this valley. You wouldn't have to spend time away from the orphanage soliciting donations."

"That's true, but selling it would come at a steep price. The monetary return would contain the seeds of destruction. If word got out that diamonds had been discovered in the Taraba Valley, we'd suffer a ruthless invasion by large corporate mining companies. In less than a year this entire jungle would be destroyed, and for what? Certainly not to benefit the people of Nigeria. It would only make the wealthy richer while doing nothing for the impoverished."

I remembered what Father Norbert said about the impermanence of all things.

She gazed across the orphanage compound. "This land around us is too pristine and beautiful to risk contamination by the outside world. There's a town of Mayo-Sina where one of the largest diamond fields was recently uncovered. It took only nine months for the little village of five hundred people to grow by over two hundred thousand, all looking to find the elusive gems. Outsiders invaded the area like swarms of locusts, bringing disease and death with them. The land now looks like a war zone. The ecology of the region has been irreparably damaged and crime has skyrocketed. I refuse to allow that to happen in the Taraba Valley. It would destroy the land, the orphanage, and result in the total elimination of the Zambuti culture, one of the purest I've ever seen."

"So why are you telling me this?"

"I want you to take the diamond with you when you return to America. Despite whatever personal issues you might have, you're still a famous and successful person. You must have contacts in the large metropolitan areas of the States, individuals who know how to be discreet in matters such as this. See what you can do with the stone. Maybe it can still benefit the orphanage somehow. Take your time though. There's no rush. Time is irrelevant out here in the jungle. It's one feature that makes it so magnificent. It's a land that time forgot. I'd like to keep it that way."

As she walked away, I placed the large diamond in my pocket and buttoned the flap. What the hell was I going to do with it and how would I ever get it through customs and back home? Who else might know about the diamonds? Like my backpack of cash, I needed to hide the gem somewhere. I looked in all directions to see if Vincent was nearby.

THIRTY-FIVE

Comboni Mission
Taraba Valley, Nigeria

Brett

In the morning, I sat on the porch listening to Father Norbert give a Sunday sermon about the "Prodigal Son," a story of how God forgives and loves all equally, regardless of their past. *I'm not so sure about that one, Father. I've already rejected God and damned myself in the process. I think it's safe to say I'm beyond forgiveness.*

After the mass was over, I spotted Sister Annie and Sister Maggie sitting together for breakfast in the dining hut. I walked over and took a seat next to them. A few tables to the left, a group of children exploded with laughter. Father Norbert was regaling them with one of his many stories. I overheard him mention the name of Sister Maggie. He stole a glance in her direction. She snapped her head toward him, her face as taught as a guitar string, ready to snap. Sister Annie gazed down at the table. The stories abruptly ended, but the good Father's shoulders continued to shake up and down while the children tried to stifle giggles. Sister Maggie's cold stare was enough to wilt a flower. A bad sign, especially if you happened to be Father Norbert. He retreated to the safety of his church.

Relieved that the impending storm was over, I poured myself a second cup of coffee. "Do you two Sisters have anything scheduled for this afternoon? I've been here for over two months and I've not been more than a hundred yards into the jungle. Thought about taking a small hike down the road. It'd be fun to explore a little, and I was hoping you two might join me."

"I'm sorry, but I have some work to do in my office," said Sister Maggie. Translation, she was about to have a serious discussion with Father Norbert.

I glanced over my shoulder in the direction of the church. "Feel sorry for you, my friend," I said under my breath.

"I have to help clean up the breakfast dishes, but it shouldn't take long," said Sister Annie. "I'm free afterward. I can join you if it's okay with Sister Maggie." She looked to the good Sister who nodded her approval. Sister Annie stood. "Give me a few minutes to change into my hiking clothes."

It was amazing how easily she was able to transition between her two different lives: nun and civilian. After she left, I turned to Sister Maggie. Her demeanor had softened. "Sister Annie's a special person."

"That she is." Sister Maggie's eyes sparkled, a look I hadn't seen until now. "We've been blessed to have her with us."

"Father Norbert told me she's a novitiate. I'm not sure what that means."

"She's never taken her final vows. I think she's uncertain as to whether or not this is the life God has selected for her. I know she prays a great deal for guidance. It's an important decision that each candidate must make on her own."

I took a sip of coffee while processing her comments. Sister Maggie smiled. Looked like I might have saved Father Norbert from a tongue thrashing.

"I'm ready," said Sister Annie as she rejoined us. She had exchanged her religious habit for a pair of khaki shorts, a black t-shirt, and hiking boots. Her new ivory crucifix with its blue stone hung from her neck. She and I excused ourselves.

"Be careful," warned Sister Maggie. "The jungle around here can be an unforgiving place. The further away from the orphanage you wander, the more dangerous it gets."

"Like from the Zambuti?" I asked, filling a canteen with water.

"You'll never have to worry about them. After saving the chief's little boy, you're both probably looked upon as family. There are many other things out there to worry about, though." She didn't elaborate any further. At the last minute, she said, "Make sure you stay on the paths."

We walked out of the dining hut and Sister Annie led me toward a path that headed east. I stopped and pointed in the opposite direction. "Isn't the entrance road to the orphanage back there?"

"Yes, but it'll be more fun this way. There's a series of back trails that head toward the Taraba River. It's pretty much overgrown by vegetation but much more interesting. We might even see some local wildlife."

"That's great as long as the word wildlife doesn't include the leopard that prowls around the orphanage every night." We took a right and continued down a dirt path bordered on both sides by thick underbrush and a canopy of tall trees.

"Have you ever walked in this direction before?" I asked.

"Yes, but it's been a while. After a mile or so it intersects the main road. That's the one you drove down when you first came to the orphanage. Once we reach it, we can head further east. I've never hiked out that far."

"So, it'll be uncharted territory for the both of us, our own private adventure. It could lead us to a place completely untainted by mankind."

"Exciting," said Annie. We continued our walk in silence, gazing at the trees and listening to the songs of the many multicolored birds, most whimsical, but others guttural and ominous. It was like walking through the middle of a living, Henri Rousseau painting. Their serenade was occasionally disrupted by the whooping calls of a few howler monkeys. We paused to search the trees but only caught a momentary glance of one as it swung from one tree to the next directly overhead. More monkeys joined in the chorus of cries.

Annie looked up. "Probably warning the rest of their tribe about our presence."

"Understandable. For them, we probably represent a threat."

Annie paused and turned to me. "What about you, Brett? What threatens you?"

"Not much except that leopard and some baboons I've encountered. Other than those, visiting the orphanage has given me some of the most exciting experiences in my life." I didn't mention the boy who underwent the tire necklacing or the dead Somalis.

"How long are you planning to stay?"

Tree branches overhead shook. I gazed up, searching in vain for the monkeys. "I don't know how long I'll stay. Haven't made any plans to leave. I'm sure I've already overstayed my visa, so I might be in a bit of trouble."

"Since you're in Taraba, I doubt anyone in the government actually cares."

I stopped, held up my hand, and studied our surroundings.

"What is it?' asked Annie.

"Listen."

She looked around. "But I don't hear anything."

"That's just it. Neither do I. A few minutes ago, the jungle was alive with different sounds. Now there's only silence, an eerie silence." The absence of sound was intense.

As soon as the words came out of my mouth, a loud rustling arose from the brush, just ahead, and to our left. It was followed by the loud cracking sound of a tree falling. Whatever it was, it was getting close, and it was large. The hair on the back of my neck bristled.

"What was that?" Annie grabbed my arm.

"Maybe it wasn't us the monkeys were so worried about. Maybe there's something else out here with us—something much bigger." That's when we saw him, just a hundred feet down the path. A large bull elephant arose from the brush, its gait ponderous but unrelenting, his long tusks pushing aside everything in its path. The huge animal turned his head, flapped his ears, and stared at us, a look of casual curiosity in his eyes. I held my breath. We remained frozen in our tracks.

"What's he doing?" asked Annie.

"I think he's sizing us up."

"Maybe he thinks we might be a threat."

"I once read that when confronted by a large animal in the wild, you should stand your ground, and never run."

"Nice theory," replied Annie, "but my feet are telling me to take off."

As if bored by our presence, the elephant looked away and raised his trunk. He stripped a branch of leaves from a small tree and shoved it in his mouth. He lumbered forward, back into the jungle, leaving in his wake a string of fallen trees. A moment later, he was followed by several females and a baby. Like the large male, they paused and stared.

"Probably aren't used to seeing humans," I said.

The baby took a few steps toward Annie, but its mother intervened and coaxed him back to the center of the group. When they disappeared, we looked at each other and laughed in nervous relief.

"I've been here in the Nigerian jungle for over five years and I've never seen anything so amazing as that before," said Annie. "I'm still shaking."

"They were magnificent!" I understood what Sister Maggie meant when she said all this could be destroyed if mining and civilization invaded the valley. These animals would be lost forever.

"So majestic!" Annie was still holding onto my arm.

"I thought the baby was going to walk right up to you."

"I know, I know. I'm not sure what I would've done if it had. Run? Pet it, maybe? I was frightened and excited at the same time."

I stared at the spot where the animals disappeared. "I never realized there were elephants in Nigeria."

"I've read about them, but until now, I've never seen one in person. They're forest elephants. You can tell by the downward projection of their tusks. Most of the forest elephant population was destroyed by ivory poachers years ago. They're making a comeback, but their survival is still in jeopardy."

"I thought most of the illegal ivory trade came from Tanzania."

"It still does, but at one time there were large herds of forest elephants that roamed the eastern Nigerian jungles and Cameroon. Now they've pretty much been wiped out. Boko Haram did most of the damage."

"Taking ivory to fund terrorist activities?"

"Probably. The few survivors generally remain in the National Parks where they're protected, but Gashaka-Gumti is only ten miles east of here, so I guess this group wandered down from the mountains looking for food. Supposedly, the forest elephants are much smaller than the others."

"I don't know. That male looked pretty darn big from where I was standing," I said.

Annie must have realized that she was still clutching onto my arm. She blushed and slowly released it. My arm tingled where her hand had once been. We watched the last of the large animals disappear farther into the bush, eating leaves and knocking down more trees in the process. "They seemed to be focused on a mission. Where do you think they're headed?"

"Probably the Taraba River. It's only several miles to the south of here and it parallels this road all of the way to Cameroon."

"A road to Cameroon?"

"That's what I've been told, but it's not actually a road and it's never used anymore. Too rugged and dangerous."

We resumed our hike, cautiously checking our surroundings for any more signs of wildlife.

"Even after five years, I still find Africa to be a land full of surprises," she said.

"Splendor or danger can be lurking in the darkness around every bend," I added.

"I wonder what other surprises are in store for us today?"

"Hopefully nothing with big fangs," I said.

THIRTY-SIX

Road to Cameroon
Taraba Valley, Nigeria

Brett

Annie stopped at a crossroads. "Here's the main road, if you want to call it that."

"Looks pretty rough," I said.

"The primary orphanage entrance is to the west of here. That's where you drove in when you first arrived."

The dirt trail we had been walking continued to snake its way straight ahead through heavy brush. It was an old path, almost completely overgrown. "Where does that lead?" I asked.

"A deserted village sitting on the banks of the Taraba River. That's where they used to load the ivory onto boats, until the ivory business died off. Once it did, the village withered away. The few remaining villagers were killed by disease or raids by revolutionaries. The old boat dock was how the orphanage had supplies shipped."

"By boat?"

"Yes, at least they used to."

"It must be two or three miles from the river to the orphanage. How'd the nuns ever manage to get goods delivered from the dock? They certainly couldn't carry the stuff."

"That old truck Mr. Vincent tried to repair. After it died, Sister Maggie tried to use Otis and a wagon, but that didn't work out. Too many deep ruts and the wagon fell apart. Now, we have to rely on deliveries overland and those were usually hijacked—until you arranged for military escorts."

"Maybe it would be interesting to head that way and see how the old village looks."

Annie shook her head. "Nothing there of interest anymore. Let's follow the main road east. Like I said, I've never been out this far, and I'd like to see what's around the next bend."

"Maybe more elephants?"

We continued with our hike as the road soon gave way to heavier underbrush. The overhead canopy of vegetation created the effect of a darkened tunnel, the trees on either side twisting and turning their way upward, fighting with each other for access to the life-giving rays of the sun. The birds resumed their songs and the monkeys howled. We were alone.

I stopped and turned to her. "May I ask you a personal question?"

"Depends upon what you'd like to know?"

"What, besides Sister Maggie, brought you to this remote part of Africa? You possess a remarkable talent for medicine. What you did to heal that little boy's leg wound was nothing short of miraculous. You saved his life. Did you ever consider becoming a doctor?"

"Actually, I graduated from medical school."

I stopped walking. "You did? What happened?" I shook my head. "I'm sorry. I keep asking personal questions. It's none of my business."

"That's okay, but it's a bit complicated." She picked a small red flower from a bush that had been partially trampled by the elephants. She sniffed the flower, and put it in her hair. Beautiful. "After starting a surgery residency, I became a bit disappointed. Don't get me wrong. I loved the patient interaction, but I soon realized that the hospital was not the place for me. It was controlled by lawyers and administrators preoccupied with economics. Too many individuals turned a blind eye to too many important issues. The practice of medicine had become driven by public image and the bottom-line financials rather than patient care. Meanwhile, millions around the world suffered from disease and starvation. I believed there had to be a different life for me, one in which I could impact the lives of others in a more significant way. That's when I met Sister Maggie and the seed of missionary work was planted. I guess the rest is history."

I chuckled. "She certainly can be a motivating force. I know this from first-hand experience."

"That's how I wound up joining the Comboni Sisters. I volunteered for Nigeria. It was the perfect opportunity for me to make a difference. So here I am." She started walking again slowly, her eyes watching every step. "I have no regrets."

I considered Annie's claim that she left medicine because of problems with hospital administrators and lawyers. Though I had only known her for several months, I was convinced she wouldn't run away from a battle. She would dig in her heels and fight. Something else must have happened, something hurtful, something deep below the surface, enough to force her to run away from her past. I couldn't figure out what it might be, but I didn't press the issue and looked to change the subject. It was getting a little darker and that gave me the opportunity. "We've talked so long I've lost track of time. With the heavy tree cover, I can't see the sun, but I suspect it's getting lower in the sky."

Annie stopped. "The road ends here anyway. Looks like the only thing left is a dry creek bed that heads up the mountains toward Cameroon. This here is the end of any vestige of civilization. There's nothing ahead but miles and miles of jungle."

"It looks as though the jungle swallowed everything up." Somewhere up in that hostile land, the Zambuti lived. How did they survive? Where did they find the diamonds? Up ahead? Unlikely. "Wait a minute," I said. I leaned over to study the creek bed, rubbing my fingers across the ground. "There are tire tracks here—and they're fresh. Look farther up the hill. The underbrush has been trampled down. Something must be up ahead of us."

"Or maybe behind us," she said.

"Any idea who might have left them?"

"None at all. I haven't heard any vehicles out here since that convoy dropped off the supplies last month. There are no villages for a hundred miles. Can't imagine what a car would be doing out here." She looked up through the trees. "We'd better head back to the orphanage. We don't want to get caught out here at dusk. That could be very dangerous."

Especially with a vehicle behind or ahead of us.

We walked, side by side, in silence for just over an hour. It was getting darker by the minute, and we were still spooked by the presence of the recent tire tracks. Annie looked at me, her eyes lingering for a few seconds. They said that she had more to say about her past, something more terrible than she had described. She started to speak but stopped when sounds arose from the brush ahead.

"More elephants?" I asked.

"I'm not sure. Sounds different than before, smaller maybe."

I suddenly grabbed Annie's arm and pulled her off the path, to the ground behind the bush with the red flowers. She started to scream. I clamped my hand over her mouth.

THIRTY-SEVEN

Road to Cameroon
Taraba Valley, Nigeria

Brett

Annie panicked and struggled to get free. She kicked at my legs and pushed my arms away. "Whuff r you doffen?" She broke loose. "Get off me." She smacked me in the face.

I held my index finger to my lips. "Shh."

"What are you doing?" She was angry, beyond angry. She was frantic.

"I saw some men in the heavy grass up ahead," I whispered.

She stopped struggling and looked through the bushes. "Who are they?"

"I don't know," I said. "The light's bad and I only saw parts of shirtsleeves. They seemed to be wearing military camouflage."

"Nigerian army?"

"Maybe." That's when I heard it, the sound of metal sliding against metal, a gun being cocked. I pulled Annie lower to the ground and covered her body with mine. She didn't resist this time. A great deal of commotion arose from the site of the shirts, but no shots were fired. Several seconds later, bizarre gurgling sounds filled the air, and then, nothing, only an eerie silence. We remained motionless for what seemed like an hour but was probably only a few minutes. Finally, I raised my head and peeked through the leaves. "I think it's over."

"What happened?" asked Annie.

"Sounded like they were getting ready to shoot, but somebody or something stopped them."

"Why would someone want to shoot at us? We're no threat to anyone."

"I wouldn't think so. Maybe they were poachers going after the elephants."

"But they didn't fire at them earlier and the elephants are long gone by now," said Annie.

I had no answers. "Keep your head down and follow me." We continued for several hundred yards, well within the protection of the brush until we gradually made our way back to the main path. We ran the final mile back to the orphanage. I wondered when the leopard would begin her nightly hunt. We agreed it would be best to avoid mentioning the men we had encountered. There was no sense in alarming everyone at the orphanage when we had such little information.

By the time we returned, dinner was almost over. Covered with dirt and grass stains, Sister Maggie gave us each an inquisitive look. I shrugged and said by way of an explanation, "We crossed paths with a herd of elephants out there and we had to hide in the brush for a while."

"Forest elephants?" said Sister Maggie, her eyes wide with excitement. "Thought they were extinct. Those heathenness poachers wiped them out. Where'd you see them? You must tell us all about it."

We ate the rest of dinner together discussing what Annie and I had encountered, but avoided the full story. When I returned to my hut, I found Vincent sitting on a porch chair with an automatic rifle cradled across his lap. I joined him. Vincent asked, "You have a good time today, Boss?"

"Yeah, it was a nice day. Why?"

Vincent stood and gazed into the darkness. "She's a beautiful woman, Boss. The only time I ever see you smile is after you've been with her."

"She's a nun, Vincent!"

"That she is, Boss, a nun with big blue eyes, a great body, and luscious legs that go all the way up to her neck."

I jumped up, my face inches away from Vincent's. "Careful Vincent, you'd better not go there or you're going to start pissing me off and that's not something you want to do." A flash of anger glowed in Vincent's eyes, the same look I saw just before he shot the Somalis. If he'd had his holster on his hip, he might have drawn on me. The look faded. "I don't appreciate your talking about her like that. I don't care if you did save my life. You keep it up, we're going to have a problem."

Vincent held up his hands and backed away. "Easy, Boss. All I'm saying is that this could become a delicate situation, and you need to handle things the right way. If you're not careful, you could find yourself headed on a collision course with a runaway freight train by the name of Sister Mary Margaret. When you're out in the jungle, you can't afford to be distracted, especially by a pretty face."

"Don't worry about me. There's no situation here. End of discussion."

"No problem, I won't mention it again."

"See to it that you don't." I stared at the rifle. "Speaking of Sister Maggie, you'd better not let her see you with that out in the open."

"I thought I'd best be prepared in case anything happened."

"Like what?'

"I overheard what you said in the dining hut and you sounded more than excited. You were worried. I don't think it was just a group of elephants that had you rattled. I suspect what you saw out there was a more dangerous kind of animal, like the kind that walks on two legs. What actually happened?"

I told him about the men hiding in the brush.

"They had loaded guns and they just suddenly disappeared when you ducked into the brush?"

"Pretty much. I figured maybe they were poachers."

"Poachers, huh? I think you and I should go out and visit that site tomorrow morning and have a look around."

"Why?"

"Something's not right. I doubt they were poachers and that was definitely no chance encounter. We need to check it out in the morning."

While I tried to sleep that night, I kept thinking about what Vincent said about Annie being a beautiful woman. He was right, of course. I kept replaying the incident when I pulled her to the ground. Her response shocked me. An overreaction, like I was attacking her. What had happened to her?

THIRTY-EIGHT

US Embassy
Arusha, Nigeria

Aryianna

Aryianna knew they'd be coming for her this morning. She had been recorded having a treasonous conversation with Minister Uguhru. There was nothing else to do but wait in the hotel restaurant and enjoy another glass of Mimosa, probably the last one she would have for a while. It was the same place where she had unsuccessfully tried to seduce Mr. Buchanan just over three months ago. Pity. At the time, she was flush with cash and the prospects for more were certain, but life had taken a drastic turn for the worse. She was trapped in an impossible predicament from which there was no escape. She'd had no other choice but to place the bug. The Americans had been investigating what they thought was a major drug-money laundering operation, and they suspected Minister Uguhru was a central figure. What they actually uncovered was her own association with Shakar. A relationship with a leader of Boko Haram would be tantamount to treason and result in a death sentence. She had been hoping to avoid this, but for now, it was what it was, and running was out of the question. They had her passport. She'd have to try to work her way out of it. She'd gotten herself out of worse jams than this in the past, and she did have one major chip she could play. Opening her purse, she checked to be sure it was still there.

Hopefully, it would be enough to save her life. All she could do was wait for the men who would be arriving soon.

When she looked up toward the restaurant's entrance, a man was standing there, flanked by two large associates, one on either side of him. All three were dressed in black suits and white shirts, opened at the neck. The two larger ones remained in place and scanned the crowd as their leader stepped forward. He had an athletic build and chiseled facial features. His eyes were cold and impersonal. Her usual feminine wiles weren't going to work this time. Without speaking, he took a seat opposite her. Her pulse quickened, and a few drops of perspiration formed along her upper lip. She attempted her old reliable seductive smile, but as expected, the man was having none of it. His face remained emotionless. The guy was all business.

"Miss Rhamani, my name is Desmond Pierce. I'm from the American Embassy."

She sipped on her Mimosa and blotted her lips with a napkin. "American did you say? You don't have any authority in Abuja."

He sneered in response. "I assume you know why I'm here."

"How should I know?"

"You are to accompany me to the U.S. embassy. Is that going to be a problem?"

"Of course, it's a problem. This is an outrage. I'm a French citizen living in Nigeria on a work visa. I refuse to go with you."

"I'm afraid you have no options here, Miss Rhamani. It's not a request. It's either come with me or I call the Nigerian Ministry of Security." He pulled his coat aside to reveal his holstered Glock for emphasis. Handcuffs would not be necessary.

As the three men escorted Aryianna through the hotel lobby, she said, "I have valuable information to share." Desmond didn't reply. After searching her purse for a weapon, he placed her in the rear seat of a black limousine with heavily tinted windows. One of the large guards sat next to her. The other drove the car while Desmond sat in the front passenger seat. Not a word was spoken during the twenty-minute drive. When she arrived at the American Embassy, the men took her to a second-floor office. The plaque outside the door read, Sebastian E. Cabot, United States Ambassador. Desmond's men stood guard in the hall as he opened the door and showed her in. Two gentlemen were seated in chairs inside the room. They didn't stand when she entered. Aryianna recognized the man behind the desk. He was Ambassador Cabot. She didn't know the other man who was seated in a leather chair next to Cabot. His expression was cold, another no-nonsense man. Desmond whispered into the ambassador's ear. Afterward, he folded his arms and stood against a far wall, next to a picture depicting the seal of the United States, Department of State. The Ambassador motioned for her to sit in the only remaining chair.

"Miss Rhamani, I'm Sebastian Cabot and this gentleman seated next to me is General Mandumo Nostafu, Minister of the Nigerian Intelligence Agency." Cabot wrote something on a piece of paper and handed it to the Minister. Aryianna shrank deeper into her chair. She knew of Nostafu. He had a reputation. Cabot allowed the Minister to take over.

Nostafu stared directly at her, a cold merciless look, his eyes boring holes through her soul. "I'm afraid you're in serious trouble here, Miss Rhamani. You have been consorting with Shakar Bhutah, a ruthless terrorist and an enemy of the state of Nigeria. That makes you guilty of treason against the people of this country, a crime punishable by death."

Aryianna said nothing in response. The fewer the words the better at this point. She simply stared at the floor and waited for an opportunity to present her case.

Nostafu read the note handed to him by Ambassador Cabot. "I'm told that you might have some information you would like to share in exchange for a more lenient disposition of your case."

She sat up tall in her chair and raised her chin, trying to project an air of confidence that she was now in control of the dialogue. "That is correct, General Nostafu. I'm prepared to provide all the information you need to successfully prosecute Minister Uguhru Muhammadi and his associates. I've kept a diary of everything they've done. I have names, dates, and details of all their plans to control the market."

"Drugs?" asked General Nostafu.

He doesn't know. She smiled, realizing her bargaining position had just improved significantly. "Drugs? Oh, no, no, it's something much more sinister. For the past five years, Minister Uguhru and his friends have been in the process of buying up large parcels of land in East Nigeria. They've been able to do so at deeply discounted prices through an Iranian shell company."

"Did Uguhru and his friends manipulate the land values through his Ministry?" asked Nostafu. He apparently couldn't figure out how an association with a terrorist leader like Shakar fit into a land acquisition scheme.

"No, he'd arrange for Shakar Bhutah and his men to raid a particular village and terrorize its inhabitants. Most of the survivors would flee and after the villages were abandoned, it created an opportunity to seize the land for next to nothing. As the Minister of Natural Resources, Uguhru could do this without attracting undue attention. On the surface, the raids appeared to be nothing more than a typical Boko Haram terrorist operation."

"Part of a money laundering scheme?" asked Nostafu.

Aryianna smirked and continued. "Those villagers who chose to remain were either killed or driven out by certain units of the army."

"What? The army?" asked General Nostafu. He leaned forward in his chair. "Are you telling me members of the Nigerian Army are involved in this scheme?"

"Yes, I can outline for you the details of their plans and names of individual participants."

General Nostafu leaned back and appeared to ponder her statement. He needed to find out what Uguhru was up to. His eyes narrowed. "And in return, you are seeking?"

"Full immunity from all prosecution for any and all hypothetical past crimes I may have committed. That's not to be construed in any way as an admission of wrongdoing on my part."

The General brushed a piece of lint from his lap. "You're a smart woman, Miss Rhamani. I'm sure you realize that a full pardon is out of the question. It's simply not going to happen. You have been a willing participant in plans to assist Boko Haram in the slaughter of thousands of my countrymen. To make matters worse, it wasn't out of any revolutionary desire to improve the lives of the poor, but only to enrich yourself and your associates by laundering drug money."

They still didn't appreciate the significance of what was happening and why. It gave her more leverage. "But I wasn't a participant in their scheme. I was little more than a pawn who did nothing but relay messages back and forth between Uguhru and Colonel Shakar."

Nostafu leaned forward in his chair. "And that alone makes you an accessory to mass murder and treason. You had ample opportunity to notify the authorities at any time, but you remained quiet."

Aryianna lowered her eyes, trying to look contrite. "But I was afraid!"

"Enough! You're lying. You would have been given all necessary protection, but you willingly chose not to come forward with the information you had. Thousands of lives could have been saved." He looked her in the eyes, "One of the villages Shakar invaded was the home of many of my cousins. They were massacred and you are partially responsible. Your inaction is unforgivable. You will have to pay for your crimes, Miss Rhamani. Now, here's what I'm prepared to offer you: ten years in prison in exchange for your testimony and successful prosecution of Uguhru and his cohorts. Otherwise, you will be hung for treason."

Aryianna jumped out of her chair. "Ten years? Look at me! I can't do ten years! I'll be raped every day."

"If it were up to me, I'd have you taken out and shot for treason right now, so this offer is more than generous."

Aryianna's mind raced. This was not going as expected.

She conjured up her best flirtatious smile and sat back down, crossing her legs, allowing her skirt to rise, showing as much thigh as possible without being too obvious. "If Mr. Cabot and his associate could leave the room for a few minutes, maybe you and I can negotiate an arrangement that would be mutually beneficial."

The General scowled. "You can put that worn out act away, Miss Rhamani. It's not going to help you here. You have just five seconds to accept my offer. After that, it will be withdrawn, and you'll be facing execution."

"Okay, okay, I accept," she said, fully knowing the negotiations were far from over. She still had one card to play, and it was a big one. She handed over her diary and her notes regarding Uguhru's organization.

Ambassador Cabot paged through Aryianna's journal. "This includes some of the most prominent businessmen and politicians in Nigeria. Why would they involve themselves in terrorist activities in exchange for land that's almost worthless? The only rational explanation is to launder drug money."

Aryianna smiled but said nothing. She had baited the hook and was getting a nibble.

Cabot studied the list more carefully and was astonished to find the name of one of the military officers on his own payroll. General Bhendari Jabba was the one who arranged for the caravan delivery to Buchanan's orphanage months ago.

He handed the list to Nostafu whose face flamed red, transforming from a look of astonishment to one of seething fury. "I always believed that General Jabba lived beyond his means but attributed it to the typical corruption seen elsewhere in the government. I never imagined that the man might be guilty of collaboration with terrorist revolutionaries. Corruption is one thing, but sedition is an entirely different matter."

Nostafu stared into Aryianna's eyes. "How can we be sure this is accurate? Maybe you've added a few names of men against whom you have a vendetta. I'm not simply going to take your word for it."

"I wouldn't expect you to, General. Feel free to check out every name. I would suggest that you focus on their financial records in detail, especially look for the influx of funds from international sources. I believe you'll find confirmation of my claims. If you decide that any of my information is deceptive, you are free to cancel our agreement and have me shot."

"Rest assured, I will definitely check into the veracity of your claims. Meanwhile, Mr. Pierce and his associates are going to place you in protective custody until arrangements can be made for your incarceration." The General stood, preparing to terminate the meeting.

Aryianna remained seated. "There's one other matter we should discuss."

"We already struck a deal on Uguhru and his partners," said Nostafu with an impatient tone in his voice. "You'll serve ten years and not a day less. I won't consider renegotiating the matter."

"That deal was for information leading to the prosecution of Uguhru and his accomplices. That is what I have just given you, but I have further information that will be of even greater interest."

General Nostafu huffed and sat back down, clearly agitated. "This had better be good, Miss Rhamani. I'm a busy man and not one to be trifled with. If I find that you are playing games with me, the consequences will be serious."

She leaned back in her chair and smiled. She had finally taken control of the discussion. The hook was set and all she had to do was reel him in.

"I can serve up over half of the Boko Haram army to you on a silver platter." She was, of course, overselling her position but knew it would be too enticing for General Nostafu to ignore.

Nostafu looked in Cabot's direction and chuckled. "Right. Half of Boko Haram's army? You? A flight attendant who moonlights as a prostitute? Please, go ahead. I'm listening. This is going to be good."

Aryianna reached into her purse and withdrew a pen and a

piece of paper. She was prepared to write something down. The General's smile faded when he realized the woman might be able to deliver what she was promising. "Okay. I'll play your game. What do you have?"

"The name and exact location of Shakar's next attack. I can even give you a one-week window of when it will occur. You take out Shakar and you eliminate the most threatening arm of Boko Haram."

The room went quiet. General Nostafu stared at Ambassador Cabot, while digesting her remarkable offer. He leaned forward. "Let's just say you can deliver on this, which I seriously doubt, what is it that you want in return?"

"Assurances that I will receive a full pardon and secure transportation on a private jet to Paris. I need the agreement in writing, and I want it immediately. If you ignore my information or try to double-cross me, the fact that you passed up an opportunity to defeat Boko Haram will be made public. A third party is prepared to post my story on the internet if he does not personally hear from me within forty-eight hours. The deaths of future villagers will be on your hands."

The General's face darkened. He did not like surprises or being outmaneuvered by a prostitute. He gazed out the window while he considered her demands. In the overall scheme of things, she was a small fish in comparison to Shakar. Still, she had willingly participated in plans that resulted in the slaughter of his family members. He stroked his chin. "I have to make a call to the President."

He left the Ambassador's office and returned several minutes later, his face more somber. "We have a deal, but if and only if you can deliver what you promise."

An agreement was drawn up and witnessed by Ambassador Cabot who made several copies. Aryianna folded the original contract and placed it in her purse. She picked up her pen and wrote down just one word on a piece of paper. She handed it to the Ambassador.

"Nguroje? The village?" he asked.

"Yes, Uguhru demanded that Shakar eliminate it within the next week or he would withdraw all financial support and protection for his army."

Cabot leaned back in his chair and exhaled. He removed a box of red pins from his desk and walked over to the large map of Nigeria hanging on the side wall of his office. He placed a pin on the site of the town of Nguroje. "It's only five miles away from a village raided by Shakar six months ago." He placed a red pin on that site as well. He turned around and addressed General Nostafu. "I'm going to need your help on this, General."

Nostafu walked over and stood next to Cabot.

"I want you to locate all the villages attacked by Shakar over the past three years."

Nostafu marked each with a pin, at least a dozen in all. The two men stood back and inspected the pattern.

"Do you see it?" asked Cabot.

"Amazing. I'm surprised I've never noticed it before. They're all within a one-hundred-mile radius of Mayo-Sina village in the Mambilla Plateau region. That's where the large diamond fields have been discovered. There are a few attacks outside the area, but I suspect those were diversionary. It explains everything. That's why Uguhru teamed up with Boko Haram. It has nothing to do with revolution or the laundering of drug money. It's all about accumulating control of Nigeria's diamond market."

Aryianna said, "And if Shakar failed, Uguhru would resort to his backup plan."

Cabot spun around and looked at her. "Backup?"

"Yes," she said. "He would contact his favorite general on the list and order him to clear out the remainder of the locals under the guise of chasing away Boko Haram sympathizers."

Nostafu shook his head in disgust. "Thousands of our Nigerian brethren and members of my own family were slaughtered for no other reason but to make money. Uguhru and his partners stood to make billions if they succeeded. It pains me to know our own military participated in this atrocity." He paused for several seconds and turned to Aryianna. "Have you delivered this message to Shakar yet?"

"I haven't had the chance."

"Here's what's going to happen, then. You'll arrange to meet your contacts and deliver Uguhru's demands—with a few additional terms. I will have bodyguards with you at all times to ensure your safety. In the meantime, you'll be kept at a secure facility until we can confirm that all you say actually happens. Once we have Uguhru in custody, and after we have destroyed Shakar's army, you will be free to leave for Paris. There's just one stipulation."

Aryianna faced General Nostafu. "And that is?"

"You are never to set foot on Nigerian soil again or the terms of our agreement will become null and void. If you do try to return, you will be immediately arrested and tried for treason. Do you understand?"

"That, I can guarantee you, General. I have absolutely no interest in returning to this wretched land." Aryianna walked out, accompanied by the two guards.

❖

The General watched her leave. He couldn't help but admire the view. *Pity. So much potential.* He turned to Cabot. "I'll need several copies of that agreement. I assume you've made a video tape recording of our meeting."

"Yes, it's already on a flash drive." Cabot understood exactly where the General was headed. There are many different forms of justice. Above all else, Nostafu was a man of his word and completely incorruptible, no matter the price. It was a character trait that had been the cornerstone of his career, something that would make him an excellent president one day. As promised, there would be no arrest and no trial for Aryianna. However, their written agreement did not preclude him from leaking a video of today's meeting to Boko Haram and Isis. Radical Islam maintained a large contingent of sympathizers in France. They would not take kindly to her betrayal. Revenge would be exacted, and Aryianna would be lucky to survive a month in Paris.

"I guess it's time to pick up Uguhru before he finds out his mistress betrayed him," said Cabot.

Nostafu replied, "I already have men stationed outside his home. They'll arrest him while he's on the way to his office. They're in an unmarked van, so it'll look like a kidnapping for ransom."

Cabot knew Uguhru would never see the inside of a traditional jail cell. He'd be spending his few remaining days at an interrogation center. Once all available information regarding his partners was extracted, he would simply disappear. His associates would experience similar treatment. Each of them would become the victim of an accidental death or suicide over the next year.

"I'll take care of the corrupt General Jabba myself," added Nostafu.

238

THIRTY-NINE

Comboni Mission
Taraba Valley, Nigeria

Brett

I ran as fast as I could, but the jungle kept holding me back. I clutched Jonathan under my left arm while holding Annie's hand in mine, pulling both of them along with me to safety. The vines reached out, trying to snatch them away. Whatever was chasing us was getting closer, lunging forward in a furious attempt to get my new family. The smell of blood filled the air. The jungle was hungry and needed to eat. I turned to look over my shoulder. Behind me, gold fangs exploded out of the darkness! Something grabbed my arm and shook me.

"It's time to get up, Boss," said Vincent.

I awoke in a sweat, flailing my arms like a man drowning, my heart pounding in my chest. I opened my eyes, the ghostly aftereffects of the dream running across my mind. It took several seconds to get oriented. "It's still dark outside."

"I hate the morning worse than anybody, Boss, but we have work to do. The sun'll be up in about thirty minutes and I want to be out of here before anyone sees the guns."

"Guns?"

"Of course. We don't want to be wandering around in the jungle without protection. Don't know if the men from yesterday are still around. Get dressed while I sneak over to the kitchen to see if I can scrounge up some garri biscuits and coffee for breakfast. Wear jeans and boots. We're not going to be on the regular paths. We have cobras and vipers in the jungles of East Nigeria and we'll be too busy to have to deal with a venomous snake bite."

"Snakes? Terrific. I hate snakes!" I murmured and got dressed.

Vincent returned with two cups of black coffee and a small pack of biscuits from the kitchen. Two assault rifles hung over his shoulder. He took a bite out of a biscuit and tossed one of the guns on my cot. "You know how to use one of these?"

"I've fired handguns at a range and shot clay pigeons at a friend's farm once, but never used an automatic rifle."

"This is an AK-47. It's just about the most common weapon found in Nigeria. It's old but almost indestructible, and simple to use. To load it, you first flip the safety switch on the right to the on position. Then, just slam a full magazine into this opening." Vincent loaded the mag and locked it in with the palm of his hand. "When you're ready to fire, pull back on this knob to rack the slide. That places a round into the chamber. If you don't do that the first time, the gun won't fire. As soon as you need to shoot, flip off the safety and pull the trigger. It can empty an entire clip in seconds, so you only need to aim in the general direction of whatever you're trying to shoot. You're bound to hit something. If not, you're sure to scare the shit out of someone. I guarantee they'll run. Just remember to keep the safety on until you're ready to fire. I don't want you accidentally shooting your foot off." Vincent racked the slide to chamber a round.

"That's the exact same sound I heard yesterday when Annie and I dove into the bush."

"Then, you're lucky to still be alive. It's a good thing we'll be armed. Eat your biscuit and let's get going before the others wake up and see us with these weapons. Sister Maggie'll skin me alive if she knows I have rifles."

We exited the hut and headed in the direction of the same back road Annie and I had hiked the day before. The first light of dawn was already fighting its way through the trees. Once we reached the path, Vincent led the way, taking us about thirty feet deep into the thick bush. It was tough going but we had no choice. "We can't take the chance that those guys from yesterday are still here," Vincent said. "Walking out in the open on the road, we'll be sitting ducks." We continued past the place where the elephants had trampled down the grass and upended small trees. Vincent knelt down to inspect the ground. "Elephant tracks. Maybe those guys you saw were poachers after all."

"Maybe," I replied but wasn't convinced.

"Let's keep moving. Keep your head down. Poachers would just as soon shoot us as an elephant."

We continued forward, crouching low for another half hour until I stopped and looked around. "This is it."

"Are you sure?"

"Yeah, I remember that bush on the right, the one with the red flowers. It's been partially trampled by the elephants. That's where we hid."

"So, the men you saw were on the other side of the path?"

I looked in the direction where they had been hiding. "About a hundred feet down."

"How many?"

"Can't say for sure—two at least—maybe more."

"Let's go," said Vincent as he led the way across the road and toward the site. After about five minutes of searching, he found the spot, an area of trampled grass where the men had been lying in wait. There was blood on the ground—a large amount of blood—more than any two men could lose and still be alive. There were no bodies to be found. "Did you hear anything?" asked Vincent. "You must have heard something for this to happen!"

"No, nothing at all. No screams or yelling, just the sound of the rifle slide being racked and the gurgling noises."

"No? Well, something happened here. There's too much of someone's or something's blood, and it's not from a poached elephant. That's for damn sure."

Vincent raised his rifle and flipped the safety switch off with his thumb. "Stay alert. Turn off the safety on your gun but keep your finger away from the damn trigger. Rest it along the side. And don't accidently shoot me in the ass." Vincent knelt in the grass and ran his hand along the ground. "Boot tracks. You were right, Boss. It looks like there were two men, but where'd they go?" He brushed some of the grass aside and added, "There are more tracks here, but they weren't made by boots."

"What the hell made 'em?"

"Can't tell for sure. The area's too trampled and distorted by all the blood. Some are definitely from an animal. Others look human." Vincent walked in a circular fashion in a ten-foot perimeter around the site until he found what he was looking for. "Here. I knew they couldn't just fly away. This should take us to 'em." We followed a trail of blood for a quarter mile until we found a single body, dressed in a frayed military uniform. It had been partially consumed. "Leopard got to him but didn't kill the bastard. His throat's been cut. No animal did that." Vincent looked in all directions. "What the hell?" he said.

"What?"

"I've done more than my share of hunting, both man and beast, but I've never seen anything like this before. We only have one of the dead guys. Where's the other one? Bodies don't just disappear into thin air like this." He looked around searching for a sign of where we might pick up the trail of blood again, but there was nothing. Vincent scanned the jungle, looking for an explanation for what had happened. "There," he said, pointing to a spot around a hundred feet away. Concealed on a tree limb, twenty feet above the ground, was the body of the other man.

"Another leopard?" I asked.

"Looks like the momma leopard's cubs have grown up and joined in the hunt. They typically hide their kills in a tree to keep them away from other predators." He studied the body. "But like I said, they don't slit people's throats. The leopards simply took advantage of an easy meal."

"Then, who or what killed them?" I looked into Vincent's

eyes and saw something I'd never seen before. Fear.

"Can't say for sure. I'm more worried about who these dead men were." He turned to me. "Let's head back to the orphanage. No need to tell 'em about what we found out here until we get a better idea of what's going on."

I scanned the surroundings. "What is going on? You think there could be any more of those guys?"

"Don't think so," said Vincent, "but I can't be sure. The good news is that the two guys who were following you are dead. The bad news is that they were probably on a mission. They failed and that means we can count on more of 'em to return."

"Mission? What kind of mission?"

"Maybe you, Boss. From now on, anytime you get the itch to hike out into the jungle, take that rifle with you, and make sure it's fully loaded."

244

FORTY

Boko Haram Camp
Cameroon Jungle

Shakar Bhutah

"What happened to your two cousins?" asked Shakar. "It was supposed to be a short reconnaissance mission, just a few days at most. They should've been back a week ago." He picked up his club and demolished a small table.

Ziyad cringed and took a step back.

"The bastards deserted, didn't they?" said Shakar.

"Neither would, Colonel," said Ziyad. "Both of them were dedicated soldiers and I have no doubt that they would follow your orders to the death."

"Then someone or something got to them."

"They were too capable to have been killed unless they were ambushed, sir."

"I doubt that a small group of nuns and orphans could've done it. Proves that the orphanage must be a front for a military operation. You don't need a convoy of trucks with an armed escort for orphanage supplies. I want to find out what's going on there and if the Americans have anything to do with it. Send five men this time. If it is a military outpost, we can return and eliminate them."

"Would you like me to lead the group, sir?"

Shakar didn't respond. He had just read Aryianna's most

recent note and was distracted. It still sat on his desk. Minister Uguhru was demanding that Shakar destroy the town of Nguroje. If he failed, all financial support would be withdrawn, and his army would be disbanded. If he succeeded, there would be a five-million-dollar bonus as a personal reward and all regular support for his army would be restored. He brought the small piece of paper to his nose. It still carried Aryianna's scent, so it was legitimate, but something didn't feel right. He turned to Ziyad. "What'd you say?"

"Would you like me to lead the group, sir?'

"No, I want you to remain here with me. We've been given an important mission and it's going to be a dangerous one. A lot is at stake this time and I'll need you at my side. I want you to gather a hundred of our best men, ones that have the most combat experience. Have them report in full gear and ready to deploy in two hours."

"May I ask where we're headed, sir?"

"Nguroje."

"That's a pretty big town sir, and it's Christian. We have no local support there, and we're not very familiar with the area. We could be vulnerable. Perhaps we should do some reconnaissance first."

"There's no time for that. We must complete the mission within the week." He pulled a regional military map from his desk drawer and studied it with Ziyad looking over his shoulder. "There's one primary road leading into and out of the town. It's probably guarded, but I doubt the local security forces are well trained. No one there will be expecting an attack. We'll come in from the side roads, through the jungle and catch them from behind. Once we eliminate the guards, we can cut right through the middle of the town. Tell the men to kill anyone they see, no exceptions. I won't be taking prisoners this time." There was a five-million-dollar reward on the table and Shakar intended to get it. The people needed to be so terrified, none of them would think of staying behind. The entire town had to be dead or gone. Anything less than total annihilation would be a disaster for him.

"If I may, sir. Nguroje is a large town with too many people to control. This is going to be more difficult than a raid on a school or a small village. You might want to take an additional one hundred men to ensure our success."

"That would leave us with less than five squads in reserve, half of whom are untrained recruits," said Shakar. He studied the map again. Why the rush to eliminate this particular town? It left him with no time for proper reconnaissance and training. He wasn't comfortable with the situation, and he had learned long ago to pay attention to his instincts. It was one reason he was still alive, that and the protection of Allah. He knew Uguhru couldn't be trusted but why would he sell out? He stood to make billions as a result of the raids. It didn't make sense. Aryianna was in the same boat. If she tried to betray him, she would pay the price. Even though the plan smelled of a possible double-cross, a five-million-dollar bonus was on the line. It was worth the risk. Besides, it was Allah's wish that he become king. Allah would protect him from his enemies.

"You're right, Ziyad. Make it two hundred men. That should be more than enough to destroy a town of farmers and small businessmen. Meanwhile, make sure you select five good men to return to that orphanage compound."

248

FORTY-ONE

Comboni Mission
Taraba Valley

Sister Annie

S ister Annie finished giving immunization shots to several of the new children. There was nothing else on her schedule that morning. Her mind had been preoccupied and she hadn't slept the entire night. She needed advice and there was only one person in whom she could confide. She walked over to the communications hut where Sister Maggie was on the radio trying to arrange for another supply truck delivery.

"Well, speak to Mr. Desmond Pierce at the American Embassy. I'm sure he can arrange for another military escort," she said into the receiver. When she saw Sister Annie standing at the door, she held up her right index finger, indicating that she would be finished in a minute. "That would be perfect. Thank you for your assistance. Would you call back later to confirm that everything has been arranged?" There was a pause while the person on the other end appeared to respond. "Thank you very much." She turned off the radio and looked at Sister Annie. "What is it, my dear? You look worried."

"May I have a word with you, Sister?"

"Of course, child." Sister Maggie always called Annie child though she was past thirty. "Just let me finish what's on my desk. Have a seat for a minute." She clicked her tongue against her teeth as she made a few entries into the orphanage ledger. She closed the large book, stood, and came around the desk. "I'm sorry. Running an orphanage, even out here in the middle of nowhere, requires some accounting work. It's tedious, but necessary." She took Annie's hand and led her outside. "Why don't we walk together? It's such a beautiful morning, much too wonderful to be cooped up inside."

They walked past Otis' pen where Sister Maggie set out a large bucket of grain. The two nuns strolled around the crop fields saying nothing for several minutes. Finally, Sister Maggie stopped and looked Sister Annie in the eyes. "What's wrong, Annie?"

Tears welled up. "I'm so confused, I don't know what to do."

"This is about Mr. Buchanan, isn't it?"

Sister Annie dropped her head and looked at the ground. "How did you know?"

"It's written all over your face every time you see him. Your eyes light up at the mere mention of his name."

"It's true. I think about him all the time. We started out as friends, but something has happened over the past several months. We have a bond of some kind, and I sense he feels the same way. I haven't experienced these kinds of feelings since I was young. I know it must be wrong and I try not to, but I can't seem to control them. It's like I'm a teenager again. When I'm around him, I feel alive, and when not, an emptiness consumes me."

"Do you think you might be in love with him?"

"I don't know—maybe. I think so. It's the first time I've allowed myself to think about a man romantically. I mean, since the incident at the hospital." Annie never could get herself to use the term rape. The word brought back the ugly memories of shame and terror. "I feel very safe and comfortable when I'm around him. He's a wonderful, kind man, like none I've ever met before."

A smile spreading across Sister Maggie's face said it all.

"And he's pretty easy on the eyes."

Annie's head popped up. "I never thought you would notice something like that, Sister."

Sister Maggie squeezed her hand. "Let me tell you something, child. I've been a nun for over forty years but that doesn't mean I'm dead. I still appreciate the beauty of God's creations, even men."

The two chuckled for several seconds. Sister Maggie continued. "Yes, he does seem to be a special person, but what do you actually know about him other than what you've seen over the past several months? What do you know about his life prior to his arrival in Africa?"

"Almost nothing, other than the fact that he was a famous baseball player in the U.S. Every time I try to guide our conversations in the direction of his personal life, he avoids the subject. It's almost as though he's running away from something."

Sister Maggie stopped walking. "Or perhaps he's looking for something. There's an emptiness in Mr. Buchanan, an underlying sadness in his eyes. I think he has a void he's trying to fill. That can lead to desperate emotions."

Annie nodded. "I've noticed it too, but I care about him. While there's something dark beneath the surface, I know he's basically a good person. What should I do about it? I know it's not right for me to feel this way. I'm in a religious order."

Sister Maggie lovingly tucked a loose strand of hair over Annie's ear. "You can't control what you feel in your heart, child. You can only control what you do about those feelings, and that's something only you can decide. It's not an accident that you have never taken your final vows. Commitment to a religious life of celibacy is not a thing one should take lightly, and certainly not based upon feelings of obligation or guilt. If you do, you'll spend the rest of your life second-guessing that decision. You should do it because you firmly believe it's the life God wants you to live. Since I first met you, I've always believed that God had a different plan for you other than a religious vocation. I sense that you've been avoiding any kind of romantic relationship because of what had happened to you at that hospital. You've isolated yourself in the jungle where you feel safe. You have been running away from your problem, much like Mr. Buchanan seems to be running from his. You must decide what you feel God wants and not what you feel obligated to do. I can't tell you what that should be. All I can say is this, you shouldn't make any decisions based upon your feelings for a man you really don't know. The success of any relationship must be based upon mutual honesty and trust. You need to find out more about Mr. Buchanan's past. At the same time, you should make him aware of the problems you have faced. Then, you must pray hard for the guidance to make the right choices."

FORTY-TWO

Comboni Mission
Taraba Valley, Nigeria

Brett

Staccato sounds of gunfire woke me from a deep sleep. Thoughts about the men who had stalked Annie and me raced through my mind as I grabbed my rifle and rushed outside. Vincent stood about a hundred yards away, near the edge of the jungle, Jenkins next to him. Sister Maggie ran toward them, her habit billowing around her. Father Norbert and Sister Annie were several steps behind. What the hell was going on? Were we under attack?

Sister Maggie got to Vincent just before me, almost too short of breath to talk. She stared at Jenkins who was holding a rifle, bracing the gun with the stump of his right arm, his left index finger on the trigger. "Exactly what are you doing, Mr. Vincent?"

"Teaching the boy how to protect himself. After what happened to Mr. Buchanan and Sister Annie, I decided it would be a good idea."

"Defend himself? From whom? What happened to Mr. Buchanan?"

Vincent looked at me. "I think you'd better tell her, Boss. She needs to know."

Sister Maggie glared at me. "What do I need to know?"

"When Sister Annie and I took our walk several days ago, we were about to be attacked by several men hiding in the brush."

Father Norbert joined the group, huffing and puffing. "Attacked by several men? Who?"

"We couldn't tell. It was all over in less than ten seconds. When Vincent and I checked the area the following morning, we found evidence of a bloody struggle."

"They had automatic rifles and were after Sister Annie and Mr. Buchanan," said Vincent.

"Who were they and where did they go?" asked Sister Maggie.

"Can't say for sure," I replied. "There were probably two of them and they're both dead."

"You killed them?" she asked Vincent.

"No Sister, but someone or something did."

"The leopard?" she asked.

"I don't think so," I said. I didn't mention the slit throats or the fact that the men were partially eaten. Didn't want to frighten Jenkins.

Vincent stepped forward. "If there were two, you can expect there might be more in the near future. You need to be prepared to protect the orphanage. That's why I'm trying to teach Jenkins how to fire a rifle. He's learning fast." He patted Jenkins on the head.

"You don't even have concrete evidence that Sister Annie and Mr. Buchanan were about to be attacked. It's mere conjecture. The two men might have been poachers. I'm not going to allow guns in my orphanage based upon what you think might have happened."

Father Norbert stepped forward. "Maybe it's not a bad idea, Sister. There's nothing wrong with being prepared."

She glared at him. "Nonsense. I'll not have guns around my children."

Vincent stared at her. "Maybe you should listen to the good Father, Sister. The world around you is not a peaceful place, even in your little isolated valley here. It's better to have a gun available than to be underground because you didn't have one when you needed it."

"No guns in my orphanage and that's final. Come on Jenkins, you have chores to do." She harrumphed, grabbed Jenkin's arm and stomped away.

I looked to Father Norbert for some support. He shrugged. "When she's like this, I'm afraid there's no changing her mind."

256

FORTY-THREE

Taraba River
Taraba Valley, Nigeria

Brett

It was late morning when Annie approached. She was again dressed in casual shorts. A light blue blouse accentuated the color of her eyes. The ivory crucifix hung from her neck. She looked even more beautiful than usual.

"How about taking a walk with me?" she asked.

I had completed my work on the water pipes. The system was working as expected and the storage tank was full. No leaks. "Sure. Where to?"

"You were interested in seeing that abandoned village and I thought it would be a nice day to head over in that direction to check it out."

"Sounds great. Just let me get something first." I headed toward my hut and returned a minute later with a rifle hanging over my right shoulder.

Annie turned her head in all directions. "Where'd you get the gun?" she asked with an astonished look in her eyes. "You know Sister Maggie doesn't allow those things in the orphanage."

"After what happened to us the last time we wandered off into the jungle, Vincent convinced me that it would be a good idea to always bring a little protection." When she showed a look of disapproval, I added, "Vincent gave me some words of advice after what we saw on the road. He said that in the jungle, it's better to have a gun and not need it than need a gun and not have one."

"You sound like my brothers." She looked skeptical. "Do you know how to use it?"

"Yeah, Vincent showed me. You just release the safety, point and shoot. I doubt we'll need it, but I think it's best to be safe."

Annie hesitated. "I guess, but don't let Sister Maggie see you with it. She's been pretty edgy since she found Jenkins shooting the gun."

We headed down the same back road we had walked several days ago. This time I was more alert to what was happening around us. There was the usual chorus of birds and the howler monkeys, but nothing threatening. We reached the path leading to the village and the Taraba River. Along the way, we talked about the orphanage and Jenkins. We discussed our futures but neither of us had specific plans to leave Africa.

The skeletal remains of several small homes sat on either side of the path, the wooden structures almost collapsing under the weight of time, quickly being devoured by the jungle. It was apocalyptic.

"They were small farms before the village was abandoned years ago, after the tragedy," said Annie.

"Tragedy?"

"Yes. I'm surprised no one told you about it. When Sister Maggie first arrived in Nigeria, she had only four other nuns with her. All she had were three tents and provisions for a month. Local tribal leaders expected her to fail, but she prevailed. It took several years, but they built an orphanage and cleared several acres for farming. Then the problems developed."

"Father Norbert told me some of it, how one of the nuns died of malaria."

"It got worse. After an epidemic hit the village, some of the locals blamed the nuns. It reached a boiling point when the nuns obtained antibiotics and started to cure children. This enraged some of the tribal elders who claimed that women had no business being involved in the treatment of disease. That was the sacred responsibility of the sangomas only."

"Sangomas?"

"It's the African word for witch doctor. The head sangoma argued that the nuns' successes were the result of witchcraft and he accused them of making human sacrifices to their devil gods. The situation smoldered for several years until an outbreak of diphtheria arose in Nigeria. Supply boat crews brought it to the area. The villagers had no immunity and many of them died. Sister Maggie and the other nuns became convenient scapegoats for the sangoma. The Sisters arranged for the delivery of vials of vaccine so they could begin an immunization program and prevent another epidemic. The locals had never been exposed to the concept of injections and they became suspicious. This provided an excuse for the sangoma to whip up some of the more radical members of the tribe. They accused the Sisters of giving the children poison so they could be sacrificed to their Satan gods. In time, the stories became more bizarre, including claims of cannibalism."

"Success breeds contempt," I said.

"Unfortunately, that's true," said Annie. "It was a peaceful afternoon when it happened. Three of the Sisters were out in the fields harvesting vegetables when men stormed out of the jungle with machetes and clubs. The nuns were hacked so badly they were unrecognizable. The attackers immediately ran into the woods and were never caught. Many of the villagers fled, fearing retribution from the nuns' gods. Those that didn't, paid the price for the treachery. The army came in and burned their homes, forcing them to flee. It remains abandoned to this day."

When we reached the village, it looked like a ghost town. In the center stood a sculpture, a pole with an ornately carved face. Annie rubbed her hand across the smooth surface. "It's an image representing a combination of their god and the spirits of ancient ancestors. It's meant to protect the village from evil."

"Doesn't look like it did a very good job," I said. The only evidence that there had ever been people living here were the remnants of a couple dozen cinder-block homes. Their scabrous surfaces were scarred by bullets and scorched by fire. A few walls had been painted, an act of futility because the scorch marks returned. *Paint over stains*. An old boat dock still extended out into the Taraba River. I looked about. "It looks like some of the homes have been torn down. What happened?"

"When the people disappeared, the buildings sat empty for several years. When it became apparent that they were never going to return, Sister Maggie decided it would be a sin to let everything go to waste. She had some of the men living in the compound cannibalize the old buildings to recycle the concrete blocks and tin roofs for buildings at the orphanage. The medical clinic was the first to be built and after that, a few dormitories. She was working on replacing more of the children's dorms when everything came to a halt."

"The villagers returned?"

"No, she ran out of concrete and was forced to abandon her new construction plans. Now that you've established more protections for the supply trucks, things are returning to normal."

Annie and I walked down to the old dock. It was still sturdy, so we sat down on the edge, took off our boots, and let our feet dangle into the cool water, drinking in the serene beauty of the lazy river. Herons and white egrets patrolled the shoreline, their beaks slashing through the water in search of a meal. A loud squeal from the opposite shore pierced the peaceful tranquility. A large crocodile had trapped some animal in its jaws and was dragging it under the surface. We pulled our legs from the water and jumped up.

"You can never let your guard down in the jungle," said Annie.

I laughed. "Especially if you want to keep all your toes." We walked back to the safety of the village and sat on a fallen log as the river slowly drifted past. It was a lovely afternoon, a rare moment to be cherished.

Annie looked up at me shyly. "I enjoy spending this time together with you, Brett."

"Me too."

An awkward silence followed. Annie seemed to want to discuss something but looked uncertain as to how to do it. She turned to me. "What happened, Brett?"

"What happened with what?"

"There's something troubling you, something deep within your soul. I've noticed it ever since you first arrived at the orphanage. I have three brothers who are great baseball fans. I've done some research on you. Why does a famous man who's worth in excess of three hundred million dollars decide to lose himself in the jungles of eastern Nigeria? I know I'm pushing, but I care about you, and I'd like to know what happened."

I care about you? That's what she said, "I care about you." What did she mean by that? Does she care about me because she's an empathetic nun and cares about everyone, or does she actually care about me specifically as a person? I pondered the thought for a second. It was time to talk about things I had rarely told anyone else before. I talked about my youth, my alcoholic father, and the violent death of my mother.

"I was a loner in the orphanage, but in high school, I discovered how hard I could throw a baseball. That's when my life changed. I'd been given a great talent, the ability to throw a baseball impossibly fast for my age, and that's what I did. I was recruited by the Cincinnati Reds directly out of high school and after three years in the minor leagues, they called up to the big show as a starting pitcher."

"Big show?" asked Annie.

"The major leagues. After my first season, I was named Rookie of the Year and was featured on the cover of Sports Il-lustrated. I became an instant celebrity and soon was a frequent guest star on television talk shows. The sudden fame was overwhelming and the invitations to star-studded parties were frequent. Beautiful women could be had everywhere I went." I stopped and looked at Annie. "Sorry about that last comment."

"Why? Remember, I had three older brothers. You were a normal young man with healthy desires."

I breathed a sigh of relief. Last thing I wanted to do was to offend her. "After my third year in the majors, I was introduced to my ex-wife. She was different from most of the other women I'd met. Think I was attracted to her because she didn't seem to be affected by my status. We eventually married and started a family, a little boy, we named Jonathan. Everything was perfect. Our lives were something most people couldn't begin to imagine."

"But?" asked Annie.

"It all began to fall apart after I won my second Cy Young award."

"That's the one given to the best pitcher in baseball?"

"Yes. It's an honor to receive it just once and I won it two years in a row. I became an even bigger celebrity than before, but there's a hefty price to be paid for that level of fame. It affected me in a bad way. I lost sight of my priorities and focused only on myself, pushing all that was truly important to me into the background."

"The Devil has a knack for coming at us in unlikely forms and from many different directions," said Annie. "He's an insidious predator, slithering around you like a snake, circling closer, so gradually you don't even notice. By the time you do, you're already trapped in his coils."

"With the fame came invitations to join other celebrities for a little partying during road trips. Alcohol and drugs were everywhere. I didn't use the drugs, but I did drink—too heavily. I didn't think it would pose a problem because I always avoided alcohol several nights before I was scheduled to start a game. In time, that became one day before a start and eventually, I would drink at any time. I was rarely sober. My coaches and teammates warned me, but didn't press the issue because I kept winning games, and was honored as the National League's Most Valuable Player. As long as I did that, and generated good ticket sales, no one really cared about my drinking."

"You become an alcoholic?" asked Annie.

I hung my head, kneading my hands together. "A very bad one. My wife eventually confronted me about the problem. Told her I was a finely-tuned athlete in perfect physical condition. I reassured her that I wasn't like most people. I had everything under control." My eyes met Annie's. "That's what most alcoholics claim, that they're in control, but it's a lie. The alcohol had already begun to take over my life. After winning my third Cy Young Award in eight years, my agent negotiated a fifty-five-million-dollar bonus with the team and a seven-year extension on my thirty million dollar a year contract. I was making ten times that amount in endorsements. All was good. I had everything I could ever want: wealth beyond comprehension, a great job, a beautiful wife, and our wonderful son, Jonathan. Then I blew it all away. I violated my most sacred commitment."

"You had an affair," said Annie. It wasn't an accusation.

I gazed at the river for a minute, watching the water drift by just as my life had. I recalled the tragic events of my past and how I had destroyed everything. "No, not an affair, though that alone would have been despicable enough. It's not that I didn't have the opportunity. Women were always hanging around the hotels when we were on the road, but I wasn't interested. I already had a mistress and her name was alcohol." Another crocodile caught one of the herons along the shore. It cried for a brief second before it disappeared under the water. "In some ways I wish my sin would've been something similar to infidelity. It would've been easier to handle. What I did was something far worse."

Annie played with the ivory crucifix hanging from her neck. "Worse than an affair?"

"Much worse. Something unforgivable." The memories caused my heart to spasm as I gazed out at the jungle on the other side of the river, looking at nothing in particular. The croc was gone. My voice quivered and tears threatened my eyes.

"It's okay if you don't want to talk about this, Brett. I understand. Maybe we should head back."

I paused to regain my composure. "With the fifty-five-million-dollar bonus, I decided to buy a new red Bugatti convertible."

"Sounds expensive?"

"It was. Very expensive." My focus blurred as I remembered that damn car. "Not only expensive, but costly. I drove it home on Jonathan's sixth birthday. He wanted to ride in it. 'Sure,' I said. My wife warned me that it might not be such a good idea, but I was too full of myself. At that point in my life, everything centered around me because I was the sports super-star. I still remember what I told her. 'I think Big Brett Buchanan is more than capable of taking care of his own son.' I told her she worried too much. I tussled my boy's hair and said, 'We'll be extra careful, won't we, buddy?' He looked at his mother and pleaded with her. 'Okay, but keep it under forty,' she warned. I can still see the worried smile on her face as I backed down the driveway, the engine rumbling. I should have paid attention to her.

"I lowered the convertible top and took off. Ten minutes later, we were driving through Eden Park. The sun was shining, and the wind was blowing through my hair. 'Faster Dad,' said little Jonathan. He was having a great time. 'Okay, buddy,' I said. 'Let's air this thing out and see what she can do.' People on the sidewalks recognized me and were waving at us. I can still see the admiration in Jonathan's eyes. 'They all know you, Dad! You're a hero.' He was so proud. It was a great day for both of us. I looked over at him. He had undone his seatbelt and was standing up on his seat to wave at everyone.

"I wanted to tell him to sit down and fasten his seatbelt, but I didn't want to destroy the moment. It was the happiest I had seen him in years—since I started the heavy drinking.

"I didn't see the other car pulling out of a parking space. The driver didn't see me. I was going too fast. I swerved, hit a large pothole and lost control. The car rolled over three times before it was stopped by a large elm tree. My left arm was broken, the bone poking through the skin. Jonathan was lying in the grass against a tree trunk, thirty feet away from the car, his head tilted at an impossible angle."

I stared at the ground, unable to hold back the tears. "Excuse me." Annie took my hand in hers.

"He died instantly. My job as a father and husband was to protect my family. I failed. Killed my own son. I don't know why or how I survived but I did. Wish I hadn't. God should have taken me instead of my boy. Why would He do that?"

Annie had no words. Finally, she said, "I can't imagine how horrible it must have been. Is that why you're here in Africa? You're looking for some kind of atonement."

"Not possible. That wasn't the worst of it," I said. "I was never held accountable for my actions that day. Celebrities often get special treatment. An investigation into the events surrounding the accident revealed that my blood alcohol level was a modest 0.05, well under the legal limit. I knew better. I had already worked my way through a half-bottle of Jack Daniels that morning before I got behind the wheel.

"At a press conference, my attorney claimed 'It was an unfortunate accident due to hazardous road conditions. The city should have repaired that stretch of road years ago. They were negligent.' When asked if we were considering a lawsuit against the city, my attorney responded, 'Brett Buchanan grew up in this city and has called it his home for his entire life. He and his wife love Cincinnati and are not interested in pursuing legal action. There's been enough pain surrounding this unfortunate incident already. They just want to be left alone to grieve.'"

I looked down and shook my head. "They called my son's death an unfortunate incident! Can you imagine that? An unfortunate incident."

Annie squeezed my hand.

"The entire press conference was a charade. I knew it and worse, my wife knew it. My blood alcohol test results were falsified, a lie concocted by a group of attorneys to protect the image of the team's sports icon. Big Brett Buchanan had become the veritable face of Major League Baseball. Thousands of people had a vested interest in my continued success, from MLB to the entire sporting goods industry. They couldn't allow the image of one of the country's star athletes to be tainted by a scandal of this magnitude. So, the truth was buried. The memory of my son was pushed aside for the sake of my career. I should have done more to protect my son. I should've been a better father. I should have confessed."

Annie remained quiet for a minute, still holding my hand, rubbing her thumb over the back of it, while appearing to process everything I'd said. "That had to have been an overwhelming burden. I can't imagine having to deal with it every minute of every day. I know you were driving under the influence that afternoon, but I also know it wasn't entirely your fault. I'm not trying to give you a pass, but it really was an accident. There's a good chance that what happened was going to happen anyway, whether you were completely sober or not. Don't get me wrong, I'm not saying you weren't wrong in what you did. You should have never gotten behind that wheel after drinking."

She squeezed my hand harder and looked directly into my eyes. "I know this, Brett Buchanan. You're a good man. I've seen it time and time again over the past several months. God has forgiven you, but you still need to forgive yourself. I know it's easy for me to say, but you can't continue to wallow in your past mistakes. Nothing good comes from beating up on yourself like that. You must somehow put it behind you and move forward. God wanted you to live for a reason. Otherwise, he would have let you die in that car crash. I think that's why you are here in Africa. God has a plan for you."

"I'm not so sure, Annie. God and I aren't on the best of terms."

"Maybe you should try praying to him."

I didn't respond. The two of us sat side by side for another half hour, Annie still holding my hand. The silence was broken when I finally said, "Thank you for listening, Annie. Outside my rehab counselor, I've never shared that story with anyone."

"Thank you for trusting me with it." She looked out across the river just as I had earlier. She looked troubled.

"Did I say too much?" I asked. "I'd understand if you didn't want to have anything to do with me anymore."

"Not at all," she said. "I've also been looking for a new life in Africa. I never expected to find one—until you arrived, Brett."

We gazed into each other's eyes, our faces drawing closer together. I hesitated. Annie didn't. It was a kiss the likes of which I had never experienced before, tentative at first, with the hint of a promise of what might lie ahead, a kiss that might happen once in a lifetime. Time stood still. All my previous personal tragedies melted away into the jungle. Nothing beyond this instant mattered.

I pulled away slightly. "I'm sorry, Annie. I'm not sure how that just happened."

"I'm not sorry. We did nothing wrong."

"But you're a nun."

"I'm not a nun yet, and I never will be. I've taken no vows of celibacy. I've realized that being a nun is not the path I should be taking in life."

"I don't want to be the reason for you walking away from your religious vocation."

She caressed my cheek with her hand. "You're not, Brett. This was a decision I was going to be forced to make with or without you in my life. You simply helped me make it. There's a reason why I've never taken my final vows. Most novitiates would have taken them years ago, but deep inside I knew this wasn't what God had planned for me. I've always felt that I had a different purpose. I'm not planning on abandoning a religious life. I'm just taking a different path, so you can push aside any guilt feelings you might have. God knows you've had enough mea culpas to endure."

She kissed me again, hard and passionately, opening her lips slightly, inviting my tongue. We held each other close as though we had been doing it our entire lives. A wave of intense feelings washed over me, carrying with it a world of new possibilities, of a new life for both of us. "I've wanted to do that from the first moment I saw you, but wouldn't allow myself to believe it could actually happen."

The brush behind us rustled. Startled, I stood, but all I could see was the dead village and the jungle that was consuming it. I unshouldered my rifle, and chambered a round, flipping the safety to the off position. "We should head back now."

We returned to the orphanage, headed toward what I hoped would be a new life together. My excitement dampened when I heard the voice of my mother. "All things end, Brett. Both the bad and the good." I refused to allow this to end.

FORTY-FOUR

Comboni Mission
Taraba Valley, Nigeria

Brett

When we returned, Annie headed directly to the kitchen to help prepare for supper. I walked to my hut, sat on the chair, and thought about what had happened between Annie and myself. It was the first time I had been excited about life since Jonathan died. I was completely happy; not the type of happiness that comes from fame, owning a collection of expensive homes, or fleets of luxury cars, but the type that comes from within. The voice returned, dark and threatening.

"Too many stains, Brett. You can't whitewash over them. You don't deserve her. You never will until you do what you should have done long ago."

The voice was right. I needed to cut the stains out of my life. I planned to call a friend of mine, a reporter for Sports Illustrated magazine. I needed to schedule an interview, to bare my soul and tell the truth about what happened to Jonathan. A sense of calm washed over me, the burden of guilt lifting from my shoulders. "No more mea culpas."

"No more what, Boss?" Vincent took the chair next to me. He set a rifle across his lap.

"Uh, nothing. Just thinking out loud."

Vincent flipped the rifle's safety to the on position. "Good thing you took that gun with you on your little hike to the river."

I jumped out of my chair. "What? You were following us? I told you to stop butting into my business."

"Settle down, Boss. Yes, I followed you. I figured it'd be a good idea to cover your ass after what happened the last time you two wandered about. It's a good thing I did. You were being stalked again."

My heart skipped a beat and I collapsed back down into my chair. "Like last time?"

"Yes. I found three men about a hundred yards behind, following both of you all the way to the river. Didn't look like they wanted to hurt either of you, but they were definitely interested in what you were doing. One of them followed you back to the orphanage where he met up with two others. Looked like they were checking out the orphanage. Why? I don't know. Then, the three of them left."

I gazed out over the fields, digesting what Vincent had said. "Wait a minute. You say there were three stalking us to the river and two watching the orphanage. That makes five but only three left. What happened to the other two?"

"Don't know. They disappeared."

"Disappeared?"

Vincent shrugged. "Yep. Into thin air."

"You think they're still around, keeping an eye on us?"

"I don't think so. I think they're dead like those two supposed elephant poachers. Part of the same group. The one guy who made it back to the orphanage looked frightened. He started waving his arms around frantically and yelling at his buddies. Must have told them their teammates were killed somehow. Then, they took off."

"Like last week! Who are those people and whatta they want?"

"Had to be on a surveillance mission, Boss. It's the only thing that makes sense. That means they're preparing for something and will return soon with more men—a lot more men. Something big is about to happen. We need to warn Sister Maggie and Father Norbert about this."

I wondered who killed the two men.

FORTY-FIVE

Comboni Mission
Taraba Valley, Nigeria

Brett

"We're not leaving, and that's final." Sister Maggie was surrounded by Father Norbert, Annie, and the rest of the nuns. "I started this orphanage thirty years ago. I've faced down deadly diseases, wild animals, and murderous tribesmen. I'll not be frightened off by a few thugs."

"More than likely, they're trained terrorists, ma'am. Men with automatic weapons," Vincent said.

"Maybe, but you can't even say with certainty that they were Boko Haram. They were probably just a small gang looking to rob us, but were frightened off by an animal, maybe our leopard."

"There was no leopard out there today, Sister," said Vincent.

"I'm not running away based upon the remote chance of a problem."

"I think it's more than a remote chance," I said and looked to Annie for help.

She shrugged one petite shoulder. "I have to go with whatever Sister Maggie says." The other nuns nodded in agreement. I looked to Father Norbert in the hopes that he might be the voice of reason. His reply was, "I'm with Sister on this."

Terrific.

Sister Maggie turned to Annie, "Maybe, you should go with Mr. Buchanan and Mr. Vincent, child. There's no reason to stay here with us. You could take the children with you."

"That's not possible," said Annie. "We could never evacuate over sixty children in Vincent's small Jeep and they certainly can't walk through miles of jungle to the nearest village. No, I'm going to remain here with you. That's our only option."

Sister Maggie clutched the silver crucifix hanging from her neck. "Hopefully I'm right about them being a small group of frightened thugs. I'll pray on it. We probably have time, maybe a month before anyone returns. We can make preparations."

"Preparations with what?" asked Vincent. "You won't allow the use of guns, and we can't fight off an army with shovels and pitchforks."

She scowled at him. "If things are looking different, maybe we can make other plans."

Vincent and I walked back to our hut. "She's wrong, Boss. Something's going to happen here and it's not going to be a month from now. Whatever it is, it's going to happen soon. I can feel it. We should clear out tonight."

"I can't just leave Annie and the children to fend for themselves. At least we have some guns of our own."

Vincent shook his head and disappeared into the evening.

FORTY-SIX

Boko Haram Camp
Cameroon Jungle

Shakar Bhutah

Shakar's army limped back into camp with only twenty-seven of their original two hundred men. They had been ambushed by a full regiment of the Nigerian Army. His men were badly outnumbered by ten to one and they faced a relentless barrage of artillery fire. It wasn't a battle; it was a massacre. Not only did his army lose most of its best soldiers, but the majority of their vehicles and machine guns had been destroyed. Shakar and Ziyad were lucky to escape with their lives. If several of his men hadn't launched a counterattack at just the right moment, both would be dead.

Shakar shouted as he entered his tent. "Uguhru, you fat bastard. You set me up. You were supposed to protect me from the army! They knew we were coming." He picked up his club and smashed a chair to pieces. "I'm going to gouge that fat toad's eyes out. Then I'll cut off his dick and shove it up his ass!" All Shakar's dreams of ruling Nigeria were dashed. "Allah has abandoned me. I can no longer rely on him for help. I need to find something else to preserve my destiny. I need prestige and my own cash to rebuild my army."

Ziyad entered. He hesitated. It was best not to enter the command tent when Shakar was holding the club, but this was important. He remained close to the door. "I'm sorry to disturb you, Colonel. The men have just returned from their reconnaissance mission."

With all the disaster surrounding their defeat, he had forgotten about the orphanage. If it was a front for a military compound, his remaining army was doomed. He was outflanked.

"What'd they find?" he asked.

"There was no military camp, but only three of our five men made it back, sir."

Shakar was surprised. "Were the others shot?"

"No sir. The men report that there was no gunfire. They just disappeared."

"Like your two cousins?" It was a statement more than a question. "But what could kill two armed soldiers?" Shakar set the club aside. "Did the orphanage have any defenses?"

"They said, minimal, sir. There was no sign of a military presence anywhere, just children and a small group of Christian nuns. Our men followed two white adults as they walked toward the river. One of them was an extremely tall man, carrying a rifle. A woman with him called him Brett."

Shakar dropped his club. "Brett Buchanan, our missing celebrity? I figured he'd returned to America months ago. Looks like he's been holed up in that orphanage all along."

"He and the woman seemed to be a pair."

"Lovers?" asked Shakar.

"They kissed."

Shakar picked up his club again and resumed pacing, trying to figure out how he could use this information to his benefit. He stopped and grinned. Shakar pulled out a map and spread it across his desk. He discussed his plan with Ziyad. "If the report is correct, we shouldn't need any more than fifty men for this mission. Can you put that many good soldiers together?"

Ziyad glanced at the club, still caked with dried blood. "We don't have many left, but I'll make it happen."

"Organize them right away and prepare our remaining vehicles. It'll take over a day to get there through the creek beds. I want us to be ready to move out immediately."

FORTY-SEVEN

Comboni Mission
Taraba Valley, Nigeria

Brett

I got up just before dawn, still tired. It had been a fitful night and I'd already been awake for hours, wrestling with the crippling issues of my life. Annie was right. In the end, I decided it was finally time to make things right with God. I would attend the Sunday church service, something I wouldn't have even considered when I first arrived here several months ago. This place and Annie had convinced me to do it.

I rolled over. Vincent hadn't slept on his cot. I got dressed and rushed outside. The Jeep was gone, and Vincent was nowhere to be seen.

"Damn him! The coward ran off." I'd never really trusted Vincent. Maybe it was the guns he smuggled or the way he gunned down the Somali boys at the checkpoint, but there was definitely a dark side to the man. "Now what's he up to?" I ran out and checked my hidden backpack with the cash and Sister Maggie's diamond. Still there. Returning to my wooden chair, I watched the predawn morning unfold. The sun was just cresting the mountains to the east as Annie approached with coffee. It being a Sunday, she was wearing her full habit, so today it would officially be Sister Annie. She set the pot and two cups on the old table and poured for each of us. After she sat down, we both sipped our drinks in silence, enjoying the peace of the early hours. Annie was the first to speak. "I had a wonderful time the other day."

"Me too," I said. *Jesus Brett, is that the best you can do? Me too?* That was pitiful. How about, it was the most wonderful day I've had since Jonathan was born? I took a sip of coffee. "Annie, we've only known each other for a few months but I think there is something special between us."

"I agree, Brett. We'll have to take it a little slowly and see what unfolds. One thing is for certain, I'll be leaving the Comboni Sisters as soon as they can find a replacement."

We remained comfortably quiet for a few minutes, drinking our coffee, unsure of what to say next. Sometimes, nothing needed to be said.

"What do you think about those men who followed us?" she asked.

"I'm not sure. Vincent has a great deal of military experience and knows what he's talking about. We might be in danger. At the same time, Sister Maggie could be right. Those men might simply have been some hapless thugs. We should probably make some contingency plans."

Annie reached over to hold my hand. She asked the same question she or Sister Maggie asked almost every Sunday, "Will you be joining us for mass this morning?"

"I think I will. We could all use a little prayer I guess."

Annie smiled and stood. "I have to help with some preparations for the Sunday breakfast, but I'll see you in church?"

"You can count on it." I watched her walk away until she disappeared into the kitchen building. I took a few minutes to finish my coffee and stepped inside my hut to get dressed in long pants and a button-down shirt. By the time I got out, Jenkins was waiting for me.

"I heard you were going to join us in church this morning."

"Sure am. Would you like to sit with me?'

Jenkins flashed a wide grin exposing his perfectly white

teeth. He and I walked side-by-side, my arm over the boy's shoulder. We selected a bench in the back. I scanned the congregation of about eighty people until I saw Annie sitting at the piano, near the rest of the nuns. I wondered how long she would continue to be with them. Would she leave with me?

The congregation stood to sing as Annie began playing "How Great Thou Art." Father Norbert entered from the back, stepped up to the humble altar, and began the mass, "I will go unto the altar of God."

"To God the joy of my —"

I felt it as much as I heard it, a distant rumble. Sounded like thunder. The ground shook. Jenkin's head snapped around to check the periphery of the compound. He looked terrified, his eyes wide and darting in all directions. He ran outside and appeared to look through the trees to the sky for reassurance. He didn't find it there. It was a cloudless day with clear blue skies. There were no signs of an approaching thunderstorm. He grabbed hold of my hand and pleaded, "We have to go. Must leave now!"

I gave him a puzzled look. "What is it? Mass is just beginning."

"I remember that day. Men are coming—very bad men. Must hurry!"

The rumble grew to a loud roar. Oncoming vehicles slammed through the brush, less than a couple hundred yards away. Shit! Vincent was right. This thing was happening right now. I tried to run to the front of the church to get Annie. Had to warn the others, but by then, panic began to spread through the congregation. I couldn't get to her. In desperation, I yelled, "Annie! Run! Boko Haram!"

When she turned to look back toward me, her eyes widened as she saw the first wave of attackers, a hundred yards away.

"Head out the back! Go to the dock!" With her outfit, she was an obvious target. "Habit!" I yelled.

She nodded in understanding. The last I saw of her, she was trying to pull Sister Maggie to safety. Failing that, Annie told the others to run and then disappeared behind the altar.

"We have to go," said Jenkins as he pulled hard on my arm. The trucks were already cutting off escape routes. I thought about my rifle still sitting next to my cot. I'd never make it in time. Jenkins and I darted behind the dining hut and ran toward the small trail Annie and I had used several times before. We raced between the onrushing vehicles. I glanced over my shoulder to see others following me, trying to escape the impending slaughter. Most were cut down in their tracks by automatic gunfire. Their deaths provided Jenkins and me a few extra seconds to make it to the brush. I felt a pang of guilt, the same sensation I felt when my mother died, but without a weapon, there was nothing I could do to save them. I could only save the boy who I wasn't about to abandon. Jenkins and Annie were my first priority, and I couldn't protect them if I were dead. A second later, we disappeared deeper into the jungle. I prayed that Annie made it out safely.

"Follow me," I said to Jenkins, sprinting as fast as I could, my lungs nearly exploding out of my chest. I held tightly onto Jenkins' hand. We remained off the road, following the jungle in the direction of the Taraba River and the abandoned village. Branches slapped our faces while thick brush and vines pulled at us and tore at our skin. When the boy could no longer keep up, I lifted him up in my arms and carried him the rest of the way until we reached the water. In the distance, the shooting became more frequent. The two of us hunkered down behind one of the abandoned cinder-block homes and waited for Annie. Soon, the gunshots crescendoed into a constant staccato of automatic rifle fire. Several loud explosions shook the ground. I pulled away from Jenkin's grasp. "I have to go back to help them. I must find Annie."

The boy grabbed me around the legs. "Stop. Please don't leave me!" He looked up with tears in his eyes and cried. "We can't help them now. It's too late. They have guns and we have nothing."

Of course, Jenkins was right. If I rushed back now, we'd

both die and any hope for the others would be lost. We sat, huddled together in silence as we listened to the painful cries of the innocents being gunned down.

I stared out over the river, lost in thought, and said to the water, "It was the damn money. How could I have been so stupid?"

"What is it?" asked Jenkins.

"We were betrayed."

"Betrayed, by whom?"

"Vincent. He's with Boko Haram. He was the only one aware of the backpack I had been carrying. The thing was loaded with American money, a lot of money, and Vincent wanted it. I knew I should've never trusted that bastard." I shook my head in disgust.

An hour later, the shooting stopped. It was over. "Annie, where are you?" I said to the river.

FORTY-EIGHT

Comboni Mission
Taraba Valley, Nigeria

Sister Annie

As soon as Brett told her to run, Annie grabbed Sister Maggie by the arm. "We have to go. It's Boko Haram!"

"I'm not leaving the orphanage, Annie. Now hurry and catch up to Brett. Don't worry. They won't harm the children."

Annie scrambled behind the altar, stopping for a second to look back on Sister Maggie. The nun shooed her with her hands and Annie rushed for a rear exit. As she ran around the generator and barrels of diesel fuel toward the safety of the jungle, she heard the beginnings of gunfire. She looked back and saw several of the adults fall. She was relieved to see Jenkins and Brett just as they disappeared into the bush. "They're headed for the village," she said to herself. She removed her outer habit, leaving her in hiking shorts, a t-shirt, and boots. She found the back road she and Brett had hiked just several weeks ago. It would lead her directly to him.

She picked up her pace and ran harder. Taking the road was faster but it was a mistake. She should have stayed in the bush. They caught up to her before she made it a hundred yards. "It's her!" she heard one of the attackers exclaim just before she was knocked unconscious.

FORTY-NINE

Comboni Mission
Taraba Valley, Nigeria

Shakar Bhutah

By the time the people realized what was happening, it was too late. Shakar's men already had them surrounded. His men fired into the air to herd the Christians together in front of the church. Only individuals trying to escape were shot. Shakar didn't want to risk the chance of killing his prized target. When all was stable, he rode into the compound in triumph, standing in the back of a military Humvee. The man next to him aimed a .50 caliber machine gun at the crowd.

Lieutenant Ziyad approached the Colonel to give a situation report. "Did you find him?" asked Shakar.

"No, sir. We've checked the entire orphanage, but the man was nowhere to be found. We searched the huts and found clothing that looked like they could belong to a tall American, so I'm almost certain he was here. I doubt he could be far."

Shakar clenched his fists. How could the American slip through his grasp? He looked up and scanned the cowering group. "Who's in charge?" When there was no response, he jumped down from the truck, grabbed a young girl by the hair, and dragged her to the front.

"Please don't hurt me!" she sobbed.

"If I don't see the leader of this orphanage within five seconds, I'm going to put a bullet into this little girl's head!"

Father Norbert stepped forward, holding his hands up. "We don't want any trouble here. We don't have much, but whatever we do have is yours."

"What I want is Mr. Brett Buchanan. Do you have him?"

"You must be mistaken. I'm not familiar with a Mr. Buchanan," the priest said. "This is just a peaceful refuge for orphaned children. We have no weapons and pose no threat to you."

Lieutenant Ziyad handed the Colonel an automatic rifle. "We found this in one of the huts, sir. It's the same one that contained the American's clothes."

Shakar took the automatic rifle and grinned at the priest. "No weapons, you say? You're lying, priest. I believe that's a sin, is it not? Tell me where the American is or the girl dies." He pulled hard on the little girl's hair. She screamed in pain.

"Please let her go. I don't know where Mr. Buchanan is. He fled."

Shakar paused, then grinned wider, showing his gold tooth. He inspected the rifle Ziyad had handed to him. It was an AK-47, his favorite weapon. He raked the slide, chambering a round. "If you can't hand over Mr. Buchanan, what good are you?" He pointed the gun at the Father Norbert. "I'm going to give you a chance to live, priest. Remove that infidel symbol from around your neck and stomp it into the ground."

Father Norbert instinctively clutched his crucifix with his right hand as if he could protect it. "I won't do that!" he replied in defiance. "This is a symbol of Jesus Christ, the Son of the Almighty God!"

"Then you will die, Christian. Your God is nothing to me." Shakar fired his rifle and three rounds exploded through Father Norbert's chest.

Sister Maggie ran out from the congregation and knelt beside the priest's body, clutching his hand. "Maggie," he said with his last breath. She stood and glared at Shakar, "What have you done? He was a good and holy man."

"He wouldn't tell me what I wanted to know, so now he's

just a dead man, an infidel on his way to hell," replied Shakar. He turned his rifle toward Sister Maggie. "Now it's your turn. Where is the American?"

She clutched her own crucifix against her chest. "Get out of my orphanage, you monster, and take your pack of heathens with you! What kind of people are you?"

"We are the children of the great Allah, the one true god. In time we will rule this world."

She stared directly in the man's eyes, boring down to his black soul. Between clenched teeth she said, "If this is what your so-called Allah commands, he isn't great. If he orders the murder of innocent children, he isn't even a god and the only kingdom he will rule over is hell, where he'll be sitting at the right hand of Satan. My God will strike—"

She didn't get a chance to complete what she wanted to say. A sudden flash of light exploded from Shakar's rifle barrel. There was no time for her brain to process the pain. The bullets shattered her crucifix and drove the pieces through her heart. She fell next to the body of Father Norbert. Her last act was to place her hand over his.

Shakar again turned his gun on the little girl who's hair he was still holding. Before he could shoot her, gunshots rang out from a small hill, a few hundred yards to the west. Bullets whizzed past his head. One of his men standing directly to his right dropped to the ground clutching his neck. A river of blood pulsated through the man's fingers. More shots erupted from the trees.

He turned to one of his squad leaders. "Take a dozen of your men and get that shooter. It's probably the American." The soldier did as ordered, but when he and his men reached the spot, they were met with a hailstorm of grenades. Most were killed within seconds.

The surviving squad leader ran back to Shakar. "There's more than just one guy out there, sir. Must be at least a dozen and they're well-armed! It's probably the Nigerian army again. I think it's another ambush. We should retreat." Those were his last words. A half second later the back of his head exploded as a bullet pierced his skull.

Shakar was livid with rage. "I want a half-dozen men to lay down suppressive fire on that position out there. The rest of you take the prisoners and anything you can carry." He nodded to his men and the carnage began. All remaining adults were immediately killed. The children were herded together, bound with ropes around their necks, and loaded onto trucks. When the raiders opened the door to the communications hut to steal the radio equipment inside, they set off a grenade booby-trap. All six of them were killed instantly. The same happened when a group tried to get food from the storage barn.

Gunfire continued to erupt from different locations in the jungle, picking off Shakar's men one by one. Shakar paced back and forth, bullets whizzing past his head as he looked at the dozens of his soldiers lying dead around him. This was becoming a costly raid, but it shouldn't have been. He'd been given bad information. He was getting angrier by the second and he needed some release. He called out the soldier in charge of the reconnaissance team that had surveilled the orphanage. When the man approached, Shakar poked a finger in his chest. "You said they weren't armed, you idiot."

"I'm sorry sir, I believe I said they were lightly armed." Those were his last words. Shakar drew his sidearm and put a bullet in the man's forehead. He looked at the rest of his men and shouted, "Anyone else wanna refresh my memory?"

Shakar felt better. "Nothing like a good shooting to calm the nerves and to keep the men focused on the task at hand." The rage still percolated inside him. Though it had been a somewhat successful raid, he'd lost over half of his men. At least he picked up a couple dozen new recruits from the orphanage. Then there were the girls and younger boys. They would fetch a few hundred thousand dollars and that was good, but his grand prize wasn't there. He hadn't found Buchanan, but he did have the one thing the man wanted above all else.

Shakar reached into his pocket and withdrew Annie's ivory crucifix. His men had removed it from her neck when they caught her trying to escape. "Ziyad!" he screamed. The lieutenant ran from behind one of the huts.

"Yes, sir."

"Show me the hut where the American had been living, the one where you found the rifle and clothing."

Ziyad pointed across the open courtyard. "It's the one directly across from the church, Colonel, the one with the wooden chairs sitting in front."

Shakar walked over to the hut and looked around. He turned the chair so it faced outward toward the bush and sat. "Buchanan, I know you're out there. I have your woman. If you want her back, you're going to have to come get her from me. I'll be in Cameroon." He was in control and holding all the cards. He grinned, stood, and draped Annie's crucifix over the chair. He then ordered his men to pack up and head out. At the last minute he yelled, "Burn down the church!"

"No, don't burn it!" said Ziyad.

"You dare to countermand one of my orders?" screamed Shakar as he pointed a pistol at the lieutenant.

"Sir, there are at least twenty barrels of generator fuel stored behind the church. This entire place is going to blow and kill us all."

It was too late. Several torches had already been thrown inside the wooden structure. As Shakar's men rushed to escape, a deafening explosion knocked them off their feet, killing many. The rest ducked, expecting to die, but it wasn't the fuel. The four-thousand-gallon water tank sitting on the hill behind the church suddenly ruptured open sending a tidal wave through the church, extinguishing the fire.

290

FIFTY

Road to Cameroon
Taraba Valley, Nigeria

Sister Annie

After skirting along the edge of consciousness, Annie finally came to, laying on her side in the rear seat of a truck, pain pounding at the back of her skull. It was a headache the likes of which she had never experienced before. Where was she and what'd happened? She tried to collect her thoughts. The last thing she remembered was running down the path in the direction of the village where Brett and Jenkins would be waiting for her. Then, nothing—until now. *Must've hit me in the head.* She pulled against the ropes binding her wrists and managed to reach the back of her head, checking on the source of her pain, fully expecting to find blood on her fingers. *No laceration or fracture. Just a concussion.*

Annie tried to sit up but couldn't. Her ankles were also bound. She reached for her ivory crucifix for reassurance. It was gone. Fighting back a wave of panic, she tried to take stock of her situation, looking for any means of escape. Sounds of children crying sent chills down her spine. It was soon replaced by rage. *The bastards took them too.* She had to save them somehow. She had to survive. She had to escape. She pulled at her restraints until they dug into her skin. It was hopeless. All she could do was pray for help. Each time the truck hit a rock, a fresh jolt of pain shot through her head.

The truck slowly came to a stop and the doors opened. That's when she heard it, the same voice that was shouting orders at his men during the attack. Shakar Bhutah.

"Select a dozen men, Ziyad. Station them on either side of the road to set up an ambush."

"Sir?"

"Buchanan will soon realize I have his woman and he'll try to get her back as soon as possible. He must know this is the way we're headed and he's going to follow us. Have the men spread out. He'll be alone and on foot, so he should be an easy target. Take him alive and unharmed. Just be sure no one kills him."

"Yes, Colonel."

"It shouldn't be more than a couple hours, a day at max. When you have him, bring him to the camp in Cameroon."

"What about those Nigerian soldiers who fired on us at the orphanage? Won't they be with him?"

"The Nigerian Army wasn't shooting at us. If they had been there, they would've attacked us head-on as soon as we lost the first dozen men. No, I think it was only Buchanan and maybe a few others, but that was it. You should have more than enough men here to handle them. Kill anyone else you see but make sure Buchanan is unharmed."

Lieutenant Ziyad selected a squad and positioned them on both sides of the road. He turned to Shakar, "What about the Taraba River?"

"The river? Not possible. He has no boat." Shakar thought for a second. "Send two of your men to the river to keep an eye out just in case."

The caravan of trucks again took off. Annie could tell they were climbing up a hill and headed across rocky terrain. *Must be the creek bed Brett and I found at the end of the road.* When the truck hit a large rock, shards of pain exploded through her head and she lapsed back into unconsciousness.

FIFTY-ONE

Comboni Mission
Taraba Valley, Nigeria

Brett

After several loud explosions, the gunfire ceased. Jenkins and I left our hiding place and saw a Zambuti tribesman standing along the river's edge.

I remembered Sister Mary Maggie's words. "By the time you see them, it's usually too late." I positioned myself in front of Jenkins to ward off the possible attack. It never happened. The pygmy warrior made several clicking sounds, which I couldn't decipher. The small man bent over and scooped up a handful of river water, which he slowly poured onto the ground. He repeated the procedure several times and pointed up river.

"What's he saying?" Jenkins whispered.

"Can't tell."

"What does he want? Is he going to kill us?"

"I don't think so. I believe he was sent to watch over us. There are probably more of them hiding in the bush. I think they've been here ever since Sister Annie cured the little boy." When I looked back, the pygmy was gone. "We'd better go," I said.

We remained in the shadows of the thick brush and slowly made our way back to the orphanage compound. As we approached, the roar of escaping trucks faded in the distance. I stopped dead in my tracks, completely unprepared for the carnage that lay before me. *Nothing lasts forever, Brett.* I pulled Jenkins close to my side. The air hung heavy with the smell of cordite. The grass was awash with pools of fresh blood from over fifty victims. There were no bodies of children, just adults, most of them Shakar's soldiers. I had trouble understanding. "Who killed the soldiers?" I asked as I searched the orphanage for survivors. There were none. The church had been burning but the fire was out, and the building was soaked with water. In front of it lay the bodies of Father Norbert and Sister Maggie. Rage boiled up from the depths of my soul. I dropped to my knees beside them. "Why God? These were good and decent people whose only goal in life was to help others. How could you allow them to be gunned down like animals? These are your people? What kind of a God are you?" The jungle had no answer. There could be no explanation. God had again abandoned me.

After a few seconds, I looked around for evidence of Annie. One by one, I frantically turned over the bodies, afraid she might be amongst them. I scanned my surroundings in all directions, but she was nowhere to be seen. Maybe she survived. I turned to Jenkins. "Check the perimeter and see if you can find her."

Calling out her name, I rushed to the clinic but it was empty. I ran around the edge of the brush hoping to find her safe and hiding, but found nothing. "Annie!" I screamed over and over as loud as I could. Jenkins did the same.

"She's gone, Boss," said a voice from behind me. It was Vincent with his nylon gun bag and a half-dozen different rifles hanging from his shoulders.

I clenched my fists and charged him. "Vincent, you son of a bitch! You deserted us."

Vincent backed up several steps and held up his hands. "Never, Boss. I knew what was about to happen here. It was inevitable. I tried to warn you and when you wouldn't leave, I grabbed my guns and hid deep in the jungle. Figured I might be of more help there. I've been setting booby traps all night. Several hours after dawn I spotted Shakar. He had five dozen men with him. I killed at least thirty of 'em but there was nothing more I could do."

I lowered my head, my stomach wanting to wretch. "I ran. Should've done more. I should've stayed and helped them."

"And do what, Boss? Beat 'em off with sticks? I was watching. You had no weapon at your side. There's nothing you could have done but die right next to them."

"You said she was gone. Is Annie dead?"

"No, they took her. Took all the children too." Vincent pulled Annie's carved ivory necklace out of his pocket. "Shakar left this in front of our hut. He obviously wanted you to find it."

Incredulous, I asked, "They kidnapped her?"

"Yes, but she'll be fine. Shakar wants her for bait."

"Bait? I don't understand."

"They came to this orphanage for a reason, and it wasn't just to kidnap some orphans and murder a few Christians. It wouldn't have been worth the risk of traveling this far from their base camp into the Christian zone. They could've kidnapped children anywhere."

"The money," I said. "Did they find out about the money?"

"They might've been aware of it and I'm sure they would've liked to have found it, but I don't think it was a priority for Shakar. He certainly didn't spend any time searching for it. No, he was interested in finding something much more valuable than cash." Vincent stared at me. "He wanted you, Boss."

"Me? Why me?"

"Because you're worth tens of millions in potential ransom and a hundred times that in propaganda. Parading you around in front of the news media would resurrect the Boko Haram cause. They'd love to beat and torture one of America's great heroes. It would humiliate the United States and make Shakar the undisputed leader of their organization in Nigeria. As long as you're still alive, Annie will be fine. We need to keep you that way. At least you were able to save the boy."

I jerked my head right and left. Jenkins? "Where's Jenkins? He was with me a few minutes ago." I no longer heard him calling out for Annie. I turned to Vincent, my heart racing. "Something's happened to Jenkins."

Vincent handed me one of the rifles and both of us rushed out to check the jungle. It was empty.

"They must have him. We have to go!" I turned to run up the road.

Vincent grabbed my arm. "Hold on, Boss! What're you doing?"

I pulled away. "They can't be far. Gotta hurry. It's the only way to save Annie and Jenkins!"

"And exactly how do you plan to do that?"

"I know exactly where they're headed. There's only one way for them and it's down the road along the Taraba. We can follow their tire tracks. They'll lead us right to Shakar's camp."

"And then what? You think Shakar's just going to be sitting there waiting for you to arrive? Maybe you two can get together and negotiate their release over a few beers? Come on, Boss. Think! Shakar's going to have men hiding on either side of that road. When we show up, they're going to kill me and kidnap you. Once he has you, the children will still be sold into the sex market. That includes Annie, if she's lucky. There's a good chance Shakar'll decide to keep her as his trophy wife." He studied our surroundings. "We need a plan."

Vincent was right, but I had to do something. I was losing Annie and Jenkins just like I lost my mom, and just like I lost Jonathan. Panic overcame me, and my mind raced out of control at the thought of what Boko Haram might do to them, thoughts too gruesome for anyone to stomach. I puked, wanting, needing a drink badly. I clutched my sobriety medal until my mind stabilized. I vowed to save them, all of them. I took Annie's crucifix necklace and tied it securely around my neck with the sobriety medal. "We have a little time now. Here's what we're going to do. First, we need to find some shovels to bury our friends. Then we're going to track those bastards down."

"But we can't head down the road, Boss. Like I said, they'll ambush us for sure, and there's no way we can catch up to them. They have heavy-duty vehicles and we have nothing but my Jeep. It'll never make it."

"But they can't drive on roads forever. Annie and I hiked five miles east of here and the road peters out. There's nothing after that other than creek beds to get them to wherever they're headed. It'll be slow going for them so maybe that'll give us a chance to catch up somehow."

"Even if we catch up to them, Shakar must still have over thirty men armed with automatic weapons. We have only the two of us with a few rifles each. We won't stand a chance."

"We'll deal with that when we find them. Go to the barn and find some shovels. Start digging the graves while I head over to the communications hut. Hopefully, we still have a radio."

"I think we just might," replied Vincent with a wide grin on his face.

I scrunched my eyebrows in confusion and looked in the direction of the tall cotton silk tree. The antenna was still there. When I reached the communications hut, I understood what Vincent had meant. The front door of the small building had been destroyed and the bodies of five Boko Haram soldiers were lying nearby. I checked inside the hut and found the radio to be intact. Reaching into my pocket, I retrieved what was by now a torn and dirty business card. Once contact was established, I said into the radio's microphone, "I need to speak to a Mr. Desmond Pierce at the United States Embassy. Can you patch me through? Tell him it's Mr. Livingstone, and it's urgent!"

A minute later, he was on the radio. "Desmond, I have a critical situation here."

❖

I returned to help Vincent with the task of burying the bodies of Sister Maggie, Father Norbert, and the rest of the adults. We didn't have time to dig deep graves, but at least the wildlife wouldn't desecrate their bodies. When finished, I leaned on my shovel. "We should say a few words." I couldn't think of anything. I hadn't bothered praying since asking God to protect my mom from Dad. I looked at Vincent who stepped forward and folded his hands. "Lord Jesus, please open your arms and accept our friends into your kingdom. They were good people. Amen." He bowed his head in silence and added, "And please help us find that son-of-a-bitch Shakar so we can send him to hell."

"What about them?" I asked, pointing to Shakar's dead men.

"Leave them for the animals. They would've done the same to us," replied Vincent.

I didn't argue with him. "Grab whatever food and water you can carry and meet back here in ten minutes." I dug up my backpack with its cash and Sister Maggie's diamond and led Vincent on the three-mile walk back toward the Taraba River. I had a plan.

"Where we going?" asked Vincent.

"To meet our ride."

"What ride?" asked Vincent. "There's nothing there. Hasn't been in over ten years."

"You'll see. It should be here by tomorrow afternoon."

An hour later we walked through the center of the same abandoned village Annie and I had explored just several days previously, the same place where we shared the kiss. It seemed like a lifetime ago. The empty shells of former cinder-block homes and market stalls appeared more foreboding now that my life had again been touched by death. Why did it follow me so? Again, there were no answers here. There never were in the jungle.

We selected a hut along the periphery, with a good view of the dock and river. It was one of the few still intact. Vincent boiled water and made rice. At dusk, we settled in for the night. Vincent and I alternated guard duty just in case some of Shakar's men backtracked for another search of the area. It was an uneventful evening except for the cries of the animals of the night.

FIFTY-TWO

Taraba River
Taraba Valley, Nigeria

Brett

Just after noon on the following day, we saw a boat pulling around the bend down river. It was an old wooden trawler with a red hull, chugging against the current, belching out thick black smoke from its exhausts. On the front of the pilot house hung a plaque with the name, "Nigerian Princess" painted in faded black letters. Even at a distance, I heard the captain cursing and screaming orders to his first mate. "You're on the wrong goddamn side! Who the fuck ever said you could work on a boat? I said the port lines! They're on your left! Now get the goddamn things tied and ready! Don't forget the goddamn bumpers either. Jesus H. Christ do I have to do everything myself!"

"Aye captain, the port side," the young boy replied.

"Get your ass moving, son. We're almost there," the captain screamed as he stuck his head out of the port window of the pilot house.

"That's our ride?" asked Vincent, standing on the edge of the dock.

"That's it," I replied.

"And where are we supposed to go in that old bucket?"

"Upriver, deep into the jungle."

"Into Gashaka-Gumti?"

"All the way to Cameroon. That's where Shakar's hiding out," I said.

"How can you be so sure?"

"That's where the road leads. One of the Zambuti showed up yesterday and kept reaching into the river with his hands. I didn't understand at first, but I think he was trying to tell me that this was the best way to find Shakar."

"But how're we going to find him?" asked Vincent. "There must be thousands of square miles of thick jungle up there. How can we possibly track down a group of men that even the entire Nigerian Army hasn't been able to find?"

I continued to stare at the boat as it approached. "If you're right about what Shakar wants, we won't have to worry about finding him. He'll find us soon enough. It's what he's counting on. Like you said, it's why he didn't kill Annie in the first place."

"And once they find us, then what? We still only have a handful of weapons. What can we possibly do against an army?"

"Improve our odds, somehow."

The boat slammed against the dock so hard it almost knocked Vincent into the water. I grabbed him just in time.

"Son-of-a-bitch, that was a goddamned hard landing," said the captain with a booming voice. "It's the goddamn river up here. Fucking eddy currents everywhere. This trip's going to be a major cluster fuck! I can already feel it in my bones." His voice betrayed a history of too much yelling and smoking.

After the bow and stern lines were secured, the captain set foot on the dock. He was a big man with a long white beard that hung down to his chest where it faded to a dingy yellow. The color contrasted against his deeply tanned face, leathered by years of squinting into the sun. His piercing black eyes scanned his surroundings, missing nothing. He chewed on the end of an unlit cigar as he walked up to me. "You must be Buchanan, the guy paying for this little adventure. Well, the river's worse'n I expected, so it's going to cost you extra. That'll be ten thousand for my trip up to this shithole and five thousand a day after that."

"That wasn't the deal, captain," said a familiar voice from

inside the boat. A stocky black man, dressed in standard military camouflage emerged. A .45 caliber semiautomatic pistol was holstered at the right side of his waist and a combat knife on the other. "The deal was five thousand for your trip here and three thousand a day afterward."

"Desmond! I didn't expect to see you," I said and rushed over to shake his hand.

"Officially, I'm not here," said Desmond. "Officially, I'm not allowed to protect you."

"And unofficially?" I asked.

The façade of civility on the man's face gave way to a stern look. "Unofficially, I'll do whatever it takes to protect you, including killing any bastard that gets in my way."

The boat captain growled, "You're a goddamn crook, Desmond. I don't know why I ever agreed to work for you."

"Because I pay you three times more than anyone else would to hire this old piece of shit you like to call a boat."

The captain grumbled some more under his breath and walked away, venting his frustration on the mate. "What the fuck is this? You call this a fucking knot? Another five minutes and the goddamn boat's gonna break loose and drift down the fucking river. Then, I'm gonna make your sorry ass swim through the crocs after it!"

Desmond turned to Vincent. "It's good to see you're still alive."

Vincent nodded. "It takes more than what they have to kill me."

"You still have those guns I gave you?"

Vincent lifted the nylon bag. "Right here. I still have several hundred rounds of ammo. Had to use up all my grenades though."

I looked back and forth between the two men. "You two know each other?"

"Since we were kids." Vincent grinned. "He's my cousin."

"Make that, distant cousin," said Desmond. "We come

from different ends of the gene pool."

"Now you've gone and hurt my feelings," said Vincent. "Like I give a shit." He laughed.

"I was afraid Vincent was playing both sides of this," I said. "For a while I thought he'd betrayed me. He did have all those guns he appeared to be smuggling."

Desmond stepped forward. "Perhaps I can explain. Vincent is what we call a problem solver. In your case, his job was to watch over you and keep you from getting yourself into trouble. We couldn't have you falling into a situation that could jeopardize U.S. interests in this part of the world."

"Like getting yourself kidnapped and ransomed for millions of dollars," said Vincent. "That's a lot of money in the hands of a terrorist organization."

I was incredulous. "You two are CIA?"

Neither man responded to my question. Desmond paused for a minute as he looked upstream. "Who raided the orphanage?"

"Boko Haram. Colonel Shakar to be specific. No doubt about it," said Vincent.

"I had hoped we killed him and destroyed his entire army last week. Looks like we failed." Desmond put his hand on my shoulder and pulled me aside. "I have some information that might be of interest to you." We walked out of earshot of the others. "When we first met, I warned you about associating with that pretty flight attendant."

"I remember the conversation well. You said she might be affiliated with Boko Haram."

"Turned out I was right. We discovered she was working on a scheme with Uguhru Muhammadi, the Minister of Natural Resources. He and some Iranian partners had been bankrolling Shakar's activities for years. At first, we believed it to be some kind of complex money laundering operation, but that was far from the case. As it turns out, Shakar was paid to drive thousands of innocent Nigerians from their villages, murdering many of them in the process. It wasn't tied to money laundering though, and it wasn't related to any kind of political revolution or religious quest. They were solely interested in the accumulation of land in the vicinity of the diamond mines in the Mambilla Plateau region."

I thought of the Zambuti diamond in my backpack. "So, Aryianna and this Minister Uguhru have been dealing with Shakar just to enrich themselves?"

"Yes. They stood to make billions."

"Then why attack the orphanage?"

"It was just happenstance when you crossed paths with Miss Rhamani on your flight from Paris. She didn't know who you were, but notified Shakar that a famous American was flying to Abuja. We believe Shakar had some interest in you as a potential kidnap for ransom, but it wasn't a high priority item for him as long as he continued to be funded by Uguhru and the Iranians. Unfortunately for Shakar, Minister Uguhru was arrested and placed in a cell for treason."

Howling erupted from the shore behind us. Desmond spun around and withdrew his sidearm. Two adolescent baboons rolled out of the brush in a cloud of dust and fur, fighting to establish their pecking order in the troop. Apparently satisfied they posed no threat, Desmond reholstered the gun and continued. "After Aryianna was arrested, she faced the same fate, so in a plea deal she agreed to help set up an ambush to destroy Shakar's army. It worked, but unfortunately, it looks like he survived. Once he was defeated and discovered that his major source of funding had been eliminated, he probably looked to you as a possible source of cash. You would command a high price in ransom, probably in excess of twenty million dollars. When he couldn't find you at the orphanage, he took the woman."

Desmond gazed up the river. "I understand what you want to do here, Mr. Buchanan, and I have to tell you it's a bad idea. You can't deal with these people. Shakar will double cross you the first chance he gets. You're going to be up to your neck in crocodiles and I'm not talking about the reptiles. Your chances of surviving this plan of yours are about nil."

"I realize that, but I have no other choice. I have to find those children."

"I told Mr. Cabot you'd say that." Desmond kicked at a loose board on the dock. "I can contact the Nigerian army and ask them to take over the search."

"That's tempting, but you and I both know they'll never find the children in time. They've had years to look for Shakar and haven't been able to locate him. Besides, I'm sure he's hiding in Cameroon and the Nigerians can't enter the country. It would constitute a foreign invasion. That means it's up to me and anyone else who wants to join me."

"Okay, here's what's going to happen," said Desmond. "Mr. Cabot has arranged for a group of newspaper reporters and photographers to come to the orphanage to document the atrocities that happened there. He'll launch an international public relations campaign against Boko Haram and their financial backers. Heavy pressure will be brought to bear to eliminate any supplemental funding they've been receiving from Iran and other exporters of terrorism in the Middle East. That will help to destroy most of the remainder of their organization."

"But that's not going to address the present situation," I said.

"You're right. That's why Vincent and I are going with you. You're going to need all the help you can get."

"It's not your fight, but I'm glad to have you with me."

"That settles it then. Let's get our gear on board and head out." He turned to the captain, "We're ready."

The captain mumbled something under his breath that sounded like, "Fucking shit show."

FIFTY-THREE

Boko Haram Camp
Cameroon Jungle

Sister Annie

Annie drifted into and out of consciousness. The terrain improved from the rocky creek bed they had been on, but the headache continued to pound away. The air grew cooler, meaning they were headed toward a higher elevation. Over twenty-four hours must have passed by the time the caravan of trucks began to slow down to a stop.

One of the soldiers jerked her out of the vehicle and dragged her to a tree. She struggled and punched him in the chest, but was rewarded with another hit to her head. Her brain seized in more excruciating pain than she could imagine, dropping her to her knees. The world around her spun as she was on the brink of again passing out. She pushed back at it and forced herself to remain calm. Slowly looking from side to side she tried to assess her situation. Surrounding her was a grassy clearing, dotted by several dozen clusters of military tents. Most looked empty and there weren't that many soldiers around the camp. Vehicles, scarred with bullet holes, hid under large trees or camouflage netting.

To the left sat several empty corrals protected by coils of barbed wire. Soldiers unloaded sobbing children from the trucks and herded them into the pens. Those who fought back were slapped into submission. It looked as though about thirty men returned from the assault on the orphanage. Another several dozen rested under trees waiting for the return of their commander. Technically, it was an army, but not large and not very healthy judging by the looks on their war-weary faces. Exhaustion and defeat filled their eyes. Absent was any sense of discipline or the enthusiastic bravado one might expect to see from troops when their conquering commander returned from battle.

A giant of a man stood in the bed of a pickup truck to address his men. It was Shakar, sporting a black beret and khaki uniform with epaulets decorating the shoulders of his shirt. He raised his right fist in the air and said one word, "Victory." His men's attempts at enthusiasm rang hollow considering they had defeated only a small group of nuns and children. Undaunted, he jumped down from the truck and approached Annie. There was nothing subtle about the look of evil in his eyes. He approached like a predator, stalking his next meal, relishing the hunt. She tried to hide her fear, but it was a difficult task. She was in an extremely dangerous situation, her head lying squarely in the mouth of a crazed lion. He flashed a sinister smile exposing a garish gold tooth, too large even for his gigantic mouth, a look that could open the very portals of hell. "I am Colonel Shakar, commander of all Boko Haram armies in Nigeria. I am told you are the American's woman." The smell of death spewed from his mouth.

Annie pushed her shoulders back and stood. She stared directly into his eyes, not allowing herself to blink. "I am nobody's property, and I'm no one's woman but my own. I demand that you release me and the children immediately." Her head hurt so much she feared that the outburst might cause it to explode. The worst was yet to come.

Shakar's smile immediately transformed into the sneer of a rabid animal. He reached out with his right hand and grabbed her by the neck, almost lifting her completely off the ground. "You need to get this straight! You're just a woman, about as important to me as a goat, less even. Right now, you're my property. I own you. If I want you, I'm going to take you. If you fail to obey me, I will kill you. If you displease me in any way, I will kill one of the children. If you scream, I'll kill two of them, and if you try to escape, I'll kill all of them. Do you understand what I say?"

She nodded yes.

"Say it!"

She tried to talk but couldn't. She could barely breathe. He relaxed his grip slightly and she managed to croak out, "I understand."

Shaker lowered her back to the ground and ripped open her shirt, exposing her breasts. He squeezed the left one hard until she grimaced. His demonic smile returned.

Thoughts of the rape raced through her mind. *Never again!*

He called for Ziyad. "Take her to the tent next to mine. Post two guards outside. She's to be watched twenty-four hours a day. If anyone besides me tries to enter, shoot them. Right now, she's probably worth at least a couple hundred-thousand dollars. That amount will be cut in half if she's been defiled, so make sure it doesn't happen."

FIFTY-FOUR

Taraba River
Taraba Valley, Nigeria

Brett

The boat headed upstream, to where exactly, no one knew, not even the captain. He had never before traveled this far up the Taraba. Nobody in their right mind would. The river sliced through a land of nothing but thick, dark green jungle, and more jungle. The captain cursed his way against the current, mile after tedious mile. It was an endless source of frustration. An overwhelming sense of urgency plagued my mind, but I was trapped by the slowness of the process. I sat on the wooden deck of the bow, undistracted, and forced to consider my own thoughts. I took stock of my life and how things had changed over the past several months. What was so important to me only a few years ago, seemed trivial. The fame, the money, the cars, the homes were all insignificant distractions. In fact, in many ways, they had contributed to my downfall. Time with the Comboni orphanage had helped me to understand that. I'd finally begun to allow myself to look forward in life, not that I could ever forget Jonathan or go a minute without missing him. I still saw him in everything around me every day, but at least I was beginning the process whereby I could forgive myself. I planned to confess to my part in Jonathan's death. I had even made the decision to return to church. I was happy for the first time since the incident.

But that wasn't enough. God suddenly decided to take it all away again. I was right about Him all along. He allowed me to hope, but then dashed that hope. God didn't give two shits about me or the children. Damn Him for not protecting them.

I found myself falling back into the dark abyss that had consumed me a year ago. The children were gone. Father Norbert and Sister Maggie were gone. Now Annie was also gone, and it was all my fault. It was me who Shakar wanted. The others were innocent bystanders forced to pay a steep price because of their association with me. It would have been better if I had died in the car crash. Then maybe those around me would not have been punished for my sins.

The familiar feelings of doubt and self-loathing returned with a vengeance. I yearned for the soothing taste of Jack Daniels, my old friend who could soften the pain. Surely the captain had a bottle hidden somewhere in the boat's galley. I had the money to pay whatever was needed to buy it. The only thing keeping me from getting drunk was the knowledge that Annie and Jenkins were still out there somewhere. I had to remain sober so I could find them before something terrible happened.

The valley, carved out by eons of erosion from the Taraba, stretched out before us. The river led the boat deeper and deeper into the darkening throat of the jungle. The still surface of the water was only occasionally disrupted by fish jumping, probably trying to escape the jaws of a crocodile. A log floated past. When it began its journey far upriver, this moment was its future. As it drifted by us, its past was now our future. I fell into a quiet meditation, contemplating the lazy flow of the water. What did the future hold for me? It was as though traveling against the current might be transporting me back in time. I feared I was heading into the bowels of the worst that mankind had to offer.

The sun settled lower in the sky, casting a purple veil of dusk along the water's surface. The engine slowed to a near stop. I rushed to the pilot house. "What're you doing?"

"Gotta drop anchor before it gets too dark," said the captain. "This is as good a place as any."

"You can't stop! We must keep going. We'll never catch up to them at this rate!"

"I can't see in the dark. It's too damn risky to try," said the captain.

"I'll double your price, even triple!" I said.

"Normally I'd take your money and do it, Buchanan. I know the lower rivers like the back of my hand, I do. Used to make ivory runs up to that old village for years when people still lived there, so running at night would be no problem for me. But we're well beyond where I used to make my trips and it's not the rainy season. The river's low, shallow enough in places to touch the fucking bottom with my toes. Rocks are hiding just under the surface and I can't see 'em at night. If I hit one, it'll tear the bottom right outta the Princess. Gut her from stem to stern. Then we're fucked for sure. There'll be no going forward and no going back. We'll either starve to death, drown, or get eaten by the crocs. All your money'll do me no good if I'm dead, and your friends out there in that jungle will never be saved."

The discussion was over. The captain turned the nose of the boat into the middle of the river and pointed it upstream as the mate set the anchor. Before long, the curtain of an absolute dark void enveloped us. There was nothing left to do but eat and turn in. We decided to rotate guard duty on the bridge. I offered to take the first watch.

Restless, I walked out on the front deck and gazed into the black of night. A huge shooting star raced across the sky. Just like I did as a boy, sitting next to Mom, hiding on the roof from my father, I searched the stars for reassurance. I found my childhood friends, the Big Dipper and the three stars that comprised Orion's belt. They were constants I could always count upon to be there. They gave me a certain sense of stability and comfort when life was spinning beyond my control. The night sky was peppered with the light of a billion different stars, more than I could have imagined, certainly more than one could see back home.

I pondered the limitless expanse of the universe. The light from most of those stars was first born billions of years ago, but was just reaching Earth at this time. I focused on Sirius, the brightest one. If I could somehow see a person on that distant star, I'd be seeing an image that was over a billion years old. Like the floating log, the past was melting into the future while the present was a thing of the past. Time became incomprehensibly blurred. If I could follow those rays of light back to their source, would they take me back in time to an earlier universe, one more pure and less complicated—maybe even carry me back to God for a chance at rebirth?

If there was a civilization somewhere up there, would that mitigate against the case for intelligent design? Would God create life on multiple planets? What would be the reason? Could it possibly be that some scientists were correct when they claimed that life was merely the result of random molecular interactions? Surely, there must be more than that. Surely there must be some purpose, some plan. Without the guiding hand of a divine being, what would be the sense in life, but if there was a God, why did He forsake us? Why did He allow little Jonathan to die? Why did He allow good people like Sister Maggie and Father Norbert to be slaughtered? He definitely wasn't a just or merciful God. He was a heartless creator playing sadistic games with our lives.

From beyond the riverbank, the cadent sounds of jungle creatures purred at the night. All I could see was unforgiving blackness, like staring into the soul of Satan. To my right a sudden, desperate cry slashed out of the darkness, the syncopated sound of some animal sinking through multiple layers of physical anguish. I jumped and raised my rifle, but there was nothing there except the emptiness. Mercifully, the cry stopped. What had been the hunter and what had been the hunted? Made little difference. One thing was for certain, something just died so that something else could live, just as the female leopard killed goats at the orphanage so her cubs could live. It was an intricate part of life's cycle, a universal necessity almost since the time of creation. Life must be sacrificed so that life could continue. Pain and loss were an inevitability but why would any god demand such?

"Faster Dad. You must go faster," Jonathan's voice pierced the night.

"But why did you have to die?" As always, the jungle offered no answers.

FIFTY-FIVE

Taraba River
Cameroon Jungle

Brett

The following morning, I awoke to an impenetrable mist that obscured the riverbank on both sides, submerging the jungle under a heavy white shroud. We were going nowhere until the fog lifted. Walking out onto the deck, I stared over the boat's railing, wondering. What's hiding behind that foreboding white curtain? Death? Mine?

An hour later, the fog lifted and the captain weighed the anchor. Our journey continued as the boat slowly plowed forward, straining against the current. All was quiet except for the belching of the engines and the occasional guttural growl of a hungry croc. The boredom was all consuming, disrupted only by the occasional scraping sounds of rocks or sunken logs as they tore along the bottom of the hull. Each tense episode was punctuated by a "son-of-a-bitch," or a "goddammit," as the captain repeatedly cursed the river.

The helpless waiting plagued me, made worse by a sense of desperation. I needed to take action, but was being held back by nature and the dictates of the river.

"Faster Dad, hurry!" Jonathan's voice tormented me, but there was nothing else I could do but sit on this deck and wait— for how long, I didn't know. My thoughts were unraveled by images of Annie. *Where was she? What have they done to her? Was she hurt?* Annie was a strong woman and probably wouldn't panic. No, she'd keep her wits about her and look for an opportunity to escape—but she couldn't do that without leaving the children behind. They would pay a heavy price, so any escape attempt was out of the question. Their situation seemed hopeless. Only God could save them, but God was unreliable. He caused everything in the first place. It was up to me, but how? I looked across the bow of the boat. The river seemed endless.

The sun sat at its peak, bearing down on us with relentless fury, the air thick and heavy, making the simple act of breathing a chore. Armies of mosquitoes and other insects waged a constant assault. I removed my shirt and wiped the sweat from my eyes, exposing even more of my skin to the attacks. Despite everything, the scene around me was one of unparalleled beauty and undeniable serenity.

Mountains towered up on either side of us, forcing the river to fold in on itself as an entangled web of vines and dark green pushed in from either side. Giant tree limbs extended out from the shadows, reaching across the water in an apparent attempt to snatch each of us individually off the boat and into the deadly throat of the jungle.

Another scrape against the hull. "The water's getting shallower with every mile. We're on a one-way course now," said the captain. "There's no place to turn around and this boat doesn't have a reverse gear." To my chagrin, the man pulled back on the throttle, slowing the boat even more as it continued its journey. Tentative. Painfully slow. Like following the light from last night's distant stars, we seemed to be time travelers, heading back beyond history. We were an insignificant speck in the lineage of mankind while mankind was an insignificant speck in the spectrum of the origins of the universe. There was no past and no future, just the present with one single purpose in mind, to survive long enough to save Annie and the children.

The farther we traveled around the next bend in the river and the next bend after that, the more distant became my memories of home and my prior life. I abandoned all thoughts of a new life and my quest for redemption. My needs were no longer the primary issue. It was Annie and the children. They were the compelling force driving me on. I had to find them before it was too late. *Faster Dad. Go faster.*

Though we had to be getting close to Cameroon, the overriding problem was that I still didn't know exactly where Shakar's camp was hidden. I expected some contact by now, but Shakar hadn't revealed himself yet. Like Vincent had said, there are thousands upon thousands of square miles of jungle around us. The river was certainly taking us in the general direction, but how would we know when we had traveled far enough? How could I let Shakar know that I was in the region and ready for a trade, my life for Annie and the children? I felt adrift with a complete lack of direction other than what the river allowed. Just like my alcohol addiction, it was a situation beyond my control. Deep within my soul, I believed that a course of action would be revealed to me, but by whom? God? The same God who had killed Father Norbert and Sister Maggie? The same God who had taken away Annie and Jenkins? The same God who had killed Jonathan?

Desmond and Vincent stood on the aft deck, guarding the rear of the boat. Guarding from what, I didn't know. We hadn't seen any signs of humanity since leaving the village dock. There was only the occasional herd of hippos and the many crocs cruising the river, probably hoping one of our team would fall overboard. To my left, the young mate used a makeshift fishing pole to catch some dinner. He was almost asleep, his head bobbing, and his legs hanging over the edge of the boat. Out of nowhere, Desmond ran forward and grabbed the boy by the back of his shirt, lifting him straight up. A pair of crocodile jaws shot out of the water and clamped down on the place where the mate's legs had been hanging a half-second earlier.

"That was close," said Desmond. "You need to be more careful, boy."

"He's bored," I said.

"Bored huh?" asked Desmond. "Then let's spend some time learning something useful. Things are going to get a little hectic out there in a few days and it'd be best if you learn how to defend yourself. Can you shoot a gun?"

"Yes, sir, if I have to," replied the boy.

Desmond handed him a rifle and showed him how to flip off the safety and rest his finger along the side of the trigger guard. "Never place your finger on the trigger unless you're ready to fire." Desmond inserted a magazine. "It holds fifteen rounds. You won't need more. By the time you fire that many times, the battle is usually over."

The mate studied the gun, flipping the safety up and down.

"Now let's see if you can shoot," said Desmond. He showed the boy how to aim. "Look down the barrel and line the front sight with your target. Just squeeze the trigger when you're ready. Don't jerk or you'll pull the gun off-target."

He aimed the rifle at a nearby croc, the one that tried to take his leg.

"Don't," said Desmond. "Only kill if it's in self-defense or for food. Aim at one of those tree trunks on shore."

The boy took aim and carefully squeezed the trigger. The rifle's recoil kick knocked him back, but Vincent grabbed him before he fell overboard. The sounds echoed down the river valley and through the jungle.

Multiple shots erupted in response. Vincent spun around. "What the hell is that?"

"It's coming from the jungle," I said. "Someone's shooting at us."

"What the fuck?" screamed the captain and pushed the throttle forward. The engine strained to follow the command. Submerged logs clawed at the hull.

Desmond returned fire in the direction of the gunshots. The boy also fired his rifle. The left pilot house window shattered and the boy fell to the deck with blood on his sleeve.

"He's been hit," yelled the captain.

From shore, more shots followed, piercing the hull just

above the water line. Desmond and Vincent fired back at the invisible enemy.

"Goddamn sons of bitches! They're trying to sink us!" said the captain.

As quickly as it started, the shooting stopped. Desmond tended to the mate. "Just a flesh wound. You weren't shot, just hit by a few shards of window glass. He removed them from the young boy's shoulder and applied a combat dressing. "You're going to be fine," he said.

"Why were they shooting at us?" the mate asked.

"They wanted to stop the boat. Tried to sink us enough to run aground," answered the captain. "Almost did it."

"Who?"

"Shakar's men," said the captain. "Must've been watching from the shore to see if we'd head this way. They want what we have on the boat." He looked at me. "Told you this was going to be a cluster-fuck, Buchanan. You should be paying me three times what you are. We should just hand your ass over to 'em."

Vincent raised his rifle to the center of the captain's chest. "That's the last time I want to hear you say that kind of shit. If it happens again, I'm going to make you swim home."

Desmond took over the wheel while the captain went below to repair the holes in the hull. Vincent and I walked out onto the bow and studied the deep recesses of the jungle for any further threat. The trees were less than thirty feet away on either side of us and slowly closing in. We could see nothing.

"If they attack us again, they'll be so close they could almost jump onto the boat," said Vincent. "They sure want to get their hands on you, Boss. If they'd hit the engine, we'd be finished. We wouldn't have been able to hold 'em off for very long." He looked upriver. "I don't understand. They had us and then just stopped the attack. Why didn't they keep shooting?"

I smiled. "At least Shaker knows we're here."

"The problem is that in this narrow river we're sitting ducks," said Vincent. "If Shakar returns with more men, we're dead."

Around the next bend, we reached a wider section of the river. The captain said, "Only an hour of daylight left. We anchor here for the night. It's going to be the safest spot until we get to wherever the hell this shit show is headed."

We ate and took turns with watch duty. Shakar's men didn't return. Clouds obscured the night sky and I could find no solace in the reliability of my old friends, the stars. The night filled with sounds of the critters of darkness, hunting for food or searching for a mate. Alone again, I had only my thoughts for company. The situation with Annie and the children seemed hopeless. Vincent was right. Even if I found Shakar and his army, my small group was badly outmanned and outgunned. I needed help, but from where?

A flurry of familiar existential questions plagued my mind. Why does a supposedly all-merciful God allow suffering? Why did He allow me to have happiness if His only intent was to rip it away from me? Was He merely some supernatural, malevolent prankster? What do I have to do? The answer came to me like a flash of light piercing the impenetrable darkness. Me. My entire life had been centered around me: My career, My pain, My failures, My addiction, and My losses. I've been searching for My new life, My happiness, and My atonement. I needed help. Sister Maggie said, "When things are darkest, sometimes the only option is God." Seemed hypocritical, to ask God to help Me.

I hadn't prayed since I was a kid, and I couldn't remember exactly how to do it. So, I simply talked to the darkness. "Lord, I know we haven't been on the best of terms and there's no reason why you should even be listening to me. I've blamed you for almost everything that's gone wrong in my life. I blamed you for the death of Mom and Jonathan. I blamed you for the end of my marriage. I even blamed you for the deaths of Sister Maggie and Father Norbert. The fact is that I'm the only one to blame for what has happened. I placed myself above everyone else, and those around me have paid the price. Even my search for atonement has been selfish. Rather than seeking redemption for my sins, I should be asking Your forgiveness for squandering the wonderful life You've given me. I realize redemption can't be attained by trying to erase the sins of my past. The answer is in the future, and I need your help with that. It's all I can control. I have no right to ask anything for myself, but could you please protect Annie and the children from harm until I can get there? Please help me find a way to save them. I'll do whatever you ask. Amen."

FIFTY-SIX

Boko Haram Camp
Cameroon Jungle

Annie

The sun was setting, and the darkness laid siege to the Boko Haram camp. Annie worried about Brett. She didn't want him to come, but at the same time she did. Without him, she and the children had no hope of escape. At the same time, she knew it would be extremely dangerous for him. Even if he were able to get some help, and even if he could find them, he would be badly outnumbered. It would be a suicide mission. He wouldn't stand a chance. She was torn, praying he would come but hoping he wouldn't. Annie beseeched God to show Brett a way to do the impossible.

She had been asleep on her cot when the guard entered her tent. She awoke to find him leering at her and holding a knife to her throat. He had the look of rape in his eyes. She had seen it before. Annie struggled but her arms and legs were still bound and there was nothing she could do to protect herself. He put his hand over her mouth. His skin was rough and smelled like something rotten.

"Shh. Be very quiet now. I don't want to have to cut your pretty face," he whispered, dragging the knife across her cheek. "Haven't had a woman in a long time." He kissed her neck. "Looks like your boyfriend's forgotten all about you. I don't think he's coming. Shame to waste such a pretty thing like you." He reached out and pulled up her shirt. "What you got under there?" He groped her left breast.

A second later, half of his face was gone. Annie was covered in blood. When he fell to the ground, she saw Shakar standing behind the body, holding a gun in his hand. He fired another bullet into the man's head. "I warned them. I warned them all. They're not to touch you. You're of little value to me if you've been sullied. If anybody's going to have you, it's going to be me."

He called out for another guard and pointed to the body, "Get this piece of shit out of here, and clean up the mess. Then bring a bucket of water so she can clean up. Touch her and you're dead."

Annie didn't sleep the rest of the night. She vowed that she would never again allow another man to do that to her, even if she had to fight back with her life.

"Please help us Brett," she pleaded into the darkness.

FIFTY-SEVEN

Taraba River
Cameroon

Brett

Except for the attack by Shakar's men, the day was a generic copy of the day before, and the one before that. One painfully slow hour followed the next as the relentless monotony on the boat continued into the afternoon. I stood guard on the bow while Vincent and Desmond covered the sides. Noticing the subtle movement of leaves in the underbrush along the north riverbank, I was thankful that we would finally be getting some welcomed breeze to abate the heat. But, there was no wind. There hadn't been since our first day on the boat. I chambered a round in my rifle and made my way to the pilot house. The captain intently studied the shore, a shotgun across his lap.

I said, "I think we're being followed."

"I know," said the captain, continuing to peer into the thick brush. "Been with us for the past hour."

"Who are they?"

"Don't know. Never been this far upriver before. There are no villages around here for over a hundred miles or so."

"Same group as yesterday?" asked Brett.

"Nope. These fellows are acting differently. More careful."

"Do you think they plan to attack us?'

The captain chewed on his cigar for a second. "I don't think so. If that was their intent, they'd have done it a half mile back where there's a sandbar and the water's shallower. No, I think they're just curious. Probably never seen a boat like this before, but we'd best be ready for them in case they change their mind and decide we're some kind of fucking evil spirits. Jungle people can be damn spooky."

Vincent climbed up. "We're being followed." He was carrying two of his automatic rifles, one hanging from his shoulder and the other aimed at the shoreline.

"We already know. I'd lower that gun if I were you, Mr. Vincent," ordered the captain, almost chewing the end of his cigar in two. "Right now, it doesn't look like they're going to be a threat, so you don't want to be doing anything that might piss 'em off."

Desmond stepped in with his rifle. "How many are there?"

"Can't say for sure," replied the captain, his eyes darting back and forth. "These guys aren't Boko Haram. They're jungle natives. For each one you think you see, there's probably a dozen more hiding in the bush that you don't see."

Sounded familiar.

For the next half hour, we watched them along the northern bank, leapfrogging their way parallel to the boat. They were so close I could almost touch them, but couldn't see their faces. We waited, guns ready, as the boat negotiated the next bend.

Vincent was the first to break the tense silence. "What the hell is that?"

Standing on a fallen log, just one hundred yards ahead of us, stood a short stocky man, his body tattooed in red ochre markings, and holding an exquisitely carved spear in his right hand. "It's the Zambuti chief, the one whose son Annie healed a few weeks back," I said.

A second later, a red spear launched from out of the foliage and imbedded itself in the middle of the boat's front deck, making a deadly thud when it landed.

Vincent immediately raised his rifle. "Damn savages.

They're going to kill us and eat us for dinner."

The captain placed his hand on the rifle barrel and forced it lower. "Settle down, Mr. Vincent. You're much too anxious to fire that goddamn gun of yours. That spear was just to get our attention. It was a calling card, their way of telling us we'd better not fuck with their chief over there. You keep making them nervous with that rifle and we're all going to wind up with a spear in our chest."

"No need to worry, Vincent," I said. "These little guys are our friends. I'm almost certain they took out Shakar's men yesterday when they opened fire on our boat. Might've been the ones who killed the poachers."

No more spears landed. The captain throttled back. As we approached, the chief raised his scepter spear over his head.

"He wants us to stop," I said.

The captain pulled further back on the throttle, maintaining just enough speed to keep the nose of the boat pointed upstream.

"Are you crazy, Boss?" Vincent spread his arms. "We can't stop here. It's in the middle of the jungle and we're surrounded by cannibals. All they want to do is eat us. That's what they do. Eat people." He again raised his rifle.

"If you don't lower that goddamn rifle of yours, Mr. Vincent, I'm going to take it from you and shove it right where the sun don't ever shine," ordered the captain.

Vincent scowled and muttered, "I'd like to see you try." He lowered his gun and hung it over his shoulder. "Damn savages are going to boil us alive."

Desmond stared at him. "Savage is a relative term, Vincent. This tribe probably considers us to be the uncivilized ones. So far, they have done nothing but protect us. Yet we are the ones standing here with assault rifles ready to massacre them with a few pulls on the trigger. So, you explain to me. Who are the savages?"

The captain gazed forward. "We have to stop here anyway, Mr. Buchanan."

"Why?"

"Listen."

A loud roar rumbled from upriver. "What is it?"

"Must be a waterfall around the bend and from the sounds of it, it's a big one. This boat doesn't have wings, so I'm afraid it's the end of the line for your expedition. I think the chief knew we'd have to stop around here and decided it was the best place to make contact."

"I think he wants to talk to me."

"Might not be a good idea, Boss," said Vincent. "We could be dinner by sundown."

"They're the ones who kept Shakar's men from sinking our boat," I said. "The chief wants to help us. If it'll make you feel any better, I'll take the dingy and row over to shore to be sure."

"Okay, but I don't trust the little red devils. If they try anything funny, I'm going to unload hell upon 'em," said Vincent, his finger on the trigger of his gun.

"That's fine, but keep your finger off the damn trigger, and make sure you don't accidentally shoot someone."

I lowered the dingy, rowed over to the chief, and stood on the log just several feet from him. The pygmy spoke in the same clicking and grunting language I'd heard when they first arrived at the orphanage with the injured boy. The chief stared at Annie's carved crucifix, hanging around my neck. He touched it with his left hand and pointed to the interior of the jungle, saying only one word, "Maageek."

"Maageek," I replied.

I returned to the boat and told my small team we were going inland. The captain said, "I'll maintain this position as long as I can. I'll give you three days and that's it. If you're not back by then, I'm leaving."

I opened my backpack and pulled out three stacks of bills. "Thirty thousand for five days."

The captain took the wad of cash. "Okay, this'll buy you five days. After that, I'm gone. Your money's no good to me if

I'm dead."

Vincent stepped forward, his nose inches away from the captain's. "Just be damn sure you're here when we return. If we get back and find that you left us high and dry, I'm going spend the rest of my life tracking you down. When I find you, and I will find you, I'm gonna feed your sorry ass to the crocs, one piece at a time." The look in his eyes confirmed that this wasn't just an idle threat. It was a promise.

Our group disappeared into the darkness of the jungle, giant leaves folding in behind us, obliterating any evidence that we had ever been there.

FIFTY-EIGHT

Cameroon Jungle

Brett

Once deeper in the jungle, I opened my backpack to be sure it still contained Sister Maggie's diamond. The chief watched me with a look of amusement in his eyes. He shrugged and without a word turned east and ran. He was joined by a half-dozen of his tribesmen. My team followed, struggling to keep up, plunging farther into the depths of the jungle. A few of the pygmies had modern machetes strapped to their waists. "Where the hell'd they get those?" asked Vincent.

"Up until a few days ago they probably belonged to Shakar's men," I said.

It was a surreal experience as I tried to follow this band of nearly naked pygmies at breakneck speed, racing across what seemed to be a prehistoric land. The diminutive size of the tribesmen might have been a problem for them in a modern society, but here, in the strangling confines of their surroundings, their small, lithe bodies were uniquely adapted to this life. Unencumbered by the restrictions of clothing and large size, they gracefully made their way around and over obstacles, negotiating through the thick vegetation with amazing agility. The unending labyrinth of green textures and twisted geometries had provided them with a verdant cocoon, protecting them from the outside world. They made not a sound, no labored breathing, no twigs snapping under their feet, and no smacks of branches brushing against their bodies as they ran. If I hadn't already been aware that they were thirty feet in front of me, I would've never known they were there. Even the chief, who was clearly twenty years older than me, ran effortlessly, slowing down only to allow my friends and me to catch up. There was no communication between them, just the pigmy's instinctive understanding of where they were headed.

My group ran as fast as we could, our arms and faces assaulted by the small limbs and thorns of the jungle. Looking at the ground, I focused my attention on possible rocks or fallen trees the tribesman effortlessly avoided, obstacles which could trip me up and end my mission with a broken leg, or worse. My mind began to wander. Had any other man ever set foot on the ground we had just stepped on? Was it possible that there were places on earth that had never been touched by humans before? It was an exhilarating thought. Whether for good or bad, modern man had drained the inaccessible swamps of southern Florida and built Miami. Las Vegas had been born out of the sands of a remote Nevada desert. Man had even set foot on the moon, but this jungle had pushed back against civilization and still remained untamed. Perhaps that's the way God preferred. Maybe this place was permanent, the closest thing to a Garden of Eden after all.

The heavy, humid air ripped at my lungs. Attacks of insects were merciless. I slipped on a rock, twisting my ankle at an odd angle. Desmond kept me from falling, but my leg throbbed with each step. Cramping seared through my muscles, but I pushed on, embracing the pain, believing it brought me closer to Annie and my soul nearer to healing. At least now I was moving, doing something more than just sitting on the deck of that boat. When one of the pygmies noticed the bug bites, he stopped the group with a distinct whistling call. He searched about until he found the particular kind of bush. He picked a few small leaves, put them in his mouth and began chewing. Several of the others followed his lead. When ready, they removed the resulting green paste from their mouths and attempted to spread it over my exposed arms and legs. I pulled back until he said, "Maageek." They repeated the process for Desmond. Vincent refused to allow the savages to touch him claiming, "They're spicing us up to be cooked later."

We continued in relentless pursuit for several more hours, until we eventually stopped at a small creek bed for water. I didn't need to check my ankle to know it had swollen to astronomical proportions. If I ever took my shoe off, I'd never get it back on. I drank as much as I could and wondered how long it would take before the effects of the unboiled water hit me. Diarrhea could be just as bad as a sprained ankle out here. It never happened. The tribesmen seemed to know what was safe and what wasn't. While we drank, one of the men dug in the jungle floor with a knife until he had harvested a dozen or so roots. He tied them together and hung them over his shoulder. Another picked several things off a nearby tree. Whatever they were, they were moving. He wrapped the treasures in leaves. The chief raised his spear and clicked. The chase resumed. How he knew where to go, remained a mystery. There were no visible landmarks. Yet the chief and his tribesmen pressed forward, never stopping to get their bearings.

Under the thick canopy of trees, sunlight was sparse, but the shade offered little respite against the temperature. Rather, it created an oven-like effect that drained me of all strength. Still, I pushed on, knowing that somewhere out there was Annie and a group of terrified children waiting for me to save them. Sweat poured down my face, burning my eyes.

The jungle floor became an impenetrable wall of green vines. Cutting our way through the web was all but impossible. Undaunted, the lead tribesman took to the trees. He leapt up on a low-hanging branch and followed it higher, about twenty feet above the ground. Without hesitation, the rest followed from one branch to the next, each several feet in diameter. It was much like following a natural jungle expressway above the tangle of vines below. The cost was that it was much more treacherous.

The results of a fall could be deadly. I refocused on my footing, learning to look ahead and plan my next steps in advance. My ankle throbbed.

When darkness began to settle over the jungle, we were forced to stop. Even these people with their amazing abilities, couldn't travel in the dark of night. As they each selected a limb for sleep, one of the tribesmen cut into the flesh of a nearby tree, removed a spongy material, and offered it to me. When I squeezed it, a sweet taste filled my mouth. The tribesman repeated the offer to the rest of the team. Even Vincent accepted the fluid.

The chief unwrapped several large leaves he had been carrying. He mixed their contents with diced portions of the roots and other things they had found earlier. It looked like a mixture of raw snails, insects, and nuts. I didn't want to know what I was eating. It was salty but surprisingly good, and I ate voraciously until my share was gone. The rest did the same. Nothing went to waste.

The tribesmen used their machetes to cut vines from the trees and handed them to my friends. "What the hell are these for?" asked Vincent. "They going to tie us up and kill us now?"

"They're safety harnesses," said Desmond. "Our friends are trying to keep us from falling out of the trees. There are a lot of hungry creatures prowling around down there at night and they'd love nothing better than to have you for dinner."

Vincent took the vine and tied it tightly around his waist. He double-checked to be sure the knots were secure. A shroud of blackness enveloped us. I could barely make out the silhouette of the chief, sharpening the blade of his spear with a rock. He would spit and sharpen, spit and sharpen until he was satisfied. When finished, he leaned his head against the tree and fell asleep. It took me much longer to relax.

The jungle came alive as the frightful sounds of the nocturnal creatures filled the night. They seemed to be all around us. Minutes later a familiar noise arose, the panting sound of a leopard, hunting directly below. A desperate cry pierced the darkness. Just like the night before, something died so another could live. I wondered how many of us would die so that Annie and the children could live. I rechecked the vines securing me to the tree and pulled my automatic rifle close. I gazed upward for the security of the stars but couldn't see them through the canopy of the trees. All was black.

My fear reached into the absolute darkness, but it pushed me away. It wasn't fear for my own safety but that of Annie and the children. I could no longer tell if my eyes were open or closed. Didn't matter. Fatigue overwhelmed me and I finally dozed off.

FIFTY-NINE

Cameroon Jungle

Brett

In the distance, I heard a scream. It was a woman's voice and there was no doubt in my mind whose it was. Annie! I jumped up and raced through the underbrush until I reached a small clearing. In the center knelt Annie, head down, and her hands bound behind her back. A group of people surrounded her and began hitting her in the face with broken branches. Blood and tears streamed down her face. The crowd chanted over and over, "Shakar, Shakar."

"Annie!" I tried to yell, but the words remained trapped in my throat.

She looked up and saw me. "Brett," she said quietly. It was then that I saw the car tire hanging from around her neck. I screamed her name and tried to run to her, but the jungle vines had wrapped themselves around my legs and kept pulling me back into the darkness. I watched helplessly as a large man walked toward her, carrying a flaming torch. He looked at me and grinned, exposing a mouthful of gold teeth. "No! No! No!" I screamed, and this time the sound exploded from my throat.

"Wake up, Boss!" said Vincent as he shook my shoulder. "Wake up! You're having another one of your nightmares." Vincent cut away the vine safety belt holding me. "Not that today is going to offer anything better than your dream."

We cut Desmond's vines and stood to find the tribesmen already waiting. Within the hour we returned to the security of solid ground. The chase resumed, but I felt an even greater sense of urgency. I pressed on, passing the chief.

"Faster. You must go faster."

Didn't know if it was the food or the water concoction the tribesmen had given us, but the pain and swelling in my ankle were gone. I ran with more energy than yesterday, more effortlessly, relying on instinct rather than planning my steps. The frantic pace seemed like an endless wild goose chase as we aimlessly rushed through the thick jungle. One hour melted into the next.

When the tribesman in front of me stopped abruptly, I almost ran into him. It happened without warning. Why stop? I scanned the area, expecting to face a threat of some type. Initially, I didn't see them. There were three, each one impossibly tall with abnormally long arms and legs like aliens in a space movie. Their moss-stained lines blended perfectly in with the surrounding flora. They were the kind of sculptures one might see in a museum of modern art. Instead of eyes, each one had a large blue stone in the middle of its forehead. The one in the center was the tallest, the ones on either side appeared to be protectors like the three stars of Orion's belt. The Zambuti bowed their heads.

"I think they're pygmy gods," said Desmond. The tribesmen withdrew their knives and machetes and began to cut away encroaching vines. The exposed statues were magnificent works, the smooth stone an alabaster color, the forms, graceful, flowing, and poetic. I looked around for a temple but there was none and there was no evidence of any prior sophisticated civilization, just these three gigantic idols in the middle of nowhere.

My friends and I helped the Zambuti clear the brush. We exposed over three dozen graves, each marked with a small spear, a miniature replica of the chief's. All were inlaid with the same type of blue stones.

"Diamonds!" said Vincent. "There must be hundreds of 'em!"

"This has to be where they bury their fallen leaders," I said. "The blue gems must have been unearthed when they dug the graves."

"How long do you think these statues have been here?" asked Vincent.

"A hundred years—a thousand years—maybe ten thousand. It all looks so ancient. If there had been an advanced civilization at one time, it had been devoured by the jungle long ago, leaving behind only this vestige of Zambuti culture." *Nothing lasts forever, Brett.* I wondered how today's major cities would look in another ten thousand years. Would they suffer the inevitable depredations of time, being completely swallowed by the jungle, a testimony to the impermanence of all things man-made? The surrounding jungle had tried to erase the Zambuti past and choke out any future. The land around us appeared to have rejected any further progress by these people. It was probably for the best. The jungle offered a sanctuary, protecting them from their enemies. Civilization brought with it greed, jealousy, and rage. Perhaps it's the absence of civilization that brought a simpler purpose to life. In some small way, these primitive people lived in their own utopia. They had all they needed and desired nothing more: food, shelter, and the bonds of their tribe. Who were we to say otherwise? Like Father Norbert once said, "Sometimes you have to lose yourself in the jungle before you can find true happiness."

I doubted that anyone but the members of this small tribe had ever seen this shrine. I was delighted that no anthropologists or scientists had descended upon this sacred ground. They would have desecrated it. I would never allow Shakar or anyone else to uncover its existence.

I restudied the blue eye of the largest idol. It was polished and as large as an orange. How could they polish a diamond without modern tools? I reached out to touch it, but the chief stopped me with the tip of his spear. He shook his head. "Maageek."

That single word sent a wave of panic through me. I thought that was their special word for Annie. Was this all the chief and his men had done, brought us through miles and miles of jungle just to see a collection of magic idols? Maybe Vincent was right about them. Maybe they just led us here to offer us as a sacrifice to their gods.

My head pounded in frustration. Had the Zambutis wasted days of precious time while Annie and the children were being subjected to unimaginable acts of violence? Then I remembered. The chief did specifically say "Maageek" when referring to Annie. It was the only English word he knew. Maybe it was an all-encompassing term they used to refer to anything special like Annie, their gods, or the diamonds.

The tribesmen finished their work. When complete, they stepped back and chanted, an indecipherable prayer apparently beseeching their gods to protect them. I bowed my head in respect. Desmond and Vincent did the same.

Suddenly, the tribesmen stopped. The chief faced me. "Maageek." He turned and ran into the bush, the tribesmen and us in close pursuit. The mission was again underway.

"Hurry! Please hurry." The voice arose from inside my head. It was Annie. The overwhelming sense of urgency pushed me forward.

SIXTY

Cameroon Jungle

Brett

For endless hours, we continued to run, until the chief stopped and raised his spear. He turned his head to the right and the left, apparently listening to the sounds of the birds around us. He leaned his head back, placed a finger against the side of his throat, and made a high-pitched shrill, different from any animal sound I'd heard before. An identical sound echoed from somewhere in front of us, probably several miles away. Nothing was spoken. One of the younger tribesmen disappeared into the brush ahead of us. Thirty minutes later, he returned and spoke to the chief in their clicking language. The chief turned to me and smiled. "Maageek," he said.

He pointed his spear forward. Our group continued with caution until we came to an open area of buffalo grass. It had been tamped down in spots and I recognized the prints of recent tire tracks. *Annie was nearby.* My heart pounded loudly in my ears and I started to take off at a full sprint. The chief grabbed my arm and pulled me back. He sent a few scouts ahead as the rest of the tribesmen and my friends slowly followed at some distance. We were only about a half a mile away when I heard the laughter of men—many men—and the desperate cries of children.

One of the younger tribesmen, Desmond, and I climbed a nearby tree. The camp was only a few hundred yards away, close enough to make out details. There were a half-dozen trucks parked under a camouflage netting. Rear mounted machine guns pointed outward. Several dozen men sat on the ground or stood guard, none of them appearing to be concerned about the potential of an attack. The children were secured in pens, tied together with ropes around their necks. They whimpered. One was defiant, yelling at one of the guards, demanding to be released.

"Quiet!" said the guard as he passed the boy and kicked him in the side. The boy scowled, hate filling his eyes, his right arm partially gone. My heart raced. *Jenkins. Thank God, he's still alive!*

I searched the rest of the camp and was horrified. "I can't find Annie."

"She's probably in one of those tents," said Desmond. "She's much too valuable to leave out in the open with all these men."

"Bait," I said to myself.

We climbed back down the tree, and I turned to Desmond. "You're the military man. How should we handle this?"

"We certainly can't shoot our way in. I'd guess there are fifty or so men in the camp. We're badly outnumbered and outgunned. Those children are certain to be the first casualties. The first thing we need to do is to improve our odds without letting them know we're here." Desmond paced the ground. "The guards look tired and inexperienced, certainly not ready for an attack. We might be able to use the element of surprise."

I looked in the direction of the camp for several seconds. "I have an idea. We have to wait until just before dawn when the mist is still pretty thick." I wanted to get Annie and Jenkins out of there as soon as possible and didn't want to waste another night sleeping in the jungle, but I had no other choice. Their safety was of paramount importance and my plan would take a little time to organize. "I'm going to see if I can somehow communicate with the chief." I remembered the words of Sister Maggie. "For every one you see, there are at least ten more you don't." I was counting on that.

While there was still light, I spent my time in search of what I needed, selecting some and discarding others that weren't quite the right size, shape, or weight. I then settled in next to a tree, put my backpack behind my head, and tried to rest, knowing sleep would be impossible.

In the predawn hours, the heavy mist hung close to the ground, bathing the area in a ghostly layer of white. I cautiously crawled closer to the guards, most of whom were sitting or lying on the ground, asleep. I approached those nearest to the children and once I was about sixty feet away, I slowly stood. It was about the same distance as from a pitcher's mound to home plate. I unshouldered my backpack and selected one of the rocks I had gathered earlier and struck the closest guard with a Brett Buchanan 98 mph fastball, hitting him directly in the temple. A quiet thud and he hit the ground. All remained quiet. I took out the remaining guards in the same fashion. Once down, one of them stood and moaned slightly, but I was out of rocks. I withdrew Sister Maggie's diamond from my backpack and quickly silenced him with another fastball to the forehead. A one-hundred-million-dollar bullseye. "That's six down," I whispered. "The children are safe from immediate fire."

I gave a thumbs-up sign. It was Desmond's cue to initiate his part in the plan. He quietly crawled through the grass and neutralized seven more guards by slitting their throats. The tribesmen took out a dozen more using arrows and spears. By now, almost half of Shakar's men were down and all was still quiet. Vincent and Desmond set about the task of cutting the children free. It was a slow process and by the time they were close to finishing the mist was dissipating.

When one of Shakar's lieutenants exited his tent to relieve himself, some of the children panicked and screamed. He saw what was happening and grabbed his gun, aiming at them. Vincent raised his rifle and fired three quick rounds through the center of the man's chest. He was down, but our advantage of surprise was now lost.

"Run!" I yelled to Jenkins.

One soldier rushed out of his tent and charged the children, hoping to block their escape. An older girl retrieved a machete from one of the dead guards and hacked the man in the belly. That was followed by a series of slashes across his face until he was unrecognizable. The girl stood above him grinning. Her face was badly bruised from the rape she had endured at the hands of Shakar's men. Desmond grabbed her and pulled her toward the safety of the jungle.

"Too late for quiet now," said Vincent. "Get the rest of those kids into the brush." He emptied an entire clip into the cluster of Boko Haram men who were now rushing forward. Desmond emptied another clip into some of the tents, neutralizing any who hadn't made it out yet.

"Careful," I said. "Annie might be in one of them."

Clouds of red arrows obliterated the sky as they flew out from the brush. The tribesmen cut down one terrorist after another. Shakar's men fired blindly into the jungle, unable to focus on any specific enemy targets. The Zambutis were like ghosts. One large man with no shirt and a black beret ran out of his tent, pulling his pants on. He wasn't grinning, but I was convinced there was a big gold tooth inside his mouth. Shakar glared with the eyes of a madman as he looked around his camp watching his men get shredded.

Seeing that defeat was imminent, several of his men dropped their weapons and ran. Shakar pulled a rifle from the hands of a dying lieutenant and shot a few of them in the back. Three ran for the protection of the jungle but Vincent followed right behind them. When he got close enough, he dropped the one in the lead. The other two turned and raised their hands in surrender. After tying them up, he began the process of extracting information about other possible camps using his own unique code of "jungle justice."

Shakar stood his ground in the middle of the gunfire and arrows, unafraid in the belief that he would be protected by the hand of Allah. He had been selected to be king and nothing would deny him that destiny. Ziyad remained at the Colonel's side, firing at the intruders, but it was all in vain. The lieutenant was hit in the belly by one of the red arrows. He spun around and was hit by a second arrow in the middle of his back. When he tried to raise his rifle and return fire, he was greeted by three more arrows in rapid succession, all of them striking him in mid-chest. Ziyad fell dead in a pool of his own blood at his Colonel's feet.

Shakar realized this battle was lost and he had to do something while he still had some bargaining power. He pulled his sidearm and rushed into the tent adjacent to his. A second later, he exited with his gun pointed directly against Annie's neck. Her eyes were wide but she remained calm. He stood with her in the middle of the camp so he could be well seen. He looked in all directions.

He grinned and said in a loud voice, "Mr. Buchanan, I know you're out there. I must admit, you've impressed me, but the game is over. It's time for us to meet face to face and make a deal."

When he received no answer, he pressed his gun more firmly against Annie's neck, causing her to wince. "Mr. Buchanan, I'm not a patient man. I'm going to give you just five seconds to step forward, or I'm going to blow this pretty lady's head off! Are you going to just stand there and watch her die?"

I stepped out from the cover of the jungle, flanked by Vincent and Desmond on either side, their rifles aimed at Shakar. Annie was only thirty feet away, so close I could almost touch her. I stared into Shakar's eyes, as black as his soul, satanic windows of pure evil. The man was capable of unparalleled atrocities. My mind went into overdrive, running through options. There weren't any. Annie's life was at stake. The slightest miscalculation on my part would result in her death.

"Okay, I'm here. Now what?"

"You and your pretty girlfriend are coming with me."

"That's not going to happen. I'm not going to let you leave with her, Shakar. Let her go. It's me you want."

"Then lower your rifle. I'm not going to ask again."

There was no room for negotiation. I lowered my gun.

"That's good, Mr. Buchanan, famous American sports hero," said Shakar with a laugh. "Now, here's what's going to happen. First, drop your weapon and slowly walk toward me."

"Don't do it, Boss!" said Vincent. "He's going to kill her anyway."

"Desmond?" I asked, not taking my eyes off Annie.

"Don't have a shot, not without the risk of hitting her."

I lowered my head, deciding how I was going to play this. A sacrifice was needed. After a second, I looked up. "You don't need her, Shakar. She and those orphans are of no value to you. They're peanuts compared to what you can get for me. I must be worth… what? At least twenty million in ransom money. If you want it, here are my rules about what's going to happen here."

"Don't, Brett," pleaded Annie. "He's crazy. He'll kill you as soon as he gets his money."

I smiled and looked at Shakar. "I'm going to drop my weapon and we're going to have an exchange, but I've instructed my men to kill me at the first sign of any harm to the woman. If that happens, all you wind up with is a dead hostage and a dozen bullets in your chest. So, what's it going to be? You want your twenty million or do you want to be dead?"

There was a tense pause as Shakar looked around considering the offer. The tables had been turned. His eyes filled with rage like he was going to start shooting, but in a rare moment of lucidity, he appeared to reconsider. He grinned, exposing his gold tooth. "I think we have a deal, Mr. Buchanan, but don't fuck with me or the woman dies."

I dropped my rifle to the ground. Annie shook her head and cried out, "No, don't do this, don't trust him!"

"Everything's going to be fine," I reassured her.

SIXTY-ONE

Boko Haram Camp
Cameroon Jungle

Sister Annie

Annie's mind raced to the point of panic. She couldn't allow Brett to leave with Shakar. He'd be tortured and the entire spectacle would be paraded in front of the world news media. She willed herself to remain calm and analyze the situation much like she would evaluate a trauma victim in the emergency room. It was a step-by-step process. She flexed her fingernails into her palms hoping the pain would clear her head. Almost on a subconscious level, the maneuver gave her an idea, more of an instinctive reflex than a plan. "Never again," she said to herself. "Never again will an evil man put his hands on me." She refused to allow herself, Brett, and the children to remain hostage to this monster. She refused to be the victim. She would become the predator.

Shakar stood over a foot taller than Annie and outweighed her by two hundred pounds, but wrestling with her older brothers when she was younger taught her that winning a fight wasn't always about size or strength. It was more about cunning, speed, and using the element of surprise, taking advantage of that moment when opportunity presented itself. That's when she felt it. Shakar loosened his grip in anticipation of making the exchange for Brett. She again flexed the fingers of her right hand so that they formed a sharp angle at the knuckles. Now! She broke free of Shakar's grasp, knowing he could easily shoot her in the head. It was a risk she was willing to take to save Brett.

She pirouetted around on her left foot and pushed upward. In one fluid motion, like an Olympic high-jumper, she lifted her right knee to give her as much vertical height and momentum as possible. With all the strength she could muster, she reached up as high as she could and drove her clenched fist into the middle of the giant man's neck. She felt a crack as Shakar's larynx fractured. Annie landed and raced toward Vincent, expecting a bullet in the back.

A startled Shakar wheezed and struggled for air as he fired his gun wildly in all directions. When the clip was almost empty, he aimed directly at her. It would be an easy shot.

A single shot rang out hitting Shakar in the right shoulder, rendering his shooting arm useless. It was Jenkins, holding the rifle Brett had dropped.

The impact of the bullet caused Shakar to spin around. A second later a red arrow penetrated Shakar's left cheek and exited through his mouth, carrying his precious gold tooth with it. By the time he returned his attention to Annie, she was no longer standing in front of him. She had been replaced by a red pygmy. In his right hand, he held a carved ivory spear inlaid with blue gems.

"You little shit! You think you can take on the great Shakar! I'll snap you in two like a tw…"

It happened so fast Shakar didn't even see it. The maneuver was only a blur to those watching. Before Shakar realized what had occurred, he saw the chief, still standing in front of him, but now the spear's blade was bloody. A huge gash opened in Shakar's neck, pulsing forth twin fountains of crimson from his carotid arteries. His large head teetered on his shoulders for a brief second until it fell backward onto the ground, his eyes blinking in disbelief that he was dead. His lifeless body soon followed its head.

"Brett!" screamed Annie. He was lying on the ground

with a bullet hole in his leg. A pool of bright red blood rapidly expanded around him.

"Oh God. No!" she cried. "He's been shot! Hit a major artery!" She looked to the others. "He's bleeding out. I need something for a tourniquet." Desmond pulled Shakar's belt and used it to stem the flow of blood. Annie cradled Brett's head in her lap and cried, "Please Lord, don't let him die!"

Brett looked up at her. "You okay?"

"I'm fine."

His voice weakened. "The children?"

"They're all safe. You saved them, Brett. You saved all of us."

He grew pale. He shivered.

"He's going into shock. I need a blanket," screamed Annie. "Elevate his legs!"

She looked into his eyes with tears running down her cheeks. "Please don't leave me, Brett. You can't go. You're the love of my life."

Brett looked up at her and smiled. "Love you too, Annie...from the first day I met you." He struggled to continue. "But it was you...you and the children who saved my life... from the darkness." He was slowly fading from consciousness. "It's okay...This was the deal...It's the reason I survived the car crash. This is what God had planned for me all along...Understand that now."

The mist dissipated. "Everything's going to be fine," he said. He gazed up at the clear blue morning sky and closed his eyes as the life-giving light of the sun washed over him. His last words were barely audible: "Redemption."

EPILOGUE: ONE YEAR LATER

Montgomery, Ohio

Annie stopped to straighten the Henri Rousseau print, hanging over the fireplace. It portrayed a jungle scene with lush green vegetation and an assortment of brightly colored birds. The painting brought back many fond memories of her hikes with Brett. It also forced her to recall the day he was shot. There was blood everywhere. She shuddered at the thought, pulled her robe tightly around her, and headed out into the cool spring morning toward the mailbox. After retrieving the mail, Annie brewed a fresh pot of coffee and sat down at the kitchen table to sort through the envelopes. There were the usual monthly bills, an integral part of living in American suburbia. She felt a gentle kick and slowly rubbed her belly. They had become more frequent over the past several weeks. She picked up the coffee pot and when she poured a cup for herself, she heard the tapping of his cane on the hardwood floor as he walked down the hall. Brett put his arms on her shoulders and kissed her on the forehead. "How's our little girl this morning?"

"Active," replied Annie. "I think she's anxious to meet her father and see what the world has to offer."

"Everything," said Brett.

"How's the leg?" she asked.

He flexed and extended it. Recovery from a total knee replacement took longer than he had expected. "Still stiff but getting better every day. Doc said I should be able to ditch the cane in another week or two."

A voice rang out from down the hall. "Come on, Dad! You need to get dressed."

Brett smiled. "It's only nine and the game doesn't start until one o'clock."

"Yeah, I know, but we should get there early to loosen up."

Brett looked at Annie. "He's excited."

She chuckled. "Don't I know? It's all he's talked about for the past two weeks."

Today was the debut of Brett Buchanan's return to baseball. He was the new coach of the Montgomery Hornets knothole team. Jenkins was scheduled to be their starting pitcher.

Brett groaned as he struggled to sit in the chair. Annie poured him a cup of black coffee, and handed him the stack of mail, including a box from FedEx. He set the bills aside and studied the box. It was addressed to Mr. and Mrs. Brett Buchanan, and postmarked from Nigeria.

"I thought that one might get your attention," she said, a wide grin on her face.

He opened the box and poured its contents onto the kitchen table. On top was a stack of newspaper articles with an attached, hand-written note. "Mr. Buchanan, I thought you might be interested in seeing these."

He spread the articles out in front of him. The first contained a newspaper picture of a body placed on display outside the village of Chibok, the same village where Boko Haram had massacred dozens and kidnapped over three hundred young Christian girls from their school. The headline read, "Boko Haram Dealt a Fatal Blow." He continued reading, "The Nigerian Army staged a successful raid on a hidden Boko Haram camp in the mountains near the Cameroon border. A total of fifty-seven young orphans from the Comboni Sisters Mission in Eastern Nigeria were freed, unharmed. The notorious Colonel Shakar Bhutah and most of his men were killed in the process. Through prisoner interrogations, two other Boko Haram camps were discovered and eliminated along the border. In all, a total of nine hundred-eighty-seven of the organization's soldiers were killed or captured. Many others fled to their respective villages. No longer afraid of reprisals from the group, locals have been quick to identify the terrorists. They are currently being rounded up and arrested. In a recent speech, newly-elected President Mandumo Nostafu claimed that Boko Haram has been completely driven out of the eastern zones." Brett smiled and set the article aside.

Next was a letter, dated three weeks ago. It said:

> Dear Mr. Buchanan,
>
> I hope all is going well with you and Mrs. Buchanan, and that your recovery from the knee surgery has been uneventful. I wanted to thank you both personally. Your actions here have provided a great service to the people of Nigeria and to all in the free world. This part of Africa is now much safer than it was prior to your arrival. Your driver, Vincent, uncovered the existence of a laptop computer during the Cameroon raid. It contained a detailed list of clients in the pedophile sex trade market. The names include many prominent business and government leaders in the Middle East. There was also a list of Boko Haram financial backers from Iran and Saudi Arabia. The information has been turned over to the U.S. State Department. The appropriate governments will be contacted about securing justice for the young children abused as the result of Shakar's activities.

The letter wasn't signed but the identity of the sender was obvious.

"Sebastian Cabot," said Annie.

Along with the letter was a newspaper article about the reopening of the Comboni Sisters' orphanage in Taraba Valley. A picture showed a half-dozen nuns posing in light-blue habits next to a sign that read, "Sister Mary Margaret School for Or-phans." Brett smiled and handed the article to Annie. She stud-ied the column intently. "They say the orphanage was reopened thanks to a significant donation from an anonymous benefactor." She squeezed Brett's hand. "Anonymous benefactor? Hmm, I wonder who that might have been?"

She checked the photograph, looking for familiar faces, but didn't know any of the new nuns staffing the orphanage. She did recognize the tall man standing behind them. He wore mir-rored blue sunglasses and had a noticeable scar along the left side of his face. A six-gun hung in a holster, low on his right hip. Vincent looked official with his new green uniform and a black beret. It looked like the same hat that used to sit on the head of Shakar Bhutah. The caption under the photograph identified Vin-cent as the head of security for the newly established Zambuti Region National Park in Taraba Valley. When she looked closely, she could make out the presence of a small red tattoo along his right neck. It was a cross. She turned to Brett and pointed to the photograph. "It's Vincent and he's sporting a new tattoo."

Brett smiled. "It looks like the Zambuti made him an hon-orary member of their tribe."

He withdrew a final thick packet from the bottom of the stack. It was from his attorney in Nigeria and it contained a deed, confirming the sale of over two-hundred-thirty-thousand acres of land south of the Taraba River, all the way to the Cameroon border and the Gashaka-Gumti National Preserve. An attached letter said:

> Congratulations, Mr. Buchanan.
> The purchase was approved by the Nige-rian Government in gratitude for what you did for their country. The original contracts have been executed and filed with the new Ministry of Natural Resources. Enclosed are your copies of the legal documents. Per your instructions, the land has been placed in the Buchanan Family

Trust. I believe this will accomplish all you requested. The Comboni Sisters have been issued a one-dollar-a-year lease in perpetuity and will never have to worry about losing their land to outside influences. The indigenous Zambuti tribal lands are now fully protected from any future encroachment by civilization. They will forever be free to live their lives as they have for centuries, protected from the rapacious greed of modern civilization. Specifically, any future mining activities or commercial development will be prohibited. You will also find enclosed the final adoption papers for your son, Jenkins. Good luck. If I can be of any further service, do not hesitate to call.

I guess some things can last forever. Brett set down the letter. "It's finally finished."

"Seems like a lifetime ago," replied Annie.

"It was. A completely different lifetime ago." Brett stood and stretched his leg. He leaned on his cane, and carried his cup of coffee outside onto the back deck. It wasn't the fifteen-million-dollar estate he once owned in Indian Hill, but it was their home where new memories were being created every day. Gone was his fleet of exotic sports cars, replaced by an electric sedan and a hybrid Toyota SUV with a baby seat in the back. Expensive cars were no longer important to him. The only other vehicle in their garage was a riding lawnmower that Jenkins used weekly. Annie came outside and stood next to him. He placed his arm around her and held her tight. All he would ever need or want in life was right here.

He gazed over the railing toward a wooded ravine where a small creek babbled its way across the rocks. Rays of early morning sunlight danced through the trees. Birds sang while a family of squirrels scurried about looking for breakfast. "Beautiful, isn't it?"

"Our own special place," said Annie. She melted her body

against his. "I wish this moment could last forever."

Brett took a deep breath of the cool air. Forever. He liked the sound of the word. "With a little help from God, we'll make that happen."

Recommended Book Club Discussion Questions

1) Thoughts on the first sentence paragraph of the story. Why did the author start that way?

2) Was the first paragraph effective in engaging your interest?

3) In chapter one, Brett is shaken by the presence of the young boy and his father at the ball game. There were hundreds of children attending. Why do you think this particular boy caught his attention? Why did Brett walk away from the game?

4) Multiple times the phrase "paint over stains" is used. How did you interpret that?

5) The 'voice" that plagues Brett is clearly his own guilt. Do you know of anyone that has experienced similar crushing guilt?

6) What is the significance of Debare (Jenkins)? How did he have the strength to overcome the horrendous conditions of his childhood?

7) What did the obese lumber merchant on the plane symbolize?

8) When Desmond picked up Brett at the Arusha Airport, Brett was hesitant to get into the limousine. What would you have done? What about Desmond convinced you one way or another to make that decision?

9) What do you think Desmond and Ambassador Cabot symbolize?

10) What was your initial impression of Aryianna? Did it change as the story progressed? What did she symbolize?

11) Vincent is a more confusing character that Desmond. Did you trust him initially? Why or why not? When did your opinion of him change.

12) Many of the Shakar and Boko Haram chapters are graphic. Do you believe the episodes are real? Did those scenes compel you to read on to see if they are vanquished, or did the scenes make you hesitate to continue?

13) Sister Mary Margaret literally saved Brett's life as part of his twelve-step program. Has anyone ever helped to turn your life around?

14) When Brett first meets Sister Anne Marie (Sister Annie), he "gets lost in her words, and the tenderness of her touch. Was this love at first sight? Do you believe in such a concept?

15) When do you think Annie developed the same attraction?

16) What point is being made about the Zambutis and their culture? Why do you think they trusted Sister Mary Margaret (Sister Maggie)?

17) What part of the story resonated emotionally with you?

18) What recurring themes interested you.

19) In the end, Brett finally achieves redemption? How?

20) Redemption is a story of relationships: Brett and his son, Brett and Jenkins, Brett and Sister Maggie, Brett and Annie, Father Norbert and Sister Maggie. Did all the relationships make the story more interesting or did they detract from the action?

21) Who was your favorite character? Why?

22) If a movie were made of the story, who do you think should play the various parts?

23) If you were to name the book, what title would you give it?

Other Blooks by T.Milton Mayer

For most of her adult life, Lisa Savich-Crawford had been a member of an elite anti-terrorist team. She retired from her career for the sake of her marriage and the pursuit of a "normal" life. Didn't work out. She had sacrificed her identity for nothing. When she discovers a body in a remote Florida swamp, it reignites in her a new sense of purpose. Although officially labelled an unfortunate accident, Lisa's investigative instincts say otherwise. Dozens of unanswered questions plague her, each answer more dangerous than the previous. As she follows the clues, they lead her to the political swamp of Washington DC. Her case is more than an isolated homicide in Florida. Powerful, international forces are in play. They are determined to stop Lisa at all cost.

The United States faces a catastrophe far worse than the Wuhan pandemic of 2020. Like before, the threat originates in China, but this time it's not just another virus. It is a powerful device that is already embedded in cities throughout the civilized world. When activated, billions could die.

Jacob Savich is the only man capable of stopping whatever is planned. Though plagued by his own personal demons, he is commissioned by the President to assemble a clandestine team of warriors with the necessary backbone and moral flexibility to protect the country. Until now, they have been successful, but this new mission poses the most dangerous challenge Savich has ever faced. He must identify the nature of the attack, when it will occur, and who is responsible. His relentless pursuit of each clue takes him a step closer to stopping the elusive mastermind behind the plot, but it also leads him toward his own death. Despite the danger, Savich must hurry. Time is running out. The day of YAOGUAI is near. Modern civilization is about to end.

A high-tech machine is stolen from a research laboratory in Oslo, Norway. A Stanford University sophomore detonates a bomb, killing himself and a hundred other students during a pre-med chemistry lecture. The country's foremost aeronautical engineer and his family are kidnapped from their yacht while cruising to Bimini Island. The events are somehow related to a mysterious shipment being smuggled into the country from Canada. Something sinister is about to threaten the very foundation on the United States…an event more devastating than the 9/11 attacks.

Veteran CIA man Winston Hamilton, FBI Special Agent John Crawford, and Dr. Jacob Savich each possess unique skills. They combine their talents to become the country's only hope of avoiding the impending disaster. They follow a convoluted trail that begins in a tiny Afghan village thirty years ago and winds its way through present day corporate America. Can they stop the threat in time?

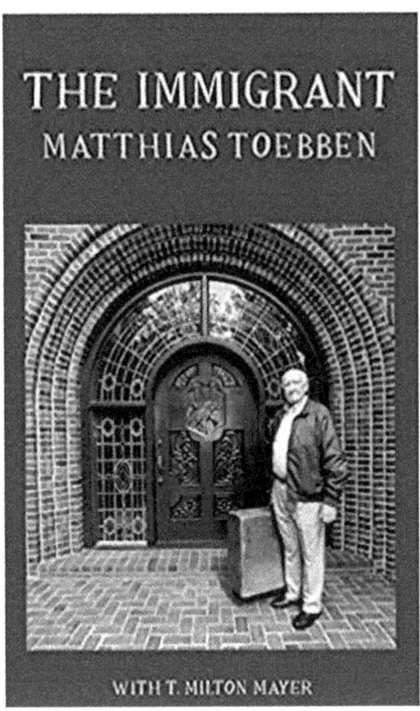

The story of Matthias Toebben begins as a tale of a young child growing up under the scourge of Nazi Germany. He was forced to witness things a boy of his age should never see. For Matthias and his family, every day was a struggle for survival in a time of overwhelming oppression.

At the age of twenty-one, he headed forth across the Atlantic Ocean to America. Although he was unable to speak a word of English and had only ten dollars in his pocket, he wasn't deterred. Those obstacles were offset by an abundance of ambition and determination. He found the United States to be a land of immense opportunity for anyone willing to work hard and make their visions a reality. He dedicated himself to the principles upon which his new country was founded: devotion to God, love of family, and dedication to the community. Through sheer determination, he succeeded, and with each success came another. Along the way, he faced multiple disasters, both professionally and personally. It was the way in which he overcame the setbacks that had defined him as one of the area's most respected and influential leaders.